In Ludd's Name

David Field was born in Chilwell, Nottinghamshire, and grew up in neighbouring Beeston. After attending Nottingham High School and Nottingham University he embarked on a career as a practising and academic lawyer, and now teaches Law at Bond University, on Australia's Gold Coast.

In his second novel for Arundel Books, David has again combined his life-long love of history with his nostalgia for the town of his birth.

David is married, with two sons and three grandchildren, who occupy his remaining time when he is not either writing or teaching. He currently lives in the Northern Rivers region of New South Wales and lists surfing among his many failures.

IN LUDD'S NAME

David Field

ARUNDEL
BOOKS

First published in Australia in 2013 by Zeus Publications

This edition first published in Great Britain in 2015 by
Arundel Books, 2, Audon Avenue, Chilwell,
Nottingham, NG9 4AW

www.arundelbooks.co.uk

ISBN 978-0-9558133-7-5

Front cover image from an original document of 1811. Reproduced courtesy of the
Local Studies Library, Nottingham.

Rear cover image courtesy of Framework Knitters Museum

Typeset in Garamond 11pt

Design and Artwork by
David Charlesworth GRA, Notions by Design, Chesterfield, Derbyshire.

Printed and bound in Great Britain by
CPI Antony Rowe Ltd., Chippenham, Wiltshire.

To the memory of Adam W. Thomas,
Senior History Master,
Nottingham High School,
who taught me to love history.

FOREWORD

THE TERM 'Luddite' has acquired a popular meaning not justified by history. Ask most people whom they believe the Luddites to have been, and their response will be something along the lines of 'a bunch of violent Lefties from somewhere in the north of England who opposed technical progress, and smashed new machines which were throwing them out of work'.

Wrong on every count except the use of violence. But it was a violence born of desperation which drove them to smash, not new machines which threatened their livelihoods, but the very machines on which they had been earning their livings for at least a generation. That desperation arose, not from any technical threat, but from hunger, disease and wretched living conditions, in the face of the seeming indifference of those whose apparent prosperity they were feeding. But the very entrepreneurs whose working capital went under the hammer, axe and tinder box almost nightly for two turbulent years were themselves victims of the same economic downturn, and were financially powerless to relieve the sufferings of their workers.

I have set out to depict what little is known of the actual events from both sides of the economic divide, through the eyes of two notional families whose mutual regard and respect for each other brings them nothing but tragedy. The main characters are obviously fictional, but the dates are accurate, and most of the background is historically sound. There really was a Town Clerk called George Coldham, and the Home Secretary of the time really was a man named Richard Ryder. The maiden speech of Lord Byron during the House of Lords debate on the Framework Bill is reproduced almost in its entirety.

There also really was a man named Gravenor Henson, and one theory puts him very close to events. We shall never know for certain, because the real Luddites kept their identities as well hidden from the modern historian as they did from the authorities at the time. Whether or not one can conclude that they came from 'somewhere up north' depends upon where one is standing. They came from Nottingham, an English Midlands town famous mainly for Robin Hood and pretty girls. Also for its lace industry, made pre-eminent in the world by the men and women on whose behalf this story is told, in an attempt to set the record straight.

David Field

"The great body of the present Mischief arises from the endeavours of the laboring classes by terror to compel their Employers to increase the price of their Labour and otherwise conduct the Manufactury in a manner more agreeable to the Interests or prejudice of the Artizan and this System must be held down by force before we can expect the restoration of Public Tranquillity"

Extract from a letter from the Town Clerk of Nottingham to the Home Office
December 6th, 1811

CHAPTER ONE

A laying to rest

A RAT foraged hopefully through a mound of rotting garbage, nose twitching, its writhing tail flicking a channel through the slime. Tommy Slack's boot missed it by half an inch, and it shot for the sanctuary of the open drain which ran through the centre of the greasy, unpaved, inner courtyard. Tommy grinned, and completed the short journey from the communal corner privy to the single low door of number seven.

The fog which had hung since daybreak over the canal and adjacent River Leen, had since crept up cautiously towards the town, searching out the overcrowded courts and narrow alleyways, packed tightly between Leen Side and Narrow Marsh. By two o'clock it had already drifted into Tanners Yard, and now, a few minutes short of three, was snaking triumphantly around the roofs of the workmen's dwellings. These were only a generation old, but their unscrupulous developers appeared to have opted for instant slums, laid out in cramped back-to-back rows around the courtyard.

It was October 12th 1809, and old Joe Slack was to be buried.

Tommy lifted the latch and rejoined the company. Many had gathered to pay their last respects to old Joe and the cramped all-purpose room was rank with the steam of cold damp clothing on marginally warmer bodies. In the upper room lay old Joe himself, on a borrowed trestle, in a simple wooden coffin donated by the chapel. A modest arrangement in itself, but no-one in the yard could recall a neighbour going off in a coffin. Nor would he have done, in all probability, had the entire family, Joe included, not been regular worshippers at that same chapel.

From time to time a mourner would mount the rickety stairs to the upper room and gaze down wistfully at their former neighbour. Grizzled, shrunken, and even greyer in death than he had been in life, Joe Slack had lived to be sixty-two, a feat of endurance for someone who had worked a stocking frame for nigh on thirty years.

It was a meet time for reflection, and Nathan Slack was ever one for that. He'd been just short of his thirteenth birthday when his father had led the entire family off the fields of Edwalton into the town parish of St. Mary's, newly swollen by the pre-war expansion of the Nottingham hosiery trade. The parish had been overcrowded even then, and Nathan's mother had been the first to succumb, a victim of the dreaded consumption, exacerbated by the fogs that frequently rose from the river as if seeking to shroud the squalor above. At the age of thirty-three she'd left a husband and three children; a common enough loss, and Joe had battled on.

In Nathan, Joe had raised a son in his own image, a strong and willing worker who'd helped to support the family through long hours at the frame. At the age of fourteen, Nathan's sister Nellie had died of the same fever, and at seventeen, his younger sister Millie had perished under the wheels of a coach and pair on Hollow Stone. Joe and Nathan had lived alone until Lily came along.

It was Lily who broke the spell, a firm hand on Nathan's arm.

"It's near time – best see ter the carryin' party."

Nathan smiled proudly as he watched her bustle back into the company; even at his own father's funeral she was taking charge. They'd managed well enough these past sixteen years and he wouldn't have wanted her any other way.

The flickering glow from the oil lamp suspended by a hook from the ceiling, essential all day during the winter months, picked out the silver in her dark brown hair, tied back, as ever, in a neat bunch at the nape of her neck. She was only of average height for a woman of those times, but even so, over the years, the low ceiling had trained her to an instinctive stoop. Her once slender figure had swollen with middle age and childbirth, and their latest – surely their last – showed only modestly beneath her coarse cloth apron. Perhaps this one would survive, making it four. Those stillborn had all been boys, and old Nancy had divined a girl this time, not that Lily believed in 'all that tomfoolery'.

Nathan was drawn back again to the business in hand as Tommy sidled alongside him. "There's still time ter change it, Dad. Will's complainin' as 'is back's bad."

Nathan sighed with irritation. "Yer not goin' in the carryin' party, an' there's an end on it. Yer place as eldest boy is wi' yer mam an' me, up the front. There's plenty more can carry the coffin."

"But Dad . . ."

"But nowt. I'm tellin' yer, lad – it's all settled. Nah go an' see after the guests, like yer mam asked yer."

Tommy grunted as he walked away, and Nathan reminded himself for the tenth time that it was the right decision. At fifteen, although tall for his age, Tommy was probably too young to be a bearer, and if he gave in to Tommy he could hardly refuse his brother Matthew, and thirteen was definitely too young. It was a pity, all the same; they'd both thought the world of their grandfather.

As usual, it had been Lily who'd had the last word. "I'm not 'avin' folks sayin' as no-one else'd tek 'im," she'd announced flatly, "an' anyroad, we must walk as a family, an' ar place is up the front."

By way of compensation, Tommy had been placed in charge of the meagre supply of ale, to fortify the mourners against the dreary uphill trudge to the burial ground.

Nathan pushed through the throng to the foot of the stairs, signalling to certain of the men as he went. Once upstairs, Bob Pilgrim secured the lid with a handful of nails, then helped the other three pass the coffin down to the room below, where it was lowered reverently to the ground. The four men then paused nervously, waiting for the word.

"Ready, then? Mind the balance as yer go. You'll be right enough, Will?"

Will Draycott grinned toothlessly. "Reckon that lad o' yourn's bin tellin' whoppers again. Mi back were a bit sore yesterday, that's all. Anyroad, it'll tek no gristle ter lift poor old Joe."

Relieved to have the final decision taken out of his hands, Nathan caught Lily's eye across the room, and nodded. Lily slipped off her apron and took hold of a ladle from the hob rack. As Joe's coffin was lifted effortlessly onto willing shoulders on a whispered command from Nathan, she struck the ladle against the pot which hung over the empty hearth.

An instant silence descended and Nathan stepped self-consciously towards the door, followed by the coffin and its four bearers. The company parted down the middle as Nathan led them out, crouching to clear the low lintel as they moved out into the yard. The rest followed, and as the full procession formed up outside, Lily dropped the latch behind the last of them. She then came round to stand alongside Nathan at the head of the line, their two sons immediately behind them as instructed and young Ruth holding onto Lily's right hand. There was a moment's hesitation, and then they moved off at what they hoped was a suitable funereal pace.

The fog now engulfed the whole of St. Mary's, swirling and twisting in unchallenged eddies wherever its whim decreed. The measured tread of the mourners rang hollowly against the crumbling archway exit from the yard as they passed under it and out into Narrow Marsh, then round the corner into Turncalf Alley. Avoiding the steep and dangerous steps of Garner's Hill and Middle Hill, they elected instead to reach the high town via Drury Hill. A carriage clattered somewhere above them, and they braced themselves against the cold dank air and the steep walk up to Weekday Cross.

They turned right at the Cross into High Pavement, stepping at an easy pace for the sake of the women and children, a humble

cortège of some forty common people. High on their left rose
the four-storied mansions of the well-to-do; the manufacturers,
tradesmen, frame owners and suchlike. To their right, the High
Pavement Chapel and School, the Shire Hall and town gaol, perched
menacingly on the edge of the steep cliff which fell sharply down
to Narrow Marsh. A hundred yards to the south, beyond the narrow
River Leen and the Nottingham Canal, lay the open meadows of
the East and West Crofts, barren now, but in summer months the
favoured picnic grounds for the workers of St. Mary's. A chance to
fill their lungs with God's good air, and their tiny back-to-back houses
with daffodils and crocuses. Today the meadows lay somewhere
behind a heaving grey wall of fog, and not even the wealthy, from
their servants' attic rooms, could buy a glimpse.

The occasional passer-by scurried in and out of the fog, and
Lily pressed close to Nathan, her left arm in his right, seeking his
warmth and his reassuring presence. He recalled how she'd shared
his arm all those years ago as they'd left the parish church, man and
wife in the sight of God. Further back still, how she'd first come into
the yard, a bundle of starved rags pursued by the Town Watch.

It had been cold then too, a wicked November night with clear
skies and a cruel early frost. The hue and cry had risen on Drury
Hill, and had followed her as she'd scampered down into Narrow
Marsh and sought refuge in Tanners Yard, a grimy scarecrow of a
girl. Nathan, then a robust young man of twenty-two still grieving
for the tragic loss of his sister Millie, had been out in the courtyard,
chipping the first hard ice of the year from the doorstep of number
seven. Lily had raced behind him and across into the corner privy;
seconds later, two burly officers of the Watch had skidded under the
archway and into the yard, each holding aloft a search lantern.

"You there! Seen a girl come in 'ere?"

Nathan disliked the Watch, and particularly Watt Griffin.

"They come in an' aht all the time. Why, yer lost one?"

Griffin scowled at Nathan then scanned the yard, his lantern
held as high as his short arms and legs permitted. His suspicious eyes
fixed on the privy. "Wharrabaht in there?"

" 'ave a look fer yersen, but dun't blame me if Scuff Needham
pulls yer ears off."

Scuff Needham was a fearsome size, and none of the Watch had
ever taken him. Griffin was not in the mood for pointless heroics, not
even with Collins to assist. With a final glare at Nathan he swaggered
out of the yard, closely followed by a relieved colleague. Nathan
waited silently until the privy door opened a few cautious inches.

"They've gone, lass – nowt ter fear."

She'd have slipped back out of the yard, but Nathan intercepted her and held on firmly to her right arm.

"Not so fast, young lady. Nah then, yer bin stealin' or summat?"

Proud eyes had burned into his. "That'll be the day as Lily Parker steals, an' I'll thank yer ter tek yer gret hairy fist off mi arm!"

"I'll do that when I'm good an' sure what brung yer 'ere. Dad!"

Old Joe shuffled carefully out over the icy threshold in answer to Nathan's summons, and surveyed the young girl with a wisdom born of experience.

"Yer can lerrer go, Nathan; anyone can see she's got nowhere ter run to."

"I reckon she's bin stealin' or summat."

"An' I reckon yer wrong. Anyroad, fust thing is ter get summat warm into 'er. She's shiverin' fit ter bust."

Nathan looked down at her more gently. "What d'yer say, lass? Like summat ter eat?"

Temptation and suspicion fought each other in both her face and her words. "I'll not lie wi' yer, if that's what yer thinkin'."

"That yer'll not, lass. Leastways, not smellin' like that."

He had to let go of her as she lashed back at him with an outraged fist. It took many days of gentleness to allay her suspicions, and at first it was only old Joe who could really set her at ease. Her story was by no means novel.

The oldest daughter in a family of seven born to a drunken, itinerant tinker and his timid, downtrodden wife, she'd stuck with the beatings, abuse and humiliation for sixteen years, for the sake of the mother and family she'd adored. Her mother had died the previous Christmas, and all the children but Lily (who was above the age of child charity) had been consigned to the Leicester Poorhouse. She'd followed her father under threat of further violence, and in the waning hope that love and devotion might even yet be his salvation.

A month previously they'd arrived in Nottingham for the annual Goose Fair, and having failed to sell any of his pots and pans, Harry Parker had tried to beat her into whoredom. She'd run blindly away, heartbroken and badly shaken. After three weeks in the open she'd still been too proud to beg, and had stayed alive from the sale of her meagre possessions, now exhausted. In a fit of rage her father had listed her as a vagrant and set the Town Watch after her. Such was the savage charity of the Poor Law that to be without the means of support in a foreign parish was a serious offence, and she'd barely stopped running for four days until she found refuge in the yard.

She'd stayed on at number seven, a new daughter for old Joe and a surrogate sister for Nathan. Her domestic skills had rapidly transformed the tiny two-roomed dwelling, and in return she'd found a peace of mind beyond her wildest imaginings. After a few months she persuaded the two men to take her to the local chapel, pursuing a curiosity aroused in her by a Wesleyan preacher she'd heard as a child at Ashby market. The recently formed Sion Chapel soon had three new converts, with Lily the most devout of them. After all her sufferings, and such a change of fortune, to give thanks to God seemed to her the most natural thing in the world.

As she relaxed into her new life, so she saw in Nathan's dependability and kindly virtue a quality rare in one of their class. Her respect slowly deepened, kindling love for this long-boned, red-headed rock with his rough gentility, and she cried herself to sleep the night that she discovered that her love was quietly returned by Nathan. No quick-burning passion, this, more of a growing mutuality. They were married in the autumn of 1793, and they owed their happiness together to the unassuming kindness of the man now being borne effortlessly in the coffin behind them.

On they trudged, hair matted down by the fog, up the slight rise towards St. Mary's Gate. The fog lifted briefly to reveal a group of people awaiting them ahead on their left, on the front doorstep of the house of Robert Bradley. At its head stood Robert himself, attired in sombre black, his face a mixture of awkward solemnity and studied sympathy as he squinted into the fog towards the sound of the approaching funeral party. A man deprived of height, he made up for it in girth, with a barrel chest and short legs which promised an ape-like energy, and betrayed the coarseness of his origins. Behind him, his wife Catherine, two of his children and several domestics. Even the scullery maid had been ordered out to mark the passing of old Joe.

As the distance between the two groups narrowed an uneasy silence fell among the mourners, which became more palpable as Nathan halted the procession by raising a hesitant hand. It was left to Robert to break the embarrassed silence that followed.

"My whole family unites in prayer with yours in your hour of sorrow, Nathan Slack. As he lived in the sight of the Lord, so now shall he reap his heavenly reward."

"Amen," echoed his wife.

Nathan stood tongue-tied, and it was Lily who replied, pronouncing her words with special care. "We thank you for your kindly words of comfort, Mr Bradley, sir. There never was a more

Christian man walked the face of God's earth than Joseph Slack, poor though he was. As ye sow, so shall ye reap, as the Good Book says."

"Amen," repeated Mrs Bradley.

There was another long silence, which was mercifully ended when Nathan coughed awkwardly and mumbled, "Our thanks to you all," before waving the procession on. As they filed past the silent Bradleys most eyes were fixed firmly on the ground ahead of them, but some of the party could be heard muttering. It was Tommy who gave voice to what many were thinking, as he looked back to his left, below the side of the coffin.

"Fine words enough, but I dun't see anyone joinin' us. Mebbe not all folks is required ter walk ter 'eaven."

There were several sniggers from behind him, and Lily turned angrily on her son while walking backwards in an effort to keep pace with Nathan.

"That's a wicked thing ter say, Tommy Slack! The Lord has chosen those who must walk, burris kingdom is open ter all. Yer too quick ter judge, mi lad; where would you an' all the rest of us be wi'aht Bradley's Hosiery?"

"Aye, an' where would Bradley an' the rest of 'is kind be, wi'aht the likes of us killin' oursens ter line 'is fat pockets?"

This time it was Nathan who whipped round sharply.

"Shurrup! Yer can mek as big a fool o' yersen as yer like, fer all I care, but I'll not 'ear yer talk back ter yer mam like that, not terday of all days. So shurrup afore I belt yer!"

Tommy subsided into a brooding silence, still smarting from his failure to secure a corner of the coffin. He was already as tall as most men, with his father's long frame and the same sinewy strength. He had his father's red hair, too, but more of his mother's spirit. He was painfully anxious to demonstrate his new-found manhood, and would have given much to have been allowed to join the rest of the men carrying his grandad's coffin along High Pavement, past all the grand houses, and with Lucy Bradley in the audience. For all her fancy schooling she was just like all the other girls of her age, and knew a fine male body when she saw one. One of these days . . .

His daydreaming grew less focused as they plodded on down the slope towards the burial ground.

⸺ ◗◖ ⸺

As the last of the funeral party passed through the veil of fog, Robert Bradley turned to those grouped around him.

"There goes a man whose example we'd all do well to follow.

Blessed are those that do hunger and thirst after righteousness. And now, my dear, I think a little tea wouldn't go amiss; we must not, in our sadness, neglect our guests."

Their guests were frequent visitors to the Bradley house and important men in their own communities. Like Robert, they were entrepreneurs in the hosiery trade, but while he had been one of the first with the foresight to establish a small manufactory in addition to renting out stocking frames around the parish, both William Mellors of Arnold and Edwin Cossons of Beeston had remained loyal to the old trade, cotton hosiery fashioned on stocking frames by home-based workers who rented their frames from the entrepreneurs who then bought up the fruit of their labours at agreed rates.

All three were merchant hosiers and members of the Hosiers' Association, and today they were met upon weighty matters. The tea, sandwiches and plum cake having been dispensed and gratefully consumed, they lost no time in getting down to the more important issue.

"If we give 'em a penny a dozen more now, we'll be payin' out for the rest of our lives."

"But surely, Edwin, they've got a good case."

"Aye, Robert, an' so 'ave we. With trade the way it is, we should be cuttin' 'em back further, not talkin' about a penny more."

"I'll not agree with you there," responded the third member of the group. "They've got ter live, same as us, and you know as well as the rest of us that the Association's dead against layin' off on principle."

"William Mellors, you'd believe owt, you would," retorted Cossons. "They're only against layin' off because o' the rents they're gettin' off the frames. Better to 'ave fifty workers payin' out a shillin' a week for a frame an' starvin', than only twenty earning a decent wage from the same number o' finished goods. Anyroad, I'm not talkin' about layin' off. What I'm sayin' is that we can't pay 'em any more, leastways I can't."

"No more can I, ter tell yer the truth, not without switchin' ter cut-ups," admitted Mellors. "But my workers won't 'ave that."

"Aye, an' that's summat else. Who runs our businesses, us or them?"

Having received no immediate reply, Cossons pressed his point.

"Between you an' me, I've nowt personal against these new workers' groups, even if they are against the law, but I'll not 'ave 'em tellin' me 'ow ter run mi own business. Mind you, I'll grant that it's high time the Association did summat about cut-ups – they'll ruin the trade yet, you mark my words."

Nobody disagreed with him. All the reputable manufacturers were suffering from those inferior, cheaper, products known in the trade as 'cut-ups'. Made on outdated, wider, frames, they were simply broader pieces of finished hosiery which were then cut and sewn into a stocking shape, rather than a single garment more skillfully fashioned on a modern frame. They sold for less than half the price of a fully fashioned garment, could be made by 'colt' workers who had not completed a full apprenticeship, and were wrecking the more skilled side of the trade for stockinger and entrepreneur alike.

But with falling markets caused by the recent wars, more and more producers were turning in desperation to what seemed like an attractive weapon against cheaper Flemish imports. In fighting this threat to the quality and reputation of their product, many employers' associations and groups of stockingers saw eye to eye, and it was only the government of the day which saw in the embryonic workers' unions a seditious threat similar to that which had so recently spawned a revolution across the Channel.

"Gentlemen," urged Bradley, "we're strayin' somewhat from the point. Do we give 'em their penny, or don't we, bearin' in mind that the others will likely be forced ter follow our lead if we do?"

"No."

"No."

Bradley sighed. "I'll go along with you, o' course, but I'll not pretend that I'm 'appy with it. We're not the only ones sufferin' higher food prices, yer know; it must be worse fer them, and we must remember our Christian duty."

"We're not all pillars o' the church, Bradley," scoffed Cossons. "An' we're not all makin' a fortune out o' fancy point net."

"It's 'ardly a fortune," Bradley protested. "And yer don't 'ave ter go ter church ter lead a Christian life."

———◦—◦◦—◦———

Down in the parish burial ground, off Barker Gate, at the top of a piece of open land behind a low wall, a fellow Christian was being lowered into his grave. The fog clung to the throats of the silent mourners, their eyes downcast towards the crude hole, as the Reverend Josiah Hepworth, Sion Chapel's current minister, monotoned a familiar eulogy.

"In so far as it hath pleased Almighty God to call each of His children into this life, even so shall He in due season . . ."

On the other side of the wall, in the anonymity of the fog, a group of small children, heedless of the solemn rites being performed only yards from them, perfected a new nursery rhyme which had only recently arrived in the town in the panniers of the packhorses.

"The Grand Old Duke of York,
He had ten thousand men,
He marched them up to the top of the hill,
And he marched them down again."

"Into Thy hands we commend the spirit of our dearly departed brother, Joseph Slack."

"And when they were up, they were up,
And when they were down, they were down,
And when they were only halfway up,
They were neither up nor down."

"Amen."

The first shower of stony earth hit the coffin lid with a rattling thump.

———◆———

The banked fire crackled cheerfully in the grate as the last of the toasted muffins was accepted with eager thanks.

"Tell me, Robert, do you always take such a personal interest in your workers?" enquired Mellors in a tone of genuine mystification.

"No, ter tell the truth, not all of 'em. But there are some people worthy of the encouragement of the likes of us, and I reckon the Slack family's a good example. Joe Slack was the best stockinger I ever had, and his son Nathan's not far behind. Lily Slack's a good Christian mother, and I've hopes for those two sons o' theirs, although the big un's gettin' a bit above himself lately."

Like many a merchant hosier, Robert Bradley was self-made. Two generations previously, the Bradleys could have been found living above a carpenter's workshop in Fletcher Gate. It had been Robert's father who had begun renting out the frames which he had been involved in making, and Robert himself who had risked all to open a self-contained manufactory of his own, in which all the processes involved in stocking manufacture could be supervised centrally in something which was slowly becoming known as a 'factory'.

On the way up, Robert had known hardship of a sort, and in

his recently acquired financial comfort he liked to think of himself as a benefactor to those less fortunate than himself. Indeed, compared with most men in his position, he was benevolence itself, a trait which occasionally caused concern to his wife Catherine, the daughter of a well-placed Sneinton vintner, who had in many ways married beneath herself. While her husband rejoiced in his promotion from the tradesman class, Catherine preferred to forget that he had ever been a member of it, and found the lower classes more appealing from a safe distance, even while conducting charitable works for the chapel.

She'd made considerable efforts to ensure that their four children were educated well above their father's lowly horizons, and was now beginning to reap the benefits of her earlier determination. Lucy, at seventeen, was acknowledged by all those whose opinions mattered as the most eligible and accomplished young lady in the Nottingham Junior Wesleyan Fellowship, as well as one of their most gifted Sunday School teachers, while her thirteen-year-old sister Rebecca showed great artistic and musical promise. Fifteen-year-old James would soon be taking some of the pressure of commerce from his father, while six-year-old Howard already knew exactly how to behave in company.

"It's risky, yer know," warned Cossons. 'Next thing yer know, they'll be expectin' ter take supper with yer!"

"Hardly. Although I'm not so sure as I wouldn't say yes ter some of 'em."

Catherine, hovering in the doorway with her two daughters in attendance, paled perceptibly and hastened to rescue the situation. "Come now, Robert, no more of that teasing of yours. That's enough business for today, surely. I thought perhaps our guests might like to move into the drawing room and hear Rebecca play a little."

***

The Beethoven prelude was faintly audible from outside and some light filtered through the heavy drapes to illuminate the rutted street, as the remainder of the mourners passed Bradley's front door again on their return trip. They were less tightly bunched this time and several had slipped quietly away to their homes in neighbouring Hockley, but the party was still over twenty strong. The conversation had been brief and intermittent since they'd left the burial ground, but the drifting piano notes and the reassuring light invited at least a comment.

"That'll be Miss Rebecca – she's a fine 'and wi' music, they reckon."

"Aye. 'ow much d'yer think Bradley charges fer a yard o' that?"

The resulting laughter was to relieve the tension, but there were some who probably meant it unkindly and Lily, as usual, leapt to Bradley's defence.

"There's worse than 'im, when all's said an' done."

"Mebbe, burra bet 'e weren't pleased when we took 'alf a day off."

Almost all the occupants of Tanners Yard worked, in some way or other, for Robert Bradley or one of his close associates in the Hosiers' Association. Most of them worked rented stocking frames in their own homes, but a few, like Nathan, had taken the trouble to master the more complex point-net or warp frames in Bradley's pioneering lace workshop in Stoney Street. Lace was becoming an important extension to the traditional Nottingham hosiery trade, and lace operators like Nathan, being more skilled and better rewarded, were by way of being the aristocrats of the workforce, just one rung below the framesmiths – the mechanics who built and maintained the frames on which the hosiery was actually produced.

"I'm sure 'e understood," said Lily. "After all, 'e even came aht 'issen ter pay 'is respects."

"Even supposin' yer right," countered her neighbour Will Draycott, "I'll still not fall fer that 'Christian brotherhood' tripe 'e's so fond o' spoutin'."

"It's truly meant," Lily protested. "There's plenty like 'im as wouldn't gi' us the time o' day. An' yer must own, it's a real treat ter see 'im wi' that family of 'is. A real family man, 'e is."

To Lily, family was everything. Once she'd settled safely in Tanners Yard she'd made exhaustive efforts to locate the six brothers and sisters left behind in the poorhouse. As was common for these ill-managed salves to civic conscience, the children had all been allowed to vanish without record. Lily had never, in truth, got over the loss, and when her own children had come along they had been almost smothered by her determination to put family above all else.

They were soon back in the cold, dripping confines of the yard, and darkness was rapidly settling in as Lily unlatched the door to number seven. She and a few of the neighbouring women soon had the table covered and several pans on the boil. The fruits of habitual economy, and two days of hectic preparations, were laid out on the table, and for some it would be the first time for many months that they had tasted cake. Cheese, herring, barley bread and potato scones completed the funeral meal, accompanied by volumes of tea, fast becoming a luxury in stockinger homes. Nathan passed around the tobacco he had been saving, despite Lily's frequent homilies on the evils of smoking, and soon several pipes were contentedly billowing acrid fumes around the small room.

The conversation was general at first, rarely extending beyond those stories which had been around the parish many times but always survived a retelling. Of the day the Watch had been chased into the Leen by a rabid dog they'd been sent to destroy, or the time when the landlord of the Ten Bells had been suspended from a meat hook in his own parlour by a group of irate navvies from the nearby canal diggings who'd caught him watering the ale.

And, most beloved of all, but now almost beyond living memory, that magic day many years ago when a disgruntled mob at the Goose Fair had taken over the stalls of cheese vendors whose prices they considered extortionate, and had set about redistributing their wares around the Market Place. The mayor had been in the process of reading the Riot Act from a temporary platform, when a rolling cheese had struck a mortal blow to both his balance and his dignity. It had required a company of dragoons to restore order.

But of late, anxiety dogged all such reminiscences, and tales of past hilarities were recounted with rising desperation. Coal was over sixpence the hundredweight and flour nearly six shillings a stone. A quarter of wheat now cost over a hundred shillings, and even cheaper items such as potatoes were threatening to enter the luxury class. Food prices had trebled overall in the past twenty years, yet in the same period the wages paid to hosiery workers had actually fallen. A man who, in 1800, could have counted on a regular income of nearly eleven shillings a week now felt himself lucky if he took home eight in a good week, and there weren't many of those to be had. To earn even that, a fourteen-hour-day was the rule.

Such underlying concerns, combined with the natural solemnity of the occasion, kept communal conversation sporadic and subdued, and in the end it came down to several smaller groups talking amongst themselves. The women, released for a brief while from the drudgery of mending and making do, closed around Lily and the baby she was expecting in a matter of weeks. The children played on the bare floor while most of the men, as usual, talked trade and politics.

Conspicuous among their voices was Tommy's, a strident complaining note above the near-defeated hum of the older men around him. Nathan, nursing a weary Ruth on his knee, would occasionally glance across at Tommy, concern in his eyes, and once or twice he caught young Matthew looking in the same direction. He, too, was uneasy about his older brother and the resentment which seemed to be building up inside him.

The night was as black as pitch as the last of them left, offering the customary condolences to Nathan and his family. Ruth roused herself and set about clearing the remains of the funeral tea from the table, supervised as ever by Lily as she sat, sewing, in the big old chair which by silent agreement was hers, her legs resting on an old prayer stool. Tommy appeared to have worked off his steam and now sat morosely at the table, toying with an old knife and a piece of kindling.

Matthew took down his Bible from the shelf above the door, and with a kiss for his mother and a cheery farewell to the rest of the family, set off for Bible study. By rights, Tommy should have gone with him, but a succession of heated arguments had ended with Lily conceding defeat out of sheer exhaustion, in return for Tommy's promise of regular attendance at Sunday School as well as morning and evening Sabbath services. Nathan puffed at the remains of his fill and stared fixedly into the fireplace, remembering.

And so the evening passed with hardly a word between them. Matthew was back home before nine, and barely thirty minutes later the heavy day began to take its toll on them all. Nathan stretched and yawned, replaced his pipe on the shelf, and saw to the crude lock he'd put on the door catch during the election riots some years previously but had somehow never got around to removing. His arm around Lily, he led the way to their bed in the upper room, leaving the rest of the family to make up their bedding on the floor of the main room.

Upstairs an hour later, each of them, for their own reasons, was still awake. Lily eased her swollen stomach over, to lie for a while on her back and gaze into the darkness above them. She sighed.

"You still awake, lass?"

"Aye. I were just thinkin' 'ow much we owe poor old dad."

"Aye, but 'e'll not be so poor where 'e's gone."

Lily laughed lightly. "It's come ter summat when you 'ave ter remind me abaht that. D'yer know there's some in the yard as call me Holy Lil?"

It was Nathan's turn to chuckle. "Nemmind, lass, I'd not 'ave yer any different."

There was a long silence.

"Nathan?"

"Aye?"

"What's gunner become of ar Tommy?"

"Nowt, wi' a bit o' luck. A lot o' the young uns get like 'im at 'is age. We just 'as ter pray that he remembers all you've taught 'im abaht Christian duty, that's all."

"Aye, burrit's not as simple as that, is it? It's 'ard on a young lad like 'im, just like it were 'ard fer you. Sometimes I get this bad feelin', like we're wrong an' 'e's right. It's not a nice feelin' at all; it's just like we're readin' it from some book, like the minister does on Sunday, only it's all lies. We are right, aren't we?"

There was an ominous pause.

"I dunno, lass, an' that's the truth. I used ter think so, but just lately I'm not so sure. It's all right fer us, we've got just abaht enough ter live on. But there's plenty 'asn't."

"I know, an' it bothers me summat rotten, but what can we do ter mek it berrer fer Tommy and Matthew?"

Nathan hesitated for a moment, then took the plunge.

"Well look, if yer mean it, I was 'earin' that they're doin' some new 'ouses aht Radford way – 'ouses just fer the likes of us. Seems like some farmer's widder needs ter sell the land after 'er 'usband died. They'll be three bob a week, mind, or at least that's what Bob Pilgrim were sayin', but there's gunner be four rooms in 'em, an' wi' Tommy comin' aht as a stockinger next year, I reckon we could manage it."

"What, leave the yard, yer mean?" Lily asked apprehensively.

"An' why not? Yer the one who's allus sayin' that it's not 'ealthy rahnd 'ere. An' if we do get right aht, well Tommy an' Matthew – and Ruth – might stand more of a chance in life."

"Wharrabaht Bradley's?"

"I can walk up every day; it's only a couple o' miles or so."

Lily lay quietly for a while, torn between her dearest desire to improve things for her family and the guilt she already felt for even considering abandoning their neighbours to their problems. A stirring beneath her ribs reminded her of another whose future might be in the balance. Nathan was almost asleep when she made her final decision.

"Nathan?"

"Mmm?"

"Who d'yer 'ave ter see abaht them new 'ouses?"

"Feller in Pelham Street. Summat ter do wi' an 'ousin' trust."

Another pause.

"When can yer go an' see 'im?"

He was more fully awake now.

"Why, are yer interested in goin' after one?"

"Aye, I am. Very."

"Right then, I'll go termorrer."

He finally fell asleep with her head on his shoulder. She took a little longer, but as she felt the new life turning and tumbling inside her, she mouthed a silent prayer and began to plan for the new house.

CHAPTER TWO

A Sunday School class and a parting of the ways

"AND NOW let us disperse to our Bible classes and consider these words of Our Lord."

The Reverend Hepworth beamed down indulgently at his junior flock, as the scramble to classes began. The smaller ones scraped and banged their way between the pews in their eagerness to be first, while their seniors assumed customary expressions of tolerant indifference to their antics. The young girls twittered and the young men swaggered; it was the same every Sunday.

Sion Chapel Sunday School was a thriving community of well over a hundred, and was far from being a mere recruiting agency for the evening congregation. It was a way of life, a social centre, and it absorbed two and a half hours of every Sunday afternoon. First came a hymn and a dedication prayer, then an hour or so of reading and writing. Even if this hour was primarily intended to give each child enough learning to allow them to read the Scriptures in adulthood, for many it would be the only education they ever received.

In the generation to come, the Noncomformist educational movement would be blamed for industrial unrest and would have hurled at it, particularly by the High Church faction, the accusation that it had handed to the working classes the very weapons with which they went on to fight the established order. Even if so, it must also be credited for having given the first groundings to many who were later to gain fame in more scholarly pursuits.

After the grammar class there was a short service, at the end of which the minister gave the Biblical text for the week. This week it was the Parable of the Five Talents, and the Sunday pupils were now forming into their Bible classes for a discussion of the implications of the chosen text for the young Christian.

Each set of classes was loosely graded according to ability, so that those who met for grammar were not necessarily in the same class for Bible. This was certainly true for Tommy and Matthew Slack, for while Tommy laboured dully at his grammar under the disciplinarian rule of Mr Tranter, Matthew was allowed to soar to his own heights in Miss Lowe's special class for those who displayed particular promise.

The two brothers did not even look alike, for while the older boy had taken his father's angular height and carrot colouring, Matthew was darker, more rounded, of barely average height for his age and with a softness of feature which made him look almost cherubic. His younger sister Ruth also took the same features from their mother, but in her case it was called prettiness.

It was a mistake even to put the two boys into the same Bible class, but here their differences in ability and comprehension were less likely to show. Matthew, for all his intelligence, was by nature shy and hesitant while Tommy was as forthright as he was bigoted, and his surly contributions displayed a practical wisdom of sorts.

Charged with the task of blending the personalities of the two for the benefit of the group was Lucy Bradley, and also in her class was her brother James, a puffy, unpleasant caricature of his somewhat pompous father, but lacking the latter's redeeming generosity towards others. James, like Tommy, only attended Sunday School under parental dictate, since Robert Bradley had determined that it would be "good for his future to get to know the ordinary folk who'll be working for him one day", despite his wife Catherine's concern that he might "pick up some of their rough ways".

No-one who watched her in action could deny that Lucy was a naturally gifted teacher. In another place and time she would no doubt have risen to great scholastic honour, but early nineteenth century Nottingham was neither of these. Her predestined role in life was as a future bride to wealth and position, for which she was equally qualified, with a dignified beauty which featured a finely cut, oval face framed by rich brown tresses which glowed on her shoulders as the last of the early winter sun shone in shafts through the lead-mullioned windows set high in the chapel walls. Her voice was sweet and calm, restrained and perfectly modulated, the proud product of Miss Humberstone's Ladies' Academy. For all her privilege, Lucy was gentle, and her concern for the welfare of others was genuine and classless. But to her Sunday School class she seemed as remote and unfathomable as one of the angels that the minister preached about, while to Tommy she remained infuriatingly unattainable.

Tommy was feigning an intense interest in the ceiling – his customary pose in class – as Lucy sat herself down in the centre of her group of twenty or so, opened her Bible at the marked passage and smiled slowly around the semicircle of faces.

"Now, the Parable of the Five Talents. Who would like to explain what Our Lord meant when he gave us this parable?"

There was the usual awkward silence.

"Come now, let's not be shy again this week. We learned so much last week, didn't we, when we agreed not to be shy? So, does anyone know what this parable has to tell us?"

A minimal interval having elapsed, James concluded that it was time for him to lighten the darkness of his less gifted classmates. He did so every week, and it had become customary for the rest to await his lead.

"It tells us," he explained, "that profit is a worthy achievement, and that it is not a sin to use what one has in order to acquire more."

There was a sharp intake of breath from Tommy, whose eyes hardened but remained riveted on the roof beams.

"I'm not sure that's entirely what the parable means, James," Lucy replied, "but it's certainly part of it. Would someone else like to add to what James has just told us?"

Another silence, then a light cough from Matthew.

"Doesn't it also mean somethin' about workin' hard an' bein' a credit ter the boss?"

Tommy ground his teeth together and shot Matthew a warning look. Lucy smiled indulgently.

"That's very good, Matthew, although you make it sound a little harsh. Could we not say instead that there is virtue in seeking the good opinions of those whom we serve, and striving for their benefit?"

"That's the same thing, as far as they're concerned. Dun't let 'em tek yer fer a donkey, Matthew." It was rare for Tommy to participate so early in the proceedings and Lucy was ever the optimist.

"Why is it the same, Tommy? Can you help us interpret the parable?"

Tommy's responding snort was not pleasant. "The Lord 'elps them as 'elps themselves, that's what the minister allus sez. Mind you, it's easier fer them that's got fifty men workin' forrem."

James spotted the allusion immediately.

"He's off again!"

"An' you can just shut yer trap fer once," Tommy snarled back. "We all know who your father is. But mine's one o' them slavin' fer 'im. It's the likes o' my dad yer all goin' on abaht, mekkin' a quiet fortune fer the boss. Well done thou good and faithful servant? That's a laugh, tharris. There's nowt in words that'd mek a good meal, so they're cheap enough. Instead o' givin' 'is servant a pat on the back, 'e shoulda gev 'im two o' them five talents!"

"Quiet, Tommy, before yer say summat rude," urged Matthew, who was embarrassed enough to forget his grammar for once.

"Say summat rude? I ain't even started yet! An' dun't tell me ter shurrup, yer little pipsqueak, or I'll belt yer a good un!"

Lucy pursued the tactful line. "Don't be angry with your brother, Tommy. Like the rest of us, he only wants to learn the true meaning of the parable."

"Oh, does 'e? All right, Miss Bradley, I'll tell yer. I'll tell the lot on yer! It means work 'ard every day 'cept Sunday till yer arms are near 'angin' off, an' dun't ask fer more than eight shillin's a week. Do that fer forty years an' they'll say summat nice at yer funeral. But dun't ask where the rest o' the money's goin', 'cos that's not yer place. It's just like all the other shit we get stuffed dahn us every Sunday – just do what we tell yer, know yer place an' dun't ask what's really goin' on. One day yer might get to 'eaven, but yer'll likely be queuin' up behind all the bosses who've got the money ter gerrin fust!"

Matthew was mortified. " 'e don't mean it, miss; 'e's allus sayin' daft things like that, but 'e don't mean 'alf of 'em!"

Tommy made a vicious grab for Matthew, but missed. Two of the larger boys held on to the sleeves of his jacket and slowly pulled him back. He struggled free, and hissed down at Matthew. "You'll gerrit when yer come aht, boss's man!"

He stormed noisily through the pews, down the left-hand aisle and out of the main door at the front of the chapel, slamming it hard behind him. Every group stopped what it was doing in order to stare; somewhere, a small girl began to cry.

Sunday School ended, as usual, with the final hymn and the blessing. Matthew seemed reluctant to leave, and sat slumped in a pew long after the others had scampered home. He got up, wandered aimlessly around the chapel, examined the inscriptions on every memorial plaque, then sat down again. Lucy was busy collecting Bibles and hymn books when Matthew finally plucked up the courage to get up and offer his assistance.

"That's very kind of you, Matthew," she said, "but I've nearly finished, thank you all the same. But if you'd like to turn up early next week and help me lay them out again, then I'd be most grateful."

Matthew turned sadly away and trudged resignedly down the aisle and through the main door, closing it carefully behind him. Lucy began counting the books she had been stacking, reflecting on Matthew's charming offer to help. Then, with a start, she realised why. Appalled by her own preoccupation she raced out of the chapel and into Halifax Lane. She was already too late.

Matthew lay in a dishevelled heap at the edge of the rutted lane, sniffling softly. His jacket was torn, his boots and trouser legs plastered with mud. One eye was already closing up and the blood from his nose flowed in a thickening stream over his lips and down his chin, having merged with the crimson line from his split lip. His collar was ripped open and his cap lay in a puddle. Young Billy Howell stood looking down at him in morbid fascination.

"It weren't 'is fault, miss. 'e didn't do any fightin'. Just sorta stood there an' let it 'appen."

"I know full well who's to blame, Billy. Help me get him up."

They lifted Matthew to his feet and began to dust him down. Lucy stemmed the bleeding with her handkerchief, while Billy retrieved the cap, flicked the muddy water from it and replaced it on Matthew's head. The sniffling had stopped and Matthew looked down ruefully at the state of his clothing.

"Mi mam'll kill me when she sees this lot."

"Surely not; not when it was your own brother?" The hesitation told her everything. "Matthew, you will tell her the truth, won't you?" His eyes shifted uneasily.

"It weren't Tommy," he lied.

Lucy fought with the lump in her throat. She wanted to hug Matthew to her, to make everything right for him, but that would only embarrass him further. Instead of the loving sympathy he had every right to expect, he was intending to go home and face the consequences – and possibly another beating – for spoiling his Sunday best for no apparent reason. Well, she wouldn't let it happen.

"Come along with me, Matthew, and we'll see what we can do about those clothes."

A few minutes later, Catherine Bradley raised two enquiring eyebrows as Lucy led Matthew into the scullery and reached for a flannel cloth.

"That awful brother of his waited for him after Sunday School. I can't let him go home to his mother looking like this."

Catherine grunted a vague acknowledgment and handed Lucy a slab of pumice. She was not accustomed to making her domestic facilities available for all and sundry, and she hoped that this was not to be the start of another of Lucy's enthusiasms. She was about to seek out her husband and register the fact, when he came through the door from the parlour, young Rebecca scampering at his heels. They had been alerted to the minor drama by the scullery maid.

Rebecca was inclined to be childish for her thirteen years, although her long dark ringlets gave promise of an impending cuteness. She had already heard about Matthew's battering, and was all agog.

"Is he going to die?"

"Don't be silly, Rebecca," replied her father. "Help your sister clean him up – he looks as though he's been dragged through a hedge backwards."

Rebecca gleefully splashed water on Matthew's muddied apparel, while Lucy took needle and thread to the jacket and collar. Finally, Lucy stood back and examined the results of their combined efforts.

"There now, that's not so bad. Now, you just stay there a minute while I get something for you."

She hurried to the sitting room, where she wrote a short note in simple language, hoping that Lily could read well enough. When she returned to the scullery, Robert was asking Matthew about his forthcoming indenture as a stockinger, learning the trade under his father. Lucy took her father to one side and explained under her breath that if she left it to Matthew to hand his mother the note, it would never arrive. Robert nodded his agreement and sent for Adam, the family butler.

"Adam, please accompany Master Slack to his home, and see that his mother receives this note."

"Yes, sir. Any reply?"

"No, Adam, likely not."

"Very good, sir."

Matthew was almost through the scullery back door when he remembered the handkerchief, now stained brown with his dried blood. Sheepishly, he offered it back to Lucy, who shook her head and smiled back at him.

"Keep it."

Even at the door of number seven, Matthew made one last despairing effort. But Adam firmly declined his invitation to trust him with the note, and instead, when an anxious-looking Lily answered the door to his imperious knock, Adam adopted his best drawing room manner, and held out the note.

"Compliments of Mr Robert Bradley, ma'am."

As he strode away, glad to be rid of the smell of the yard, Lily stared first at her grubby, crestfallen son, and then at the note. She signalled for Matthew to come inside, while she painstakingly spelt out the message, letter by letter. No Sunday School had provided for her education.

Nathan was about to lay into Matthew for his late return and the state of his clothing, but Lily placed a protective arm around him.

"You all right, lad?" Her tone mixed tenderness with sadness.

"Yes, Mam – it weren't much, 'onest, an' 'e didn't mean it."

"Who didn't mean what?" Nathan demanded. There was no point in handing him the note, so Lily explained.

"The bogger! I'll flay 'is arse fer 'im when 'e gets 'ome!" growled Nathan.

Tommy had not yet returned from Sunday School. He had still not put in an appearance when the family left for the evening service and was not even home when they returned. Lily was now both annoyed and worried, and Nathan was even more angry to see Lily upset.

When Tommy lifted the latch as quietly as he could just after eleven, his father was waiting for him in a state that was little short of fury. It was a brief confrontation, and Tommy got the biggest leathering of his life. He choked back angry tears, and threw himself down on the bedding that a wretched Matthew had prepared for him. In the upper room, Lily could be heard weeping quietly, her sobs muffled against Nathan's comforting chest. Soon it grew quiet, except for Tommy's harsh breathing. Matthew felt desperately sorry for him.

"Tommy?"

There was no response.

"I didn't tell on yer, Tommy – it were Miss Bradley."

Still no response.

"Tommy?"

A grunt.

"I saved yer some o' mi tea; look."

Tommy cautiously shifted his position on the bedding, reached out and took the bread. He ate hungrily, without looking up.

"It don't matter ter me, Tommy. I . . . I . . . still love yer."

With some effort, Tommy raised his head, and there was moisture running through the dust just below his eyes. He leaned over, arm outstretched, to grip Matthew's shoulder, and felt pangs of shame when Matthew instinctively flinched back from his grasp.

"Yer all right Matthew; it's me that's the bastard, sometimes."

Matthew fell happily asleep, wondering idly where Tommy had been since Sunday School.

One day, he was to find out.

It was cold up in the frame room, but then it usually was in late November. Flanked by a line of tall windows the length, and almost the height, of one wall, it was a room designed for maximum daylight. That same design also guaranteed a working environment which was an oven in the summer and a blue-fingered torture in the winter months. It would be even worse come February, but this was bad enough.

The point-net frames clattered and clonked their steady rhythm, nine of them, each extruding unfinished garments at a crawling pace which seemed to mock the efforts of the men who worked them with their hands and feet. Each of the stockingers sat at his frame, slightly stooped, for hour after dismal hour, barring technical mishaps. Today they were on a run of standard Derby Rib, and it was boring work. After a few years, it was claimed, you could tell a framework knitter by the shape of his back and the weakness of his eyes.

Conversation was difficult above the persistent rattle, and in consequence most frameworkers tended to shout, even at home. Nathan and his nearest colleague, Sam Pinkney, had got into the way of it over the years.

"Three bob a week, yer say?"

"Aye, but I reckon it'll be worth it, specially fer Lily, wi' the new one on the way."

"I'm not sure as my Eliza'd agree wi' yer there. When d'yer reckon you'll be goin' then?"

"Steady on, we've only just purrus names dahn! Anyroad, they'll not be startin' till the spring, an' the fust lot's already tekken. I reckon it'll be a couple o' years afore we actually move."

"You 'ope! God only knows what things'll be like bi then. You'll mebbe not 'ave three bob a week ter spare."

"Aye, there is that."

Nathan had taken the plunge. Mr Endicott had recorded his name as a potential tenant in the proposed Newnham Family Trust Artisans' Dwellings development, on the strict understanding that the landlords reserved the right to increase the weekly rental before entry, and that the final entry date itself would depend upon a whole host of unknown factors, particularly the weather and the ground conditions. But still, the hope was there, and Lily had beamed with pleasure when he'd told her. The rest of the family had shared her enthusiasm, even if Tommy had seen fit to pass some remark about deserting a sinking ship.

It was Tommy who now sauntered towards them with the grease pot, essential for the easy running of the frames. Morose and distracted as ever, he was the most unenthusiastic of apprentice journeymen. In accordance with the now firmly entrenched tradition he was apprenticed to his own father, as Nathan had been to Joe, and while his technical progress could not exactly be faulted, his heart wasn't really in it. Not like Matthew, who was eager to begin to learn, even though it would be a couple of months yet before he could start officially. For the time being, he worked upstairs with the young girls, bailing the lace goods which they had 'hand-run' to a final finish.

"Ey up then, Tommy," Sam Pinkney greeted him, "yer dad's bin tellin' me as 'ow yer all clearin' off to a swanky new 'ouse."

"So I'm told; all the same ter me."

"Try thinkin' abaht somebody else fer a change," growled Nathan. "Yer mam's 'appy enough. Dun't that mean anythin' ter you?"

Tommy ignored the question, and countered with one of his own. "Yer seen Stan Cadby anywhere?"

"No," replied Nathan, "an' I dun't want ter, neither. An' I'd advise you ter keep yer distance."

Nathan was concerned to see Tommy seeking the company of men such as Cadby, who worked for Bradley as a bag-hosier, a job which involved touring the area daily to collect the basic plain rib produced by the 'home' workers on rented frames. He also acted as paymaster, paying in cash for the work he collected, an ideal opportunity for sharp practice which, rumour had it, he grasped with both hands. His mobility during the working day also allowed him to indulge in even less savoury practices, and he was shunned by the majority of decent workers.

Despite Nathan's stricture, Tommy eventually found Stan, and their furtive conversation lasted several minutes. Cadby then climbed the two flights of stairs to the garret where another group of women sat in rows, adding to the final product the 'needlerun' patterns demanded by fashion, which not even the relatively new point-net frames could produce.

Stan's crude repartee was appreciated by some of the older, harder, women, but the majority of the younger girls kept their eyes demurely on their work. He dumped his bags of home-produced work on the floor, and then sat, toad-like, on the topmost bag. From the centre of the cramped room, his watery gaze swept over the group of women in a silent but unnerving assessment of their physical assets.

"An' who's the lucky gel who's goin' ter wrestle wi' me fer this lot?"

The girls were paid by the 'piece', and in these days of falling orders, stood to gain much by keeping well in with the bagger. There were several coarse replies, and a good deal of general vulgarity, following which Cadby distributed the work according to his whim, then sidled alongside Dinah Watson, and whispered in her ear. Dinah glanced across at Annie Beckett, grinned wickedly, and nodded. Cadby slipped the extra bag of work under Dinah's stool and started to walk away.

"Oh, Annie," called Dinah in her most innocent tone, "Mr Cadby's got some more work fer us dahn on the landin' – gi' 'im an' 'and wi' it, there's a good gel."

Annie didn't know any better. She was just fourteen years old, and Dinah was by way of being the uncrowned Queen of the Needlerunners. The young girl rose without a word and followed Cadby faithfully down the stairs.

Off the landing below was a storeroom piled high with raw cotton bales. In a matter of seconds, Cadby had one hand on the door handle and his other arm around Annie's waist. Then, in a single movement, he threw her down on the bales, followed her inside and slammed the door behind them both.

Her screams were so loud and piercing that Dinah panicked. She rushed down the narrow flight of stairs and hammered on the storeroom door.

"Stan, fer pity's sake leave off afore the little bogger brings the place dahn!"

The screams died to hysterical choking sobs, the door handle rattled, and a second later Annie flew out, her bodice torn and her hem above her knee. She dashed, screaming, down the next staircase and ran out through the frame room, on through the far door and all the way down to the first landing – straight into the arms of a startled Robert Bradley.

———— ◁▷ ————

Tommy approached the door of number seven with foreboding. He didn't believe for one moment that his father had accidentally forgotten their break-time food, and he had a fairly shrewd idea why he, rather than Matthew, had been sent home for it. The one thing he tried to avoid – whatever the cause – was a direct confrontation with his mother, who was usually more than a match for him when it came to an interrogation. All the same, it looked as if he was in for one, and he could guess why. He slipped the latch and sauntered in with what he hoped was a preoccupied look.

"Ah, Tommy. Come back fer yer dinners?"

"Yeah, Mam, an' I've to 'urry back, dad says. Lot o' work on terday."

"Yer'll do fer a minute; siddahn."

"But Mam . . ."

"I said siddahn! Ruth, go an' see Mrs Morton abaht that there apron." Ruth scuttled away on cue, and Tommy's worst fears were realised. "Nah then, mi lad – just what's gorrinter yer these past few weeks?"

Tommy was familiar enough with his mother's direct approach to everything, but the suddenness of the question floored him temporarily.

" 'ow d'yer mean?"

"Yer know fine wharra mean. Yer so narky these days that there's no talkin' ter yer. An' that were a terrible thing ter do ter yer own brother."

"I said sorry to 'im, an' anyroad, 'e asked fer it."

"What, bi tryin' ter stop yer mekkin' a fool o' yersen in Sunday School?"

Tommy warmed to the theme. "I weren't mekkin' a fool o' misen, just tryin' ter show the rest of 'em that the church is allus on the side o' the bosses, no marrer what."

"We'll not go inter that, just at the moment. Wharram askin' yer, right 'ere an' nah, is what's mekkin' yer so ratty these days?"

"Ain't tharrenough?"

"No, it ain't. I know mi own son berrer than that."

Tommy paused, then retorted. "O' course, it's all right fer you. Yer 'appy enough wi' this place, an' the family. But the likes o' me, well we can see further than that. Me – and others like me – can see what's really goin' on, an' who's gerrin' the benefit of it. An' it's gerrin' worse, yer know. What's gunner be left fer the likes o' me when I'm your age?"

"Tommy Slack, yer daft in the 'ead, you are! Yer a lot luckier than some I could mention; a lot luckier!"

"An' why should it need luck, then? Tell me that. Yer allus tellin' us that all we need ter do is work 'ard an' we'll gerrus rewards. That's what they tell us at chapel, an' all. Yer all kiddin' yersens, tek it from me!"

"There's more rewards than money, lad. No man need ask fer more than a good wife an' . . ."

"Aye, an' that's summat else. What girl's gunner look at me, in mi boots an' 'omespun?"

"There's plenty o' girls'll be pleased ter tek you on in a few years' time. Yer a fine strong lad, just like yer dad, an' yer'll not be lackin' fer offers. But yer too young ter be thinkin' on that yet."

"I'll never be old enough ter drill the likes o' Mary Draycott and Hannah Needham, if that's who yer've gorrin mind."

"Dun't be coarse, Tommy, there's no call forrit! An' what's wrong wi' Mary Draycott, or Hannah Needham, anyroad? Or d'yer think some fine lady should set 'er cap at yer? Somebody like Lucy Bradley, mebbe?" Tommy coloured unexpectedly, and Lily pressed home the advantage. "Is tharrit? Yer think yer good enough fer the likes o' Lucy Bradley?"

"An' why not? We're all equal under God, or so yer allus tellin' us. Only it's not really true, is it, not when it really comes ter summat? We're only equal as long as the likes of us keeps ar place. What sort o' religion d'yer call that, then? D'yer send us all ter chapel ter learn that?"

Lily felt genuinely sorry for him, and her tone softened. Her guard dropped, and she made a tactical mistake. "Tommy, yer must see that girls like Lucy are used ter berrer than ar class can give 'em. She's 'ad the best that money can buy – teachin', clothes, everythin'. Yer couldn't bring a girl like that inter the yard, could yer?"

"Ar class – that's what yer just said. 'ow come there's classes if we're all s'posed ter be equal? Answer me that, then. Yer right, o' course. She'd never lower 'ersen ter look at the likes o' me. But then, that's only 'cos o' the fancy ways she's bin taught, an' the money fer that came from the likes o' dad an' me."

"I didn't say it were all perfect, nobody expects that. The Lord requires 'is servants ter labour long fer their rewards, but 'e never fails 'em. God provides everythin' in due season."

"That's what we're allus bein' told bi them that's already gorrit! But tek a good look rahnd yer, Mam. What's 'e provided fer folks in this yard?"

Lily was weakening, and fell back on reminiscences. "Yer shoulda seen it a few years since – things was really bad fer a time then."

"An' yer reckon it's so bloody marvellous nah? Livin' like this, five to a room? An' wharrabaht poor sods like the Draycotts an' the Plummers? They'll still be 'ere, yer know, when we've slunk off ter Radford!"

Tommy had hit a vulnerable target, and he knew it. Time to leave, while he was still winning.

"Anyroad, I'm off back ter Bradley's. Tell God tea's at nine."

Lily was too shocked to get in a reply before the door slammed shut behind him.

That same afternoon, Robert Bradley conducted two interviews. The first was with Stan Cadby, angrily recalled from the hovel in Narrow Marsh where he'd hoped to skulk until things quietened down.

"Come in, Cadby, and stand there, where I can get a good look at yer."

Stan had planned a variety of defences and was wondering which to try first. But first he needed to assess the strength of the case against him, and planned to keep his silence, at least to begin with.

"Now then, I've 'ad a most serious complaint from young Annie Beckett."

"She's lyin'. "

"I 'aven't even told you what she said yet! Or maybe yer know already?"

"She's a liar, that's all. Allus was, an' allus will be – you ask Dinah Watson."

"I suppose she tore 'er own clothes as well?"

"I wouldn't know abaht that. But she'd do owt ter cause trouble, that one."

Robert had already lost what little patience he had managed to muster for the occasion.

"Cadby, you're a lyin', two-faced, snivellin', hypocritical bastard, and may the Good Lord pardon my sinful language on this occasion of sore temptation. I want you off my premises inside the next ten minutes, and I want yer lace bags, stock tallies and piece tokens back in 'ere by tomorrow afternoon. I'm givin' the money that's due to you to Annie Beckett instead, and I'll make bloody sure that no-one of my acquaintance gives you as much as 'alf a day's work from now till Judgment Day. Now get out before I strangle you as well!"

"But Mr Bradley . . ." The confident tone had reverted to a whine.

"I said get out!"

"It weren't me, 'onest! Leastways, I were only 'avin' a bit of a lark, but . . ."

"A bit of a lark?" Robert's facial expression had turned almost murderous. "You were all set ter ruin the poor girl, by all accounts! By rights I should've 'ad yer taken in charge by the Watch, yer filthy animal! As it is, yer can thank me fer mi Christian forbearance, not that you showed any."

"Can't I just . . . mek it up to 'er?"

"Make it up to 'er! You just stay away from 'er altogether, do you hear me, or I will 'ave yer taken up. I've said mi piece and I'm not one fer going back on things. Yer finished 'ere, so clear out now before yer get what yer really deserve!"

Cadby recognised defeat, and his manner changed as rapidly as his fortunes. "Yer've not 'eard the last o' this, Bradley. You an' yer precious Christian charity! Yer'll not do this ter me an' gerraway wi' it! I've got friends, I 'ave, an' yer'll get paid back fer this soon enough, yer miserable old bogger!"

He just managed to dodge the flying ledger as he shot backwards through the door. As he took the stairs down, two at a time, Robert raced to the head of the stairwell armed with an inkstand. On an impulse he changed his mind, pulled his ruffled frock coat back into place and took several deep breaths. He then walked sedately back into his office and closed the door quietly behind him.

Even so, nearly an hour elapsed before he felt sufficiently composed to call for Nathan. His forced cordiality was a shade overdone, and Nathan took the proffered chair with a mixture of surprise and apprehension.

"Now then, Nathan, you and me 'ave known each other fer that many years I reckon I can speak mi mind to you without formality."

Nathan was sometimes at a loss for words in the presence of his employer, and no real response seemed to be called for, so he simply nodded and waited politely for what Robert had on his mind.

"I've got summat ter say about those two lads o' yours, startin' with Matthew."

"What's 'e done?" blurted out Nathan, genuinely bewildered.

"Nowt at all, so don't take on. It's more a question o' what other people reckon 'e could do, given a chance."

Not one for riddles, Nathan awaited enlightenment.

"Yer know, of course, that 'e's in our Lucy's class at Sunday School, and you 'eard about what happened last Sunday?"

Nathan nodded sadly; he'd hoped that the incident had already been forgotten.

"Well, 'e's quite clearly bein' 'eld back by that brother of 'is, at least that's what Lucy reckons. The fact is that Lucy's always wanted ter be a teacher – a proper teacher, mind, not just Sunday School. Anyway, 'er mother won't 'ear of it, so there's an end ter that. But after she'd brought young Matthew 'ome last Sunday she 'ad a word with 'er mother, and naturally 'er mother spoke ter me about it, and I promised I'd 'ave a word with you. What I'm gettin' to is this; 'ow would it be if our Lucy was ter take your Matthew on as a pupil in the evenings? It'd cost yer nowt, obviously, all free of charge, only Lucy reckons 'e's a bright lad and could really learn summat. 'er mother's agreeable, since she's hopin' it'll get all this teachin' business out of 'er system. Fer miself, I wouldn't know, but I'm not a man ter stand in the way of mi own daughter's 'appiness, so what about it?"

Nathan was dumbfounded. It was all too sudden, all too organised. He needed Lily's advice, and it only seemed right to ask Matthew first, although he could guess what the two of them would say, Lily particularly. Robert sensed the hesitation.

"I'll tell yer what – think on it fer a day or two then come and see me again. 'ow would that suit?"

"Er . . . aye, all right. Thank you, Mr Bradley." He half rose from his chair, believing the interview to be over.

"Not yet, Nathan. Mind I said I had summat ter say about Tommy as well?"

"Oh, aye." Nathan's heart sank to his boots.

"Yer'll 'ave ter do summat with him, Nathan, he's gettin' out of 'and. I know 'e's only young yet, even if 'e is almost as tall as you, but the way 'e's goin', 'e'll come to a sticky end before 'e's much older."

"Aye, I know," admitted Nathan. "Burre means well, it's just that 'e's got this bee in 'is bonnet abaht some people bein' more fortunate than others. Reckons it's not fair, that's all. Yer can see 'is point."

Robert frowned slightly, before continuing. "Then it's up ter you and 'is mother ter teach 'im that yer get nowt in this world without yer work fer it. Now, take me fer example . . ."

"We 'ave tried," interrupted Nathan, "but lately 'e allus seems to 'ave an answer ready. Sometimes we almost believe 'im oursens."

"Well, that's up ter you, o' course," Robert replied, the frown deepening, "but I'm tellin' you that 'e needs a firm 'and, and preferably across 'is backside."

"Aye, yer right there," Nathan agreed.

"Maybe 'e's not a bad lad at heart, but 'e's got ter be sat on."

"Aye."

"Anyway, what I'm leadin' up to, I'm afraid, is that we 'ad a trustees meetin' at the chapel yesterday evenin', and we came ter the reluctant conclusion that fer the time bein' at least, it'd be best if yer kept 'im away from Sunday School. We'll expect ter see 'im at the regular services, mind, just not at Sunday School."

Nathan couldn't help himself. "That's a bit much, beggin' yer pardon Mr Bradley. 'e's a wild un at times I know, but Sunday School's the only chance 'e's got of betterin' 'imself."

"I appreciate that, Nathan, but it's the only chance fer the others as well. We can't 'ave the classes interrupted like that by every young tearaway that fancies 'imself as another Robespierre. No, we think it best if 'e keeps away fer a while. By all accounts, 'e doesn't learn a sight from the grammar classes anyway."

The conversation switched to work-related matters, and a few minutes later Nathan was back at his frame, confused and angry. Like most fathers, he wished that his sons could be more like him. As it was, one already had more learning than he would ever have, while the other had more spirit. What on earth was he going to tell Lily about Tommy? He still thought the trustees were wrong, and keeping Tommy out of Sunday School wasn't going to help him one bit.

Back at home, tea was a dismal affair of bread and herring. Nathan's morose preoccupation cast a gloom over the simple proceedings, and it was a relief to everyone when he finally broke the silence.

"Well, I've got a right pair o' sons, an' that's a fact."

No-one spoke.

"I said I've got a right pair o' sons . . ."

"We 'eard," Tommy growled.

Nathan shot from his chair, leaned across the table, grabbed Tommy by the front of his jacket and hauled him bodily off his stool. The move had been so swift that Tommy had no chance to avoid it, and now, as he stood almost on tiptoe, only inches from his father's darkened countenance, there was fear in his eyes.

"Oh yer did, did yer?' thundered Nathan. 'Well 'ear this an' all, yer cocky little know-it-all. I 'ad ter sit in Bradley's office this afternoon an' listen while 'e told me that mi eldest son's bin thrown aht o' Sunday School!"

Lily cried out, a hand to her mouth. Nathan's grip had relaxed sufficiently for Tommy to sense that the crisis might be over, and a contemptuous smirk crossed his face.

"They're finally learnin' summat dahn there, then. Suits me, anyroad."

He learned his mistake as Nathan's left hand transferred to Tommy's collar, and twisted. His father's voice was unnaturally soft and determined, and only increased in pitch as he promised further physical retribution.

"Well, it doesn't suit me! We've all 'ad just abaht enough o' you an' yer mytherin' manner. As of nah, yer not settin' foot aht o' that door unless it's ter go ter work or chapel. An' yer comin' ter chapel wi' the rest of us mornin' an' evenin' every Sunday. An' every time I

'ear yer as much as cough in the wrong place – abaht anythin', mind
– yer'll get mi belt across yer arse. Yer gorrall that?"

Tommy's eyes met Nathan's in a brief, unequal, struggle.
Determination triumphed over the unpredictable, and Tommy's eyes
dropped dutifully to the table.

"Aye, 'appy wi' that, anyroad," was all he could muster in an
effort to save some face. But as Nathan pushed him roughly back
onto his stool, his mind was already working tactically.

Lily had so far been a silent but horrified witness to all this.
Now, as she recovered her composure, she remembered Matthew.

"What's ar Matthew bin up ter, then?"

"Eh? Oh, nowt. Leastways, nowt ter be ashamed of. Fact is, 'e's
won such golden opinions fer 'imsen that there's some would like ter
see 'im educated proper."

Lily eagerly dragged the details from him, while Matthew sat
silent and bewildered, glancing shamefacedly across at Tommy's rigid
expression. As the conversation continued, he could also not fail to
be aware of his mother's mounting excitement. As usual, nobody
consulted him, and it was a foregone conclusion.

"Matthew!" Lily was almost breathless. "It's yer big chance, lad!
There's nowt yer can't do wi' the right schoolin' – it's God's
doin', is this!"

"Aye, Mam."

"Tommy, didn't I tell yer, only this morning, abaht God providin'
in good season?"

"Aye, Mam, yer did."

Tommy's tone of voice was equivocal, and Nathan looked hard
into his face for an excuse to take his belt off. But Lily's enthusiasm
distracted everyone.

And so Nathan was instructed to see Robert Bradley first
thing the following morning, accept his offer, and remember to
say thank you.

Later that evening, as they prepared for bed, Matthew had
thought it through. He'd never be like Tommy, never big and fearless
like him, but here was something he could do, and perhaps help the
family in his own way. It would make his mother happy, and maybe
in the end Tommy might come to accept him as he was. He'd often
wondered about the scholars he'd heard about in Sunday School,
and wondered whether he was more like them. Here was his chance
to find out.

He was excited, and grinned as Ruth skipped back and forth

between the table and the bedding on the floor, singing "Matthew's goin' ter go ter school, Matthew's goin' ter go ter school" over and over again, to the tune they called 'The Mulberry Bush'. She didn't really know what it was all about, but her mother was happier than she'd seen her for weeks and that was good enough for her.

Matthew even found it easy to ignore the foul looks he got from Tommy, and the silent obscenities which he mouthed at him from the corner of the room furthest away from the staircase leading to the upper room where their parents had retired to bed. Matthew was taking the first adult step in his life, and he was pleased.

Late that night, the first stone crashed through the upper windows of Bradley's Hosiery.

CHAPTER THREE

A meeting of minds

THE SNOW came early in the winter that ushered in 1810. By mid-afternoon, one dull day in early December, the warning signs were there for all who cared to stand in the elevated grounds of St. Mary's Church and gaze upwards to the east. An endless bank of grey-white clouds, eerily translucent in the gathering dusk, bore down from the distant Humber like the marauding Vikings of an earlier century. First came a fine drizzle, then the first sleety flakes, soon heavier and more disciplined. The children home to tea cheered their good fortune, chasing the gently drifting flakes around in circles and praying for enough to make snowmen. Grandparents sat silent, knowing the truth from bitter memory.

Next day, a slate-hued dawn pulled up the curtain on four inches of pure white mischief, unbroken even by carriage ruts, through which the early workers plodded in their leaky summer boots. It snowed all that day, and all the next. Then came the cruel, sharp, clear skies, and everything froze solid.

Some died within hours, dozens in the first few days, and hundreds in the weeks that followed. The first to go were the elderly and sick, coughing and shivering to their last rasping breath. Soon the victims were younger, heads of families whose daily intake of nutrients proved insufficient defence against the rawness of that winter, and whose damp and draughty hovels were no match for the east wind.

Pneumonia and bronchitis joined forces, scything through the parish like avenging angels. Carts carrying away the dead jammed in rock-hard slush ruts in the roads, and from them, frozen corpses slithered to the ground. The horse-drawn water carriers gave up their trade in hopeless despair and their carts remained frozen in their yards. The poor were reduced to shoveling snow or chipping away lumps of ice to melt over their meagre fires, assuming they could afford fuel, and for six whole weeks St. Mary's reeked of death, disease and neglect. In the public burial grounds, three inches of frost denied entry to the sexton's spade. It was to go on like this for weeks, and all the time the price of finished hosiery fell.

Nathan was luckier than most. He was still working, even if his Saturday pockets jingled less as the weeks wore on. But he was one of a diminishing band; Bradley was down to four frames and a handful of girls before Christmas, and several hosiers were on the point of closure. As the terms of trade worsened for the local product, cheap imports tightened the stranglehold and none but the finest gentry – themselves a depleted class – now wore Nottingham's pride upon their calves. The same inexorable laws of international trade made food imports dearer by the week, and life for most in St. Mary's, always hard, was fast becoming impossible. Their stomachs empty, and their lungs full, they died what for many must have seemed a merciful death.

The Nottingham Corporation began to review its options. Nothing was likely to improve until the spring, of that they were certain, even if their public utterances adopted a more optimistic tone. Winters like this were not unknown in the town, but the desperate poverty made matters more serious than they had ever been.

Some consequences were inevitable. No-one doubted that hundreds would die and none could deny that more burial space would be required almost immediately. Many feared an epidemic, but above all else the town elders were apprehensive of civil disorder. Such law enforcement as could be mustered in normal circumstances would be worse than useless if hunger and despair took a hold in barely governable areas such as St. Mary's. Indeed, there was every indication that the tenuous system had already broken down, and it was with some anxiety that the Corporation met in early January to review the Poor Law arrangements.

Conceived in the more pastoral age of Good Queen Bess, the Poor Law proceeded on the premise that every parish would, and indeed could, look after its own. Even by 1800 the system had become a scandalous farce in already festering slums like Narrow Marsh and Leen Side, or the Rookeries to the north of the town centre, in which almost all the residents were also potential recipients. And in a parish like St. Mary's, which depended so heavily on one trade, a failure in that trade meant a reduction in the financial circumstances even of those who were expected to contribute most to the common purse, and who consequently baulked at doing so. In short, while thousands struggled in clamorous need, a hundred or so looked on in resentful bewilderment.

From the outset of the meeting even the meanest alderman felt that some further aid should be granted to the parishes, but most only did so out of fear of the alternative. It took hours to agree on the method of delivery, and when a majority was finally attained on the last of many formal motions it was the most insensitive that could have been conceived in the circumstances.

Fired with the spirit of Christian charity, the authorities solemnly created an annexe to the established workhouse on Mansfield Road, utilising a number of old buildings in Barker Gate – convenient for the nearby burial ground – which were owned by a member of the Corporation and had been standing empty for some time. This meant that one hundred and twenty additional wretched souls could die slowly and institutionally, rather than quickly while surrounded by their loved ones. To further demonstrate their concern for the welfare of the community, the Corporation authorised the magistrates to appoint a further six officers of the Watch – at a stipend of three shillings a week each – to patrol the parishes, lest the local populace should take such a charitable gesture to be a sign of weakness.

To the moment of her confinement, Lily battled day and night to keep together the bodies, if not the souls, of her neighbours in Tanners Yard. Nathan's earnings, depleted though they were, and the pittances now being paid to both Tommy and Matthew, were converted each Saturday into a seemingly endless stew, hot jugs of which were always available for the asking to those in the yard in the direst need. Inspired by her literal understanding of the miracle of the loaves and fishes, Lily had the satisfaction of seeing others follow her example, and within a month or so of her first selfless gesture sustenance in the yard was virtually communal. But late one morning, shortly before Christmas, the telltale twinges she had kept silent about for the previous two days quickened and intensified beyond denial, and old Nancy was sent for.

They had been through it all before, but never under such terrible conditions. The house itself was as clean as scrubbing could make it – Lily had seen to that – but the very fabric of the mean dwelling, with its pitted timbers, roughcast floor and lath and plaster walls, served as a breeding ground for every form of infection which the yard could offer. Bedding, such as it was, was continually damp despite the fires which they somehow managed to keep burning, and the icy wind cut effortlessly through the rattling shutters which Nathan had thrown up from what he could scavenge, while the freezing fogs which alternated with the easterly gales had a choice of many gaping crevices in the walls through which to seep into the house itself.

As she went into the early stages of labour, Lily became

increasingly troubled by the tickling cough which had plagued her since old Joe's funeral and the first of the fogs. As her breathing became more erratic, and the need for longer draughts of air more urgent, the cough worsened. None of Nancy's remedies could shift it, and after the first few hours her talents as a midwife claimed a higher priority. By midnight on that first day Lily was well into labour, and Nancy was worried.

"It ain't normal," she confided to Nathan and the family as they sat huddled around the fire, boiling water in anticipation. "She's slow in 'er movements an' the waters were late. I've seen it time enough, burrit's allus a bad do when it starts like that."

"What can we do?" implored Nathan, who always felt helpless at times like this, not comprehending but fearing the worst.

"You? Nowt you can do, lad. It's up to 'er nah."

She went back to tend to Lily in the upper room, leaving Nathan wringing his hands and mumbling to himself. Tommy leaned back against the wall and closed his eyes while Matthew stared into the fire, white as chalk. Ruth followed silently after Nancy, and slipped into the upper room behind her, anxiously scanning her mother's fevered face and wincing at the hoarse coughs which now came every half-minute or so. She sank to her knees beside the bed and reached out to take Lily's hand; Lily smiled back at her, then began again to heave and bark. Nancy put her hand down inside the bedding and gently explored as another contraction rippled through, provoking another round of helpless coughing.

"Come on, lass; a bit more ter do yet."

All that night they waited, and as a late dawn crept under the shutters, the boys were sent to Bradley's with a message from Nathan. Ruth saw her chance to play the housewife and nobody stopped her, least of all Nathan, glued to his chair with his fingers twisting back and forth in nervous apprehension. Nancy came down from time to time, a drawn look on her face. The day came and went, the boys returned, and the darkness fell again. Then at half-past nine, Nancy poked her head down the staircase.

"Ruth – quick!"

Nathan, sick with fear, began quietly praying. Tommy pretended to read a crudely printed pamphlet which had been crumpled inside his pocket, while Matthew stood by the door, as if about to run. It was so quiet that every movement – and every moan – from the upper room seemed deafening. Lily's cries intensified, growing almost continuous. A long shriek was followed by a terrible silence, and nobody breathed. Then came the sound of footsteps, a soft slap and a feeble whimper, which jerked suddenly into a sharp cry. A baby's cry, and a shout of triumph from Nancy.

Nathan stopped praying and waited for the footsteps. Ruth was the first down the stairs, scampering eagerly, her face alight with wonder. "Dad! Come an' look!"

Nathan climbed the stairs two at a time, lowering his head just in time to enter the upper room without mishap. His eyes and nose smarted at the heavy stench of sweat and worse, and his eyes took in the blood and the mess before they rested on the scrawny outcome of Lily's terrible ordeal. It was purple and skinny, plastered in drying mucus and protesting feebly from within the shawl.

"It's another boy, Nathan," said Nancy gently.

"God be praised! Thanks, Nancy – thanks."

A tear of relief rolled down Nathan's creased face as he looked down at Lily, drained and sleeping, her breathing heavy and still rasping. He looked back at Nancy, a question in his eyes.

"Aye, she'll be right enough, I reckon, but not fer a good while yet. She 'ad it rotten this time, an' it'll tek a week or two at least. An' I wish I 'ad summat fer that cough."

"I'll send Ruth up ter that woman in Hockley. We'll find summat, dun't worry."

"Well mind yer do. An' dun't waste yer time wi' goose grease, I've tried that already. An' nah yer'd best go back dahnstairs; there's still things left ter do up 'ere."

He went down and told the boys, and they all sat round the Bible and said a simple prayer of thanks. They called him William, and even Tommy seemed pleased.

The unforgiving winter ground on slowly and relentlessly and every day the death toll rose. Mother and child made hesitant progress at first, but by early February the family's worst fears had subsided. Within a week Lily had been forcing herself around the yard, making up for lost time, coughing and spluttering her advice on the best ways to obtain nourishment from next to nothing. Nathan protested at her self-neglect, but neither he nor the boys could stay at home all day to keep her confined by the fire, and Ruth could keep a secret. William, although underweight for the first few weeks of his life, continued to fill out slowly, and as the first signs of spring peeped through the receding snow the memory of that harrowing labour began to dim with the lengthening daylight, leaving only Lily's cough as a lasting reminder.

As the surviving townsfolk began to thaw out and count the cost, a new and bitter atmosphere could be detected in the yards and alleyways of Narrow Marsh and other deprived neighbourhoods. While many – perhaps the majority – had been content merely to try and stay alive, huddled together against the cold, others had been pooling their discontent in isolated groups around the town. In courtyard, workshop and tavern, they could be heard muttering darkly, each group at first unaware of the others, but all sharing a common grievance.

Barely a family had survived without bereavement, none had enjoyed full bellies and all feared for the future. To a man, ignorant of the finer laws of commerce, or the wayward winds of foreign trade, they felt betrayed by those for whom they toiled for such long hours, and to a man they looked to those same people for deliverance. The seemingly obvious remedy for their suffering was an increase in the rewards for their labour, at least back to the levels enjoyed in better times. The stubborn denial of such a just demand was taken as proof that, whatever else he might say in public, the wealthy hosier was, in private, indifferent to the imminent extinction of the hosiery worker upon whose back he had risen to a position of material comfort.

There were some among the workforce who did grasp the evidence of their own eyes and ears and could deduce, however imperfectly, that the employer was also suffering, albeit at a lesser level. But such men were not present during those early, furtive, meetings.

Among those who were present were men with interests of their own to serve. For every nine men fired by a genuine and understandable fear for his family's future welfare, there was one who sought to harvest the growing crop of resentment he had helped to sow. It was these men who met together on a wider front, once each of them realised that the others existed, and slowly a network spread across the town, a cobweb of links woven by self- appointed leaders of men. The Nottingham mob had always been a force to be reckoned with, but never before had it been properly organised. Day by day, that organisation began to yawn and stretch.

Once the movement had became anything like a coherent organisation it was predestined to become illegal under the Combination Act, a panic reaction by a previous Parliament to France's cataclysmic revolution, which they thought might somehow cross the channel via 'Jacobins' posing as group organisers within the many trades and industries on which Britain depended for her prosperity. Under the Act, any attempt at association, be it by worker or employer, was classed as sedition and attracted a prison sentence of several years.

In reality, such groups formed by employers were quietly tolerated, although in the Nottingham of 1810 there were virtually none. Even groups of workers were tactfully ignored by the Watch as they sidled in and out of the local inns and alehouses, on the grounds that ' . . . it surely can't be agin the law ter 'ave a sup of ale wi' yer pals after a hard day's work . . .' and initially no magistrate could be found within the town with either the energy or the will to entertain a case, even had anyone been insensitive enough to raise one. Only later was the Home Office to exhort the Nottingham justices of the peace to 'weed out the troublemakers' when it was, for all practical purposes, already too late. Until then, the Combination Act remained merely a potential weapon to be wielded spasmodically and arbitrarily when the common law failed to provide a remedy against what was, in reality, nothing more pernicious than hunger and despair.

If the employers were aware of these early rumblings among their workforce, they chose not to show it. Indeed, even when, months later, it became clear that the workers were uniting, there were some hosiers – Robert Bradley included – who misguidedly believed that any positive action, from whatever quarter, would be directed at Parliament rather than at the hands that fed the town, and that stockinger and employer alike would then benefit from any government action aimed at curbing imports and correcting abuses in the trade. They were tragically naïve as events were to prove, but in any case, in early 1810 the employers themselves were too disorganised to prepare for anything, and any unity that did exist among them was squandered in futile attempts at price-fixing.

By April, no employer was free from the undercurrent, not even Bradley. His diminished workforce had heard the whispers, and several were attending meetings. Stoney Street had several hosiery establishments along its length, and these in turn had daily contact with stocking workers throughout nearby Sneinton and Hockley. No-one denied that the hosiery industry as a whole needed a champion, an organisation and a united front. They had already endured too much to have any real hope for the future unless someone took the initiative.

Nathan shared these views but shied away from meetings; a man of few words who was as uncomfortable listening to speeches as he was making them. Perhaps, more than most, he could see beyond the partisan demands and counterclaims and could grasp the overall problem in its basic form. His family's needs were no less than any other's, and his hopes for the future were no different from theirs. Where he differed from most was in wishing the same upturn in fortunes for the employers from whom their livelihoods were derived.

It was Sam Pinkney, his neighbour on the point-net frames, who persuaded him to attend his first meeting, in the belief that Nathan's quiet wisdom would be an asset to the group with which Sam had already become associated. Together, one evening in mid-April, they left Bradley's during a chilly sunset and walked down Stoney Street towards the Union Flag. Each believed, in his own way, that he was about to contribute to the future of his family. Nathan in particular, although somewhat apprehensive, could not suppress an inner hope that he was about to hear something comforting regarding the future of the trade which supported them all.

Darkness was falling rapidly as they entered the Union Flag and went straight through into the back room, already heavy with tobacco smoke. Its muddy floor was pungent with the smell of spilled ale as neighbours and colleagues jostled noisily for space under the solitary oil lamp in what was a cramped area at the best of times. Nathan was known and respected by many, and indeed there were some who thought of him as a potential champion of 'the cause', as it was becoming known, a leader of sensible men whose undoubted moral character might impress those to whom the workers' grievances would need to be addressed. A welcoming arm directed him to a corner, where he chatted in a jovial way with some of his neighbours from Tanners Yard and the surrounding courtyards, until someone rapped an empty ale pot against a table in what was clearly the customary signal, and an instant silence fell.

Nathan listened to what followed, and at first chose to say nothing. He was familiar enough with the mens' grievances, since they were also his own, and he was waiting anxiously for those men with ideas to emerge. He was annoyed to notice Stan Cadby in the company, and was uneasy with the popularity he seemed to enjoy with some of the others. He knew of Cadby's reputation and was well aware of what had led to his dismissal from Bradley's employment. He certainly wanted no part of any group of which Cadby was a member.

Nathan grew increasingly restless and irritated as platitude followed platitude in the general conversation, but no progress was made beyond the restatement of old grievances. Then slowly Cadby began to draw the meeting out.

"Right then, we're all agreed as summat's needed ter get things goin' arahnd these parts. We've all suffered, even those who've still got work, an' 'aven't bin cast aht like a dog, like I were."

Nathan fixed Cadby with an icy stare, but said nothing.

"What I say is," continued Cadby, "that we need summat definite ter put ter the bosses – summat that we're all agreed on. I'll be seein' Caleb Mason from Goose Gate termorrer, an' I promised 'im we'd 'ave summat worked aht. Nah, wharrabaht it?"

No-one spoke.

"Right, well look, I've gorra few ideas we might start wi'. It's up ter you, mind, but someone's gorrer start the cheese rollin'."

Several chortles from his audience confirmed that his allusion to a happier past had not been missed. Encouraged, he moved up a step.

"We'll start wi' fifteen bob fer a full week's bag, guaranteed."

There was a communal gasp, then a stunned silence.

"An' what's wrong wi' that?" Cadby demanded. "We 'ad nearly twelve shillin's fer the warp-frame men ovver two years since, an' wi' food the price it is nah, we're needin' more than that; obvious, ain't it? All right, we're seein' more like seven at the moment, but whose fault's that? Yer dun't 'ave ter look far fer an answer ter that – go an' ask the likes o' Gibson, Solley and Bradley." No-one contradicted him. "Well come on, wharrabaht it? Sam Pinkney, Jack Cossall, wharrabaht it?"

Sam Pinkney wriggled his shoulders uneasily. "Well, yer right o' course, Stan, but God knows it's an 'ell of a jump."

"Like I said," Cadby persisted, "not if yer think back a couple o' years."

"If yer purrit like that," Pinkney admitted, "yer right, I s'pose."

"Course I'm right. An' I 'ain't done yet. I reckon they should get extra when they 'as ter work Sat'days an' all."

This time, rumblings of discontent could be heard.

"Come on," Cadby urged them, "dun't be daft – every man 'ere knows 'e's worth it."

"Aye, but . . ."

"Aye but what, Jack Cossall? Are yer sayin' yer not worth it?"

"No," Cossall conceded weakly.

"Anyone 'ere think they're not worth it?" Cadby challenged them all.

No-one did, or if they did, chose not to say so.

"Right," Cadby continued with more confidence, "an' if yer worth that, then it's time that some o' them bosses saw to it that blokes like you – an' yer families – is looked after proper when yer poorly. 'ow many o' you've seen the inside o' that so-called free 'ospital up bi the

Castle? No, I thought not. I reckon a few o' them beds ought ter be kept fer the likes of ordinary folks like us, but paid fer bi the big nobs that's gorrall the money. If every boss chucked in a sovereign every week, I reckon that'd tek care on it. What d'yer reckon?"

"I reckon yer bloody barmy."

Nobody moved. Nathan had listened to Cadby in mounting disbelief, but had suddenly seen through him, and his anger had overpowered his natural reticence. Cadby glared back at Nathan, his eyes narrowing in challenge.

"Say that again?"

"I said yer bloody barmy. No, yer worse than barmy – yer a bloody liar!"

"Nah look 'ere, Nathan Slack . . ."

"No, you look 'ere Stan Cadby," thundered Nathan, not one to back down from something he had started. "We've all listened politely enough ter all yer shit, an' any man 'ere wi' an 'ead on 'is shoulders could tell yer that fifteen bob a week might as well be fifteen sovereigns. No boss in Nottingham can afford fifteen bob a week when 'e's only payin' arahnd seven at the moment."

" 'e could if 'e took less fer 'issen!"

"Where yer bin lookin'? The bosses 'ave suffered an' all, yer know – that's why they've bin layin' off so many. It's not their fault, what's bin 'appenin' this last winter. There's not the call fer Nottingham hosiery there was, that's all. I'm not sayin' they couldn't squeeze a bob or two more if they tried, but not fifteen. An' what do you care abaht 'ospitals? Yer dun't even wash regular!"

There was a roar of laughter, and Cadby would have struck Nathan had he dared. Instead, he lashed back angrily with the only weapon that came to mind. "I thought you'd be a good bloke ter 'ave at ar meetin's, but I'm glad we saw the truth in time."

He paused for effect, then turned to survey the still-grinning group. "Not all o' you 'ere know Nathan Slack, do yer? Well, 'e works fer Bradley, an' allus 'as done. All the time Bradley were layin' off, Nathan Slack were still workin' regular, an' nah we know why, dun't we? A bloody boss's man, that's what 'e is! I reckon Bradley sent 'im 'ere ter spy on us, an' tell 'im what we're up ter. That's the sort o' dirty trick Bradley'd do, 'im an' 'is precious bloody Christian charity!"

"Aye, that's more like the truth, ain't it?" Nathan retorted angrily. "Yer dun't give a shit abaht the likes of us – yer just want ter get yer own back on Bradley, 'cos 'e paid yer off, an' there's some of us 'ere as knows why! That's why yer askin' fer fifteen bob – yer know yer won't gerrit, an' then yer can turn folks even more agin Bradley an' others like 'im, who do care, in their own way. Well, not me. I'm not that daft, an' I'm 'avin' no part on it. I'm leavin' this so-called meetin' 'ere an' nah, an' them's that gorrany sense'll be leavin' wi' me."

He stepped past Cadby, who shrank back to allow Nathan access to the door. Once it was safely shut again, Cadby yelled after him. "Aye, go on – bogger off, boss's man!"

He turned quickly to the others, some of whom were mumbling uneasily amongst themselves.

"That's just why we're 'ere ternight, ter fight the likes of 'im! It's 'cos sheep like 'im 'ave sat on their woolly arses an' said 'yes sir' an' 'no sir' ter the bosses that the rest of us is starvin'. I'll tell yer summat else an' all – an' some o' yer will know this fer yersens – there's allus plenty o' food in their 'ouse. Ask yersens where that comes from, then. An' 'ow many of you can go 'ome ternight an' eat summat?"

Several of his audience knew first-hand about Lily's kindness to others, but were frightened to speak out. Encouraged by the resulting silence, Cadby pushed his point further. "You all 'eard wharre said – dun't ask fer more than another two bob. Where did 'e get that idea from, if not from the likes o' Bradley? Dun't kid yersens, I know wharram talkin' abaht, an' we needs ter watch aht fer shit like 'im all the time. Dun't get me wrong, Sam Pinkney, you weren't ter know who sent 'im; we're not blamin' you. We just 'as ter watch oursens, that's all. Right then, who else wants ter leave nah, before we get dahn ter mekkin' a list o' what we want?"

There were some who agreed with Nathan that fifteen shillings was too much. But none had his courage or clear-sightedness, and for most of them the dream was too tempting. They kept their silence, and Cadby had won the day.

Except with Nathan, who swore under his breath for most of the short walk home, and startled his family by slamming the door on his way in.

———————◦◦◦———————

Cadby's insinuations might have seemed well founded to anyone walking along High Pavement some evenings later, and who happened to notice a scrubbed and glowing Matthew seeking admission through the front door of the Bradley house. He had a copy of Bellamy's English Grammar under his arm, and he was apprehensive of his first lesson with Lucy. They had waited a few months because of the inclement weather, and also to allow Matthew to absorb some of the grammatical rules contained in the book which Lucy had loaned to him. Rebecca had protested at first, since it was hers, but now she looked forward with girlish curiosity to renewing her acquaintance with the young man whose previous visit to her house had been in muddy tatters.

Heavy footsteps approaching down the hallway preceded the grinding of the bolts. The door opened a foot or so, and behind it stood Adam. All memory of his trip to Tanners Yard the previous November having been gratefully erased, he had no recollection of Matthew and surveyed him silently and with suspicion.

"Yes?"

"Er . . . I'm Matthew Slack."

"Indeed?"

"Yes."

This fact firmly established, silence once more descended.

"Er . . . I think Miss Lucy's expectin' me."

Adam savoured this suggestion for a moment, then came down in favour of it being a wild improbability. However, he had learned to be wary of employers as unpredictable as Miss Lucy.

"Wait there."

The door closed firmly in his face and Matthew was sorely tempted to run all the way home. He glanced down at the book laced tenuously by his nervously twisting fingers, and decided that the prospect of justifying any such retreat to his mother was worse than the certainty of a polite rebuff. He would wait until Adam returned to order him off the doorstep, and would then simply hand the book to him.

"Come in."

He had not heard the door reopen, and he jumped in surprise.

"Pardon?"

Adam sighed. "Come in, you're letting in a draught."

"Oh, sorry . . . sorry."

Matthew tumbled in through the doorway, and started down the hallway after Adam. Then he remembered his mother's last instruction before he left his own house, and returned to the front door to wipe his boots on the mat. Adam turned back from the sitting room door and waited in mounting exasperation.

"There's no need to wear a hole in it! Wait in here." As Matthew slipped past him into the empty sitting room, Adam lowered his voice to a whisper. "And keep your thieving hands to yourself. Is that understood?"

Matthew was stung by the insinuation, and the change in tone.

"But I wouldn't . . ."

He was wasting his breath; Adam had withdrawn.

Matthew stood in the room, not daring to move. He gazed, awe-stricken, at the thick velvet furnishings, the oil paintings on every wall, the standing clock in the corner and, directly underneath the cut-glass candelabra, the polished mahogany table on which lay a supply of paper, an inkstand and a heavily decorated pot which held a collection of quills. His boots felt rough and clumsy in the soft deep pile of the carpet and he wondered if he should perhaps take them off. He listened to the sounds of the house; he could hear crockery being moved, and Mrs Bradley's imperious commands from somewhere deep in the confines of the scullery. His back to the open door, he hadn't realised that he was being watched.

"Hello."

He turned quickly, expecting to see Lucy. It wasn't her, and in his confusion he dropped the grammar book. Rebecca giggled, a pleasant, ringing sound. "Oh dear, aren't you clumsy?"

Matthew grinned through his embarrassment, and bent to pick up the book.

"I hope you've been keeping better care of it than that. It's mine, you know."

"Yes; Lucy – sorry, Miss Lucy – told me. And I have been looking after it, honest. I wouldn't have dropped it if there hadn't been a carpet."

Rebecca giggled again, tossing her ribboned ringlets. "You're a funny one. Has your brother been hitting you again?"

"Oh no. He doesn't do it all the time; only when he's angry at summat – something."

The conversation flagged, and Matthew searched for something to say. "That's a pretty dress."

"Do you think so? Mama says I have to give it away to charity soon. I've had it over a year now and I'm getting too big for it. Still, it's nice of you to say you like it."

"I like blue. Always 'ave – have – done."

There was a rustling sound and Lucy appeared in the doorway, smiling over Rebecca's shoulder.

"Hello, Matthew. I'm sorry to have kept you waiting, but we've only just got back from shopping. We've been to Leicester, and the coach got stuck for almost half an hour near Bunny."

"My mam's from Leicester."

"Is she? It's nice there. But let's not waste any more time. Has Rebecca been keeping you entertained?"

48

"Oh yes, I was telling her what a pretty dress she's got on."

"That'll please her; it's one of her favourites but she's going to have to part with it soon." She patted her younger sister affectionately on the back of her head, then leaned forward to look into her face.

"Anyway, Rebecca, off you go now. You've got that tapestry to finish for the Sunday School Union."

Rebecca's face fell, and she pouted. "It's not fair! Goodbye, Matthew."

"Goodbye." He watched her shuffle unenthusiastically out of his line of sight. "She's very nice."

"She's very spoiled, you mean," Lucy said. "But she's got a kind enough heart for all that. Now, which part of the book have you been reading?"

"All of it," Matthew replied, slightly confused by the question.

"All of it?" queried Lucy. Her smile was indulgent, but her eyebrows were raised quizzically. She motioned Matthew to a chair at the side of the centre table, and took the vacant chair at its head, reaching for paper and pen. "All right then, here's a pen and some paper. Let's see how much you've actually learned."

After only a few minutes Lucy had revised even her estimate of Matthew's potential, and was silently ashamed of her initial condescension. After an hour she was both astonished and excited. She rang for Adam, and ordered tea.

"Will that be for two, miss?"

"Of course it will." Her brow clouded slightly as she stared defiantly at Adam, who beat a hasty retreat towards the scullery.

"I don't think he likes me," Matthew explained unnecessarily.

"He's not used to you, that's all." She thought carefully before she gave voice to what was occupying her mind. "Matthew, how long did you spend reading this grammar?"

"I'm not very good, am I? I know I made some mistakes, but you see mam had William, and then she was poorly, and I didn't get much time . . ."

"Matthew, listen to me. Carefully. You've had that grammar for just over five months, and you don't go to school. Rebecca goes to Miss Humberstone's and she got it when she was eleven. She's fourteen now, and you're already further through the book than she is."

"But if she's been doing that tapestry for the chapel and things like that, and she has to practice at the piano, it's mebbe – maybe – not her fault . . ."

Lucy laughed, and gave in to the temptation to lean across and pull his left ear lobe playfully. "Matthew, you silly goose, I'm not criticising Rebecca. She's quite good for her age, if a little lazy at times. Can't you understand what I'm saying?"

He gazed at her blankly.

"I'm saying that you're very, very bright. Very intelligent."

Matthew thought for a moment, identified the word, and immediately turned scarlet with embarrassment. Lucy rose from the table, walked to a bookshelf near the curtained window and from it took a red volume which she handed to Matthew.

"Do you know what Latin is?"

"I've heard about it. Don't they do it in big churches?"

"They don't do it, Matthew, they speak it. It's a language."

Adam entered with the tea tray, placed it in the middle of the table and retired with a sniff. Matthew stared in horror at the china cup and tried to refuse it, but Lucy showed him how to hold it properly, forced a piece of cake into his hand, and began to explain the basic principles of Latin.

When Matthew left later that evening, he had parted company with the English Grammar book. Under his arm he now carried Henson's New Latin Grammar, written sixty years previously by the schoolmaster vicar of Beeston, widely used and universally detested by the pupils of the Free Grammar School in Stoney Street. Boring it might be, but Matthew carried it as proudly as if it were a Sunday School prize.

Matthew's excitement was nothing compared with Lucy's. She deferentially interrupted a conversation between her parents in the drawing room, then breathlessly recounted her discovery.

"Well I never! You mean he's a bright un?"

"Bright? Papa, he has the potential to be a scholar!"

"A scholar, eh? Well, I wouldn't know about that. But if he's that good, he should make a promising apprentice – he starts next month, you know."

Lucy made a dismissive noise with her throat, and continued. "Papa, look, I don't want to seem, well, too pushy and so on, and I know he's my first pupil, but do you think you could find a position for him as a clerk?"

"A clerk? Well, I don't know about that, princess. I've got stuff going all over the Midlands these days, and even the two clerks I've got at the moment find things a bit difficult sometimes. You've got to be good, you know, to be a clerk."

"But he is good, Papa, honestly! You should see how quickly

he learns things! I don't mean to sound demeaning or anything, but I think he's got it in him to be better even than a clerk. I mean it!"

Her mother frowned slightly over the top of her spectacles, and looked up from her crochet work. "Lucy, I think that's enough for the time being, don't you? You hardly know the boy yet, and he may prove to be a disappointment. Heaven knows, for one of his class to even rise to be a clerk is almost unheard of."

"But Mama . . ."

"No, your mother's right, Lucy," interrupted Robert. "It's early days yet. But I tell you what, we'll start him as an apprentice to his father, just like we planned, but every now and then I'll give him some packages to address and some stock tallies to reconcile. If he shows promise at that, we'll talk some more. How does that suit you?"

Lucy flung her arms around her father's neck, narrowly missing the cigar in his left hand. "Oh, thank you, Papa! I know you'll be simply astonished by him. Just give him the chance, that's all I'm asking." She breezed out into the hallway, and Catherine looked sceptically at her husband.

"Be careful, Robert."

"I know, I know. But if the lad's got it in him, why not? Lucy's not often wrong about people, and if I give him his big chance I get a loyal worker for the rest of his life. In any event, I'm going to have to replace old Danby if his eyes get much worse."

Catherine furrowed her brows in thought. "They're an odd family, the Slacks. Every one of them seems, well, different somehow. Even that ruffian of theirs has an air about him."

"That ruffian could do with a bit more discipline. He'll not make half the stockinger his father is."

Catherine paused briefly, then enquired. "That young girl of theirs – is she called Ruth?"

"Wouldn't have a clue, why?"

"Oh, nothing much, only Mrs Barrett was mentioning at the Ladies' Guild meeting a couple of weeks ago that she's a very nice young girl, and apparently very advanced in domestic duties."

"And how would she know?"

"Well, evidently young Ruth offered to help at the Sunday School Christmas tea, and Mrs Barrett was amazed at how good she was in the kitchen. It seems that the mother's been ill or something, and the girl's had to take over managing the house. And she can't be any more than eleven-years-old."

"I don't suppose it takes much effort to look after one of those dreadful places in Tanners Yard. Have you ever been in there?"

Catherine huffed indignantly. "Really, Robert, when would I have occasion to go in there? You know my charitable works are all in Hockley these days."

"Sorry. Anyway, where's all this leading? Are you suggesting we take her on here?"

"Here? Certainly not! Martha's the best scullery maid we've ever had and I'm not parting with her. No, I was thinking of Letitia."

"If I were you, I'd let your sister hire her own domestics."

"I promised I'd look out for a suitable girl for her, that's all. It's not so easy to find them, you know, out there in the country."

"Well, take my advice, and leave well alone. Oh hello, here comes the last hope of the Empire."

James had stalked right past both his parents without speaking, and was now searching through a shelf of books on the drawing room wall. He turned back towards Robert, his nose wrinkled in displeasure. "Really, Father, the stink from those cigars of yours is truly unbearable."

"When you're man enough to smoke one without going green, then you can criticise, and not before."

"You won't catch me even touching one of those filthy things. Mother, where's my Latin Grammar? Did it get moved out of the sitting room with the others?"

Robert laughed derisively. "Your what? You never read the blessed thing when you were at the Grammar School, so why start now?"

"I've a wager on with Toby Solley about the genitive case of puella. He says its puellae and I say it's puellam."

"I haven't the faintest idea what you're talking about. Why don't you ask Lucy? She knows where the books are in this house."

"I think she may have loaned it to Matthew Slack, dear," added his mother helpfully.

"Who?"

"Matthew Slack. You know, her new pupil."

"What, her poor scholar from Narrow Marsh? Damned cheek!"

"By all accounts he's not a poor scholar," Robert chortled gleefully. "In fact, from what Lucy was saying, I'll wager he's a damned sight better than you."

"Rubbish! You wait until I'm running the business, then you'll see."

"No, you wait till you're running it. And it'll be a while yet. You've got a full two years at Gibson's before you set foot in my business."

"That's another thing – why send me off to another hosier to learn the trade?"

"Because he's the biggest in the town, that's why. Come back when you've learned something."

"Honestly," James protested in a whining voice which was far from pleasant, "it's insufferable! My own father sends me off to another employer, while my sister runs a charity school in the sitting room!"

He slammed the door noisily behind him. Robert stared thoughtfully into the fire.

"He's got a lot to learn, that one."

CHAPTER FOUR

Choosing sides

"EY UP THEN, Tommy Slack!"

Tommy stopped in his tracks, then turned back towards the side door through which he had just passed on his way out of Bradley's Hosiery. There, half-hidden in the darkening alleyway, leaned Stan Cadby.

"Ey up Stan, yer dun't want ter be seen lurkin' arahnd 'ere, surely?"

Cadby grinned. "Not much risk in that, I reckon. The rest'll not be aht much afore nine, will they?"

"Mebbe not. But 'ow did yer know I were leavin' early terday?"

Cadby tapped his nose with his forefinger, to indicate that his source of information was a secret. "That's my business – an' so are you."

Tommy began to walk away from the workers' entrance, afraid that they might be seen together.

Cadby yelled after him. "Ey, come 'ere!"

"Not 'ere, Stan; let's walk up the road a bit."

Cadby shuffled after him out of the narrow alleyway, and they walked two abreast up Stoney Street and into Wool Pack Lane. They were oddly matched as they passed under the oil lamp at the corner, the taller, younger man casting a firm, lean shadow, the older reflection squat and toad-like. They were safely into the shadows at the back of the parish burial ground before Tommy slowed down and broke the silence.

"Well, what d'yer want?"

"There's a meetin' ternight."

Tommy felt the familiar lurch of excitement, and a tightening around the temples. "Ternight? That's a bit sudden, ain't it?"

"It wouldn't be if yer'd bin to the last few meetin's. Yer goin' soft or summat?"

"Course not. Burrit's norreasy, yer know. It were bad enough before, burrafter you an' dad 'ad that big row . . ."

"It weren't a row, I've told yer that already. 'e just won't see sense, that's all. Either that or 'e's not got the guts ter do what's right bi folk. Anyroad, that were weeks since."

Nathan had refused to discuss the details of his confrontation with Cadby with anyone in the family, and Tommy had been obliged to rely on second-hand accounts. Cadby had his own interests to serve in playing down the incident, particularly so far as Tommy was concerned.

"Well, yer comin' or not?" Cadby demanded.

"I dunno. I'm s'posed ter be gerrin' summat for mam's chest."

"You'll do fer 'alf an hour, surely? It's summat special, I promise yer."

Tommy wavered. He had lost none of his fervour for the cause but he was unimpressed with the way in which it had so far been promoted. He'd been hoping to see a direct challenge to the employers, a threatened withdrawal of work until some demands were met. But so far, all he'd seen was a bunch of his neighbours with no sense of direction, seemingly led by Cadby, who in turn appeared to be dancing to someone else's tune.

Had they been better able to communicate at this early stage, father and son would have realised that their opinions were not all that far apart. As it was, Nathan had stuck firmly to his ruling against Tommy attending anything other than Sunday worship, and had inevitably driven the boy further than he might otherwise have ventured, out of sheer defiance. Tommy had been to several meetings whenever he could slip away unnoticed, and in this he had been encouraged by Cadby, who stood to gain advancement in the movement by bringing in recruits.

They stood in uneasy silence for a moment or two more, then Tommy weakened. "All right, but only fer 'alf an hour, mind. Nah, what's so special abaht ternight?"

"You'll see soon enough. Come on, we're late as it is."

"Where we goin', anyroad?"

"Same place as usual, Newton's Head in Glasshouse Street."

A few breathless minutes later they knocked at the rear door of the pub and were swiftly admitted once their identities had been established. They slipped into a smoky back room, and Tommy hovered uneasily near the doorway. Of the thirty or so men in the noisy company, the only one he knew apart from Cadby was a former neighbour, Jack Cossall, and he, too, looked apprehensive as he treated Tommy to a curt nod and a weak smile of recognition.

A dark, sturdily built man with a full beard surveyed Tommy from the edge of the table on which he perched, one foot on the floor, the centre of attention. He smiled welcomingly at Tommy.

"Hello, young feller. I don't think I've met you before, have I?"

" 'e's one o' mine," chirped Cadby, "name of Slack – Tommy Slack."

"He's a bit young, isn't he?"

"I'm old enough," protested Tommy, who was not prepared to be treated as a mere lad, but was still unsure of what he might be letting himself in for.

"Let's hope so, we've got a long hard road ahead of us. My name's Henson, Gravenor Henson."

A potman entered with a tray of ales, and Tommy, who had no money of his own, was about to refuse a drink when Henson placed a dripping tankard in his hand.

"There you are, Tommy Slack; you're old enough, remember?"

Tommy grinned and took the tankard. Conscious of the eyes upon him, he took a long draught and tried to stop his eyes watering as the bitter fluid hit the back of his throat. The busy hum of conversation closed around him, and Tommy was no longer a newcomer. A few moments later, Henson called for order.

"Right then, gentlemen – to business. As you know, this was originally to have been a meeting just for group commanders, but at the last minute it was decided that seconds-in-command should turn up as well."

Tommy turned back to Cadby, a horrified look of enquiry on his face. Cadby refused to return his look, and instead kept his eyes firmly on Henson as he continued.

"The fact is we're in danger of losing ground. Now that summer's just about on us again and the trade's picking up a bit, a lot of our people have forgotten last winter. If we don't do something to remind them – and keep reminding them at regular intervals – well, before we know where we are we'll be into another winter and nothing to show for the months in between. And I don't have to remind you all what another winter like the last one is likely to mean."

Low murmurs confirmed this last point, and Henson pressed on. "You represent the people of this town – the real people, that is – and all of us together must do everything in our power to make sure that our friends and neighbours don't forget and leave it too late. They can't do anything without us, and we can't do anything without them. That's why we've got to make a real effort, right now, to show them the way."

"Let's bust some winders!" came a suggestion from the back of the room. There were several shouts of support, but Henson shook his head.

"Steady on, we don't do that unless we have to. For the time being, let's try another tack. Up to now we've only met in private, in rooms like this, and in back courts and dark alleyways. I think it's time we met in the open, in public, and in large numbers. Let's get everyone involved."

"That's agin the law, ain't it?" enquired the same voice from the back, this time loaded with sarcasm. There were hoots of laughter and someone belched derisively. Henson joined in the joke, but with a hard edge to his laughter.

"That seems to depend on who you are and what you're meeting for. It certainly is illegal to meet for the purposes we've got in mind, but I've yet to hear that said about a meeting of hosiers. I'm planning to do something about that too, shortly, and when I do I'll be needing your help there as well. But coming back to the main business, what I'm suggesting is that we make our presence felt in places where there are lots of people already gathered for perfectly lawful purposes."

"Goose Fair!" someone shouted.

"Goose Fair certainly," agreed Henson, "but I'm not waiting until October to get things moving. What's wrong with Saturdays? We have markets then, don't we?"

The rumble of excitement was broken by a loud chuckle from near the front. "Remember the mayor an' the cheeses?"

Henson grinned, but shook his head. "Before my time, I'm afraid. But I'd love to have seen it, and that's just the sort of thing I've got in mind. Which is why you're all here in extra force this evening. I propose that we use this meeting to plan some little incidents on market days which will give us the chance to slip in some speeches of our own. It can hardly be called an illegal combination when all you've got is a thousand or so poor souls going about their normal business on market day, now can it?"

Cheers and more laughter greeted the idea. The same voice from the back of the room took it to the next stage. "What sort o' thing d'yer want us ter do then?"

Henson obviously had a detailed plan. "Anyone who's lived in this town for a year or two knows just how easy it is to get something going on market days; the prices alone are enough to start a riot. So we just arrange for one of us to pick a row with a trader – better be one from out of town, I think – and two or three more of us join in. Before you know where you are, you've got hundreds of them, all spoiling for a fight. Then we put up our speakers."

"An' who's goin' ter do the speakin', then?"

"Me, for one. I can yap if nothing else, so leave that side of it to me. You're not the only workers with a grievance, you know. Up in Manchester they've been complaining for years, and they're finally beginning to get somewhere. They've got speakers like Kingsley, Keegan and Crosby who some of you met when he was down here the other week. I've fixed up for some of them to come down here, and trust me when I tell you that they're very good at moving a mob.

What I need from you are a few planned incidents – just let me know when they're planned for."

Small groups began to form and ideas began to take shape. Henson left the centre table and moved closer to Tommy. "Well, young man, what do you think?"

Tommy flushed. "Yer can count me in! It's abaht time somebody like you got things goin' arahnd 'ere."

"Like I said, it's almost too late. Where do you live, by the way?"

"Tanners Yard."

"Isn't that somewhere around Narrow Marsh? I've been down there once or twice, but not lately. Your man Cadby's got the whole of that area, hasn't he?"

Tommy coughed awkwardly, hesitated, then took the plunge.

"Excuse me askin', like, but why are you . . . well, I mean ter say, yer not . . ."

Henson smiled. "Why am I taking sides? You think I shouldn't, just because I talk a bit different from you and the others? Listen, Tommy, until this year I used to be in the trade myself, and as a stockinger, mind, not a hosier. I talk the way I do because it's the only way to get yourself heard around here these days. I hope that once we've shown those who matter that we mean business, I'll be able to petition Parliament so that the local politicians won't be able to ignore us any more. To do that, you can't go around sounding like Ned Ludd from Leen Side."

"Who?"

Henson chuckled mischievously. "It doesn't matter – just a name I borrowed from a lad in Leicester. Mind you, if I get my way, a lot more people will be hearing that name before much longer."

At that moment, someone tapped Henson on the shoulder, while someone else caught at the sleeve of his jacket. Henson smiled back at Tommy. "Looks like I wasn't wasting my time, but I'd best see what these folk have in mind. I hope we'll see you here again."

"Oh yeah, count on it. An' thanks!"

Tommy left the Newton's Head deep in thought, much affected by his first meeting with Henson. Here at last was the man they needed, the one who could unite all the workers in the cause. Men like Cadby were all very well, but Henson seemed to have different connections, and important ones. He could do it, if anyone could.

Somewhere down in the town, a clock sounded. Tommy started in surprise – ten o'clock! He raced along Broad Lane into Goose Gate, and then down the hill into Hockley. Banging furiously at the door of the herbalist's, and thrusting the money Nathan had given him into the hand of the startled trader, he waited long enough to snatch the bottle that was handed back to him, then ran all the way back up the slope by way of Bellar Gate and Hollow Stone into High Pavement.

He was just approaching the Bradley house when the front door opened, and Matthew emerged into the road. Tommy dived into a darkened recess a couple of doors back and waited, chest heaving from his recent exertion, as he listened to Matthew bid someone a cheery farewell and set off down the slope towards Garner's Hill. Tommy followed at a discreet distance, then caught up with him at the entrance to the yard. They entered the house together, and no-one thought to ask Tommy where he had been.

Matthew, too, had made a new friend. At least, he had finally come to realise that friendship was being offered from a quarter where, only a few months before, he would not have dared seek it.

If Rebecca was somewhat childish, and occasionally given to petulance, this was the almost inevitable consequence of the privileges she had enjoyed all her life. Until her tenth birthday she had been under a governess, whereas Lucy and James had both attended local schools. This was partly because Rebecca had, as a young child, displayed a certain delicacy of constitution, and partly because the rising fortunes of the Bradleys had necessitated – or so her mother imagined – some outward recognition. At ten years of age she had joined Lucy at Miss Humberstone's Ladies' Academy, and now that Lucy had long since left, was its most important pupil.

These were hardly the ideal conditions to nurture a patient disposition. To Rebecca, needs and desires were something to be met immediately, and physical comforts existed as of right. Her social contacts thus far had been confined to her own class, and although she occasionally glimpsed signs of despair and resentment in the neighbouring streets, they seemed to her like scenes from a theatrical performance in which there could be no contact with the performers themselves.

Matthew had changed all that. On that November day when Lucy had slipped his bedraggled form through the scullery door, he had brought with him her first real contact with that other world. Like a theatre player still in costume he had later spoken to her, and she was fascinated.

Once his visits became regular, she sought every opportunity to listen to him speak. A subtle change slowly occurred; he was still different from her, still from that other world outside the carriage window, but he gradually grew reassuringly familiar. Eventually she realised that it was the boy himself who fascinated her, and not simply the drama of his background. She was, at one and the same time, both appalled by the glimpse he gave her of the life he was forced to lead, yet somehow vicariously proud of the courage and quiet patience with which he seemed to accept his lot in life. She soon realised, without resentment, that he was as clever as she was; what she could not accept was that, being so much like her, he should be forced to live in a place like Tanners Yard.

For his part, as he grew more socially at ease in her presence, Matthew began to relax and enjoy the company of someone soft and gentle, someone who smelt of lavender instead of camphor, of Otto of Violets instead of herring and pork fat. He loved to gaze at her smoothly coiled dark ringlets which he could not help contrasting with the matted hanks of the 'needle-run' girls he worked with; and at the jaconet, lace and silk expertly draped around her softly curved body, whilst his mother and sister bustled angularly in coarsecloth and calico. He could not share Tommy's resentment of the elegance of the wealthy, because he came close enough to it to appreciate it with an inborn artistic sense which was beginning to emerge in small ways in his own mannerisms and dress. Rebecca was the touchstone of beauty and grace, and his welcoming guide to this pleasant, sensual new world.

Lucy, sensing the innate compatibility of the two, and seizing her chance to have two pupils instead of one, persuaded her mother to allow Rebecca to learn with Matthew. Across the big sitting room table from each other they sat for many evenings, now competing to complete a Latin sentence, now smiling in friendship, now giving each other harder and harder English words to spell, now giggling and exchanging funny faces in some private joke. Pupil with pupil, friend with friend, as the summer opened before them.

There was no mistaking the major religious event in Nottingham during that summer of 1810. The spirit of John Wesley rode triumphant through the town in which a generation or two previously his horse and mule had trodden a more humble path. From the middle of the previous century, church after church had been hastily but lovingly dedicated to the cause of Nonconformity. Some, like the Unitarian Chapel opposite the Bradley house, had begun to grow in size and congregation; the early Methodists, more mindful of their founder's teachings, restrained their impulse to imitate the Anglian tendency to build towards the heavens and sublimated their zeal in piety.

Big or small, the chapel communities cared particularly for the children and for the nurture of their faith. Not content with a Sunday School for every chapel, they now sought a union of such schools, lest the chain should break and the wonderful truth be lost to a generation of young people. In August that year the Nottingham Sunday School Union was founded, and several thousand joyous souls met one Saturday to give thanks, many of them to the memory of an itinerant preacher whom their grandparents had once pelted with offal.

"I still say it'll kill yer."

"Dun't be daft, Nathan, anyone'd think I were really ill or summat. D'yer think I'm gunner miss a chance like this?"

"She should never 'ave asked yer; yer not well, Lily."

"I'm as well as I've ever bin. Nah pass me that basket an' stop yer fussin'."

Nathan picked up the basket and glared at it accusingly, as if it were somehow to blame. Cursing under his breath, he handed it over. Lily slipped the loaves and herrings into it – a Biblical gesture not lost even on Tommy – and off they strode.

At the end of Narrow Marsh they joined the gaily coloured stream of people coming down Drury Hill and the steep steps of Garner's Hill. Dogs followed them in curiosity and hope as they swarmed across the Leen by way of Turncalf Bridge and into the river meadows.

They followed the southern bank of the Leen as it stirred sluggishly through the acres of calf-deep marsh grass and clover, and passed eventually under the cool brick archway that supported the Leen Bridge, and into the wide expanse of the East Croft. To their left, the Leen oozed eastwards, while below them to their right flowed the peacefully glittering broad ribbon of the River Trent. Between the two, humanity at play filled the grasslands with lively noise and colour.

It had required considerable organisation, and the initial burden had fallen on the elders of the constituent churches that had agreed to form the union. Catherine Bradley was not one to be left unnoticed on such occasions, and she rapidly appointed herself the commanding officer of the Sion Chapel contingent. To them had been allocated the substantial task of providing one of several stalls which would be required to produce the many gallons of tea to be eagerly consumed as each family attacked the provisions which they had saved for this special picnic.

Seizing her opportunity to make her own assessment of young Ruth, while at the same time delegating much of the actual physical labour to others, Catherine had politely but firmly invited Lily and her daughter to assist at the tea trestles which had been gruntingly erected earlier that day by Robert Bradley and Adam, together with a group of conscripted male 'volunteers' from the Halifax Lane congregation. Lily shone with pride at the honour paid to the family, while Ruth bubbled with anticipation, and between them they exerted a force too powerful for Nathan when he protested about the likely effect on Lily's health. Into the East Croft they went, with mixed emotions.

There was a miserable irony in the choice of venue, although few would have been aware of it unless well versed in Nottingham politics. The East and West Crofts, which together made up the meadows area immediately south of St. Mary's, and which offered a green-carpeted entrance to the town on either side of the London Road once it had crossed the Trent Bridge, were privately owned. But they were also 'commonable' in certain seasons of the year, and accessible to the townsfolk at all times. The Town Corporation administered the commonable area on behalf of the townsfolk, and was implacably opposed to having it enclosed for additional housing, at least, officially. The freeholders were mindful of the potential fortune to be derived from the sale of their lands, but burgesses with grazing rights were equally ruthless in their self-interest, and they dominated the Corporation. As a consequence, the area was to lie under grass and wild flowers for another thirty years and more.

To the majority of the townsfolk, in their verminous courtyards and damp tenements, the meadows and other green spaces which encircled the town were a lifeline, a source of recreation and pastoral sanctuary from the grimy town itself. But to the early pioneers of public health they represented an insurmountable bureaucratic obstacle to progress. St. Mary's and other parishes were horribly overcrowded even in those days, and the entire town population, if properly housed, could already have stretched right through to the banks of the Trent. Instead, they squatted on in sordid and contagious squalor in a cluster of streets which had changed little since Saxon times, all the while praising providence for the proximity of their pleasure grounds across the Leen.

"Purrit dahn ovver there. An' mind that fire – them boots is new, remember."

Nathan sighed, and deposited the basket on a stretch of

grass which was already well worn by the passage of feet. He looked back across the East Croft, to the seemingly endless line of refugees from the town.

"There's a lot 'ere already; 'ow many are yer expectin'?"

"Many hundreds," replied Catherine, who appeared behind Nathan as if from nowhere, "and we shall be needing all the help we can get from your good wife and daughter."

"Aye, well we need 'er an' all," Nathan reminded her, "so dun't go lerrin' 'er ovverdo it, not wi' 'er chest the way it is, an' . . ."

He was silenced by a withering look from Lily who turned back to Catherine with a smile. "It's a real honour ter do anythin' we can ter 'elp. 'ow much water d'yer want in them pans?"

Nathan turned away sadly and searched for company of his own. Tommy and Matthew each had his own reason for slipping away from the family group as soon as Lily's attention had been diverted, and Nathan had given up even attempting to control the day. Only little William remained with him, cradled in his right arm and looking quizzically back over Nathan's shoulder. Nathan spotted a couple of acquaintances on the riverbank, and strolled slowly down towards them.

Matthew knew exactly where to find Rebecca – by her father's side as usual. But they were part of a larger group standing under the shade of a mature elm tree, and for a short while Matthew hovered uncertainly nearby until Rebecca looked up, beamed with pleasure at his sudden appearance, and nudged her father in the ribs, indicating Matthew with a slight jerk of her head.

"What? Eh? Oh, yes – yes, come and join the party, young un."

The invitation was clearly addressed to him, and Matthew proudly walked the few yards in order to join the group.

He was introduced to the company as 'Lucy's bright young pupil', and a possible future clerk in the Bradley enterprise. Lucy glowed with almost proprietorial pride, Rebecca giggled and flushed both at the same time, and the rest of the group gave him the benefit of a formal 'Good Day'. Only James Bradley appeared to ignore him completely, engaged as he was in a losing battle to open a parasol for Rachel Gibson, who stood with her hosier father in the select company gathered around the Bradleys.

"Well," declared Robert, who that afternoon was benevolence itself, "I don't suppose you two young uns want to listen to business talk, so off you go for a walk or something. Not far, mind, Rebecca, I promised your mother I'd keep an eye on you."

Matthew thanked Robert in the manner he had been taught, and extended a crooked right arm for Rebecca's hand. Blushing again, and suppressing another girlish giggle, she placed her arm in the crook of his as they sauntered off towards the riverbank. Only Rachel Gibson heard James offer the additional suggestion that she take good care of her purse, and she sniggered in appreciation.

"Why did he do that?" Matthew asked as they moved out of earshot.

"Who?"

"Your dad – sorry, your father."

"Why did he do what?"

"Come on, don't pretend you don't know what I'm getting at. Why did he let us go walking like this?"

"He trusts you, I suppose. Why shouldn't he? You're not going to drag me off to a fate worse than death." Her eyes rolled mischievously. "Are you?"

It was Matthew's turn to blush. "Of course not. It's just . . . well . . ."

"Well what?"

"Well, it's almost as if . . ."

"As if what?"

"You know . . ."

"No I don't."

"Well, it might look as if we were . . . well, you know . . ."

"What, sweethearts, you mean?" Her eyes had never seemed so large.

Matthew turned a deeper shade of crimson, and Rebecca now giggled with pure pleasure. They fell silent, each wondering where the conversation might go from there. Somehow, Rebecca's arm slipped from Matthew's. As his arm also dropped, their hands touched, moved away, then touched again. They remained, for an electric moment, palm against palm, and as each became aware that the other would not object, their fingers eagerly entwined. Not a word was spoken for a full ten minutes as they ambled blissfully through the ankle-high grass towards the riverbank.

Robert, like Nathan, had been allocated responsibility for his children for the entire afternoon, as each of their wives attended to the feeding of the multitude. Robert was no better at it than most men, before or since, and once he was deep in conversation with Edward Gibson and Paul Solley, two of Nottingham's most prominent hosiers, the rest of his family might have taken ship for the Indies for all he would have been aware.

As a result, little Howard, the youngest Bradley at only seven years of age, was free to pursue his natural curiosity. He had never seen so many people in his entire life, and he had only twice before seen the River Trent, both times from a carriage window. Family holidays had a habit of occurring in a hired villa in Derbyshire, or his aunt's country house in Eastwood, and although he had been to the Lincolnshire coast several times he had never been allowed beyond the edge of the sand, and he wondered if the river had big waves in it like he had seen at Mablethorpe.

Slowly, he made his way down through the milling crowds of revellers, sombrely dressed preachers, tinkers, peddlers of religious tracts, a juggling troupe that had somehow escaped the stern disapproval of the church trustees, and large family groups in their Sunday best. Here and there, groups of boys could be found playing 'longbullets', banned by the magistrates and therefore twice as exciting, and from time to time a rough and tumble could be seen taking place well away from parental surveillance.

It was a group of boys pitching stones at a crudely constructed target who spotted Howard as he sauntered happily towards the riverbank in his blue velvet suit and lace choker.

" 'ere, Smacker, look at this!"

"So what?"

"It's ever so pretty, look. Ain't it pretty, Smacker? Dodge?"

"Leave 'im alone an' come back 'ere. Just 'cos yer losin'."

"I ain't losin'! 'ere you, what's yer name?"

Howard stood frozen to the spot, staring at the big boy in bewilderment.

"I said what's yer name – cat got yer tongue or summat?"

"Howard," he replied, his voice hoarse with nervousness.

"Ooh, lah-di-dah! 'oward, eh? 'oward what?"

The big boy's friends made another unsuccessful attempt to rekindle his interest in the game they had been playing, then wandered across to join him in front of Howard, who was now visibly trembling with fear. One of them took pity on him.

"Leave off, Pockets – 'e's only a young un."

"D'yer 'ear that, young un? They wants me ter leave off. What do you want?"

Howard had no idea what he was expected to say, so responded as politely as he had been taught. "I'd like it very much if you would, sir."

Pockets laughed mockingly. "Tell yer what, young 'oward wi' the fancy ways. I'll leave off if yer do summat fer me, right?"

"I haven't got any money."

"I ain't talkin' abaht money, is I?"

Not sure precisely what he was talking about, Pockets looked around for some challenge for the boy. He spotted a rotten willow whose shattered boughs still overhung the darkly moving river.

"Climb up there!" he commanded.

"Where?"

"That there tree – yer blind as well as daft?"

"I can't climb."

"Yer'd berrer!"

Howard walked up to the base of the tree, then looked out fearfully at the river flowing strongly past the bank and under the overhanging boughs. He started to scramble up the trunk, his highly polished boots scraping on the rough and rotting bark which peeled off with each tentative foothold. He wondered what his mother would say, and whether Adam would secretly cuff his ear for the extra trouble involved in restoring the boots to an acceptable shine.

When he reached the first of the broad overhanging branches, he crawled along it and paused briefly to regain his breath. He looked back, for confirmation that he was doing what he had been asked, but the boys, tiring of the joke, had already left.

Sighing with relief, Howard tried to sit up and turn his body, in order to jump off the tree and back onto the bank. But he overbalanced in the process and fell into the river with a splash and a loud squawk.

The water was only three feet deep near the riverbank but the current was strong. Had Howard stood up immediately he could simply have waded ashore. As it was, completely unused to water in its natural state, he spluttered and splashed about until the current had drawn him over a five-foot trench, and there was no touching the bottom. He screamed as loudly as he could, and continued splashing around in his frenzied efforts to find a firm foothold. Those who paid attention simply laughed and waved back at him, sharing in what they took to be his exuberant celebration of the day's festivities.

Matthew and Rebecca were still enjoying a happy silence as their hands remained clasped together, and each of them gazed idly at the small boy squealing and splashing about in the water. Matthew smiled indulgently at his frolics and remembered his own feeble attempt at swimming when his grandad was still alive, and the family would come into the meadows on Saturdays. Rebecca wondered what the boy's mother would say when he climbed out, his blue suit ruined. Suddenly she became fully alert and uttered a sharp scream.

"Matthew – it's Howard!"

"What? Where?"

"Over there, in the water!"

"He'll cop it when he gets out. Just wait till your mother sees him and . . ."

"Matthew, he can't swim!" Her voice became more shrill with rising panic. "Get him out! Get him out! Oh please, Matthew, get him out!"

Matthew raced the few remaining yards to the riverbank, pulling off his jacket as he went. He waded in, bracing himself against the cold shock as the dark water soaked instantly through his calico breeches. Just as he was reaching out to clutch the still-wriggling Howard by the shoulder, he tripped on a submerged rock and fell forward into the current. He came up spitting rank water and bits of bulrush from his mouth, wiping his eyes as he searched the surface for Howard. He was only a foot or two away, and Matthew managed to grab him by his soggy lace-trimmed collar to keep his head clear of the water, then reached for the bottom with his feet. At full tiptoe he could just feel the rocky, uneven bed, but then the current pulled them both downstream and outward, beyond even Matthew's depth, and he joined Howard in struggling and splashing with his free arm, all the while holding Howard's head above water with the other.

A crowd began to gather, shouting advice. One or two men waded in a few feet from the bank, arms outstretched to grab them, but no-one would venture any further, either reluctant to ruin their best apparel or fearful of the river's reputation for hidden trenches. Rebecca looked about in wild desperation, and then her eyes lit upon one of a group of men talking casually together. Even with his back turned to her she was confident that she knew this man from the church, and ran towards him, screaming for help.

Nathan turned at the sound of his name and was startled to see a distraught young lady running towards him. He knew of Rebecca, but only by sight, and she was barely coherent by the time that she reached him, but he grasped that Matthew had somehow finished up in the river and, handing baby William to her, he ran towards where she was pointing.

Pushing through the gathering crowd on the riverbank, Nathan sized up the situation, and without breaking stride he plunged into the water and came up again alongside the two boys. He was able to stand, chin deep, in the swirling current, a firm arm around each of them. Slowly but surely he began to edge his way back to the bank, feeling carefully for each foothold as he went, his back to the flow and a boy on each side. The current lost its strength as he got into shallower waters, and eager hands grabbed for them as the water receded to Nathan's thighs.

They sprawled out on the bank, a hundred yards downstream from where Howard had originally entered the water, Howard coughing and crying, Matthew bringing up weed and mucous and Nathan trembling with exertion but mouthing a silent prayer of thanks.

The crowd parted on a shouted command, to reveal Robert, purple with the effort of running down the slope, followed by Lucy who was now carrying William. There was no sign of Rebecca, who had collapsed at her older brother's feet after alerting her father to the unfolding drama.

Robert raised Howard gently to a sitting position and checked him over, before turning to look down at Matthew, who had rolled onto his back and was noisily sucking in air. "What happened, young un?"

"Dunno," gasped Matthew between breaths, "he must've fell in the river . . . couldn't get him . . . dad got us out."

Nathan was back on his knees, picking the weed from his hair and clothing. "All I done were pull 'em aht – Matthew can't swim, yer see."

"Either way," concluded Robert, "it looks as if I owe the Slack family a very deep debt of gratitude. For the moment, the best I can do is get my carriage brought down here to take you home. I'll send Adam to tell Mrs Slack what's happened."

"Bloody 'ell, no!" Nathan blurted out instinctively, before checking himself. "Beggin' yer pardon, like, but these clothes is near new, an' I dun't want 'er knowin' what's 'appened till we get 'em cleaned up a bit. She'll find aht soon enough, anyroad. It's a warm enough day; we'll just lie 'ere an' dry off a bit fust."

"As you wish, but at least let me get some hot tea brought down here for you. Lucy, would you ask Adam to see to that, please? And make sure that he gets it from your mother, and not Mrs Slack."

Lucy handed William back to Nathan and set off in search of Adam.

Mark Cropper had seen better market days, and was seriously thinking of cutting his losses and hitching the fruit cart to the donkey for an early trip home to Gedling. Since hardly anyone had expressed any interest in his fruit that day, he had no reason to expect an offer of custom from the gangly youth who stood eyeing him from the front of the stall. Waiting for a chance to steal an apple, more likely.

" 'ere, mester," called the youth, " 'ow much fer a plum?"

"Penny fer three, like it sez on the list."

"I can't read, an' I've only got a farthin'."

"Then yer can't buy any plums, can yer?"

"They was only a farthin' each last week."

"Not on my stall they wasn't."

"Well, they was on all the other stalls."

The youth had apparently noticed, for the first time, a sallow-looking man who had appeared at his elbow. "That's right, ain't it, mate?" he said, addressing the man.

"Yeah, that's right. Farthin' each, they was."

"I reckon they should only be a farthing each this week, an' all," the youth added.

Mark Cropper was fast losing patience. "Look, I'm tellin' yer, it were a penny fer three last week, an' it's a penny fer three this week. If yer can't afford it, bogger off."

"If the lad sez they was a farthin' last week, then they was."

A swarthy man and his murderous-looking companion had appeared from around the side of the stall as if by magic. Now five men, a woman and the original youth all stood staring defiantly at Cropper, whose eyes darted from one to another with the first faint stirrings of unease.

"I'm not sayin' as the lad's a liar, just that 'e's wrong, that's all."

"All I want's a plum."

"After callin' 'im a liar," whined the woman, "the least yer can do's gi' 'im a plum."

The crowd had now miraculously grown to over a dozen – by far the biggest he'd had all day – and Cropper began to sense real danger. "Look," he reasoned, "if the lad just wants one plum, all right, 'ere's a plum; nah dun't say as I'm not generous. Nah then, ladies an' gentlemen, what can I interest you in? Fresh Arnold raspberries, the main crop o' the season, still in fine condition, an' only . . ."

"This plum's rotten."

Now Cropper knew he was in trouble. The plum had come from the prime pile, the one reserved for the top of each punnet on display, and could not possibly have got mixed up with the overripe ones he kept just under the stall on a concealed shelf. And yet the youth had a partly rotten plum in his hand, which he must have brought with him, and for one reason only. It had happened to a friend of his last year, and he had finished up badly beaten, with his stocks of bacon flitch pilfered.

The swarthy man turned to address the swelling crowd. "Did

yer see that? This young lad 'ere – just a poor Nottingham lad like one o' yer own – 'e just asks fer one plum from a bloke who's got 'undreds of 'em, an' what does this robber do? Gives 'im a rotten un, that's what. I bet if we 'ad a look under this stall we'd find lots o' rotten plums, all waitin' fer poor innocent folk like us. It's not right, is it?"

Loud murmurings from various parts of the crowd confirmed his opinion, while a new voice from the back took the matter a stage further.

"Show us yer bad uns, Cropper!"

Cropper peered out into the growing mob, wondering who it was that knew his name. He tried to stop his limbs from shaking visibly as he shouted back as confidently as he could. "There's no bad uns, 'onest! Well, mebbe a few, like. You allus gets a few. But not a lot. I bin standin' this market fer eight years, an' I've allus given good value, ask anybody yer like. You ask 'em in . . ."

" 'ow come yer overchargin' then?" asked someone else. There must have been over forty of them out there now, and Cropper was openly terrified.

"I ain't overchargin', 'onest! You look on all the other stalls an' yer'll see the same prices."

"Aye, but they're not sellin' rotten fruit," countered the swarthy man. "Three for a farthin', that's all yer should be chargin' fer this lot."

Cropper's eyes widened in disbelief, and a nervous laugh escaped him before he covered it with a choking cough and made one last attempt. "I can't sell 'em at that price, 'onest I can't! I've gorrer mek a livin', just like you good folks. Look, I'm sorry if the boy got a rotten plum – 'ere, 'ave some more, lad – tek yer pick from this lot."

As he pointed to the good pile, the crowd surged forward, but the swarthy man and his companion blocked their way. "Just a minute," cried the swarthy man, "let's 'ave some order rahnd 'ere. We dun't want ter damage the stall, nah do we?"

Already, a punnet of strawberries had been knocked to the ground, and the contents hurriedly grabbed from the dust by eager hands. Other hands began to go for plums and raspberries, but the swarthy man and his companion held them off.

"See what yer've started nah?" the apparent ringleader complained. "I reckon yer'd better offer this lot summat real special, or yer stall's gunner get busted."

"I tell yer what, then," croaked Cropper, now prepared to agree to almost anything, "all the fruit 'alf-price, just ter show there's no 'ard feelin's, like."

The swarthy man grinned in gap-toothed triumph. "All right, but not 'ere. We got somewhere special we can go. We'll tek yer up there when yer've packed yer cart."

He shouted instructions to several accomplices in the crowd and together they dispersed the mob, making sure that everyone knew where to go for the bargains. As the thoroughly shaken Cropper began to transfer his stock from the stall into the cart, the swarthy man cuffed the original youth playfully round the ear and grinned again.

"Well done, Tommy Slack. Nah gerrup ter the square an' tell 'enson we're on us way."

While Cropper was loading his cart, Lily was packing her basket and asking, for the fifth time, if they were all right. Nathan and Matthew, more or less dry apart from a telltale squelching from their boots, assured her that they were, and helped her pack. A search for Tommy having proved unsuccessful, they left a message with neighbours who were staying on a while longer.

Rather than go back along the East Croft, and expose themselves to the stiff breeze which was now blowing off the river as the heat of the day diminished, Lily decided that they should cross the nearby canal footbridge onto the London Road, then walk briskly up to Red Lion Square and along Narrow Marsh, where the tall houses would have retained some of the day's warmth, and would prevent father and son from taking a chill on the way home.

But as they approached Red Lion Square, and even before they could see right into it, it became evident that a crowd had already gathered from somewhere. Half a dozen empty carts on the perimeter recorded the fate of other traders such as Cropper, and the lively crowd, pleased with their purchases and thefts, were now quite content to listen to a speaker who had suddenly appeared, standing on one of the carts, hurriedly pressed into use as an improvised platform. He had just begun; a small fair-haired man with an unfamiliar accent.

"Good folk of Nottingham; I'm only going to take up a little of your time today. Kingsley's the name – Bart Kingsley – from Manchester. That's up north from here, but we've all got the same problems as you people. I happened to be passing through when I heard about the market traders who'd been caught cheating the townsfolk, and I just wanted to say how much I admire what you did today. There are lots of folks like you up north – cotton workers – and they have to live just like you."

" 'ow many to a privy?"

The gale of laughter reminded Kingsley of the warning he'd received about the wits in the Nottingham mob, which could turn nasty at the drop of a hat.

"About twenty, if you can get in for the rats!"

More laughter suggested that he might be winning them over, and he continued. "And talking of privies, some of the food I've seen in this market should have been chucked down one, instead of being put up for sale!" There were mutterings of assent from near the front of the crowd.

"And what about the prices, then? How in hell's name do they expect you folk to live with food at those prices, when wages are falling the way they are?" The crowd grew even more attentive.

"Let me say this, though, in fairness to the bosses – they've had it bad as well." He quelled a mounting roar of protest with a raised hand. "No, they have, fair's fair, and I don't want anyone thinking that I'm blaming it all on the bosses. It's not all their fault."

"Like bloody 'ell it's not!" came a shout from just in front of the platform. Those who knew him recognised Cadby's voice without taking their eyes off Kingsley.

"Well, that's as may be, but my concern is with the real people of towns such as this. I know the cloth trade well myself and I know the effect of colt working on the livelihoods of skilled men, not to mention the rising cost of renting frames. And I know what cut-ups are, as well. How many of you can honestly say that none of these are killing your livelihoods?"

He had them now, since not a single hosiery worker in his audience, which was growing by the minute as word got around, had not, in some way or another, seen his living standards fall at the same time as the introduction of untrained colt labour, the steady rise in frame rents, and the switch to ready-made lengths of hosiery. There were no more hecklers.

"Up in Manchester, we tried to do something about it. Quite simple, really. We just got together a few respectable folk from among the workers, and asked to talk to the bosses; just trying to put our concerns to them and see if something couldn't be worked out between us. But the magistrates stopped us, saying we were breaking the law. Called us an 'illegal combination', whatever that's supposed to mean."

"It means you had a damned good point which they didn't want to hear," remarked a large bearded man who had just joined Kingsley on the platform. "My name's Henson. A lot of you might know me; I live not far from here."

Cadby now climbed up onto the platform. "I know Henson, an' 'e's a good bloke. I reckon we should listen to 'im. When Mr Kingsley's done, mind."

So far, the Slacks had stood watching out of idle curiosity, but Nathan saw the warning signs and turned to Lily. "Right, come on, I've 'eard enough. I'm listening ter nowt from Cadby!"

Lily was still staring at the platform. "I reckon this bloke's got summat, Nathan. S'posing yer did ask ter see the bosses. They'd agree, wouldn't they? I reckon Bradley would."

"Aye, an' 'e'd be abaht the only one as would. Can't yer see what they're abaht? They know what they're suggestin' is agin the law, an' they're just lookin' fer trouble. If Cadby's mixed up in it, it's trouble, tek mi word on it."

"But 'ow can it be agin the law, just fer 'onest folks like you ter want ter talk wi' Bradley an' the like?"

"Me? Leave me aht of it, anyroad. I know wharram talkin' abaht. Nah come on!"

"No."

It was a direct challenge and he should have risen to it. But he was weary, anxious not to provoke Lily while her health was still low and, if he were honest with himself, half-interested in the idea which had just been put forward. So he chose an indirect response instead. "Well, yer'll 'ear nowt that's sensible, I promise yer."

Back on the platform, Henson had taken over from Kingsley.

"Mr Kingsley's right, you know. All over the north it's the same wherever you go. The workers are near starvation and the bosses won't listen. Illegal combinations they call them, right enough. That's people like you and me getting together for meetings like this. You can go to prison for it."

"Is that right?" Lily asked Nathan.

"Dun't ask me; let's just get 'ome, shall we?"

"Not yet. I want to 'ear what this bloke's got ter say. Who is 'e, anyroad?"

"Dunno. 'e talks local, even if 'e is a bit lah-di-dah."

Henson had been warming to his theme, and now, with a theatrical gesture, he pointed high in the air, northwards towards the high town. "Look up there! High Pavement, Stoney Street, St. Mary's

Gate. You can see the houses even from here, because they've got four floors each. How many of you have been inside one of them?" He quickly resumed, in case too many of them had. "You know who lives in them – hosiery bosses, almost every one of them. Are they hungry? Are they losing family every winter? Do they have to make do with stale bread and rotten fruit?"

He turned back to Kingsley, who did his best to look embarrassed. "Mr Kingsley here is an honest man, well respected in his community. He said just now that he had no argument with the bosses, and we must respect his opinion, even if some of us do believe that the bosses ought to care more about what's happening to those who make their wealth for them. Maybe there are some bosses in this town who'd be prepared to listen to us."

"Name one!" challenged Cadby from the side. Henson glared round at him, and he slid back off the platform into the heaving crowd.

"I could name several, but that's not the point. The point is that we're not allowed to talk to them, at least not in a group. That's because of the law, like Mr Kingsley says. But it's a bloody stupid law, that's what I say!" Amid shouts of agreement, he pursued the point. "I've been doing a bit of finding out lately, and it seems that any meeting of people is illegal at the moment, whether it's us or the bosses."

"Are we breakin' the law nah?" came an anxious voice from near the front.

"No we're not, because it's market day, and these kindly stallholders here offered to give us a bargain or two."

The laughter was loud and coarse and several of the still-nervous traders, under fire from the less edible remnants of what had earlier been their stock in trade, looked far from happy with their contribution. Henson kept up the momentum.

"But it would be against the law otherwise. And yet I happen to know for a fact that most of the bosses have been meeting in their own houses for months, fixing prices and so on." He was shouting now, to be heard above the rising noise of discontent.

"Well, what's sauce for the goose is sauce for the gander, as they say. I'm going to see to it that either we're allowed to meet together, and then meet with the bosses, or they're not going to meet either."

"An' 'ow d'yer reckon yer can do that?" Cadby was right on cue.

"By presenting a petition to Parliament, if I have to. Or maybe I'll report the next boss's meeting to the magistrates!" He waved down the loud applause, and went for the kill. "But I need your help. I need your ears and your eyes, and maybe I need your voices as well, in more meetings like this. We'll divide ourselves into groups inside the parishes and pass on everything we find out. So first I need some volunteers from each parish."

In a timely and well-orchestrated move, half a dozen or so men – all well known to, and already hand-picked by, Henson – leaped onto the platform. They began shouting out the names of the parishes they would represent, and Cadby claimed St. Mary's. That was enough to provoke a final determined response from Nathan.

"Bogger this. We're not stayin' 'ere a minute longer!"

Lily was still of a mind to stay, intrigued by all she had heard, but just then Ruth tugged at her sleeve, and whispered urgently in her ear as she lowered her head. "All right, we'd best be gerrin' back. It's gerrin' chilly aht 'ere, an' Ruth needs ter go somewhere, anyroad."

They were almost out of the square when, on an impulse, Nathan looked back into the surging crowd. Among those rounding up volunteers near the front, he spotted a familiar figure. Without a word to Lily, he elbowed and shoved his way to the front and grabbed Tommy by the hair. With a mouthful of oaths which would have both surprised and shocked Lily had she been within earshot, Nathan hauled Tommy savagely back through the mob. As they reached its outer perimeter, he pushed Tommy ahead of him, and kicked the seat of his breeches so hard that Tommy shot out into the open with a look of pained surprise on his face, clutching his burning rump with both hands.

Nobody said a word as they walked briskly along Narrow Marsh and down into Tanners Yard. The seething look on Nathan's face was enough to deter all conversation, and no-one dared risk even a casual remark which might provoke another outburst. They had not seen Tommy at the front of the mob, but they had seen his rapid reappearance at the edge of it, and the means by which it had occurred.

In truth, Nathan was more worried than angry. First of all Tommy, and now Lily, seemed impressed by the arguments put forward by these self-appointed peoples' champions, and while he agreed with the general complaint, he also knew the true characters of the Cadbys and the Perrys who hung around such meetings, and he had a pretty good idea of their reasons for being there.

Apart from the obvious risks which he and his family might run if they became too closely associated with anything that smacked of violent resistance to the established order, there was also the damage which any prolonged disruption might have on the already weakened hosiery trade. So far, he had avoided any long period without work, but he had seen, all around him, the terrible consequences which it could have.

At the same time, he could not expect his family simply to ignore what was clearly beginning to build up in the town, just because he said so. He had to have reasons for keeping them out of it and he had to explain them carefully. As the supper was being cleared away, he faced up to it.

"All right, I can see yer all upset wi' me, but I've got mi reasons."

Lily looked up at him from across the table as she carefully rewrapped the cheese in a muslin cloth. Matthew looked apprehensively at Tommy, who pretended that he hadn't heard. Ruth, who really hadn't heard, hummed away at her sewing in the corner of the room, next to the fire which was now burning brightly in the grate as the clothes hanging in front of it steamed quietly. Nathan tried another approach.

"Tommy, d'yer think I enjoy losin' mi rag wi' yer?"

Tommy shrugged, and his buttocks sent him a warning ache. He decided to be diplomatic. "S'pose not."

"Well, I did it terday 'cos I could see that yer gerrin' in wi' the wrong sort o' folks, an' messin' in things that yer dun't rightly understand."

"That bloke 'enson seemed all right," Lily argued, "an' that bloke from up north – Kingston or summat."

"Kingsley," Tommy corrected her.

"Aye, that's right – Kingsley. They seemed all right ter me. In fact, ter my mind they was talkin' a lot o' sense."

"Some of it were sense, I grant yer," Nathan conceded, "an' that's just the point. Everyone knows that things is gerrin' slowly worse, or will do once the winter comes, but they're goin' abaht things the wrong way."

"An' you know a berrer way?" Tommy challenged him.

"No, ter be 'onest, I dun't. But I'll tell yer this – they're all headin' fer serious trouble if they carry on holdin' meetin's like that one terday. You 'eard 'em admit that they're agin the law."

"Not terday it weren't," Lily countered, "they said that an' all. An' there must be summat far wrong wi' the law when decent workin' folks can't be allowed ter meet together like that. Mebbe 'enson's right. Mebbe someone should tek it up wi' London."

Nathan sighed. "An' a fat lot o' good that'd do. I've 'eard abaht them lawyers an' suchlike in London; they just do what they're told ter do. An' if there's a law agin meetin's, then Parliament musta said so. Are yer suggestin' that they'll change their minds just 'cos the likes of us asks 'em to?"

"Well it's berrer than doin' nowt," Lily persisted. "It's time them in London 'eard all abaht us up 'ere, the way folks is starvin' an' everythin'."

"Yer've forgotten summat else," added Tommy. "When the bosses meet, that's all right! Call that fair, do yer?"

"No, that's not all right," Nathan told him. "I were listenin' an' all, yer know, an' I 'eard 'enson say that boss's meetin's is agin the law too. 'e said 'e were gunner do summat abaht that while 'e's at it. 'e's gunner be mighty busy, is your Mester 'enson."

"An' 'e's gunner need 'elp," Tommy suggested.

"Well 'e's not gerrin' any from us," insisted Nathan.

"Nathan, I dun't often argue wi' yer in front o' the family, but this time I've gorrer say mi piece." Having secured everyone's attention, Lily continued.

"The way I sees it, there's some bosses tekkin' advantage of the situation an' summat's got ter be done abaht it, or we'll all starve. The likes of 'enson an' 'is friends mean no harm ter the decent bosses like Bradley. In fact, by standin' up agin the bad uns, they're even doin' 'em a favour, like. They're God-fearin' men, as I judge 'em, an' there's no 'arm in standin' up an' tellin' the truth."

"P'rhaps not," Nathan acknowledged, "but look at the folks they've got 'angin' arahnd 'em doin' all the shoutin' – Cadby, Perry an' the like. Yer not gunner tell me they're not aht ter mek mischief."

"There's more than them," Lily said. "In fact, most o' the folk I knew there terday was decent folk. Yer can't say they're all bad, just 'cos of a few."

"Well, I still say there'll be trouble, an' we're 'avin' nowt ter do wi' it. Particularly not wi' Cadby – 'e's in enough trouble already, bi all accounts."

Tommy remained silent, and Nathan turned to Matthew.

"Yer not sayin' much, as usual. I 'ope yer not gunner pass any o' this on ter Bradley when yer go fer yer lessons. We're 'avin' nowt ter do wi' any of it, on one side or the other, d'yer 'ear me?"

"Yes Dad," replied Matthew quietly. He was already finding his position at home awkward, and was glad to leave it at that.

That night, the whole household was kept awake by Lily's hoarse and frightening cough. Her breath was coming in shallow rasps between spasms of choking barks, and as dawn broke, Nathan slipped out of the house for old Nancy. A selection of her homely recipes and a measure of gin helped Lily to sleep at last, but not before she had berated Nathan, in a grating gargle that terrified him more than the tongue-lashing, for slipping the liquor into her medicine cup without asking.

In a day or two she was on the mend, but the warning was plain. It was still high summer, and her recurrent illness was clearly brought on, not so much by cold, as by anxiety. Nancy asked pointedly, and more than once, if anything had upset her, and although they denied it they all wondered if the real cause of Lily's relapse was in fact the family argument. As if by telepathy, no-one made any further reference to the meeting in Red Lion Square, and Nathan somehow never got round to challenging Tommy when he came in late of an evening.

Young Ruth took on more and more of the household chores, while Lily sat in her chair, nursing baby William and thinking deeply.

CHAPTER FIVE

All in a good cause

JOHN BLACKNER surveyed the new gadget cynically, his suspicion bordering on certainty that it augured nothing good for any of them. Half a dozen of his fellow stockingers were also gathered round it, trying to guess its purpose. Their employer, Joseph Rankin, looked on nervously, his smile more forced than usual, and with a wary eye on Blackner. All the workers were journeymen hosiers, but Blackner usually spoke for them all and it was his opinion which mattered.

"All right, what does it do?" Blackner eventually asked.

"It measures finished goods," explained Rankin, in what he hoped was a reassuring tone.

"Which means, o' course," suggested Blackner in case his colleagues had missed the point, "that cut-ups are not goin' away just yet."

"Well," said Rankin, "with trade the way it is, we have no choice. And I think you'll grant that by switching to cut-ups, you men have stayed in work a lot longer than you might otherwise. But we need a new system for measuring the finished product."

"An' what's wrong wi' the present system?" queried Blackner.

If there was one question which Rankin could have anticipated, it was that one, and his answer was altogether too glib to be convincing. "Ah well, yes, the present system, as I'm sure you'll all allow, isn't always as precise as one might wish, and in the circumstances . . ."

"Mr Rankin, beggin' yer pardon an' all that," Blackner interrupted, "but we've been paid bi the length ever since yer purrus on ter cut-ups, an' a foot o' stockin' is a foot o' stockin'."

"Well yes, of course, but by using this device we'll know for certain that we're getting an exact foot."

"This thing can be bent!" exclaimed Jake Fletcher, who had been toying idly with the spring mechanism.

"What do you mean, bent?" demanded Rankin indignantly.

"Like I said," Fletcher persevered, "bent. Yer puts a length o' stockin' on this thing, an' if yer stretch this wooden bit 'ere, yer can mek a foot look like ten inches."

Rankin reddened, and his eyes narrowed. "Are you calling me dishonest?"

"Not yet," Fletcher replied breezily, "but who's gunner work this thing?"

"Well naturally, either me or Mr Bentley."

"An' 'ow," enquired Blackner, "do we know that we're gerrin' 'onest measure?"

"Well, you'll just have to trust me, won't you?" responded Rankin. "I fail to understand what all the fuss is about. To tell you the truth, it's only a measuring device to help me."

"Oh aye, it'll help you all right," agreed Blackner. "That's what worries me."

"And what exactly do you mean by that?" Rankin had used up his daily supply of easy-going tolerance. After all, they were his workers, and if they didn't like it, they could go elsewhere.

"What I mean is," continued Blackner, choosing his words carefully and pronouncing them slowly, "that none o' my work is goin' on that thing. We'll carry on usin' the foot rule, just like before."

"Oh no we won't," insisted Rankin. "I paid good money for this measure, and it starts work today."

"In which case," countered Blackner just as firmly, "I stop work today." He looked around at his colleagues. "Any of yer comin' wi' me?"

It was a difficult position to be put in, particularly on the spot like that. It was now October, and winter was probably only days away. While they could always return to the old life, making stockings on rented frames at home, there was no guarantee that they could find a market for their finished product, with so many homeworkers now chasing too few merchant hosiers. Then there was the direct challenge posed by colt workers, who could be brought in to make cut-ups without serving any formal indenture. All in all, not a good time to leave the relative security of the small factory in Hockley which had given them steady, if under-rewarded, employment for several years, give or take the odd seasonal recession.

On the other hand, journeymen hosiers didn't grow on trees, and there was always a serious quality risk in bringing in colts. It would take Rankin at least a year to train up new men from scratch to work the new broad frames which he had only recently installed, even if he poached good, time-served stockingers from trade rivals. In that time he could be out of business, either through lost markets for his specialised product or because styles had moved on. He'd certainly be in a mess if all of them walked out.

In the end, four of them did and three of them didn't. The four who did, led by Blackner, made straight for the Newton's Head, where they knew they would find Henson.

"Well, I admire your courage, gentlemen," was his immediate reaction, "but it's not going to be easy. I reckon Rankin can just about hold out with the ones he's got left."

Blackner stared darkly into his ale pot, then looked back up at Henson. "D'yer think I dun't know that? An' I feel bad abaht Jake an' the others 'ere. Jake's got eight of a family, did yer know? I just 'ope we can sell from our own frames, that's all. I 'aven't been 'ome ter see the wife yet, an' I'm dreadin' 'avin' ter tell 'er, what wi' winter comin' an' all."

Henson placed a reassuring hand on his shoulder. "I'm pretty sure the lads'll pitch in when they find out, and we've still got a bob or two left in the pot after getting Kingsley down here. But there's an important principle involved. You're not the only ones who've been faced with this new measure. Some of the lads in Arnold and Beeston have been dealing with it for a month or so now, and they reckon they've lost at least a couple of bob a week by it."

"I bet they 'aven't walked aht, though," commented Fletcher despondently.

"No, they haven't," acknowledged Henson, "but now that you have, perhaps some others will follow your example. It only takes a few dozen of the best men like you and there'll be little enough hosiery coming out of Nottingham."

"A few dozen?" snorted Blackner derisively. "Yer dun't seriously expect a few dozen ter be as daft as us, do yer?"

"Who knows?" Henson speculated. "Perhaps. But look John, if you and the lads here aren't happy, no-one's going to think any the less of you if you go back. After all, you're all family men."

Blackner rose from his bench, wandered over to the lead-framed window that looked out over the busy thoroughfare and glared at the heavy drizzle outside. He turned round and stared first at his colleagues and then at Henson. "No, bogger it. We'll stick the bastard aht!"

Matthew accepted the piece of plum cake with a polite thank you, and Lucy smiled with pride as she recalled the clumsy manners of the young boy she'd taken on as a pupil less than a year ago. He could now read and write almost as well as her brother James, even if his style was still a little lacking in flourish, and if anything his grasp of Latin was superior to James's. At the same time, she wondered what use he could ever make of it all in his present situation, and although her father had promised to find him 'something clerical' in due course, she hoped it would be soon, before his interest began to wane and he fell back into that helpless indifference which fate had taught to so many of his class. She saw them in the Sunday School, lively and intelligent, but imprisoned by the lottery of their birth, meekly convinced that all they were fitted for was hardship and drudgery.

"So Matthew said, 'Let's see if it likes me', and the man let him have a try. He only fell off once, and honestly, you'd think he'd been riding all his life."

Lucy, Rebecca and Matthew had been out to Wollaton for the day, to the orchard estate owned by Catherine's cousin Andrew Blatchford, and Lucy had been intrigued by how quickly Matthew had taken to every new experience. The trip had really been intended for Rebecca, who had not yet fully recovered from an early bout of bronchitis, and for whom a day in the country air had been prescribed. Now, as the whole family sat round the sitting room table taking a late tea, it was Rebecca who was singing Matthew's praises as she relived his first attempts at horse riding.

"It's quite simple once you get the hang of it," Matthew explained modestly, and again Lucy noted how easily and naturally he now joined in the family conversations. "The worst part is getting on it in the first place."

"I've never quite taken to horse riding since I once fell off as a lad," confided Robert as he walked over to the cigar box on the table near the window, "so it's perhaps as well that Mrs Bradley and I weren't with you. In any case, you wouldn't have been interested in that sort of thing, would you dear?"

"No indeed I would not," confirmed Catherine somewhat frostily, "and I hardly feel that it's a suitable activity for a child with such a delicate constitution as Rebecca. Really, Lucy, I'm surprised at you allowing it."

"I'm not a child," Rebecca protested. "I'll be fifteen just after Christmas. And in any case, it was Matthew who got on the horse, not me. I'm not brave enough."

"There was no harm done," added Lucy, "and just look at the colour in Rebecca's cheeks. She looks so much more lively now."

"That's because she's talking about Master Slack," sneered her brother James, who had, up to that moment, devoted himself relentlessly to the eating of cake. His mother shot him a venomous look, then checked the clock on the mantelpiece.

"It's almost seven-thirty, and it's been fully dark for a while now. I really feel that the young man should be thinking about going home. It's hardly safe to walk the streets at all these days, and as for those dark alleyways in Narrow Marsh – well!"

"I'll show him out," offered Rebecca enthusiastically, as she jumped to her feet and thrust her half-eaten cake back onto its plate.

"Indeed you will not," declared her mother sternly. "That's Adam's job, and the night air is far too unhealthy for you to be breathing it in. Goodnight, Master Slack."

Matthew thanked them all profusely for the happy day out, but as Adam appeared in answer to the summons on the bell rope, Rebecca slipped out of the half-open door ahead of Matthew, giggling all the way down the hall.

"I'll just show him as far as the hat stand!" she shouted back, and her mother looked long and hard at her father.

"Really, Robert, I don't know what's come over you, allowing all this."

"Allowing all what?" Robert was genuinely puzzled.

"Well, you can see for yourself how slipshod Rebecca's manners have become since you allowed that young Slack boy into the house. And to my mind, he comes here far too often. I didn't mind when he came here for lessons with Lucy . . ."

"I should think not indeed! It was your idea in the first place," Robert reminded her.

"Don't interrupt, dear, it's most ignorant," Catherine chastised him. "As I say, I didn't mind when he came here for lessons, but this is the second time this month that he's accompanied Rebecca on some social outing which had nothing to do with his education. And if it comes to that, surely he's progressed as far as he can? Lucy tells me that he can read and write now and can even manage some Latin, although what on earth a stockinger needs with Latin I really can't imagine."

"He won't be a stockinger," interposed Lucy, who was determined not to let the matter drop by default. "Papa promised to take him on as a clerk, didn't you, Papa?"

"Well," Robert replied hesitantly, "I did say that I'd keep him in mind, certainly, but he'll have to wait till Danby's finished; or at least until he's nearly finished, so he can show him the way I like things kept."

He turned to his wife, who had been sadly shaking her head, and whose eyes he had so far managed to avoid.

"And I really think you're worrying without cause, my dear.

Young Matthew is a very pleasant, and a very respectable, young man, and we should be mindful of our duty to those less fortunate than ourselves. The way things are going in this town just at the moment, I count myself fortunate to enjoy the goodwill of families like the Slacks. There's been no real trouble in my business as yet, and there won't be, so long as good men like Nathan Slack keep their heads."

"And their places," added James, who had eaten all the cake he could manage, and was now engaged in picking his teeth. "Don't forget their places."

"And don't you forget yours!" retorted Robert angrily. "It's people with your attitude as are causin' most of the trouble lately."

Catherine winced at his grammatical lapse – a common failing of his when under stress – and tried to steer the subject back to her original point. "What you do in your own business is entirely up to you of course, dear, but I really don't think it's very healthy for young Rebecca to get too friendly with anyone from that dreadful yard, even if he is a pleasant enough young man. If I didn't know it was quite impossible I'd say she was getting rather sweet on him, and he may well be getting the same idea. You know how people from his class like to take advantage of the kindness of others."

"May I remind you," stated Robert in the tone of voice which always signified that the subject would be closed once he had finished speaking, "that the young man in question saved Howard's life not three months ago. I would hardly call that 'taking advantage'. And as far as Rebecca's concerned, you can see for yourself how it's perked her up no end having a friend her own age. They're only children, for goodness sake, and they're hardly of an age to have any silly romantic notions. Now we'll let the subject drop, shall we? Lucy, would you see where Rebecca's got to, then go and see if Martha would like to make some more tea? All this talking's left me quite dry."

As Lucy slipped from the room with a satisfied smile, and her father reached across for the newspaper that lay on the ottoman, Catherine and James exchanged pensive looks across the table, and Catherine sadly shook her head once again.

They stared, fascinated, at the notice, but only Matthew could read it all. He stood at the head of the family group, his long dark hair blowing in strands across his broad face as he proudly and slowly read from the official-looking board in the top corner of what had, until recently, been a gently sloping orchard.

"To be let. New brick homes, with slated roofs, two storeys high, two rooms on each floor; particularly adapted to stocking-makers, having room for two or three frames. Apply to R. Broadstone Esq, Solicitor and Land Agent, Pelham St."

"A room fer the kids an' all?" Lily smiled for the first time that day and Nathan was glad that they had come. A sharp wind had warned them for days that another winter was almost upon them and they needed no reminder of what winters could be like in Tanners Yard. Lily had already begun to cough her way through the night as the first hint of frost tore at her delicate chest, and Nathan prayed nightly that the new house would soon be ready for them.

His heart began to sink again as he looked down the sloping land, cleared of most of its trees but with very few of the promised houses even begun. He kept his disappointment to himself, since he had been the one to suggest the trip down the Ilkeston Road to the new development in Radford. They were in the second group of families on the list, and little enough land outside the town boundaries ever got freed up for new housing.

His intention had been to raise Lily's spirits. She seemed to lack energy for just about everything these days, and the rest of the family had realised how much importance Nathan attached to the outing when he had insisted that everyone was to go. For Matthew, this meant missing Sunday School, and he had protested loudly and vigorously about being kept away from Halifax Lane. There had been quite an argument about it, which had only been made worse when Tommy jibed that Matthew was more interested in Rebecca Bradley than in the teachings of Our Lord, and Matthew had retorted that Tommy – and anyone who agreed with him – was little better than a Philistine, whatever one of those was.

Nathan was also worried about the change which seemed to have overtaken Matthew throughout the course of the past few months. He'd always heard a warning voice in his head about letting Matthew go for that extra schooling, but as usual he'd held his tongue because it had seemed to be what Lily wanted at the time. Now even she seemed uneasy when Matthew fell into one of his 'distant moods', as she called them, and sat in the corner for hours on end, deep in some book or other, or writing things on all that paper he always seemed to have in his pockets.

He certainly seemed to have lost interest in working at the frame, almost as if it was beneath him. Whenever he got the chance to slip away, he could be found in the Counting Room, sitting with Bradley's senior clerk, Richard Danby, watching and learning the procedures for counting, batching, pricing, dispatching and billing the finished goods. He was clearly more interested in the ledgers than in the frame, and when Nathan took him to task for not paying attention while he was trying to teach him something, Matthew would simply apologise in a vague sort of manner, his mind obviously far away somewhere else.

They began the trek home. At least it was mostly downhill once they reached Sion Hill and started to drop down the Derby Turnpike towards Chapel Bar on the western perimeter of the town proper, and Lily seemed to have regained some colour in her cheeks.

"Dad," chirped Ruth as she skipped back and forth among the group, making her journey twice as long, " 'ow long afore we move?"

"Dunno, lass," said Nathan. "It'll not be this winter, anyroad, bi the look on it."

"When we do move, can I do all the cleaning? Can I?"

Nathan laughed, and squeezed Lily's arm tighter as they shared in the pride of their daughter's development. "We'll see. I leave that sort o' thing ter yer mam."

Lily smiled at Ruth, only eleven and so keen to learn. "O' course yer can 'elp," she assured her, "but before long, yer'll need ter find yer own position in a big 'ouse, an' see 'ow the proper gentry does it."

Nathan had hoped that she'd forgotten that particular idea. "Ey, steady on, lass. Yer not as strong as yer used ter be, yer know, an' Ruth's a real blessin' ter yer some days when yer real bad."

"All the more reason why I shouldn't get ter need 'er too much," Lily countered. "She's got 'er own way ter mek in the world, an' the new 'ouse'll be small enough fer me once I'm back on mi feet."

No-one was convinced, not even Lily, but out of respect they said nothing. Lily seemed to be the only one who wanted Ruth to have the chance to enter domestic service and hopefully, thought Nathan, it would slip her mind, like so many things seemed to these days, before someone made Ruth an offer. Ruth in particular knew just how much her mother had come to depend upon her, day after day, and couldn't imagine what might happen if she weren't there sometimes. Nor could she imagine her life without the family her mother had brought her up to love and cherish.

It was darkening rapidly as they walked along Bridlesmith Gate, and they could hear the crowd even before they had turned the corner towards Weekday Cross. A large group of men was ranged in front of the town gaol, and above the subdued mumbling could be heard the occasional more strident voice of complaint. Despite Nathan's warning, Tommy ran towards the rear of the group, and as the rest of the family disappeared towards the unlit gloom of Garner's Hill, and home, he grabbed the sleeve of one of the onlookers.

"What's goin' on, then?"

"Dirty bloody business, that's what. They're bringin' Blackner in."

"Who?"

"Blackner. John Blackner, from Goose Gate. One o' them blokes as walked aht o' Rankin's. You bin asleep fer a week or summat?"

Tommy had been far from asleep for a week and knew all about Blackner and his colleagues from the second-hand accounts he got from Cadby. Indeed, they were the talk of the town and the main topic of conversation at local meetings. But the way Cadby told the tale, four men had been forced to leave their employment because a new machine had been brought in to replace them, while their employer had reported them to the authorities for calling him a cheat. Cadby never let the truth get in the way of a good story against a merchant hosier. Now, listening to the conversations outside the front doors of the gaol, Tommy was confused.

"If yer asks me owt," said a man in front of him to his neighbour, "this new system'll do forrus all in the end. They reckon the journeymen in Solley's are already losin' one an' six a week by it."

"Aye," agreed his neighbour, "an' it'll not stop there, neither. The next thing'll be a machine what does the patternin' an' all."

" 'scuse me," Tommy interrupted, "but what's this bloke Blackner done, exactly?"

"Nowt at all," grumbled the first man, " 'cept stick up fer 'imself an' everyone else in 'is position. 'e won't allow 'is work ter be measured bi a fancy machine, that's all."

Tommy had heard mention of it at Bradley's, but nothing in detail. "This machine," he enquired further, "is it called the rack?"

"Aye, the rack. S'posed ter measure a foot, but the way I 'ear it, it measures fifteen inches."

His companion laughed bitterly. "If yer lucky. There should be more like Blackner, refusin' ter work wi' it."

"So this – this rack thing – it doesn't actually replace workers?" Tommy persisted. For the first time, the two men turned to peer curiously at him through the dusk.

"God 'elp us, d'yer know owt, lad?" one of them demanded.

Tommy blushed, and wished he'd paid more attention to conversations among the workforce. Then again, he was evidently not the only one who'd been misled by Cadby, and he badly wanted the truth of the matter. "An' this bloke Blackner – 'e's not bein' brought in just fer callin' Rankin a cheat?"

The two men laughed again, and were clearly beginning to enjoy themselves. "Look, lad," replied the kindlier of the two, jerking his head in the direction of the gaol, "if it were agin the law ter call the bosses cheats, we'd all be in there."

The creaking front doors of the gaol had just been opened, and in the light which flooded onto the darkened road, the burly shapes of three waiting turnkeys cast long and ominous shadows.

"So what's Blackner done, exactly?" asked Tommy.

" 'e walked aht on Rankin, that's what. An' 'e took three others wi' 'im – they're in there already, bi all accounts. It's a combination, ain't it? Yer've 'eard o' them, surely ter God?"

"Oh aye," Tommy confirmed, glad to be on familiar ground at last, "but is that all 'e's done?"

"All? That's all yer needs ter do these days. Dirty bloody business. Ey up, there's summat 'appenin' up there."

The crowd surged instinctively towards the open doors of the gaol, and shouts of protest could be heard from the front. The turnkeys moved cautiously down from the front step and ordered the crowd back, wielding long batons at shoulder height to emphasise their authority. Tommy moved round the edge of the crowd into the open road, in time to see a shaken-looking man being escorted to the steps and handed over into the custody of the turnkeys by three officers of the Watch who, to judge by their facial expressions as they passed into the pool of light from the open doors, had no taste for what they had been detailed to do.

The crowd hung around for a while, uncertain of what was to happen next. In the event, the doors of the gaol were noisily shut and rebolted, and after a few half-hearted shouts of challenge the protesters hurried back to their homes as a sleety drizzle began to fall, reminding them that another winter was almost upon them.

Lucy let the heavy velvet curtain fall back into place and turned to smile comfortingly at her sister, a frightened child in a lace nightgown, her dark eyes wide as she sat up in bed.

"There, it's all over, and there was nothing to be afraid of, now was there?"

"But they were all shouting, and I thought they were coming here."

It was, in truth, barely a hundred yards from the town gaol in Weekday Cross to the imposing façade of the Bradley residence in

High Pavement, but it might as well have been a hundred miles.

"Rebecca, it was just some unfortunate being taken in charge by the Watch, and some of his friends were obviously upset. No doubt some of them had taken some drink as well, but they wouldn't come here to harm us, now would they?"

Her sister looked far from reassured, and Lucy made a mental note to discuss with their mother the wisdom of allowing Rebecca to sleep at the front of the house, albeit two stories up from the road below. She sat on the edge of Rebecca's bed, and stroked her hair soothingly. "Do you want me to stay and talk with you a while?"

Rebecca caressed her sister's hand as it ran through her tousled ringlets. "Yes please. I'm still a little frightened."

"All right then. What shall we talk about?"

"Oh, I don't know. Yes I do – princes and princesses."

Lucy smiled. "I'm afraid I don't know any, although mama met the Duke of Newcastle the other day. He's the Lord Lieutenant of the County, you know."

"Is that something like a prince?"

"No, not exactly," answered Lucy with another smile. There was a long silence before Rebecca picked up the conversation again.

"Lucy?"

"Yes, dear?"

"Have you ever been in love?"

The older girl was taken by surprise, and sat back a little to look Rebecca more fully in the face. "Well, what a strange question from someone who's not yet fifteen!"

"But have you?"

"Have I what?"

"Ever been in love? Don't treat me like a child."

"Of course not."

"I don't know why you say 'of course not' like that. After all, you're eighteen now, and Dorothy Gibson got betrothed when she was eighteen."

"Ah yes, but her husband-to-be's an officer in the Blues, and he has to go and fight in France soon. Which reminds me; she wants us both to be bridesmaids, did mama tell you?"

The younger girl's eyes lit up. "Yes, isn't it exciting? Do you think Dorothy would mind if I were to ask her?"

"Ask her what? Honestly, you do have a jack-in-the-box mind, sometimes."

"What it's like to be in love."

"Oh well, you just feel very happy, and you sought of know that he's the right person for you."

"I thought you'd never been in love," Rebecca challenged her.

"I haven't. I told you."

"Then how do you know what it's like?"

"From what I've read, and from what people have told me."

"Did they tell you how awful it can be if you think that someone you love might not love you?"

"I don't know; I don't think so. But why are you filling your head with all this silly nonsense at your age? Is that what they teach you at Miss Humberstone's these days?"

"Oh no, she'd have a fit if she heard us talking like this."

"And she'd be quite right, too. Anyway, I think it's time you tried to sleep again."

"Lucy, before you go, just tell me something."

"Yes?"

"What do you think of Matthew?"

"Matthew Slack? Oh, he's a splendid boy, quite remarkable when you consider his origins. I've never heard of anyone from his position in life taking to education so naturally. I'm very proud of him."

"So am I."

There was something in the way she said it which made Lucy stop and look more carefully into her sister's face. "Rebecca, when you were asking me about love just now, were you thinking of Matthew?"

Rebecca's face flushed an instant scarlet, and her immediate response was the usual unintended giggle. She tried to cover her embarrassment by playing with some loose lace on the shoulder of her nightgown.

"Rebecca, I asked you a question," her sister teased.

"Well, what if I was? You said yourself that he's a very nice young man."

"Yes he is, but that doesn't mean that you're in love with him."

"No, but I might be."

Lucy smiled again, but refused to take her seriously. "Well, when you do meet the right one, you'll know straight away. And knowing you, he'll probably be a prince or something. Now come along and snuggle down; you've got your lessons tomorrow and it's almost eight o'clock. You know that mama wanted you asleep early after your sneezing bout today."

Lucy tucked the bedclothes firmly round her younger sister and checked the nightlight. Kissing her gently on the forehead, she said a blessing and reminded Rebecca to say her prayers, before quietly crossing the room and gently closing the bedroom door behind her.

Rebecca turned her head on her pillow and stared through the window, as she did every night, towards the place where Matthew was. She fought back the tears as she remembered the empty seat in Sunday School. Then she said quietly to the window, "I do love you, Matthew. I do."

The next day, shortly before noon, a very angry man splashed uncaringly though the stagnant water in the carriage ruts as he stormed up Broad Lane on his way to the Newton's Head. The three companions who had left the Guildhall with him were dim figures in the rear as Henson stalked, head down, along the middle of the busy thoroughfare, muttering wildly to himself, and heedless of the carriages and carts that were forced to take evasive action, and the fellow pedestrians that he all but cannoned into doorways and walls.

A walk that would take an average man fifteen minutes took him barely five, and if he was breathless it didn't show as he flung open the main door to the inn, crossed the half-empty taproom in four strides and burst into the back room, startling the half-dozen or so who had been waiting there for him.

"A month! A bloody month! And for what? That settles it, good and bloody proper!" In his rage, he kicked over an empty trestle as everyone waited anxiously. A braver soul slid a half-full ale pot along a table towards him and he drank from it greedily, belching as the spiced ale hit his empty stomach. "Well, that's it! The bastards have really asked for it this time. If they can use the law, then so can we!"

Henson had come straight from the travesty of the hearing of the complaint against Blackner and his three companions, before a hastily convened Bench consisting of three local magistrates of dubious ability and questionable sympathies, two of whom were themselves merchants in the hosiery trade. All four accused had been found guilty of offences under the Combination Act which consisted of little more than being in the same room at the same time when they refused to work with 'the rack', and all four had been sentenced to one month's imprisonment.

The Chairman of the Magistrates, mindful of the likely reaction of the clamorous mob inside the courtroom, and their numerous and vociferous reinforcements outside, whose protests and obscene jeers could be heard even through the tightly closed doors and windows of the stuffy chamber, advised the accused of how lenient their sentences were in the circumstances, before the entire majesty of the

Bench left hurriedly via the door to a rear corridor, while those in the public gallery angrily voiced a contrary opinion.

Henson lost no time in recounting these details to his 'colonels', as he had recently taken to calling them. The three men he had so easily outdistanced on his way back from court had finally caught up with him in the back room, and added their own earthy descriptions of the injustice they had just witnessed. Everyone waited respectfully for what they suspected was coming next.

"That's it, then," confirmed Henson. "They've left us with no choice. It's just a question of who, and when."

No-one was in any doubt about what he meant. Henson had been threatening for weeks now to test the Combination Laws in the manner he had foreshadowed months previously in Red Lion Square. It was Henson's belief, which few others privately shared, that the same law which had just been used against John Blackner and his colleagues could be made to work equally effectively against any group of hosiers who met to fix low rates of payment to journeymen for finished goods, or to concur on the use of unindentured labour. While some close to him were now openly advocating the use of physical violence, Henson was arguing strongly for one last attempt at working within the law in which he had so much, perhaps unwarranted, faith.

"Yer'll be wasting valuable time," urged Cadby. "Winter's just abaht 'ere, an' the magistrates'll never go agin their own kind."

"They have to, if we have the evidence. They can't go against facts, now can they?"

Some of the harder men exchanged glances with Cadby, but said nothing for the moment. Their time would come, when Henson had played his last card using the legal system, and another cruel winter had increased the desperation on the streets. For the time being, they would go along with it.

"What sort o' facts d'yer need anyroad, d'yer reckon?" asked Jacob Rawlings, one of the more moderate of the inner circle, but a stockinger whose hungry family never ceased to remind him that something – anything – had to happen, and soon.

"Anything that I can use to show a conspiracy by the bosses against the frame men," Henson reminded them eagerly, yet again. "Any meeting of two or more hosier bosses at which I can prove that they talked about keeping the rates down, or taking on colts, or something along those lines."

"D'yer want the colour of their drawers an' all?" asked Arthur Peters sarcastically. Everyone laughed except Henson.

"All right, so it's probably not going to be easy, I grant you. We need eyes and ears everywhere. Any of the bosses will do, but the bigger the better."

Tom Ives had said little so far, but he had the germ of an idea.

"Is Jarvis Bentinck big enough fer yer?"

"Bentinck of Eastwood?" enquired Henson excitedly. "Yes, definitely. Why?"

"Well, it's just that mi eldest gel, Jane, works as parlourmaid up at their big 'ouse. The missus is nice enough, but Jane reckons as old Bentinck 'imself's a bit of a gripper, if yer get mi meanin'."

There was no need to elaborate. Sexual abuse of domestic staff was never far below the surface in many of the wealthier households, in which appearances were everything and most marriages lost their warmth after the fourth child.

"So?" queried Henson impatiently.

"So," continued Ives, "she 'ates the old bastard. She's allus goin' on abaht tea parties an' dinners she 'as ter do fer 'im an' 'is fancy friends in the trade. I've 'eard 'er talk abaht some o' the really big uns lately. Allus talkin' business, they are, an' I reckon she'd gladly keep 'er ears open a bit wider, if I asked 'er."

"But would she go to court against him if need be?"

"I dunno fer sure, but I reckon so. She's not feared of 'im, anyroad. Every time she comes 'ome on 'er day off, she's threatenin' to leave 'er place there."

"Splendid! This might be just be the lucky break we need, but the rest of you keep your ears to the ground as well, just in case this comes to nothing."

"An' if it does come ter nowt," demanded Cadby, "then what do we tell folk, wi' the next winter on us an' everythin'?"

Henson first stared intently at Cadby and then round at the rest of them, and began to wonder whether they were all still fully behind him. "I think you know better than me what happens if this fails. But we'll need to plan that carefully as well. Innocent people could get hurt if that were to go off half-cocked."

The sigh of satisfaction was almost audible, and several among them smiled to themselves. At long last they had brought Henson around to considering the physical action which a small handful of them had wanted from the very beginning. The Nottingham mob only required a bit of generalship to turn it into a virtual private army, and several of those who had patiently risen to positions of trust and responsibility under Henson had always seen in him the potential to lead the mob, even if he preferred gentler methods when possible.

Henson could currently command the full attention of the town and its people, and those who wanted to realise their dream of being at the head of the mob had to stay close by him for as long as he was in that happy position. What would happen to the leadership once the violence broke through the surface was anyone's guess, and few of them cared anyway at this stage, so long as they were among the candidates.

It was almost winter and the trade had never been so depressed. Starvation, disease and deprivation were about to return. But for some at least – those intent on direct action – things appeared to be going their way.

———— ◆◁▷◆ ————

One Monday morning in mid-November, Tommy sat on an empty herring crate which someone had left in the alleyway, his head down against the driving sleet, listening to the chatter and excitement of the gathering crowd in the bustling street outside the House of Correction, on the north side of the town. From where he sat, just off Parliament Row, he could see them arriving by the dozen, and he wished he were somewhere else. He was also cold, wet and hungry, and he would be in serious trouble for not attending work, and not for the first time. Tommy was well aware that he only kept his place on the frames because his father was so well thought of by Bradley himself. So was Matthew, of course, but for different reasons. Fancy bloody ideas, that was Matthew's problem – too blind to see that he was never going to 'gerron in life', as their mother called it. Lucy Bradley shouldn't keep encouraging him, either. Stupid bogger would only get himself hurt, in the end.

"So there you are. I thought I told yer ter wait at the front?" Cadby confronted him, clearly annoyed. Tommy raised his head for long enough to notice that the sleet had turned to swirling snow.

"Is it nine yet?"

"What does it matter what bloody time it is? Yer were told ter wait at the front."

"They dun't gerraht till nine."

"Dun't get cheeky wi' me, yer little shit. You gerraht there – nah!"

Tommy was not prepared to argue. Cadby was too powerful these days and his local group had grown to be one of the largest and meanest. Tommy was far from happy with the way things were developing but he was still committed to the cause, as most people were now openly calling it, and he knew that for him there could be no turning back. Several had already tried, and he didn't want the same punishment handed out to him.

As Tommy rose from the fish crate and began to leave the alley in sullen silence, Cadby reached out to place a hand on his shoulder. "Come on, Tommy lad, let's not you an' me fall aht – I'm gunner need mi second-in-command pretty soon, ain't I?"

Tommy squirmed inwardly, but thought it best not to risk brushing the hand off. "There were no need ter lie ter me abaht Blackner," he protested as he looked back over his shoulder at Cadby. "A right bloody fool I looked, an' no mistake, tellin' folk that 'e'd bin thrown aht o' work bi a piece o' wood!"

"I weren't lyin' ter you, Tommy lad, but I 'ad ter put it in a way as the others would understand. I were gunner tell yer the 'ole story, 'onest, but the chance never came."

Tommy thought a lot, but said nothing as they emerged from the alley and turned right into Parliament Row. Down the road, some four hundred or so people were already waiting outside the main doors of the House of Correction. It was a month to the day since Blackner and his colleagues had disappeared behind its walls, and today was their release date. Tommy looked sideways at Cadby, who in turn was looking pleased with himself as he gazed at the gathering crowd. "Yer certainly fixed 'em up a good welcome 'ome."

"Oh, it weren't just me," Cadby conceded, "although it 'elps to 'ave contacts. There's four or five commands 'ere. See that lot, up bi the pump? They're from Beeston."

Tommy was impressed, despite his earlier misgivings, and again he reminded himself that it was as well to be on the right side while the cause was bringing them in so quickly.

The first shout went up as soon as those at the front heard the massive bolts being drawn back, and the noise was almost deafening by the time that two nervous turnkeys opened up one of the massive entrance gates just wide enough to let the four men scuttle through, then slammed it firmly shut and rebolted it before any of the crowd could rush the gates. They need not have worried.

Tommy made as much noise as he could, just as he had been instructed, but the first he saw of Blackner and the other three was after they had been hoisted onto the shoulders of several in the crowd and were being carried round in triumphant, if somewhat wobbly, arcs in front of the prison gates. For several minutes they careered round and round in dizzy circles, until Cadby elbowed his way to the front and yelled further instructions. The men acting as carriers were all from the 'Narrow Marsh Command', as it was now known, and they had been well drilled.

They turned north almost in unison and began the short journey to Glasshouse Street, where Henson was waiting for them at the Newton's Head. Tommy kept the bobbing heads of the newly released heroes in sight as he followed the noisy mob to the door of the pub, then realising that the establishment was far too small to accommodate even a quarter of the crowd, he reasoned that he had done his bit, turned on his heel and hurried back towards Stoney Street, and Bradley's. Cadby saw him leaving, but did nothing. He would save the recriminations until later, when he needed Tommy for something else.

There was a good deal of pushing, yelling and jostling as those at the back of the crowd fought to get into the pub. A window somehow got broken as those at the front were heaved up against it, and then Henson himself appeared in the doorway, pleading for order. He shouted above their heads for the men he wanted, but couldn't see, and grudgingly the mob parted to let them through. The remainder were allowed in, a few at a time, until the place was full, and those still left outside were urged by Henson to disperse in an orderly manner.

He might as well have commanded the increasing snow flurries to turn to rose petals. There were still over two hundred of them left, and many had travelled in from outlying areas. They had turned up for some fun, and some fun they were determined to have. Once the doors of the Newton's Head had been closed for the final time, there were lively discussions about where they should go next, until one of the locals came up with the most attractive idea.

"The Golden Fleece!"

Many of the alehouses in St. Mary's experienced fluctuating fortunes, and it was the turn of the most disreputable establishment in the lower town to suffer the consequences of soliciting the custom of the worst elements of the mob. Situated in Fisher Gate, on the fringes of Red Lion Square, it was close to the scene of Henson's first triumph on the day of the Sunday School Union picnic, and it had opened its doors too willingly to those who had dragged the terrified market traders into the square to distribute their wares. In the ensuing months, landlord Abel Wrigley had begun to have second thoughts about the arrangement, as brawl followed brawl inside his crowded taproom and burly troublemakers began to treat the place as their own.

As the chanting mêlée snaked its way down Lower Hockley in his direction, Wrigley heard it coming and feared the worst. He had been stacking barrels by the front door to await the drayman's horse and cart, and as the first of the mob came round the corner out of Carter Gate, he made to scuttle back inside, hoping to close the front door against them. He was too late, and as the leaders picked him up bodily and carried him back into his own premises, some of those in the following ranks sent an empty cask rolling down the hill towards the square, its metal hoops rattling and grinding on the uneven, rutted road.

Wrigley knew it was already too late to protest, and he called anxiously up the stairs for his wife to leave their upper room and help him serve the mob. She responded by hiding behind a drape under a table, shaking uncontrollably as the din intensified. The odds were heavily against a peaceful end to the proceedings, and such furnishings as there were in the taproom soon crashed to the ground against the crush of bodies. Wrigley himself strove desperately to appease them by keeping the serving jugs filled direct from the barrels, and gave up any attempt to collect payment as quart jugs were lifted, emptied, spilt and smashed. Three or four more determined drinkers climbed over his counter and drove in the top of a barrel with the hammer and spike which Wrigley used for breaching the bungs.

Those still outside, unable to fight their way in and join the growing mayhem, became more frustrated by the minute, cursing Wrigley himself for keeping them out. Two of them spotted a speedier means of ingress, and, lifting one of the empty barrels above their heads, they hurled it through the window, showering many of those inside with shards of glass and splinters of wood, some of which caused deep and painful wounds.

This was all that was needed to spark off the biggest all-out brawl which Hockley had seen for a generation, and by the time the authorities eventually arrived, the only ones available for apprehension were the badly injured and the hopelessly drunk.

CHAPTER SIX

A rattling of sabres

"WHERE IN GOD'S NAME were the militia? That's what I'd like to know!"

Alderman Jennings was very keen on law and order, and would have been happier had a company of dragoons been permanently installed on every street corner. For once he had an attentive audience; everyone charged with the governance of the town was concerned at the turn events were taking, and this special meeting of the aldermen had required little persuasion; indeed, the feeling of most members was that it was long overdue.

Town Clerk George Coldham tried once again to clarify the position. "As I have endeavoured to explain to members of this chamber on numerous occasions in the past, the town militia is a volunteer force which can normally only be assembled once we have prior warning that its services will be required."

"Good God Almighty!" thundered Alderman Jennings, to the visible discomfort of several clerical members present. "Do you mean to say that these ruffians have to give notice before we can catch them?"

"Unless we mobilise the militia on a permanent footing, or establish a much larger Watch, both at civil expense," conceded Coldham, "then yes, that would appear to be the position."

The mention of expense temporarily stemmed Alderman Jennings' righteous wrath, and it was Alderman Willis who took the argument to its next logical stage. "But surely we can ask Parliament for help?"

Coldham smiled politely. "We can ask, certainly, but as members will be only too aware, our standing army is currently engaged in hostilities on the Continent, and is even now drawing from militias all over the country in order to keep our troop levels at fighting strength. It is hardly to be expected that His Majesty's military advisers will be easily persuaded to dispatch much-needed fighting men to Nottingham in order to protect alehouses in St. Mary's which, in any case, should have been closed down by the magistrates long before now."

"It's not just Wrigley's alehouse we're talking about, as you well know," countered Alderman Bassett, himself a magistrate. "So far as I'm concerned," he added, with an obsequious glance towards

Alderman The Reverend George Hutchinson, Vicar of St. Mary's, "dens of iniquity such as the Golden Fleece can be demolished tomorrow, lawfully or otherwise, and the Devil take them. I'm more concerned about what this godless crew will do when they get tired of throwing barrels about the streets."

"That's a very important point," agreed Alderman Bates, immediate past mayor and not normally a supporter of Jennings and his faction. "Matters do seem to have got out of hand somewhat since this fellow Blackner and his accomplices were sent to prison. My very good friend Gilbert Preedy, as you know, has a place of business on Parliament Row, and has on several occasions been seriously alarmed by disturbances in that vicinity. The release of Blackner and the others was only the latest excuse for a riot outside the House of Correction, and we must be mindful of our duty to the tradesmen who elect us."

"Quite right," added Alderman Plowright, in private life the owner of a poultry business in Bottle Lane which had suffered two broken windows in as many weeks. "Something's got to be done, and quickly – certainly before Christmas."

All eyes reverted to Coldham, who sighed with resignation. "We can, of course, put the militia on a more permanent footing," he confirmed, "but I would remind members of the expense which that would entail."

"Damn the expense!" shouted Jennings, who had overcome his natural parsimony in such matters. "This is serious, and it's not going to improve until we give these oafs a taste of steel!"

There were murmurs of protest, and Alderman Bates was quick to capitalise on Jennings' intemperance. "May I remind Alderman Jennings that we are referring to human beings and fellow residents of this town, whose only failing is that they are frightened and hungry, and being led astray by a small handful of malcontents who, for all we know, may well be Jacobins."

"A small handful, is it?" challenged Jennings. "I am reliably informed that in excess of four hundred men were involved in the riot outside the prison, and as for Jacobins . . ."

"Gentlemen, please!" urged Hutchinson, whose Christian office and clerical garb were usually sufficient to command silence. He turned to the Town Clerk and addressed him in a tone normally reserved for difficult parishioners. "We all appear to accept that some additional expense may well be incurred in extending the efforts of the militia. Nevertheless, it is an expense which must be borne if the unseemly violence of recent weeks is to be suppressed before it degenerates further. At the same time, Alderman Willis may well be correct in suggesting that we are entitled to expect some help from Parliament. Your further guidance, Mr Coldham, if you would be so good."

Coldham pondered for a moment before responding. "Certainly, if we faced anything which might properly be described as a civil insurrection, His Majesty's Government would be statutorily obliged to render military assistance which . . ."

"Talk in English, man!" Jennings demanded.

"What I am saying," stated Coldham with barely concealed contempt, "is that if things get much worse, and we can persuade the Home Secretary that there is a real threat to public order on a regular basis, then we have a legal right to ask for troops."

"Thank you," replied Jennings sarcastically. "Now, what about the militia?"

"If we are obliged to use our own local militia first, in the circumstances which I have just described, then yes, we can look to London to defray the cost."

"Excellent!" enthused Jennings. "How soon can they be ready?"

"It's not as straightforward as Alderman Jennings seems to think," Coldham explained. "The latest estimate which I have received indicates that a force of some two hundred men could be ready within the week, with a further two hundred or so, currently in training muster at Chesterfield Barracks, by the end of January."

"So you have been making enquiries," observed Willis.

"Yes, I have, on the instructions of the Lord Lieutenant who, as you know, has the security of the entire county under his responsibility. What is more, I am further advised by him that, following an exchange of correspondence with Whitehall, it is possible that a detachment of the Scots Greys, followed by the Fifteenth Hussars, may be deployed from Lichfield Camp to a short term of duty at the Park Barracks, prior to each of them embarking for France or Spain."

"Why didn't you tell us all this before?" queried an indignant Plowright.

"Because," continued Coldham, unruffled, "the situation has not yet arisen when we can claim to have a civil insurrection on our hands. It is far from certain that the Scots Greys can be delayed from the front line, and I would not wish to mislead this chamber with information that may prove to be overoptimistic."

"He never gives us any damned information, optimistic or otherwise," grumbled Jennings to Plowright, but Coldham chose to ignore it in the hope of moving the meeting on to another urgent item of business.

"In the absence of the mayor, who is of course indisposed, may I respectfully remind members that we still have the Poor Law provisions to review?"

———————

Well might they have been apprehensive of the winter to come. There were some who believed that Nottingham never suffered two bad winters in succession, and who confidently predicted – against all the signs – that it would be 'a mild affair'. The last of them was silenced well before Christmas, as the snow flurries which had first greeted the release of Blackner and his colleagues grew persistent but unpredictable. To begin with they came from the northwest and were slow to settle, so that only the blustery wind and the pervading dampness proved hazardous to health. Then, at the end of November, as it had the previous winter, the wind swung round to the east.

Some of the snowfalls which heralded the festive season were the heaviest on record, and most of the roads into the town were blocked for several days. As usual, it was those who lived in the crowded yards and alleyways who suffered the most, not just from lack of regular food and fresh water, but from the rapid thaws which released enough dirty slush to flood their homes and wash the contents of the open privies into the lower houses, in time for the January frosts to turn the yards into skating rinks studded with rock-hard excrement and stained with human and animal urine.

There was little enough to draw them out of their houses anyway. Barely one man in ten could rely upon a regular wage, and even those who were earning something found that it was far less then they could have expected a year earlier. Indeed, the previous winter seemed easy by comparison, and no-one dared predict where it would all end. Christmas came and went, and the more religiously inclined among the depressed and anxious workforce reflected ruefully that although Our Lord had been born in a stable, at least it had been warm and dry.

The death toll was scandalous, those first two months of 1811, but then they'd come to expect it. Very few people now living in St. Mary's were much over forty years of age, and men like Nathan Slack were rapidly becoming senior residents. Barely a week passed without a frost-tinged corpse being lifted out of each yard and carried by hand to the second common burial ground to be opened in as many years. Had anyone bothered to keep accurate records, pneumonia and bronchitis would have been the commonest causes of death and would have exceeded even the previous year's record numbers.

There were those who cared, of course, but their concern was misunderstood, or cynically misrepresented by those with an interest to serve. The miserable wretches of the poor parishes dotted throughout the town regarded themselves as abandoned forever, and it was no use explaining to them that plans for public sanitation were being drawn up by the recently appointed Water Engineer, but had been delayed by frost and lack of immediate finance. Nor would the sick and dying have been overimpressed to learn that the authorities had held an emergency meeting at the insistence of surgeons from the local hospital, with a request that extra beds be made available for those brought in with diphtheria and scarlet fever, and that twenty more beds had appeared within the week. Twice that number were dying every day, somewhere in the icy warrens of the town.

As usual, the principal preoccupation of the authorities was with the threat of public disorder. In fact, had they taken the time and effort to visit some of the areas marked on their town plans as workmens' dwellings – where, in truth, they probably would not have been physically safe anyway – they would have learned, no doubt to their collective relief, that there was no spirit of rebellion, indeed little spirit for anything. It was an act of endurance simply to stay alive and there was no energy to spare for rioting, even had the streets been navigable for such purposes.

It was therefore ironic that the most humane action decided upon by the mayor and aldermen that winter should have provoked such community violence, and added further fuel to calls for a tightening up of law and order.

The workhouses had been filled to capacity since early November, and not another solitary soul could have been crammed within their grim walls. The authorities therefore had to further extend the more common 'outdoor relief' as it was officially named, and in return for some form of food and clothing, a lucky few were employed in cleaning up the streets, frost permitting. This lasted a month, not because the streets were then clean but because the weather rendered further work of that type impossible. A hasty survey of hosiery employers produced the alarming intelligence that less than ten per cent of the population of St. Mary's and St. Peter's had any hope of income from the only lawful source of livelihood in those parishes, and that so far as could be estimated, the great majority of the local populace must have reached starvation level weeks before.

Letters were therefore quickly dispatched to London, bearing tales of imminent riot, bewailing lack of town finance, and hinting darkly at a total breakdown of civil government in a town which already enjoyed a fearsome reputation in Parliamentary circles for the savagery of its mob. At least one Member of Parliament for the area, Daniel Parker Coke, had good reason to remember what the good people of Nottingham were capable of when sufficiently incensed or prompted, having been obliged, several years previously, to petition Parliament to annul the election of his rival after an election contest from which Coke had been forced to withdraw in the interests of his own personal safety.

Fortunately for the town, George Coldham, maintained a regular correspondence with the Home Office, whose clerks and minions were therefore well abreast of the situation even before the official letter arrived. No time was lost in consigning grain and bulk flour from London to the Humber Dock, where it was transferred to barges which brought it up the Trent, and down to the canal wharves at Leen Side. There it was met and escorted into the town centre by the Scots Greys, whose own embarkation to warmer climes had been delayed while the Emperor Napoleon turned his attention to his eastern front. For most people of the town, it was their first sight for years of 'real sojers', and they believed that the grain carts were destined for the kitchens of the Exchange Hall, as the local government building in the Market Place was known.

Even when the first rumours began to circulate about massive quantities of loaves being turned out of ovens day and night by private bakers all over the town, the ordinary townsfolk had no idea that they were intended for them. Those who still ventured out to sporadic meetings in half-empty alehouses were led to believe – by those who believed it themselves, and by others who were content to fan the collective grievance until the warmer weather arrived – that there was to be a huge civic banquet on an unprecedented scale inside the Exchange Hall, at which more food would be consumed in one evening than most of them would see in their entire lifetimes.

The authorities put up notices announcing the distribution of free bread, most of which were either silently removed by unseen hands at dead of night, or defaced by the illiterate during the day. As the first of the bread carts rolled into Weekday Cross, St. Mary's Gate and Red Lion Square, it was far from clear to most people what was taking place, and the militia who were sent with each cart almost outnumbered the crowds. As the first loaves were handed down from the pile word quickly spread, and within minutes the cart in Red Lion Square had been overturned and much of its load squashed into the icy road by the fighting wretches for whom it had been intended.

In St. Mary's Gate, a woman carrying her infant child was crushed to death under the metal wheels of the cart as she stumbled and fell in the act of grabbing despairingly for a loaf as the cart trundled past her, and the two militiamen who abandoned their weapons in order to save her child were savagely beaten and trampled underfoot. They were retrieved, mercifully unconscious, by terrified colleagues who left the cart and its driver to their fate. They were later flogged on the orders of their commanding officer for losing their muskets.

Only in Weekday Cross did the cart itself survive the initial onslaught, but only because it was surrounded almost immediately upon its arrival by a group of local ruffians armed with wooden staves who had clearly come prepared, and who, having threatened the accompanying militia with a brutal death if they interfered, drove the cart off to a prearranged alternative location at which the loaves were shared out, at knife-point, among a select and appreciative crowd. The cart was never seen again but its driver was found, face down and convincingly deceased, in the nearby River Leen, while the wood from which it had been constructed was rumoured to have fed the chimneys of the Golden Fleece for several days.

Similar fates befell the carts sent to St. Peter's and the Rookeries, and the experiment was never repeated.

The Slacks survived somehow, but for Lily it had almost been too much this time. Whereas the previous winter she had been a tower of strength for everyone in the yard, this winter she had been forced by illness to rely upon those around her for just about everything. The cough and the chest pains had continued to plague her from the first hint of cold weather, and within weeks she could not even summon up enough strength to shuffle across the yard to the privy without Nathan or Tommy to cling on to for support.

They had enough food, for which they all gave thanks to God, although Tommy would frequently remind them that it was not God who worked the frames to earn the money which fed them, but himself, his brother and his father. As if God had been listening, Tommy himself was laid off work just before Christmas by an apologetic Bradley, who pointed out to Nathan that this still left two of his family in regular work, and that as a Christian employer he had to do his best to look after all the families which relied upon him for employment. Everyone except Tommy understood, and even he accepted it, if for different reasons.

"What d'yer expect?" he growled when they came home to Lily with the news. " 'e'd be daft ter keep me an' Dan Willett on, when there's blokes prepared ter keep their traps shut, say nowt an' just keep doffin' their caps."

A year previously, he would have earned a thick ear for a comment like that, delivered as it was with a knowing smirk at Nathan. Instead, the rebuke he received was only verbal, and delivered with a weary resignation. "While yer yappin' the way you do, yer not watchin' yer frame."

"What's ter watch?" argued Tommy. "I can run a length o' rib along wi' the best o' yer. You should know, you taught me. An' if I can do it wi' mi eyes shut, so can you. Yer only blind ter what's goin' on!"

This time he might have qualified for a backhander, had not Lily interrupted. "It dun't marrer; it's only fer a while, till things pick up again. We can manage, an' Matthew's earnin' a bit nah, not like last winter." If Lily was hoping to change the subject, she'd chosen the wrong one.

"Oh aye," Tommy retorted, but with less tolerance this time, "Matthew's earnin' all right. Earnin' good opinions of 'issen, 'e is! Mind yer, yer could blink an' miss the time's 'e's actually learnin' summat abaht the frames. No, yer'll find young Mr Matthew in Danby's room, sharpenin' pens wi' 'is good manners an' writin' little notes ter Miss Rebecca. Dun't worry abaht 'im, Mam – as long as yer can mek lace out o' fancy words, 'e'll allus be workin'. Mind yer, 'e won't be bringin' the money 'ome ter Tanners Yard in years ter come. You mark my words, there's one little sparrow that won't be in the nest fer long!"

The door had slammed behind Matthew long before Tommy had finished, and as the tears welled in Lily's eyes, Ruth braced herself to see Tommy take a thrashing from their father. Instead, Nathan folded Lily in his arms and cradled her greying hair against his chest. As she began another round of coughing, he glared at Tommy over the top of her head.

"Yer stupid, 'eartless, pig-'eaded shit! Can't yer see 'ow it upsets yer mam when yer go on like that? Go an' find Matthew an' bring 'im back – nah!" He paused for a moment, and added, almost in a whisper, " 'e shouldn't 'ave gorras far as 'igh Pavement yet. See if yer can't teach 'im some proper ideas, while yer abaht it. But dun't flog 'im – yer mam's bad enough as it is."

Tommy went out with another smirk, content to have made his

point. He eventually found Matthew in the darkness of a doorway across the road from the Bradley house, staring up at the light from an upper window. There were tears running down his cheeks and Tommy reminded himself yet again that the two of them would never be alike, and that come what may he'd do his best to stop his silly prat of a brother from making a fool of himself, or becoming a target for the mob.

"Mam's cryin' an' dad says ter come 'ome nah."

Matthew turned towards him, a silent plea for understanding mingled with the tear streaks, but a hint of stubborn pride still evident, reminding Tommy of himself. Tommy pulled Matthew, almost playfully, towards him by his jacket collar, slid his long right arm round Matthew's neck and guided him back to the yard. No words were really called for, but Tommy felt obliged to say something anyway.

"Yer'll either finish up one o' that lot, or yer'll get yersen killed. I dunno which, but right nah let's worry abaht mam. That's summat we do 'ave in common."

By the time they re-entered number seven, Lily was in bed upstairs and Ruth was heating up the gruel. Nathan sized up the situation with a quick look and motioned for them to keep the noise down. Lily coughed and wheezed, then called downstairs for both her sons to come up together. They knelt awkwardly at her side, and she took a hand from each of them and made them promise to love one another as brothers should, the way that God had taught the world. They both promised, and they both made a secret vow to keep that promise. In the event, they both did.

As Lily slowly recovered from her latest setback she caused a good deal of embarrassment to the entire family, even Matthew, by praising Robert Bradley loudly to anyone who came into the house, on whatever errand. To her, he was the epitome of the Christian employer who would one day sit on the right hand of God. It was true that many families – some of them in Tanners Yard – had good cause to be thankful that Bradley, and a handful like him, chose to cut their profits closer to the bone rather than see their loyal workers starve during the lean times in the trade. But the developing atmosphere in the lower town was such that it was not safe to say such things openly.

It was also distressing for the family to see such a proud woman begin to lose her faculties and, from time to time, even her short-term memory. Nathan passed it off to the rest of the family as simply the result of worry and the strain of making ends meet. Inwardly, he knew it for what it was, having seen others like her grow old before their time, defeated by drudgery and racked by recurrent illness.

More than anything, Nathan feared that Lily would have a serious lapse while he was at work.

At least they still had Ruth to keep an eye on things and follow behind Lily tactfully while she was, in her own mind, cooking and cleaning. But it was a terrible burden to place on the shoulders of a girl just turned twelve who already had almost total responsibility for her baby brother. What made it worse was that Lily's 'wobbly turns' were only spasmodic and occasional, sometimes lasting barely an hour, and poor Ruth was never quite sure when to take over and prevent an accident or hang back rather than risk a stern admonition for 'gerrin' in the road', as Lily called it.

In her more lucid periods, Lily was still adamant that a suitable place be found for Ruth in domestic service so that she might 'gerron in life'. Nathan was terrified of the consequences if Ruth were not with Lily all the time, and he prayed nightly that the new house would soon be ready, since even Lily conceded that when that happened Ruth's services would be required, if only to begin with. How they would manage to pay the extra rent was another matter altogether, which Nathan banished to the back of his mind. And with so much to worry about he could hardly be blamed for not paying closer heed to what Tommy did with the free time now at his disposal. Even had he done so, it was probably already too late.

It was a raw and blustery day in early March when fate set the ultimate seal on the tragedy just around the corner. Henson had finally secured the evidence he had been seeking against a group of master hosiers, including Jarvis Bentinck of Eastwood Mills, who was also a freeman of the borough. Jane Ives had performed her role to perfection, and, because she was illiterate, she had an almost limitless ability to recall trivial conversational detail, a gift which many of those in a similar position often possess by way of compensation.

In Jane's case, it was also combined with a cold desire for revenge which had been fuelled by the many attempts on her virtue in the scullery, the parlour, and even the attic room which she had shared with the scullery maid. Sometimes they were accompanied by offers of money, sometimes by threats of dismissal. She had resisted them all, not from any natural desire for chastity, but from an innate sense of what was 'right and proper', and from fear of the consequences, so regularly evident in the workhouses, brothels and alehouses of the less salubrious areas of the town.

Preserving her honour to the last, she had several days earlier voluntarily left the service of the Bentincks with neither testimonial nor money. She had been obliged to walk all the way home, and she now stood calmly in the centre of the family's ground floor room, answering question after question from the eager man with the silent companions.

"This second meeting, on the twenty-third. There was Bentinck himself, along with Bolton of Arnold, Hollingworth of Bulwell and Jenkins of Ilkeston. Is that right? Are you sure you have it exactly right?"

She showed her irritation for the first time. "Look, I bin ovver everythin' lots o' times in mi 'ead, right? I might only be a domestic, but there's nowt wrong wi' what's up 'ere. Ask mi dad – ever since I were a lass I've bin able ter mind things as 'appened years ago, ain't that right, Dad?"

"Right enough, lass," beamed Tom Ives, proudly. " 'onest, Mr 'enson, yer can trust every word she sez."

The big man sank back in the chair with an apologetic smile of relief. "I'm sure I can, Tom. I'm sorry, Jane, it's just that this is so important to the cause, and we have to make sure that every single fact is in the right place."

"Oh, it's in the right place, Mr 'enson – it's in mi 'ead, that's where it is, an' that's where it'll stay till I've said mi piece ter the magistrates."

"And you're still content to do that?"

"I'm more than content – I've set mi 'eart on it. It's time the likes of 'im was brought dahn a peg or two. All fancy talk an' wanderin' 'ands, 'im an' 'is sort. Thinks yer easy meat, just 'cos yer come from poor folk. Well poor folk 'as eyes an' ears, dun't they, an' the likes of 'im forget that when yer servin' aht all them fancy cakes an' suchlike. It's like yer not there at all, when 'im an' 'is lah-di-dah friends is goin' on abaht 'the basic classes', as they calls us lot. Five bob a week they was talkin' abaht – 'ow's dad an' us s'posed ter live on five bob a week?"

"So they actually talked about forcing the rate down to five shillings?"

"Five bob, or the Lord may strike me dead as I stand 'ere. And a ha'penny less on a dozen cut-ups. An' like I said, eightpence a week more fer the tied frames."

"They actually sat there and agreed all that while you were listening?"

"Didn't even notice me when I dropped mi cloth on the carpet, I were that excited! Like I said, Mr 'enson, yer just like the furniture ter them – 'cept when the lady o' the 'ouse is aht visitin'."

Henson sat back, savouring the moment. Then he smiled slowly round at each of his companions. "We have it, gentlemen. As clear-cut a case as we could ever have wished for. Come with me, Jane my girl – we're off to swear a Complaint!"

The news swept through the parishes like the announcement of the Second Coming. The courtroom was full to capacity when, three days later, four indignant merchant hosiers stood briefly inside the dock of the Shire Hall, before being allowed to withdraw to the padded chairs which had been provided, for the first time in living memory, a few yards behind the place ordained for lesser accused.

Not only was the courtroom itself filled, but also High Pavement all the way down to Weekday Cross, for what promised to be the social event of the year. It was rare indeed for the wealthy and privileged to stand accused of anything, but for four of them to stand in line facing a charge which carried the prospect of a term of imprisonment was an entertainment too good to be missed. It was alleged that only workers would ever be convicted of an illegal combination; now Henson was preparing to put that theory to the test.

Robert Bradley stood gloomily at the window of his first storey front drawing room, from which he commanded a perfect view of the heaving crowd below him, and the front doors of the Shire Hall. He could clearly make out a few decent, honest, frameworkers for whose skills he had happily paid the best rates going, and who now seemed drawn like sleepwalkers to the doors of the courthouse. They were ragged and thin, for the most part, although he couldn't help but notice the animation of some among them as they passed back and forth through the crowd, a word here, a nod there, and on to the next. He scowled down at Cadby's greasy, balding head, and wondered what he did now to keep body and soul together, not that he looked any the worse for it. There was that wild young Slack boy, too – silly devil would never amount to anything, associating with people like that.

He had closed the factory for the day, naturally. As far as he could tell, the whole town had come to a standstill as the tidings reached not only the alehouses, street corners and yards but also the drawing rooms of the wealthy, that Henson was taking on the frame owners in an attempt to prove that their honest business meetings were illegal combinations.

The man must be deranged, reasoned Bradley, and tried again to reassure himself that if there was to be trouble, it would pass over the heads of decent Christian employers, just as the Angel of Death had passed over the chosen ones at the Feast of the Passover, smiting only the wicked. All the same, it was time that he sought assurances from his regular workers that they would stand by him if need be.

The authorities had no such illusions, and had mobilised every able-bodied member of the Watch, plus what was immediately available of the town militia, all of whom had been instructed to keep a tight ring around the crowd once it had formed, and to pluck out any troublemaker against whom any plausible criminal charge might be brought.

Less publicly, they had met with the Lord Lieutenant of the County, His Grace the Duke of Newcastle, under whose direct control lay the jurisdiction of the county magistrates. Eastwood lay in the county, and it was not so easy for the town aldermen to ensure the correct verdict in the Shire Hall as it was in the Guildhall, where most of them sat on the Bench themselves in matters arising from within the town itself.

They need not, as it transpired, have concerned themselves unduly about the formal outcome of the court proceedings. Since the county magistrates were all laymen, they relied for legal guidance on a Clerk of the Peace, and Henry Bebbington was not the stuff of which legal history is made. Within minutes of the Complaint having been sworn before him, news of it had been dispatched to the Castle, the ducal residence in which His Grace was that day entertaining a distant relative who was the commanding officer of the Fifteenth Hussars, currently occupying the Park Barracks following the departure of the Scots Greys on their embarkation march to Gravesend and the troop ships which would take them across the Channel.

The recently ensconced hussars being somewhat in need of active service experience, it had been decided that on the day of the hearing of the Complaint, a full company would be held in mounted state on the Castle ramparts, from which the town centre could be entered within minutes on horseback. As for the legal formalities, Bebbington was advised that it was for just such occasions that his ample stipend was payable, and that if the magistrates were permitted to arrive at a verdict prejudicial to good order, a more worthy recipient of said stipend might rapidly be identified.

Bebbington was neither heroic nor stupid, and shortly after receiving his instructions, and rereading the terms of the Complaint, he had found the solution which those responsible for his immediate career clearly required.

Henson stood before Their Worships in dutiful silence as the terms of his Complaint were read out by Bebbington, who was obliged on three occasions to break off in order to warn those in the public gallery regarding their behaviour. Three nervous-looking justices of the peace sat above and behind him, while as many Watch officers as could be spared from duties outside stood stoically in line across the Bar of the courtroom.

Bebbington completed the formalities, and looked up to address the Complainant himself, while a grim-looking Jane Ives looked on from where she stood beside the witness box.

"Is this your Complaint, Mr Henson?"

"It is."

"And there is nothing you wish to add to the narration of the Complaint itself?"

Henson frowned. "Your Worships will observe that I have in court today a witness, Miss Jane Ives, who will . . ."

"Mr Henson," interrupted Bebbington, "have you anything further to add to the narration of the Complaint? Since you appear not to be versed in legal matters, I will assist you by adding that the 'narration' of your Complaint is simply its outline."

"It's outline? No. I am grateful for your assistance sir, but no, I have nothing to add to the outline of what is alleged."

Bebbington hastened over to the Bench, and spoke on whispered tiptoe to the magistrates. Their Chairman nodded, and looked down at a puzzled Henson.

"Complaint dismissed."

"What!!" thundered Henson, as his protest was echoed a hundred times from the heaving public gallery. The Watch began to move forward purposefully in a line, but Henson succeeded in restoring silence by waving his arms frantically at his supporters, before he turned back to Bebbington. "How can the Complaint be dismissed? No evidence has been taken yet."

"The Complaint itself," explained Bebbington, "is lacking in particulars."

"How?" demanded Henson, restraining a sudden impulse to rush forward and strangle the smug little clerk.

"Because," continued Bebbington, in a tone of voice more appropriate to explaining the perils of fire to a five-year-old, "it does not narrate the parish in which the matter is alleged to have occurred. This is required in order to confer jurisdiction on this court."

"That is nonsense, sir!" boomed Henson, fast losing self-control. "Eastwood is in its own parish; everyone knows that. And if the Complaint required that Eastwood be named twice, why was I not informed of that when I swore the Complaint in the first place?"

"The parish must be narrated separately, Mr Henson," Bebbington confirmed in measured tones. "That is a matter of law, and as to your second question, it is not the function of Officers of the Peace to give advice on the law of the land."

"In that case, sir," bellowed Henson, now thoroughly enraged and humiliated, "damn your office, damn the so-called process of justice and damn the law of the land!"

He stormed from the courtroom as the crowd in the gallery erupted behind him. The Watch concentrated all their efforts on protecting the officers of the court and the members of the Bench, and several items of furniture within reach of the mob suffered grievously in consequence. The main body of followers, however, left the building hurriedly and lined up behind Henson on the courtroom steps outside, as he strove to be heard above the baying crowd of several thousand which stood its ground defiantly in the gusting wind.

"When the history of this cause is written down," Henson raged at the top of his voice, "it will be recorded that on this day, those who sought justice did not receive it in that place in which it ought to be found!" He jerked his thumb backwards in a gesture towards the Shire Hall, before continuing.

"This day, those in authority in this county have demonstrated before God and before the people that justice is not to be found in courtrooms. Therefore, let our cause be its own witness, and let God and the elected leaders of our people be the judges of the justice of that cause. Who is with us?"

A mighty roar threatened the crumbling roof copings, as some two thousand declared their loyalty to the new chapter which was opening. A buzz of excitement ran through the spectators as neighbour rejoiced with neighbour that the day of action had finally come. Even his most constant followers had never witnessed oratory this powerful from Henson. An anxious militia began to move in from the outer fringes, but Henson had their measure.

"To your places. Ned Ludd awaits you!"

Within minutes, the street was empty, as each man moved silently and without further protest in the direction of his home. A few of the militia followed at a safe distance, only to return minutes later with bemused expressions and shrugs of relief. To all intents and purposes it was all over, the angry mob dispersed among the warrens without a blow struck in anger or a man taken into custody. The doors of the Shire Hall opened a few inches and Officer Dunning's face appeared around it. He opened it fully and stared out in disbelief.

Above them and across the street, Robert Bradley let the curtain fall back, scratched his head thoughtfully and disappeared in search of a cigar.

———————◆◆◆———————

Captain Chesney Corbett signalled to the water carriers to stand back from the troughs as he led half a dozen of his hussars and their horses forward to take the first draught. They had stood in readiness for an hour and a half, and the mounts had grown restive as the chill spring wind which swirled down the parade square from the Castle had sent paper and other discarded litter dancing past their bridled noses. The clouds scurried by in shifts, allowing the sun to launch occasional shafts of light onto the highly polished brasses of horses and riders, and steamy breath rose from their closed ranks as greys and chestnuts chafed and jingled while awaiting human command.

An hour had passed since Henson's reappearance on the steps of the Shire Hall, and they had just this moment received the order to stand down.

"Damned piece of nonsense, if you ask me," complained Corbett to his ensign, Tobias Gunn. "We should be in France, fighting Boney, not sitting here waiting for a bunch of sweaty plebs to create a street disturbance."

"Any word on that, sir?"

"On what, France? Only that the Froggies seem to have met some resistance in the East. The best reports from Colchester suggest that we can expect to be sent to Spain by early summer, to head them off if they make it to the western seaboard."

"By jove, sir – we may see some real sport yet!"

"If this dismal hole doesn't infect us with its pestilence first. Have you been into the town yet?"

"Only on the way in, sir. Must admit, not impressed."

"I've been here twice already, both times on royal escort, passing north to York. It rained both times, and last time some damned doxy cut my purse in an alehouse and tried to blame the landlord. We'd turned the place into sawdust before I realised she'd been lying, and by then she must have been halfway to Newark."

Ensign Gunn tried to hide his amusement, and as he turned his face away was the first to catch sight of the bugler running to his post.

The Market Place lay eerily quiet, so silent that the shouts of the crowd which had gone up around the Shire Hall some half-hour previously had been heard in the Rookeries, which lay to the north of the ancient Market Place, almost half a mile away as the rooks used to fly.

Most businesses were closed, fearful of the mob, and heavily shuttered doors and windows looked out onto the open muddy space like blind beggars seeking alms. Scavenging dogs had more freedom than usual from the kicks and oaths which normally confined them to side alleys, and no-one with any mind for his health had ventured out – until now.

Three men emerged from behind the Exchange Hall, having crept along Chandlers Lane keeping close to doorways. They surveyed the open space with evident satisfaction, and one of them disappeared down Bottle Lane. From Cow Lane to the north came a growing rumble, and a horse and flat cart came into view, carrying bulky sacks which sprang to life on a word from its driver as the cart came to a halt in the centre of the Market Place. Fully a dozen men leapt from its boards and ran to their appointed places. They were coming in from the south now, too, and Wheeler Gate witnessed more scurrying figures in the space of the next ten minutes than it had seen all day.

From the cramped courtyards of St. Mary's down to Leen Side, from Hockley and Goose Gate, from Sneinton, Beeston and Arnold, they gathered in their silent dozens at the prearranged spot. The underpaid and the starving, the hapless and the hopeless, all answering the call which had gone out even before the farce in the Shire Hall had been finally played out.

Each area commander had passed the word on via his seconds-in-command, and each of them had passed it down the chain. Some three thousand were now privy to both the rendezvous point and the time; some eight hundred were on their way into the Market Place, but not a soul had betrayed the secret. The authorities had not the faintest inkling that the mob was regrouping after feigning dispersal, until it was way beyond normal control.

Henson was standing on the back of the cart before half the crowd had assembled, and as he gazed up into the streets which fed the Market Place and saw the numbers still pouring in, he felt the first fear since the whole business had begun a year ago. He hoped they would all be able to hear him, and he hoped that they would listen.

Above all, he hoped he could control them. He signalled his closest advisers to the side of the cart and squatted down to speak to them.

"I can't believe it – there must be five hundred people here!"

"More like seven," said Cossall. "There's five 'undred expected from the south side alone."

"How many were told?"

"As many as we could find. Dun't worry, there's not a man 'ere would betray us."

"They won't have to," Henson responded warily. "The authorities won't let this go on for long. Tell the men to close off the side streets as soon as they can."

"Already covered," replied Cadby with a grin, "an' wi' a few surprises in store fer the Watch."

"No violence, please!" ordered Henson. "We must show the authorities that we mean no violence – not yet, anyway. There's still a hope that they'll listen to reason."

"Very likely," sneered Cadby sarcastically. He looked slowly around him, his eager eyes taking in the sheer numbers. Then he glanced insolently back up at an apprehensive-looking Henson.

"Well, yer've gorrem. Best speak to 'em."

Henson stood back up and surveyed the heaving crowd. He raised his arms in the air, and a deafening response echoed through the centre of the town. He waved for silence time and time again, and slowly the noise subsided until those at the front could hear his shouted words. Those further back had no such hope, and relied for their information on those who weaved their way among them with a different agenda.

"People of Nottingham," began Henson, "the time has come to seek justice elsewhere than in the courts of this town."

"What's 'e sayin?" asked a man ten rows back in the crowd, who was twisting this way and that to catch Henson's words as they died in the noisy air between them.

" 'e sez it's time ter tek action," offered a neighbour.

"Yeah, an' bloody action at that!" added a man three feet away, precisely on cue.

"We have seen how the authorities are determined to treat us," continued Henson. "It's time to go outside Nottingham with our cause."

"What?" enquired a stockinger twenty yards from the cart.

"We're goin' ter Arnold ter bust some frames," said Cadby enthusiastically from just behind him.

"Our cause is just, and the remedy lies in the hands of the people, and those whom they have elected," insisted Henson.

"I can't 'ear a bloody word," complained a man from Beeston who had arrived late, and was near the outer edge of the Market Place.

"Yer must be deaf, then," grinned the man at his side. " 'e's talkin' abaht fightin' wi' us bare 'ands if we 'as ter."

On it went, a silent monologue to the deaf, the man on the cart a soundless marionette with waving arms to all but those in the first few rows. A hundred different versions of his words rippled through the mob, aided on their way by those with ambitions of their own. Henson spoke of petitioning Parliament, and the excited whisper was of smashing stocking frames. Henson preached hope for the future, and the received message was of revenge for past wrongs. For every word of restraint there were ten of violent retribution. Patience became frustration, Christian tolerance mindless class bigotry. The man called for a workers' charter, and the mob were duped into baying for blood.

They came out of Angel Row in formation four abreast, before wheeling and fanning out in a circle, classical fashion, as they entered the Market Place at the point where the Derby Turnpike ran into it. Captain Corbett, with an escort of four, rode out from the centre and pushed his horse at a stiff trot towards the cart. Henson stared him out as he clattered closer, scattering men, women, and occasionally children, in his path, his restless mount treading on ill-shod workers' feet in its anxiety to do its master's bidding and avoid the spurs.

He reigned in a yard or so from the cart, and allowed Montpellier to sidestep along its length as he gazed arrogantly up at the man with the dark hair blowing in the wind.

"Captain Chesney Corbett, His Majesty's Fifteenth Hussars. I am commissioned by His Majesty to guard his dominions and put down insurrection anywhere within his realms. You, sir, appear to be in command of an insurrection."

"We mean no disloyalty to His Majesty," Henson protested indignantly. "There's not one man here that would not lay down his life for his country. Many of the best men of this town recently lost their lives in France. Before that, my own father . . ."

"Yes, yes," interrupted the captain, "but none of that excuses what is taking place here and now. I'll not pretend to understand your perceived grievances, nor do I have any time to waste on them. I simply advise you that you have five minutes to clear this area before my men are commanded to unsheath their weapons. This I do in the name of the Lord Lieutenant of the County, whose written authority I hold to put down insurrection in this town. It is here in my tunic pocket – if you can read."

"I can read," retorted Henson hotly, "and do not doubt either your word or your written authority. If, however, I was of a mind to test your ability to exercise that authority, then I would remind you that there are almost a thousand of us, and barely sixty of you, by my reckoning. Fortunately for you, we meet only for the peaceful purpose of considering a petition to Parliament, as law-abiding subjects of His Majesty. Do you call that an insurrection?"

"You meet, sir," Corbett corrected him haughtily, "in a potentially riotous mob which already breaches His Majesty's peace. Further, on your own admission, you meet in combination and that, too, is unlawful."

"No sir, it is not!" shouted Henson, his colour rising rapidly. "We have today established that fact in a so-called court of law. As of today, we recognise no pretended combination laws."

"Then perhaps," suggested Corbett coldly, "you recognise this." He drew his sabre from its sheath, and held it high in the air. Reacting to the familiar 'prepare to engage the enemy' signal, his men reached uneasily for their own hilts, ready to unsheath on the next command. "I have only to point my weapon to the front," continued Corbett, "and my men will begin the work for which they have been training these many months. Which is it to be, sir, bloodshed or peaceful dispersal?"

Henson looked helplessly out into the surly crowd, some of whom had formed an ominous semicircle around the captain and his horse. Each hussar found his own mount hemmed in by a similar press, and here and there some of the more adventurous townspeople were beginning to tease and irritate the horses. Several of the younger troopers were displaying signs of unease, and it seemed only a short time before blood would be shed. The victims, as always, would be the innocent on both sides.

Henson looked back again at Corbett and immediately behind him saw Cadby's grinning face, eyebrows raised in a silent question as he passed a butcher's knife suggestively across his own throat. One word from Henson and His Majesty would be minus one captain of hussars. Henson shook his head hurriedly, and the moment passed. Once more he addressed Corbett, who would never know how close he had just come to an ignominious death.

"Very well, since you seem determined to uphold by force what cannot be justified in law, we will disperse – for now. But be warned, and be sure to advise His Grace the Duke, that what has begun today will not be ended until we have justice for all the people of this town, and until the labours of honest men are justly rewarded. You may command your men to stand down, and be assured that, if allowed to leave peacefully for their own homes, these good people will constitute no ongoing threat to either His Majesty or his brave, if ill-directed, soldiers."

Corbett allowed his sabre hilt to pivot slowly in his hand until its blade pointed to the ground, then he replaced it carefully in its sheath. His men unhanded their own hilts, some with obvious relief, and Corbett turned his horse. Before commanding it back across the Market Place, he looked back quizzically at Henson.

"You are a brave man, sir, if a misguided one. Your name?"

"Henson. Gravenor Henson."

"Henson, we are in sore need of men of your spirit in our fight against the self-appointed Emperor of France. I shall see to it that your name is passed on to the recruiting officer for this town. If, as I predict, you find yourself in irons before long, through your foolish support for this rabble, it may be that we can find a better use for your spirit than treading the air on the gallows."

Henson smiled dryly. "Your concern is touching, Captain, but it might perhaps be more usefully employed at this moment in ensuring the safe withdrawal of your men. My own comrades have already shown considerable forbearance."

Corbett kicked Montpellier into a canter, once again causing many to dive for their lives. Various missiles sailed after the troopers as they made the most dignified and orderly withdrawal that circumstances would permit. One hussar was pulled from his terrified mount by numerous unseen hands, and several of his colleagues were obliged to wheel their own horses and beat back the crowd in order to give him space to remount. The full detachment then reformed close to the Malt Cross, watching intently as the crowd began to disperse.

Cadby and Cossall stood at the side of the cart, muttering to each other under their breath. Henson remained aloft until satisfied that there was to be no bloodshed, then jumped down to join them. "An interesting encounter, gentlemen," he observed. "I think we established our point."

"You shoulda let me put my point through 'is poxy throat!" complained Cadby. "That'd soon show these cunnies the road back ter London."

"And risk the lives of innocent people? What would that achieve?"

"There'll be plenty lives lost afore this is all ovver," argued Cadby, "an' there's plenty aht there'd agree wi' me that yer too soft ter get this business settled."

"Really?" enquired Henson icily. "And you're just the man to take over and lead the cause, I suppose?" He walked towards another group, shaking his head dismissively. Cadby allowed him out of earshot before he had the final word.

"Bloody right, Mr 'igh an' mighty fuckin' 'enson. An' startin' ternight!"

CHAPTER SEVEN

Ludd comes calling

CLARRIE SHARP tossed fitfully for a moment then became fully awake. Beside her, husband Ben snored innocently and unaware, but Clarrie knew better than to ignore the signs. She'd been nearly seven the first time it happened, and that same night her older brother had drowned on board The Vanity. Aged ten, she had seen a tearful lady dressed all in white pass through the garden of their cottage, two days before smallpox arrived in the village. Five times since then she'd been warned by 'them' when something threatened her or hers. Tonight was the eighth.

Her first thought was for her other brother Job and his family, miles away on Dickinson's farm. She prayed hard, and in what she called her 'middle eye' she could see them all peacefully asleep. But if not them, who was it? She stared intensely into the darkness until her eyes began to water, and she rubbed them wearily. As she opened them again, a dull red glow became visible under the door. Fire!

She leaped from the bed and pulled the door inwards. Bracing herself for the heat and smoke, she lunged forward into the other room. Nothing. Nothing but the ball of red light which danced teasingly in midair above the table, then drifted slowly towards the window, seeming to pass through it completely and hover momentarily in Church Lane before fading from sight altogether. Clarrie weaved her way through the cluttered room until she reached the window, just as the full moon drew back a shutter of cloud and filled the village with a pale ghostly light. Then she waited, motionless, in the relative darkness of the room. Whatever was out there, she reasoned, would not see her inside.

It was simply a matter of patience; she knew that. They had never let her down, those unseen friends of hers, and there was a purpose to all this. She gazed across the field to the empty old mill, and recalled when she and her sister Jessie had whiled away the summer afternoons talking to the old miller, before Jessie succumbed to the smallpox. Those old days were long gone, worse luck, and even in villages like Arnold they had to do 'town work' to make ends meet. She looked back into the darkened room, and could just make out the shape of the hated frame which Ben was forced to work at, hour upon hour, in return for the few measly shillings a week he was paid for the finished stockings by Thomas Bolton up the road, from whom he also rented the frame. Not much of a life for a village boy who had been raised to drive a horse and plough, and who could even now drill a furrow straighter than any man in the village.

Somewhere close by a dog barked in warning, and, shivering with apprehension and cold, she turned back to the window just in time to glimpse a shadow in the field. It loped awkwardly across the recently ploughed potato mounds, which only last week had received the seed for this year's crop. Close behind it came a second, then a third, and even from this distance she could tell they were not local. Her instinct also warned her they were up to no good. From the height of the moon it must be well into the small hours, and no Christian man was abroad at that time.

Luckily she heard the muted voices in time, else she would have jumped and maybe given herself away. As it was, she was able to slip behind the window frame just before some half a dozen men crept down the lane a matter of feet from her hiding place. Each one swung a cudgel or a stick, and one of them had something shiny. Town men, by the cut of their clothes. As they passed, one of them stared straight into the window, and Clarrie nearly screamed out. He said something to the others with him, and one of them laughed. They stole on furtively towards the church and the crossroads, and Clarrie knew that she had to waken Ben.

Those who had come directly from the south, making partial use of the coach road that eventually ran all the way to Mansfield, had made faster progress than the others, who were forced to leave the better surface just short of Brecks Hill, and enter Arnold via the fields. Jack Cossall cursed the mud on his boots and the heavy soil which threatened to suck his weary legs down into the furrows between the mounds. His companions were strung out for more than half a mile behind him, as each did his stumbling best to reach the appointed meeting place on time. A dog barked a warning from beyond the church, a pale medieval tower in the intermittent moonlight, and other dogs took up the chorus.

"Damn the mud," swore Cossall for the tenth time, as he pushed his aching calves to the limit. He was a town man, sod it, not a fucking ox. Trust Cadby to save the easy route for himself.

At the same time precisely, Jim Collishaw's men were coming down the lane which opened directly from the Mansfield Road, only feet away from the terrified Clarrie, and at least one of them had been there before.

"That's Ben Sharp's cottage," sneered Luke Johnson as they skulked past, weapons at the ready. "We'll have that one on the way back."

"Yer'll mebbe be runnin' fer yer life on the way back," warned one of his companions anxiously. "What's so special abaht that one, anyroad? It's only a tiny cottage."

"Mebbe," said Johnson, "but 'e married Clarrie Bishop, 'er as I were courtin' fer two years afore she fell fer the local ploughin' champion."

"Mebbe 'e ploughed 'er berrer than you did," Collishaw suggested, and there was a loud chortle from Will Draycott before Collishaw hushed him into silence.

" 'ow come yer was courtin' an Arnold lass, anyroad?" asked Tom Darby. "It's bloody miles away, as we've fahnd aht to us cost ternight."

"Not if yer drivin' a flour cart, it ain't. Mind, I used ter work fer Baxters in Barker Gate."

"Shut yer row, the pair on yer!" hissed Collishaw. " 'ere's the church; nah where the fuck's Cadby?"

Cadby had been in the village for a full half-hour already, and as he lurked in the church doorway he jumped apprehensively at every dog bark that warned anyone who happened to be awake that his men were approaching from all sides. In twos and threes, and then in larger groups, they flitted in shadowy silhouette against the moon-yellowed walls as they centred in on the church. That wasn't the target – simply the one place that those strange to the village would be able to find on a dark night. Mind you, with this moon they might as well light a bloody bonfire.

He'd just sent out messengers to locate and redirect the stragglers and pass on the final plan of action, which he'd kept to himself until now, in case anyone was taken on the way. There were too many soldiers around the town for his liking, and they could have been followed. He'd come ahead of all the rest, partly to spy out the land, and partly for his own safety – he was too important to get caught. Geordie Packer was the last of them to scuttle back with confirmation that everything was in place.

"Is Jack Cossall in yet wi' 'is lot?" asked Cadby.

"Aye, just this minute in. An' 'e's not 'appy, neither. Reckons yer sent 'im the wrong road or summat."

"Piss off! 'e's just not got the stomach, that's all. Ey up, we're off!"

A sharp crack from somewhere near the bakery several doors down was followed almost immediately by the crash of wood splintering in a neighbouring cottage door. Then from all sides came the din of broken latches and shattering bolts, and family after family leapt from slumber in confusion and terror. Shouts and screams mingled with the yelping of dogs, and the combined racket was enough to set off even the cattle in adjoining outhouses. In cottage after cottage, men wiped the sleep from their eyes in time to hold their wives and children to them, and watch helplessly as the wide frames they rented were smashed to matchwood by unfamiliar men with blackened faces and merciless weapons. Here and there, a local man offered a futile resistance to his livelihood going under the hammer and the axe, and more than one was left with a useless arm hanging by his side, or a head running with blood.

Ten men had been hand-picked by Cadby to assist him with the main target of the night, and four of them forced open the door to Bolton's as the others tumbled in behind them and headed down to the lower level. They lit the lanterns they had brought with them, and with their targets well illuminated it was the work of minutes to smash the newly constructed wide frames and drag them into the centre of the room, where flint and paper was added to sawdust, and finished lace goods were piled underneath the broken wood to encourage the blaze. They danced up and down, cackling with glee and freshly released tension as the flames licked upwards in search of sustenance.

"Right, that'll do," wheezed Cadby. "Tell 'em all ter gerraht nah an' meet termorrer at the Fleece – nah run forrit!"

They turned towards the door but found their exit blocked by a formidable figure at the head of the short stairway, brandishing the cutlass he had used to good effect for His Majesty's Navy in his younger days. Thomas Bolton was not the forgiving kind, and was not easily intimidated by ill-led ruffians.

"Hold hard there!" he commanded. "Word's gone to town by fast horse, and you'll be staying right there below decks until the authorities arrive. Then we'll see who's the brave boys!"

Two men appeared in the space immediately behind him, each armed with something long. Between them, the three men blocked the entire stairhead as they glared down at Cadby and his crew. Cadby blasphemed loudly as he summed up the situation, then saw his chance as the two latecomers moved out from behind Bolton and ran down the stairs to beat out the flames.

"Jump 'em, lads!"

It was so sudden that Bolton's two men, young and fit as they were, had no chance against the flurry of fists and boots which came in at them from all sides. One of them fell into the rising flames and screamed as his hair caught alight. One of Cadby's men took pity on him, and smothered the singeing mop with an old sack before joining the rush to the stairs, where the older, heavier man, stood his ground and prepared to make a fight of it.

Cadby hung back, and it was Rob Possett who led the charge and took the cutlass blow across his face. He screamed, and dropped to his knees near the door as blood welled instantly from the deep gash on his forehead. Blinded by the blood, he flailed around in panic, catching another swinging cut to his hand before his companions could disarm Bolton and throw him bodily down the stairs into the lower room. He landed awkwardly, breaking his shoulder, and Cadby sunk a boot into his ribs before running up the stairs, the last to leave.

Outside, he found himself alone in the street with the sound of anger and confusion reverberating through the entire village. Whimpering with fear, he raced down a narrow track between two neighbouring cottages and into the meadow which lay beyond them, where he could just make out, ahead of him, two of his men half-carrying the injured Possett between them across the rough ground. Behind him lay chaos, as men, women and children all cried out for help and proclaimed from all corners of the ravaged community the injustice of the night's work.

Their mission accomplished, most of the raiding party had long since beat a hasty retreat down the lanes, footpaths and highways which led, five miles further south, to the northern outskirts of the town. Only Luke Johnson had something left to do, an old score to settle, and he had willing helpers. Back down Church Lane, they stopped outside Sharp's cottage, which lay in total darkness.

"Right, in we go!"

Johnson put all his weight behind a savage blow to the door with the metal bar he had picked up in a nearby farmyard. The wood splintered, but held, and a repeat attack fared no better. Three feet away on the other side of the door, Ben and Clarrie had used their borrowed time to good advantage, and a buttress of bedding was packed tightly between the door and an old wardrobe which they had placed hard up against it to absorb the blows. Long strips of wood, hurriedly brought in from outside, had been nailed across the inside of the window frame, defending the only other entry to the cottage. Clarrie thanked God that they had no back door, as they stood there with their fate in His hands.

"Yer bastard!" yelled Luke Johnson, frustration fuelling his fury. "We'll 'ave yer, yer cunnin' sod! Yer'll not keep us aht fer long, Ben Sharp – nor you, Clarrie Bishop!"

The attack was renewed, and Ben and Clarrie pushed hard

against the wardrobe, praying as they had never prayed before. The centre of the door was soon a mass of dents and holes, and a few more blows would have been enough. Then down the lane raced a young man soaked in sweat and breathing like an over-spurred horse. He was the last of a chain of lookouts posted earlier by Cadby.

"Sojers! Comin' up the Basford road – run forrit!"

They abandoned all thought of the cottage door as they scattered for cover over walls, into pigsties and on to low roofs. At the southern end of Church Lane they jumped, fell and staggered in the darkness through back alleys and ditches until they reached the open fields. There, they lay low in the furrows and ruts, gulping in air and praying that their pounding chests and rasping breaths would not betray them.

The seconds passed, and nothing happened. The seconds became minutes, then slowly and cautiously they moved into the hedgerows, into which they safely melted as the first of the dragoons clattered past them a half-mile south of the village. They let them all pass, then hurried back the way they had come two hours previously. By the time that daylight came, they were back in the courtyards and alleyways of home, recounting the night's adventures only to their immediate families. Not a man had been taken.

The river meadow still lay under its spring carpet of crocuses and late daffodils, while the young birds fluttered excitedly in the first rituals of courtship. Sunday School over, many scholars raced and tumbled through ankle-deep marsh grass, while others promenaded to and fro across the many informal pathways which skirted the glittering River Trent. Through the warm but fading sunshine came Lucy and Rebecca, with Matthew in attendance as always, while a bored but dutiful Adam kept a watchful, but ever discreet, distance to the rear. Bradley had been most insistent; in these troubled times it was not wise to allow one's family out alone, and Adam would not easily find another master quite so generous regarding his occasional lapses with the brandy bottle.

"Look Rebecca, there's a swallow, the first of summer, most likely. It's flying high, too, so the good weather's sure to last for our trip to Eastwood." Matthew swelled with pride as he looked at Rebecca, and noted that her eyes were only on him. The swallow could fly upside down for all she cared.

"You're so clever, Matthew! Where do you learn it all?"

"In books, mainly. But it was dad – sorry, my father – who taught me about swallows. I think his father taught him, when they lived in the country."

Lucy smiled across at them both, as they walked three abreast along the wider pathway that had just opened up before them.

"There's nothing you can teach country people about the ways of nature," she explained to Rebecca, "and Matthew's grandfather probably came from farming stock, like so many people in St. Mary's."

"That's right, he did, Edwalton, actually," Matthew confirmed, before his face clouded and he added, "but that's a long time ago; my future lies in commerce."

Lucy studied his face. "Are you still happy working for papa?"

"Oh yes, he's very good to work for. Sometimes, when we're quiet, he lets me sit with Mr Danby and check the ledgers. He's nearly blind you know, Mr Danby, and I might get to do his work when he can't manage it any more. Then perhaps one day I'll be senior clerk – that's a good enough position for any man, isn't it?"

"Yes of course," Lucy reassured him, "but have you thought of other possibilities, like being a schoolmaster, or even a lawyer?"

Matthew frowned, then replied hesitantly, "I couldn't do that, could I? You need to go to one of those universities like Cambridge to do that."

"Yes you do," Lucy conceded, "but there are free scholarships, and you could at least take the examination one day."

It was Rebecca's turn to frown, and there was more than a hint of petulance. "I don't want Matthew to go away, not ever! And what's wrong with being papa's senior clerk? He could easily support a family doing that, couldn't he, and perhaps one day papa might take him into the business."

Lucy chuckled at her enthusiasm, blind to the real significance of what she was saying. Adam was not so naïve, but it was none of his business. Butlers weren't required to have eyes and ears – only airs and graces. He slowed his pace, allowing the distance between him and his charges to lengthen to the point at which he could always claim to have heard nothing. He was, however, slightly alarmed when Lucy dropped back to join him, leaving Matthew and Rebecca to walk ahead alone.

She had barely done so when Rebecca glanced quickly over her shoulder, making sure that it was safe to whisper. "You wouldn't leave me to go to Cambridge would you, Matthew?"

"No, course not."

"Nor anywhere else?"

"No, you know I wouldn't."

She squeezed his hand in gratitude, and deliberately forgot to let go. Lucy and Adam, each for their own reasons, chose not to notice, as the young pair chatted away, suddenly oblivious of all around them.

"Do you think that papa really will take you into the business one day?"

"He might, if I work hard enough. I can manage all the ledger work already, and I reckon I might be able to do the work of both clerks one day; then I'll have to be the senior clerk, won't I?"

Rebecca paused, then chose her words carefully. "Of course, there's one way you could make sure that you came into the business."

"How?"

"Well, it is a family business, isn't it?"

"Yes, but I'm not family."

"Not yet. But there's one way you could be."

It was a second or two before he realised what she meant, then he reddened. "Steady on! Your mother would scream the place down if you even suggested that."

"Mama's just old-fashioned, that's all. When you're papa's senior clerk she'll have to think of you differently."

"I think James might have something to say about that. He's coming into the frame room in the summer, and I heard your father telling Danby that he'll be taking over soon, to give your father more time for the Hosiers' Association."

"James is just a pig," protested Rebecca, "and you're much cleverer than he is. Surely papa must see that."

"But even if he does," commented Matthew, "I heard someone say once that 'blood is thicker than water'. Do you know what that means?"

"No, but it sounds revolting. Matthew, are you sure you still love me?"

He squeezed her hand in reassurance, but looked quickly behind him, just in case. "Of course I do, but you're a hosier's daughter and I come from Tanners Yard. It's only a hundred yards away, but it may as well be a hundred miles."

"I hate it when you talk like that! Mama's always talking about what she calls 'class' and I think it's just horrible."

Matthew lost his customary cheeriness as he gazed across the meadow to the forbidding line of buildings that rose high on the cliff escarpment that was High Pavement. The most prominent sight of all was the back wall of the town gaol.

"They're starting to talk about class all over the place now," he observed. "Even in Tanners Yard. There's never been much mixing between my sort of folks and yours, but it's getting worse. That business in Arnold hasn't helped, either, and from what I hear there'll be more to come before this year's out."

"Papa was talking to some of his business friends about that the other evening. They're thinking of fighting back, did you know that? But he won't hold any of that against you, will he?"

"Your father? Not unless he has to. But it's not going to help us, is it?"

"Matthew; whatever happens, promise me you'll always love me."

"Of course I will," he promised.

"And if things get too bad, promise me we'll run away?"

Matthew hesitated.

"Matthew, promise me – please!"

He glanced nervously back at Lucy and Adam, walking in silence. He sensed that their time was nearly up, and he hated to think of them parting this way for another week.

"Of course I promise. One day, somehow I'll come and claim you, wherever I am."

"Oh Matthew!"

Despite all her mother's careful grooming, she leaned across and kissed him on the cheek. Adam coughed discreetly and steered Lucy back towards the flushed-looking couple. He couldn't help liking the cheery lad, despite his earlier misgivings, but enough was enough, particularly these days.

The Arnold raid proved to be simply the first, albeit the best orchestrated, of the early round. Two nights later a row of cottages in Strelley received a visit, and four framework knitters were forced to stand by and watch in fear and dread as their only means of supporting their families was smashed into kindling.

Within two weeks of the Arnold raid a mysterious fire put paid to a frame-shop in Gedling, and even closer to the town itself, in Basford, the premises of John Barnes, merchant hosier and lay preacher, suffered the loss of several windows, and was only saved from further destruction by the fact that some of his workers living in tied cottages nearby rushed out in time to beat off what turned out to be a relatively small party of raiders. It was later learned that the main body of the mob had been heading for Bulwell, where greater havoc was wreaked on the premises of Jasper Platt and Son. All in all, in those first two weeks, over two hundred wide frames – and some standard ones - were totally destroyed, as matters rapidly got out of hand, and those responsible began to forget what their original grievances had been. Five business houses were even consumed by fire, further proof that those who were leading the mob had hidden agendas. Many innocent workers lay injured as the result of defending their livelihoods, and not a single culprit had been identified, let alone apprehended.

Then, in the autumn, it began again. If the frame-renters and hosiers of Bulwell thought that they had already paid their dues, they were rudely disillusioned one night in early November, when it was the turn of another of those whom Henson had failed to prosecute, Peter Hollingworth, to feel the wrath of the disenchanted.

Hollingworth had, as an elementary precaution, sent some of his frames into the town, and had employed guards with loaded muskets to watch over those that remained. His defences were put to the test when a fusillade of musket shots announced to a waking village that a large body of men was seeking unauthorised entry to Hollingworth's Bulwell premises. It seemed initially that law and order had prevailed when one of the raiders, a local man named Westley, received a fatal musket shot in the chest, requiring his companions in crime to drag his body away before returning, even more incensed, and forcing the defenders to run for their lives as they broke in the door and smashed seven frames to smithereens.

Twelve more frames suffered the same fate in a single business house further up the road in Kimberley that same night, while a few nights later the mob changed their tactics, and intercepted a consignment of frames being taken into the town under cover of darkness from Sutton-in-Ashfield as they passed through Basford, leaving what was left of them as a burning beacon of welcome to the contingent of dragoons who clattered into the village long after the town men had made themselves scarce.

Two nights later, it was Sutton-in-Ashfield itself which received a visit by a force estimated at ninety strong, which battled it out with the local militia in a mêlée which resulted in the loss of some seventy frames, and the arrest of a handful of the mob, who all turned out to be local men and could give no useful information to the authorities as to who might be behind the recent unrest.

In vain did more moderate men like Henson try to remind those who had taken the initiative that the focus should be on bringing pressure to bear on the frame-owners to adjust their policies. The only legitimate grievance could be against the wide frames that were used for cut-ups, and not the standard frames on which so many innocent workers earned their livelihood. By destroying these, and setting fire indiscriminately to the workshops in which all frames were manufactured, the lawlessness was harming more working men than it was helping. But as those who had broken free of all such moderate restraint rapidly acquired a taste for what they were actually doing, their actions were destined to give the cause as a whole a bad name that it would never live down.

The biggest open confrontation of that year was reserved for the funeral of the Leicester-born Westley in the churchyard of his adopted Arnold, which attracted the attendance of almost a thousand of those dedicated to the cause, and as great an array of enforcers of the public peace as the county had seen in many a year. There was only a handful of family mourners, but the best part of a thousand 'of the worst sort' who were determined to see Westley off in style, and provoke an all-out brawl if possible.

Westley himself no doubt looked down with amusement as his service of departure was graced by the presence of no less a person than Thomas Wright, High Sheriff of the County, together with his very reluctant Under-Sheriff, a clutch of local magistrates, every local constable who could be bribed or threatened to turn out in support, along with a company of the Queen's Bays, still smarting from their inability to even find Basford, let alone defend it, several nights earlier.

Any ambitions which the mob leaders might have entertained of proclaiming their first martyr to the cause were drowned out by the slow but repetitive single beat of the regimental drum of the dragoon contingent, as a constant reminder to any potential troublemakers that while the Bays might have been held back from the troubles in France, this was not because they lacked courage and pride, and they would happily grasp any excuse to reclaim their manhood in the eyes of the local populace.

Almost in counterpart to the solemn drum beat, which was kept up by a succession of regimental drummers for the entire graveside service, was the booming voice of the High Sheriff as he intoned that portion of the Riot Act which the law required be read to any assembled multitude before any subsequent violent action on their part could be deemed in law a 'riot', and punished with death. It also provided the lawful justification for the orders which had been secretly issued to the dragoon commander that sabres were to be drawn, and used, should those deemed to be 'rioters' not disperse within an hour of the Act being read.

Amidst all this tension, the minister could be forgiven for his wavering voice as he quivered out the final passage of the official Church of England Service for the Burial of the Dead, conscious of the contrast between his own reedy words and the power with which the High Sheriff had bawled out the extract from the Riot Act, and trying his best not to read the prayers in time with the rhythmic slap of the regimental drum at the rear of the noisy congregation.

Also moving through the rear of the crowd were two agents of George Coldham, the Town Clerk, intent on locating and identifying a man bearing obvious signs of having sustained a serious blow to the face with a cutlass earlier in the year. He was the only possible line of enquiry they had as to who might have been responsible for that first Arnold raid, and it had been with high hopes that Coldham had, some months before, sent word out to all local hosiery employers for information regarding a regular worker who might recently have ceased working his frame due to some unspecified injury.

The employers of thousands of home workers had in turn instructed their bag-men to look hard into the faces of those from whom they collected the finished product. Some merchant hosiers had even offered a tempting financial incentive to whoever found the man, but either the bag-men had remained staunch to the cause, or they were more terrified of the consequences of betraying it. Or perhaps it was simply the case that whoever had taken the cutlass blow from Thomas Bolton had not been in regular employment beforehand, a distinct possibility given the uncertain times in the trade.

Whoever he was, he appeared not to have attended Westley's funeral. Unknown to those who were searching for him in vain in Arnold, Rob Possett had in fact attended his own funeral in the upper town in August of that year, as the wounds for which he dared not seek the services of a surgeon at the local hospital had festered in the Rookeries slum in which he was tended to the last by his wife and sister, who kept his secret and arranged for a hasty burial at dead of night, with Possett's ravaged countenance and bloated septicemic corpse hidden inside a potato sack.

But the long fingers of coincidence had not yet fully relaxed their grip on those who had carried off that first raid. As the sexton and his boy began to fill in Westley's grave, the magistrates passed among the crowd, warning them that they had only minutes left in which to disperse before the law took its course. Meanwhile, the officers and men of the Queen's Bays put into action the manoeuvre which they had been rehearsing for two long days at the Park Barracks and adjacent Castle grounds, and spurred their horses into the crowd at a steady trot in a predetermined and well-choreographed pattern which split the potential troublemakers into columns which were then easily driven out into the road alongside the churchyard.

From there many of them began to leave, after yelling a few idle insults at the mounted men in their orange-flashed uniform jackets. All except a handful who had turned out to see some sport, and were not yet ready to wend their way home through the early November sunset. Among them was Simon Ackroyd, a native of Arnold who had lost all he possessed during the March raid, and had since been drinking himself into oblivion at the expense of a family which had finally disowned him two weeks previously.

He had drifted into Nottingham seeking casual work as a labourer, and had attained random success as a pickpocket, before being sent back to Arnold on the orders of a magistrate who had threatened him with imprisonment if he were found imposing on the town for one more day. As the crowd began to break up without his having acquired anything to sell in exchange for the strong liquor which would ease his mental suffering, he took exception to being told to move on by an officious constable of the Watch who was young enough to be one of the two sons who had thrown him physically into the lane outside the family cottage on the day he had left Arnold in disgrace.

A scuffle ensued in which the much weaker Ackroyd rapidly came off second best, and as he was being pushed by the scruff of his neck towards the local lock-up, he sought to bargain for his freedom.

"If yer tek yer 'ands off me an' let me go, I'll tell yer summat abaht that do last spring."

"Not interested," replied the constable dismissively. "Nah keep yer legs movin' or I'll break 'em w' mi staff."

As Ackroyd became more desperate, he raised his voice to the level at which it was overheard by Anthony Brailsford, one of the two agents commissioned by George Coldham, who was walking ahead of them on his way back to the hostelry in which he and his colleague had secured accommodation for the night, with the 'reckoning' to be forwarded to the Town Clerk.

"There was plenty 'appenin' 'ere that night, an' if yer let me go I'll tell yer who were in it. P'rhaps yer'll reap a fair reward fer wharra can tell yer abaht it."

Brailsford stopped in his tracks, and waited for the struggling pair to draw level with him before holding up a sheet of parchment for the constable to view. Although the constable couldn't read he was familiar enough with the Nottingham Coat of Arms at the top of it, and was heartily tired of prodding Ackroyd up the road anyway. He handed over his prisoner to Brailsford with less enquiry than would normally have been merited, but these were strange times, when all was said and done, and the middle-aged man in the frock coat seemed to enjoy some sort of authority.

By the time the sun had finally set, Ackroyd was happily nearing the point at which he would slide from his chair onto the taproom floor in the White Lion, with a sovereign in his pocket and instructions left with the landlord to load him onto the next cart heading out of the village. Brailsford lost no time, on his return to the town, in seeking an audience with the Town Clerk in which he passed on what he had learned from Ackroyd. He was well rewarded for his lucky break, and a few months later began a thoroughly undistinguished career as Superintendant of the Barker Gate Workhouse. He was also successful in being reimbursed his sovereign.

George Coldham, for his part, called urgently for fresh quills and a supply of ink, and began penning yet another letter to the Home Office.

In those early days the authorities had no intelligence network, and therefore no way of knowing where the raiding parties would strike next. Their initial targets had all been lonely groups of cottages and outlying villages, where the only resistance which the town gangs encountered was from simple countrymen wielding the leftovers of a bygone cottage-garden era. But rusting ploughshares and broken pitchforks were no match for the cudgel, knife, axe, firebrand and occasional pistol, and the element of surprise usually neutralised any hope of an organised defence.

Some of the larger villages attempted a Watch system of their own, and at first it seemed to hold promise. A raid at Bobbers Mill was prevented after an alert lookout in a tree fired off two shots from a pistol, warning the menfolk of the village in time for them to chase off the town men, while at Beeston a raider was almost caught when a family mongrel held onto him on a command from its owner, and the would-be frame smasher only made good his escape by leaving most of his breeches in the village as a memento of his brief visit. But these were isolated triumphs, and in the main the raids were swift, bloody and destructive.

As the attacks drew closer to the town itself, two ominous

features began to emerge. The first was that, far from contenting themselves with merely targeting the hosiery trade, some of the raiders transferred their energies to petty theft from their victims, and on one occasion a serious sexual assault was committed against a young Sneinton girl while her father lay helplessly nursing a broken leg. His stocking frame was not even touched. Almost from the start, some of those involved in the nightly excursions were cynically using the cause as an excuse for general lawlessness, and more than one victim could tell a depressing tale of having bought off his attackers with a handful of coins originally intended to feed his family for the next week.

The other disturbing feature was the apparent existence of a shadowy leader whose confidence in his own anonymity was such that he gleefully left his calling card wherever he went. Many a villager, while cleaning up the remains of his parlour kitchen, found a note from Ned Ludd, or sometimes 'General' Ludd, promising to return whenever the fancy took him, and pronouncing the invincibility of the cause which soon became associated with his name, as the authorities became aware of his existence and dubbed his followers 'Luddites'.

Town records and parish registers were scanned in vain for some clue as to his origins and likely present location, and it was widely rumoured that he held court in a hidden back room of a public house in the lower town, which was carefully concealed behind a secret panel. More than one publican suffered the indignity of a visit from the Watch, backed up by armed soldiers, plus the cost of damaged wall panels, but all to no avail.

Ned Ludd was never to be captured, and Gravenor Henson grew to wish that he had never borrowed and adapted the name of a dim-witted Leicestershire boy who, some years before, had smashed his frame needles in a fit of rage during an argument with his disciplinarian father. Indeed, Gravenor Henson came to regret a great deal as he watched helplessly while what he had worked so hard to create was wrenched from his grasp as soon as his usefulness had expired, and those who had pretended to respect his leadership proved that they had not been worthy of his trust, as they scattered the now disgraced name of Ned Ludd indiscriminately around the surrounding villages.

In vain Henson pleaded with the likes of Cadby, and the other self-appointed generals, to have more sympathy and respect for the ordinary folk who were all too often the ultimate victims of their ill-disciplined activities. Most of the stocking frames which were destroyed were rented by those workers in whose cottages they were located, and yet those who led the mob were still contending – if challenged – that they were striking a blow against the actual owners of those frames, who charged exorbitant rents for them. Instead, they were simply causing further hardship and misery for the workmen themselves, who not only had no machinery left with which to support their families, but were also held financially responsible for the loss of the frames which were destroyed.

But this combination of legal argument and economic logic was lost on those for whom all forms of crime had become both a way of life and a sadistic addiction. The original cause had been both just and noble, but those who had leapt upon the bandwagon were neither, and they claimed to act in the name of working men who were appalled at what was happening. It also failed to occur to those creeping out of Nottingham in the dead of night that they were themselves descended from families which had, in some cases within living memory, been forced into the urban slums of the town by the agricultural recession which had coincided with increased employment opportunities in the hosiery trade. Without realising it, some of Ludd's followers were in fact attacking some of their own distant relatives.

It might have gone on like this for many years into the future, had not the real leaders of the mob grown overconfident. As their arrogant belief in their own invulnerability drew them closer and closer into the town centre, their victims became more powerful and influential. It was one thing to attack sleeping villagers in insecure and leaky cottages, but another thing altogether to mount an attack on substantial hosiery manufactures under the very noses of the only regular law enforcement agencies which existed at the time.

Not only were those communities which were targeted increasingly to be found within a relatively short walk of the town boundaries – for example, in Basford, Sneinton and Lenton – but night-time attacks soon began on hosiery interests within the town itself. The smashing of frames in establishments in Trumpet Street and York Street might have been rationalised on the basis that they were 'wide frames', used in the manufacture of inferior cut-ups by colt workers. But it was less easy to justify the challenge to the established economic order which was posed by the indiscriminate mayhem inflicted on some of the largest and most important businesses in town, whose only offence seemed to be the fact that they existed at all, and that their owners had reacted to the threat to their wide frames in the outlying villages by bringing them into storage in the town under military escort.

It was therefore hardly surprising that, after countless informal discussions in smaller groups, one of which had been energetically convened by Robert Bradley, the entire newly formed Nottingham Hosiers' Association met to discuss tactics in the parlour of the Flying Horse Inn one Saturday afternoon in the New Year of 1812. There were over a hundred men there altogether, and between them they represented almost nine-tenths of the local industry. Bradley himself was one of the first to arrive, and Cossons and Mellors, arriving later, found him already in animated conversation with Paul Solley.

"I find it 'ard ter bear; very 'ard ter bear," Bradley was complaining. "I wouldn't mind so much, but what 'ave I ever done but perform mi Christian duty? I kept 'em on a lot longer than most o' the members 'ere, even when times were really bad."

Solley nodded in sympathy. "There's no gratitude, you can be sure of that. When your lad James told me how many men you still had working last winter, I said to Margaret – 'a fat lot of good it'll do him, you mark my words' – and of course I've been proved right, though I take no satisfaction from it. Sheer ingratitude, that's what it is." He became aware of Cossons and Mellors hovering behind them. "Welcome, gentlemen. Have you heard about Robert's trouble?"

"No," said Mellors, who, as an Arnold-based hosier had enough troubles of his own, and was not best placed to sympathise with a town colleague who up to now had benefited from the proximity of the Park Barracks. Even so, he listened in gloomy silence as Bradley bemoaned his first violent encounter with the cause.

"It was all right until Wednesday, and I really thought that local folk 'ad more sense than ter go fer an employer who's always 'ad their interests at 'eart. Then the Watch got me out o' bed at nearly midnight ter tell me that the upper windows 'ad been put in at Stoney Street. There was glass all over the frame room, and it took mi men two hours ter clean it up. Then blow me if the next night someone didn't force entry through a window and smash a couple of mi frames. Right under the nose o' the Watch, too! If they 'adn't 'eard the noise and shouted up, Lord knows where it would've ended."

"At least you got some 'elp from the Watch," grumbled Cossons. "We don't get any 'elp from anyone until it's all over. We 'ad a raid last Thursday night, an' the troops finally arrived while Betty was layin' out the breakfast table on Friday mornin'. Because they're not local, they'd been ridin' round an' round Lenton looking fer Brown Lane in Beeston – God 'elp 'em when they get ter France, that's all I can say!"

"Robert's certainly lucky in that regard," agreed Solley. "He's about the only one yet who's got any cause to thank the Watch.

They're usually in the wrong place when anything happens, and run in the opposite direction if it does."

More of them were arriving now, and a few moments later Solley, as the recently elected Chairman of the Association, brought the meeting to order, and confirmed the reason for its calling.

"Quite simply," he announced across the sea of well-fed faces, "we can't afford to sit and wait any longer. All we've had so far from the mayor and aldermen are promises and excuses. We need urgent protection, and we need renewed respect for law and order."

"I couldn't agree with you more," shouted Michael Bird, himself a recently elected alderman, as well as being the owner of a Sneinton frame-shop which was currently minus a window or two, "but to hear George Coldham talk, you'd think we were asking him to part with his own money!"

The mention of the Town Clerk provoked a general round of grumbling and complaining, and it was a somewhat hesitant Christopher Booth who rose to his defence. "To be fair," he argued, "he is aware of the problem, and when I had occasion to speak to him last week he assured me that he was keeping London fully informed of what's going on."

"That's all very well when your brother-in-law is the Mayor," sneered a voice from the back, "but I don't suppose anyone's going to listen to the rest of us, and it's the rest of us that's being threatened."

"Gentlemen!" pleaded Solley, "let's keep this civilised, shall we? The last speaker had a very good point, but there's no sense in us degenerating into a rabble and falling out amongst ourselves. What I propose is a petition to Parliament for more direct military assistance immediately, and an end to the free-trade policies which are holding down our profits."

"And increasing the price o' food," added Bradley. "If you ask me, 'alf the trouble is caused bi starvation. Men don't riot on full stomachs, and they wouldn't be breakin' up frames if they could earn a decent livin' on 'em."

"Good God!" bellowed Michael Bird. "You're not seriously suggesting that we pay them more? How in God's name can we buy them off, when we don't even get a decent bottom price for the product?"

"That's precisely my point," rejoined Solley, keen to minimise any potential rift among the members, who in truth represented a wider range of political persuasion than was generally imagined by outsiders. "The same government policies which keep up the price of food also keep down the price of finished goods. It's free-trade policies which are to blame, if only those ruffians out there could appreciate it. We're all in the same boat!"

"Then why are they taking it out on us?" demanded a sceptic with free-trade loyalties.

"Because they don't know any better!" shouted Bradley, who rose to his feet in frustration and began to go red in the face. Cossons rose alongside him, placed a restraining hand on his shoulder, and gently but firmly pushed him back into his seat.

"Whatever may be the rights and wrongs of it all," persisted Solley, "we need the urgent restoration of law and order before matters get completely out of hand. That means troops, and not just that posy of toy soldiers in The Park. We also need a much stronger, and permanent, Nottingham militia – local men who know the town; that must be our first priority. Then we can start on free-trade reforms if we wish, but that will obviously take more time than we can afford at present."

By no means all of his audience was convinced but it was the best plan which anyone had yet come up with, and by an overwhelming vote it was decided that Parliamentary Agents would be hired in order to put their demands into petition form, with a suggested Draft Bill attached, should that be required. Before long, those who had travelled the furthest distances, and were anxious to return home in order to secure their premises before darkness fell, paid their farewell respects to the chairman and took their leave.

Eventually only a handful were left and the meeting grew less formal, since those remaining were regular business associates and genuine friends. Nevertheless it was still Paul Solley who led the discussion.

"There's something else I wanted to suggest, gentlemen, but it was best left until there were only a few of us here, and all from the lower town. First of all, do each of you have at least one worker you can trust? A senior man, preferably, but a journeyman, not a clerk. And he must be trusted by the rest of the workers."

Each of them thought for a moment, and most of them nodded, including Bradley, as Solley continued.

"Well, it seems to me that we have part of the solution in our own hands. The people behind all this trouble are clearly frameworkers – we know that because they seem to know how best to destroy the frames they attack. It's reasonable to assume that at least some of them are still working, and that some of us are providing that work. What I'm suggesting is that we use our own men to tell us what's going on and who's organising it all. The authorities don't seem to know where to start, so perhaps we can give them a few names to be going on with. One name leads to another in this business, and before we know where we are half the ringleaders will be in irons."

There was a murmured agreement, as Solley expanded his thoughts. "Even if we can't guarantee that the authorities will act, at least we can take steps to cut the poison out of our own systems and prevent it travelling any further. As well as collecting and passing on names, we must agree, right here and now, to lay off any man even suspected of being involved in all this. Are we agreed?"

Again, there was no reason to disagree, and there was some comfort to be gained from the thought that at least someone was taking positive action. But as each of them made their way home in the fading light, it was with a thoughtful countenance and a slightly preoccupied air.

CHAPTER EIGHT

The net tightens

IT WAS the Feast of St. Valentine, but those who ruled the nation were about to profess little enough love for the people of Nottingham. On an evening when the freezing fog rising off the Thames, to cluster in ghostly silhouettes around the lamplights of Westminster, had kept a quorum of members of the House of Commons in the Members Dining Room – rather than dispersing to their various lodgings and clubs – The Right Honourable Richard Ryder, Secretary of State for the Home Department, rose from his seat on the Government benches and shuffled his sheaf of papers, before clearing his throat noisily and addressing a late sitting of the House dominated by his Tory colleagues.

"I move that the members of this honourable House proceed to read for a second time the proposed legislation known as the Framework Bill, which has previously been before this House, and which provides for the more exemplary punishment of those found guilty of breaking stocking frames and for more effectually preserving the peace of the County of Nottingham."

"How many have you caught so far?" enquired a port-soaked Whig from across the floor, to the accompanying guffaws and hoots of several party colleagues who had recently enjoyed dinner in his company. Ryder ignored the question, and continued.

"It is notorious to this honourable House, and to the people of this nation, that the dwellings of individuals have been entered by armed men, who destroyed varieties of machinery and carried on a system of riot bordering on insurrection, in a manner which has never before disgraced the history of this nation. Since the 14th November of last year, His Majesty's Government has been obliged to dispatch between 800 and 900 cavalry and 1,000 infantry into the town of Nottingham, a greater force than has ever been necessary, in any part of our history, to be employed in the quelling of a local disturbance."

"Did they find Napoleon?" asked the same member, mischievi-ously, as he settled himself in for an evening of light entertainment.

"Indeed sir, they did not," retorted Ryder. "Nor are they likely to, when they are deployed in this fashion, quelling insurrection by an ungrateful populace that should be honouring their bravery on the Continent, not pelting them with cow dung and other unseemly missiles. With your permission, Mr Speaker, I will continue."

The Speaker nodded, a gesture which gave every indication of having been achieved in his sleep, and Ryder warmed to his theme.

"The progress of these disturbances has been most extraordinary, notwithstanding the assistance which has been rendered by my Office. They arose between the workmen and the manufacturers; the machines they destroyed were not the property of the persons in whose houses they were, but were hired out by the manufacturers, or by persons who made a sort of trade of them. The whole system was carried on with the greatest secrecy and management. I am sorry to have to confess to the honourable members that there never appeared in this country a system of depredation so completely organised; so organised was it that the magistrates were completely powerless to act. There were actually instances of frames being broken by parties of thirty or fifty, without creating alarm, and while the military were within one hundred yards of the scene of the mischief."

"And safely out of harm's way, as usual," observed the Whig member for Pendlebury, who had never seen military action first-hand for himself. He was 'noticed' by the Speaker, and slunk back further into his pew. Ryder continued as if there had been no interruption, having used the interlude to refresh himself from his carafe of water.

"As the law now stands, the breaking of frames is a simple felony, punishable with transportation, a punishment the dread of which has regrettably not been sufficient to deter parties from committing the offence."

"How do you know, if you haven't actually caught anyone yet?" demanded the original Whig member, who was rewarded by supporting hoots of derision from his colleagues on the Whig backbenches. Ryder stared at them pointedly, and one by one they fell silent.

"His Majesty's Government's proposal is therefore that we make the offence capital in nature. I share the opinion of that noble and eminent jurist Sir Matthew Hale that when offences become sufficiently enormous and dangerous to the State, they should be punishable with death. I so move."

The Second Reading motion was seconded, somewhat predictably, by fellow Tory Colonel Eyre, who took time to point out that while its provisions "might be severe in enactment, nevertheless they would be humane in effect", after which extended piece of sophistry he resumed his seat. Following what was described in subsequent Parliamentary papers as 'an extended debate', the Second Reading was followed hastily by the remaining stages of the lower House process, and the unamended Bill was handed upstairs to the Lords by 49 votes to 11.

But if the people of the town had received little sympathy from those 'commoners' elected to represent their interests, they enjoyed passionate support from an unlikely source just under two weeks later, when the matter was debated in the Upper House.

The hereditary peerage system in Britain had, in its time, produced many anomalies, but perhaps none more so than in the person of George Noel Gordon. He was the unlikely owner of Newstead Abbey in Nottinghamshire, some twelve miles north of the county town, and with it came the title of 6th Baron Byron. Both natural advantages were acquired by him from a great-uncle, but he was far better known in contemporary London society as the club-footed, slightly stocky and effeminate-looking romantic poet who enchanted the ladies and was despised by their husbands for his flaunted bisexuality.

As Lord Byron, he was one of the landed gentry of the county, and one who might be expected to join in the chorus of outrage against any perceived attack on the established order. If he needed any incentive other than that of heritage, it was a matter of record that many of the villages to the north of the troubled town which had received unwanted visits from 'General Ludd', as he had now become generally known, and his informal army of the great unwashed, lay within Lord Byron's feudal jurisdiction.

But as plain George Gordon, he was to prove himself both a humanist and a vocal social reformer, and an early indication of where his heart truly lay came on February 27th 1812, when he rose, on the occasion of the Framework Bill receiving its Second Reading by their Lordships, to make his maiden speech in the House of Lords, which by ancient tradition would be received without interruption, and in total silence. Bearing in mind his audience, this was perhaps as well.

With his characteristic black locks curled over his forehead, and his voice the same mellifluous liquid which so enthralled them in the drawing rooms of the privileged, but raised a pitch so that the important message he had to convey could be heard above the background rustling of order papers, Lord Byron began formally, lulling them into a false sense of security regarding what was to follow.

"My Lords: The subject now submitted to your Lordships for the first time, though new to the House, is by no means new to the country. As a person to some degree connected with the suffering county, though a stranger not only to this House in general, but to almost every individual whose attention I presume to solicit, I must claim some portion of your Lordships' indulgence, whilst I offer a

few observations on a question in which I confess myself deeply interested.

"*During the short time I recently passed in Nottinghamshire, not twelve hours elapsed without some fresh act of violence; and on the day I left the county I was informed that forty frames had been broken the preceding evening, as usual, without resistance and without detection.*

"*Such was then the state of that county, and such I have reason to believe it to be at this moment. But whilst these outrages must be admitted to exist to an alarming extent, it cannot be denied that they have arisen from circumstances of the most unparalleled distress: the perseverance of these miserable men in their proceedings tends to prove that nothing but absolute want could have driven a large, and once honest and industrious, body of the people, into the commission of excesses so hazardous to themselves, their families, and the community. At the time to which I allude, the town and county were burdened with large detachments of the military; the police was in motion, the magistrates assembled; yet all the movements, civil and military, led to . . . nothing.*

"*But the police, however useless, were by no means idle: several notorious delinquents had been detected — men liable to conviction, on the clearest evidence, of the capital crime of poverty; men who had been nefariously guilty of lawfully begetting several children, whom, thanks to the times, they were unable to maintain.*

"*When we are told that these men are leagued together not only for the destruction of their own comfort, but of their very means of subsistence, can we forget that it is the bitter policy, the destructive warfare, of the last eighteen years which has destroyed their comfort, your comfort, all men's comfort? These men were willing to dig, but the spade was in other hands: they were not ashamed to beg, but there was none to relieve them: their own means of subsistence were cut off, all other employments pre-occupied; and their excesses, however to be deplored and condemned, can hardly be the subject of surprise.*

"*Why were the military called out to be made a mockery of, if they were to be called out at all? Such marchings and countermarchings! From Nottingham to Bulwell, from Bulwell to Basford, from Basford to Mansfield! And when at length the detachment arrived at their destination, in all the pride, pomp and circumstance of glorious war, they came just in time to witness the mischief which had been done, and ascertain the escape of the perpetrators, to collect the spoils of war in the fragments of broken frames, and return to their quarters amid the derision of old women and the hootings of children. Now, though in a free country it were to be wished that our military should never be too formidable, at least to ourselves, I cannot see the policy of placing them in situations where they can only be made ridiculous.*

"*At present the county suffers from the double infliction of an idle military and a starving population. In what state of apathy have we been plunged so long, that now for the first time the House has been officially apprised of these disturbances? All the cities you have taken, all the armies which have retreated before your leaders, are but paltry subjects of self-congratulation, if your land divides against itself, and your dragoons and your executioners must be let loose against your fellow citizens.*

"*You call these men a mob, desperate, dangerous and ignorant. Are we aware of our obligations to a mob? It is the mob that labour in your fields and serve in your houses, that man your navy and recruit your army – that have enabled you to defy all the world, and can also defy you when neglect and calamity have driven them to despair. You may call the people a mob, but do not forget that a mob too often speaks to the sentiments of the people. And here I must remark with what alacrity you are accustomed to fly to the succour of your distressed allies, leaving the distressed of your own country to the care of Providence – or the parish. When the Portuguese suffered under the retreat of the French, every arm was stretched out, every hand was opened, from the rich man's largess to the widow's mite, to enable them to rebuild their villages and replenish their granaries. And at this moment, when thousands of misguided but most unfortunate fellow-countrymen are struggling with the extremes of hardships and hunger, as your charity began abroad it should end at home. A much less sum, even if these men could not have been restored to their employments, would have rendered unnecessary the tender mercies of the bayonet and the gibbet.*

"*Setting aside the palpable injustice and the certain inefficiency of the Bill, are there not capital punishments sufficient in your statutes? How will you carry the Bill into effect? Can you commit a whole county to their own prisons? Will you erect a gibbet in every field and hang up men like scarecrows, or will you place the county under martial law and restore Sherwood Forest in its former condition of a royal chase and an asylum for outlaws?*

"*Are these the remedies for a starving and desperate populace? Will the famished wretch who has braved your bayonets be appalled by your gibbets? When death is a relief, and the only relief it appears that you will afford him, will he be dragooned into tranquility? Will that which could not be effected by your grenadiers be accomplished by your executioners? If you proceed by the forms of law, where is your evidence? Those who have refused to impeach their accomplices when transportation only was the punishment, will hardly be tempted to witness against them when death is the penalty.*

"*Sure I am, from what I have heard, and from what I have seen, that to pass the Bill under all the existing circumstances, without enquiry, without deliberation, would only be to add injustice to irritation, and barbarity to neglect. The framers of such a bill must be content to inherit the honours of that Athenian law-giver whose edicts were said to be written, not in ink, but in blood.*"

The silence endured even after he had sat down, and was finally broken by an elderly earl towards the rear of the Tory benches. "And I always thought he was one of us."

Even if they had been listening, they could not have been paying attention, because the Bill was passed well within the time allocated for its debate. It passed into law a few days later, signed into infamy by the Prince Regent, ruling the nation on behalf of his father, the elderly monarch who had recently lost the American colonies and was currently subject to one of his increasing bouts of insanity. It was to survive on the statute book for only a few days short of two years, but, for some, that was long enough.

And not only did Parliament make frame breaking a capital offence that February, but in April the Town Corporation introduced, with the full backing of the law, a system of 'Watch & Ward'. A ten o'clock curfew was imposed, and all able-bodied men in the town were required to do their turn at 'watching' by night and 'warding' by day, keeping an eye out for any possible outbreaks of violence, to enforce the curfew and report suspicious activities to the authorities. Unpaid work, of course, and if ever a move was likely to aggravate the situation even more, this was it. Especially since many of those required to do their watching and warding duties were sympathetic to the cause, if not actually involved in it.

It was a long corridor, hung with oil portraits of former occupants of high office under the British Crown. The floors were of polished timber, and echoed to the sound of military boots as uniformed men entered and departed from the various doors down its length. The predominant smell was of polish and sealing wax, and the two men sitting on the bench outside the very last door on the left were both wishing that they were somewhere else. Each had his own reason.

For Alfred Conon it was fear of dismissal from the only occupation he knew. Raised in Whitechapel some forty years earlier, he had grown up among the horrors which can attend lengthy periods of grinding poverty, and when the recruiting officers had visited the Aldgate alehouse in which he had been earning a precarious living as a potman and trouble-fixer, he had gladly taken the king's shilling.

Ten years as an artilleryman fighting for His Britannic Majesty on the Continent had hardened his sensitivities, while at the same time introducing him to the rugged art of pugilism, at which he had proved himself particularly adept. So adept, in fact, that he had narrowly escaped the gallows after killing a fellow sergeant with his bare knuckles during a prizefight which the army officially claimed had never taken place, particularly since the heaviest bets had been placed by officers.

Instead, Alf Conon's life had been bartered for forty lashes and a term in a military gaol which even now he could not recall without having to suppress a scream. That term had been mercifully foreshortened after Conon had consistently demonstrated his enthusiasm for 'peaching' on fellow prisoners, and it was considered that there was a better reward for his information-gathering talents than a sordid death at the hands of his disgusted comrades in irons. Sniffing out Jacobins and other threats to the established order had become not only a comfortable way of life for Alf, but the only life he knew, and he hoped that the unfortunate sequel to his most recent assignment, in company with the man seated to his right, was not going to result in his return to the stews of Dorset Street with no means of sustenance, and nothing to offer the family which he hoped might still take him back after all these years.

Frederick Baker, by contrast, had no such apprehension. After all, he had talked his way out of bigger holes than this, and if Alf stuck to the story which Fred had concocted, and which they had both tirelessly rehearsed, there could be no suggestion that the constable of the local Watch had died as the result of anything said by either of them as they sought to ingratiate themselves with the patrons of the Square Rigger in Plymouth dockyard some three weeks since.

By rights, Baker should have been hanged by the neck many times for his repeated acts of forgery, usury and debasement of coinage, and he no doubt would have been, had not his common-law wife, Elizabeth, been an extremely attractive lady of negotiable virtue when it came to deflecting the law from its proper course. A natural-born perverter of the truth, Baker could always be relied upon to obtain the truth from others by the same methods that he had so frequently used in the past in order to obtain financial benefit for himself. His anxiety this morning was not that their services would not be retained, but that this meeting would delay his departure to the Barnet racetrack, where he and Lizzie could always earn a sovereign or two playing the old 'angry-husband-turns-up-unexpectedly' routine among the attending gentry. He listened to the clock of St. Clement Danes chiming ten o'clock in the forenoon as he and his partner in perfidy waited on the bench just to the right of the door painted with the name of its occupant – Alexander James Gillies Esq., Assistant Third Secretary to the Home Office.

Eventually they were admitted by an emaciated elderly underling in a wing collar who looked as if holding the door open for them would be his last act on this earth, and they stood in line abreast in front of the enormous mahogany table which contained just one document, which Gillies continued to read, and without even looking up he ordered them to take a seat.

"Nottingham, gentlemen," he announced in a soft Edinburgh burr which was in sharp contrast to the steel-blue eyes and close-cropped white hair.

"Where?" enquired Baker.

"Quite," confirmed Gillies. 'It's a two-day coach ride north of here, and a full two-days' march south of York, apparently. They have a serious problem with a seditious mob which seems intent on destroying the hosiery industry from which the town derives its main source of income."

"Jacobites again?" queried Baker ingenuously. Gillies raised his eyes from the document with an icy stare.

"Jacobites, Mr Baker, were supporters of the late pretender to the English throne, Charles Edward Stuart. His was a lost cause from the very beginning. Jacobins, on the other hand, are still very much alive and well, and seeking to impose their dangerous revolutionary theories on the working people of this nation. It is up to you and Mr Conon here to put a stop to their efforts."

"In Nottingham?" asked Conon in a tone of disbelief.

"I share your reservations, Mr Conon, but I am instructed by Mr Ryder himself to send agents to Nottingham without delay in order to identify the ringleaders of this ruffian band. Do either of you know anything about masonry?"

"My dad were a Mason," offered Baker helpfully. "At least, that's what me old ma used to say. Grand Master 'e were," he added by way of enlightenment. He was rewarded with another icy stare from Gillies.

"I was referring to the sort of masonry which involves dressing and hoisting blocks of stone, not the sort with secret ceremonies and unusual handshakes."

"Why do we need to know about that?" said Conon.

"Because," Gillies replied, "they are currently undertaking extensions and repairs to the Exchange Hall, which is a local government building in Nottingham. You will be posing as visiting stonemasons, and this will explain your hopefully frequent visits there to report progress in the search for a man named Ned Ludd."

"Who's 'e?" Baker enquired.

"If we knew that," observed Gillies in a condescending tone, "we wouldn't have to send you up there at considerable cost to the public purse. But I want him found without delay."

"So we just knock him over the head and drag him down here," Conon suggested.

"Of course not. You will be reporting directly to the Town Clerk of Nottingham, a Mr . . . (here, Gillies was obliged to consult the document on his desk once again) . . . a Mr Coldham. Either him or someone deputised by him. You will report all discoveries to him, and it will be his job to secure any apprehensions. Hopefully, this arrangement will avoid any repetition of what happened in Plymouth."

"Look sir," began Baker, "about that, we can explain . . ."

"I have no doubt you can," Gillies cut in sharply, "but I'd prefer that you didn't even begin. It's your God-given talent for lies and deceit which makes you so valuable in matters such as this. Even the Devil could find gainful employment in this modern society of ours. Now, are there any questions? You will leave via the nightly coach which departs from the Marble Arch at seven p.m. sharp."

"Can I take Lizzie wiv me, sir?" requested Baker.

"If you are referring to Miss Smollett," stated Gillies coldly, "I rather think not. This is not an assignment which will be likely to require her unique talents, and so far as I am aware, stonemasons are not traditionally accompanied by their women."

"Only, if it's workin' men we 'as to mix wiv, well my Lizzie can come in a bit useful, if you see what I mean."

"I do see what you mean, Mr Baker, but I do not like what I see. It will be you and Mr Conon only. Now, if there is nothing else, I have a meeting to attend in Whitehall. As usual, Mr Tolhurst will see to your detailed requirements. Good morning. And good luck."

They scuttled from the building as fast as decorum would permit, each of them relieved that it was over. Baker stopped on the front steps to light his battered old pipe, and as the smoke began to issue from it, he grinned triumphantly.

"See, I told ya! Just follow Freddy Boy's lead and you won't go far wrong. A free 'oliday in Nottlingum, or whatever the 'ell it's called. Lizzie will be pleased." He grinned across at Conon through blackened teeth, and before the latter could remind him of their last exchange with Gillies, added, "Coach drivers gets lonely, don't they? I'm sure this one won't mind an extra passenger in exchange for a warm and friendly night in a coaching inn!"

Conon grinned back, and shook his head in silent admiration as they walked back down the steps.

Nathan looked up suddenly from his frame, and all but lost his fingers under the treadle bar which came down with a clatter in response to the routine instruction his foot had given it a second earlier. It was the finest April that anyone could remember, and the late afternoon sun blazed through the high windows on the west side of the building, through which a commanding view of the tower of St. Mary's led on to a distant vista of St. Peter's and the Castle. His back to the window, with his frame located so as to make the most of the light, he sensed that someone was watching him. He turned and saw the figure shadowed in the light from the window, some six feet away from him. The body was bent with age, and the knees slightly splayed with the sheer physical effort of standing. Nathan's heart lurched in his chest, and his breath left him as if he had been punched in the stomach. He was staring at the father he had buried some two years earlier.

A chill swept over his body as the left hand of the apparition rose in a beckoning motion. There could be no mistaking it – he was meant to follow. His eyes blinded by the sun's glare, he peered hard at the face, trying to make out more detail as his mouth dried from the fear of being proved right. He remained rooted to the spot, paralysed by shock, as the figure cocked his head to one side in a querying gesture.

His neighbour Sam Pinkney had looked up from his own frame as he saw Nathan turn, and had been watching the silent pantomime with amusement. He shouted above the clatter of the frames. " 'e ain't goin' ter bite yer, Nathan – 'e's 'ardly gorrany teeth left, fer one thing."

Nathan started out of his trance as he registered that Sam was speaking to him. "Eh?"

"Danby," Sam added with some impatience, " 'e won't bite yer, I said."

He nodded in the direction of Bradley's senior clerk, who stood politely in front of the window waiting for Nathan to follow him. He knew better than to try to make his feeble voice heard above the racket of six frames, and to tap a man on the shoulder while he was engrossed in the intricate maneouvres of a warp frame was to invite an accident, or a punch in the head.

Another shiver ran through him and his breath returned in painful spasms, as Nathan's whole body adjusted to the decrease in adrenalin. He hadn't been so affected by fright in his entire life, and now he stood foolishly alongside his frame, embarrassed by his stupidity and appalled by his gullibility. And yet, for a moment or two, he could have sworn that the man had been wearing the old hat which his father had always kept perched on his head, a keepsake from his earlier life in the fields.

"Mr Bradley wants ter see yer," croaked Danby as loudly as he could. Nathan stepped forward a couple of paces, peering into the face in trepidation, terrified that the man would change once again into the old familiar figure.

"Pardon?" Nathan hadn't really been listening the first time, but Danby put it down to the weakness of his own voice against the constant din of metal upon wood.

"Mr Bradley – 'e wants ter see yer downstairs right away. Yer ter come wi' me."

Nathan wiped his hands as best he could and threw the cloth onto his now silent frame. He straightened his hair and brushed down his jacket and breeches as he negotiated the downward flight of stairs, apprehensive now for a different reason. His work had been satisfactory, he knew that, and at this time of year it wasn't normal to close down any frames, just when work was picking up. He could only hope that Bradley wasn't going to go the way of many others and switch to cut-ups.

Danby knocked on the half-open door and went straight in without invitation. Nathan remained in the narrow passageway, from which he could see Bradley and Matthew examining a large ledger which occupied most of the desk space.

"Yer probably right," Bradley was agreeing with Matthew, "but I've got used to it that way round. If yer start puttin' all the week's product on the one page, I'll not know who ter send the accounts to. Oh, come in, Nathan."

Matthew looked up sharply at the mention of his father's name, and appeared as surprised as Nathan that the latter had been summoned to Mr Bradley's office. He looked back enquiringly at Bradley, who nodded. "Yes, leave us fer the moment if yer would, Matthew. No, leave the ledger there – I'll 'ave another look at it later, and see if yer newfangled idea will work."

Matthew smirked contentedly as he passed his father on his way out, and Nathan was reminded painfully of how much his manner had changed over the past year or so. He was like a stranger back home, and father and son now seemed to have nothing to talk about that didn't lead to an argument within less than half a minute. And always the superior manner, and the know-it-all attitude. It wasn't hard to see how he'd come by it, and a lot of good it would do him when his time came to work a frame.

Bradley seemed to read his thoughts. " 'e's a bright un, that lad o' yours," he confirmed, "yer must be very proud of 'im. Lucy's fair taken with 'im, and Rebecca, fer that matter. Let's 'ope 'e's passin' on some better manners ter that brother of 'is as well."

Nathan refrained from pointing out that in reality he had little idea of how Tommy was behaving himself these days. Or, indeed, where. He was missing from the house most evenings, and Nathan was devoting too much paternal energy to his arguments with Matthew to have anything left for checking up on where Tommy spent his time. From time to time he heard snippets of gossip from neighbours about Tommy always being at Jack Cossall's side at meetings around St. Mary's, and about how well Tommy preached the cause there. Not that there seemed to be so many meetings any more, not since the night raids had started, and one thing that Nathan did insist on was that Tommy be home before the ten o'clock chime from St. Mary's Church tower, which could normally be heard all the way down to the Leen. He was even more insistent on this since the curfew had been introduced in April, for there were serious consequencs for anyone found out and about after this time.

Apart from that, Nathan had given up challenging Tommy's actions, words and movements. For one thing, he had his hands full with Lily's poor health and Matthew's newly arrogant attitude towards his family, and for another he didn't want to drive Tommy out of the house, like so many young men of his age around Narrow Marsh seemed to have been by those fathers who still fought to prevent their sons from joining the raiding parties. Nathan still secretly supported what the men were attempting to bring about, but he could never approve of their methods.

"I said yer must be very proud of 'im," repeated Bradley, and Nathan realised that he had been daydreaming again.

"Who?"

"Matthew, of course," replied Bradley, who was beginning to wonder if this was quite such a good idea after all. Still, Nathan was the obvious man when it came to honesty and loyalty.

"Oh . . . yes." Nathan fell silent again, and Bradley pointed to the visitor's chair.

"Sit down Nathan, I want to 'ave a talk with yer. No, don't bother wipin' yer clothes – you'll do as you are. Would yer like a cigar?"

Nathan shook his head, but watched in polite silence as Bradley selected one from the silver box on his office desk, and carefully snipped off the end before lighting it. Bradley waited until he had all but disappeared behind a wall of acrid smoke before he got down to the business in hand.

"We've been very lucky so far, it seems ter me." He knew better than to expect a reply, so he continued. "Only two incidents so far, and no lost production worth talkin' about. The people behind all this trouble evidently feel that they've got no dispute with me. I've always been fair, yer must admit." He paused, and Nathan realised that a response was called for.

"Yer've allus bin fair wi' me, anyroad, an' ter be perfectly 'onest wi' you, Mr Bradley, I've 'ardly 'eard a word said agin yer. Mind yer, nobody in the yard dares say owt bad where you're concerned, not while Lily's in earshot, anyroad. She proper speaks up fer yer, does ar Lily."

"Aye, she's a good 'onest woman, your Lily. Mrs Bradley was only sayin' the other day what a good example she sets ter folks around 'ere. And your Ruth seems to 'ave followed in 'er mother's footsteps, which brings me ter one of the things I was wantin' ter talk ter you about. Yer've 'eard of mi wife's sister, Letitia? She lives up Eastwood way – Amberwood House, to be exact."

"Can't say I 'ave," stalled Nathan, uneasily aware of what might be coming next.

"I'm surprised Matthew 'asn't mentioned the Beardsalls," continued Bradley, undeterred. " 'e's been out there visitin' several times with Lucy and Rebecca, and Letitia's quite taken with 'im, it seems."

" 'e never said owt ter me," said Nathan, "but then 'e don't 'ave a lot ter say fer 'imsen at 'ome."

" 'e makes up for it in our 'ouse!" chortled Bradley. "But I'm strayin' from the point. The thing is that Letitia's lookin' for a good 'onest lass ter train up as a kitchen maid, and Mrs Bradley's told her all about your Ruth. And when Letitia saw 'ow polite and respectable Matthew was – and after all the good things which she'd already 'eard about Ruth – well, yer can see what I'm gettin' at."

"Yer askin' if Ruth's ready ter go inter service?"

"She'd be well looked after, mind – well dressed and properly fed. Ter be 'onest with yer, Nathan, there's been quite a number of girls mentioned already, but Lettie insisted that Mrs Bradley ask about Ruth first. So what about it?"

Nathan shuffled uneasily in the big chair, and the soft leather squeaked under his shifting weight. "It's not that I'm not grateful, Mr Bradley, but it's just not as easy as that any more. Lily's not keepin' in the best of 'ealth these days, an' there's young William ter be looked after, an' ter be perfectly 'onest wi' yer, I'm not sure what we'd do wi'aht Ruth these days. A proper treasure, she is."

"All the more reason why she should get the chance ter make the most of 'erself. Most girls would give their right arm for a position like this one, and I reckon you owe it to 'er, to at least give it a go. I bet I know what Lily'd say."

"Aye, that's the trouble," Nathan replied gloomily, "but she don't know 'ow ill she is most o' the time, an' I'm not sure 'ow long she'd last on 'er own all day long."

"Promise me you'll mention it at least? That'll keep Mrs Bradley quiet – she's on at me all the time, and I've been meanin' ter ask yer fer days."

"Aye, all right," promised Nathan, grudgingly. Before he could rise fully from the chair, Bradley raised a delaying hand.

"No stay there, Nathan; there's summat else. In fact, the main reason I called yer down 'ere. It's about what's got to 'appen 'ere in the future."

" 'ere?" echoed Nathan, at a loss to understand how the future of Bradley's might concern him, unless he was about to be laid off.

"Aye, here. 'ow much longer before the raids come 'ere? They've already hit Solleys and some o' the other big concerns. Like I said before, we've been lucky so far, but 'ow long will that last? According ter what I've been 'earin', there's at least one o' these ne'er-do-wells in every frame room in town."

"Well it ain't me!" protested Nathan, genuinely hurt. Bradley couldn't resist a chuckle.

"Yer daft ha'porth, I'm not sayin' it's you!"

"An' I know that Tommy were a bit rude abaht yer when yer laid 'im off, but 'e's ovver that nah, an' deep dahn 'e's not the sort ter . . ."

"Nathan," interrupted Bradley, "don't get 'et up like that, I'm not blamin' Tommy neither."

"Who then?"

"That's just it. I don't know, and that's where I need your help."

"Me?" Nathan's face froze, a picture of horror and disbelief. "Oh no – not me!"

"Steady on, yer've not 'eard what I'm proposin' yet."

"An' I dun't want ter, beggin' yer pardon Mr Bradley. I'm not one fer peachin' on mi workmates."

"I'm not askin' yer ter do that, Nathan. It's just that if I can find out what the men are complainin' about, maybe I can do something about it, before things get out of 'and, so ter speak."

Nathan laughed ironically. "Beggin' yer pardon again, Mr Bradley, but I can tell yer right nah what all the men in this tahn's complainin' abaht, an' there's nowt you can do abaht it."

"Yer mean more money?"

"Aye, more money. An' there's nowt yer can do, is there?"

"No, not really, ter tell yer the truth," Bradley admitted sadly. "That's one thing everyone in the Association's agreed on. And even if I wanted ter pay more, I couldn't anyway, not with the trade the way it is."

"I know that," Nathan added more sympathetically, "an' I know that yer doin' yer best. I'm right glad I'm workin' fer you an' not some o' the others in the tahn, but I can't peach fer yer, 'onest I can't."

"But surely, Nathan, it's just as much in your interests as mine ter stop the frames gettin' smashed?"

"Aye, yer right there, an' I'd not stand by an' watch that 'appen, yer can be sure o' that. I don't 'old wi' what's bin 'appenin' as far as that's concerned."

"Well then, that's all I'm askin'," argued Bradley, "but I'm not askin' yer ter do it fer nowt. Five shillings a week extra to be General Overseer. 'ow does that sound?"

Nathan was both shocked and confused. Five shillings a week extra was a great deal of money to a man who was lucky to see nine at the end of six days' work – when he could get it – and he suddenly appreciated how frightened and desperate Bradley must be to offer him that much. This made him even more cautious, despite the loyalty he felt to the man who had always shown loyalty to him.

"Look, Mr Bradley, I'll not peach fer yer, an' I'll not tek yer money, but yer can rest assured that no-one's goin' ter smash up yer frames while I'm arahnd. An' if yer want ter know one person who'd like ter see yer ruined, then I'd say that yer did the right thing when yer saw off Stan Cadby. But I'm sayin' no more – for the present, anyroad."

"I knew about Cadby already," confessed Bradley. 'Some say 'e's more mixed up in all this night-time nonsense than is generally known. But there's nowt I can do about 'im except keep 'im off mi premises. It's the ones who're still inside I'm worried about. 'ow can I tell if some o' the others are workin' with 'im, or others like 'im? I need to know if I'm due another night visit from Ned Ludd."

"Who?"

"Nathan, don't pretend yer don't know what I'm talkin' about; everybody knows Ned Ludd's behind all this."

"Never 'eard of 'im, 'onest."

"Neither had I until recently, ter tell yer the truth. I don't think 'e's local, anyway. But let's leave it like this, Nathan; you go 'ome and talk it over with your Lily, and remember to ask about young Ruth, mind, and you and me'll 'ave another chat in a day or two. Just think it over, and talk ter Lily. That's fair enough, isn't it? Any decent man would want ter talk things over with 'is wife, I know that, and I also know that you and 'er are a good close couple. So ask 'er before yer make any final decision; after all, it's 'er family's future as well. I'll call yer back down 'ere in another couple o' days, all right?"

"Aye, all right," Nathan agreed reluctantly, glad to put off making any hasty decision.

As Nathan politely and quietly closed the door behind him on his way out, Bradley smiled with satisfaction. "If you're 'alf the woman I think you are, Lily Slack, I reckon I've got both mi answers already."

"Fer God's sake, woman, let me be!"

Lily recoiled as if she'd been stung. They'd been married for over eighteen years, and he'd never spoken to her like that, not once. Nor did he normally take the Good Lord's name in vain. She stood uncertainly by the side of the table, the hand she'd stretched out to him in a comforting gesture hanging in midair. The tears welled in her eyes, and Nathan looked up in time to see her lip quiver. Mortified, he lurched from his chair and crushed her to him awkwardly.

"Sorry, lass. Sorry."

"What's up, Nathan? Yer've not touched a bite o' food since yesterday, yer was mutterin' things in yer sleep last night, an' poor Matthew's scared ter open 'is mouth lately."

"Poor Matthew opens 'is mouth often enough at Bradley's, from what I've bin 'earin'. 'e's well enough thought of there, anyroad. Mebbe 'e should get 'is meals there regular."

There had been the predictable confrontation around the tea table when Matthew announced that he had been invited to take supper with the Bradleys, to explain his new idea for the ledgers. Lily had sided with him, of course, and had marvelled at how he was 'gerrin' on in the world'. Nathan had a shrewd suspicion that this was another ploy by Bradley to get him over to his side, and he resented Bradley using his own family against him. He also found it hard not to side with Tommy when he began verbally berating Matthew for being a traitor to the cause.

Somehow he'd kept the peace between them, although only at the expense of his appetite, and as usual Tommy had taken this as a sign that he, too, was 'in wi' the bosses'. What would Tommy say when he heard the latest? Nathan knew he had to put Bradley's proposals to Lily that evening, and he'd waited until the boys were out of the house. He would have liked Ruth out of the way, too, but she just sidled around as usual. Wherever Lily went, Ruth was her constant shadow. 'Little Lily', they called her in the yard.

"Is it Bradley's?"

"What?" He seemed to spend half his life lost in his own thoughts these days.

"Summat's botherin' yer – I can see that. Yer won't tell me 'cos yer dun't want me worryin', although the Good Lord alone knows why not. 'usbands an' wives is supposed ter share their worries, yer know. Yer looked after me right prahd when I were poorly, burram better nah. I want ter share yer burdens, Nathan, like a good wife should. If yer've lost yer work, just tell me. We'll manage somehow, an' it'll be better than 'avin' yer all quiet an' miserable like this."

Nathan almost laughed out loud, but he could see the pain in her face and he realised that the truth could only come as a blessed relief to her, whatever further misery it meant for him.

"Dun't tek on, lass; I've not lost mi work. In fact, I've bin offered a step-up."

"A step-up? Oh Nathan, that's right good news!" She was about to clap her hands but a fit of coughing got the better of her. Ruth rushed over, and together they lowered Lily into a chair. Ruth brought a cloth for her chin, then looked back quizzically at Nathan.

"Dad – there's bad news as well, ain't there?"

He had to smile. Thrteen years old and you could no more fool her than you could her mother. "Not fer you there ain't, young lady. Yer gunner live in a big fine 'ouse in the country, wi' the well-ter-do."

Ruth looked as if she'd just been smacked in the face. "I'm not goin'!"

"Oh yes you are, mi gel." Lily had recovered sufficiently to take in what Nathan had said, and another of her dreams was about to come true. She struggled out of the chair, as if to emphasise the importance of her words. "It's the best thing yer can be offered if yer a young girl in ar class. Yer'll be taught the finest manners, an' yer'll mebbe get ter see a bit o' the world. The Beardsalls is a respectable family, not like some yer can get. It's the chance of a lifetime, mi gel, an' yer goin'!"

Ruth shook her head vigorously in denial, as tears of anger and betrayal rolled freely down her reddening cheeks. "Mam, yer can't do this! I've allus looked after yer proper, 'aven't I? I've allus bin there whenever yer've needed owt. Why are yer sendin' me away? Yer don't love me any more; yer can't, else yer wouldn't be doin' this ter me!"

"Ruth, o' course I still love yer – don't be silly. We all love yer, but we can't stand in yer way any longer. Come 'ere, yer daft ha'porth, give us a big cuddle an' let's start workin' aht what yer'll need ter tek wi' yer."

Ruth backed away from her mother's outstretched arms, her head still shaking in rejection and disbelief. "No! No! I won't go – I won't!" She somehow managed to slip past the pair of them as they tried to comfort her, and she got the door open despite the stinging tears which were half blinding her. She ran, screaming, into the yard and as they stood in the doorway she had just left, Nathan made to follow her, but Lily held his arm.

"Leave 'er be, Nathan, she's only gone ter the Needhams. Alice'll see to 'er fer nah. As fer later, you leave 'er ter me."

Nathan suddenly realised what had been puzzling him. " 'ow did yer know it were the Beardsalls?"

Lily smiled one of her satisfied smiles. "Nathan Slack, I may 'ave bin ill, but I've not lost mi senses altogether. We've bin talkin' abaht Ruth goin' inter service these two years past, an' Catherine Bradley's made no secret o' the fact that 'er sister wants first refusal. Yer've bin in a funny mood ever since yer come in yesterday, an' Matthew said as 'ow Bradley 'ad asked ter see yer. Nah, am I right?"

"Aye, yer dead right, as usual. But shouldn't we 'ave bin talkin' abaht it fust, afore lettin' Ruth tek on so like that?"

"There's nowt ter talk abaht, leastways, nowt that's not bin said already. An' we agreed that once I were back on mi feet an' back ter mi old self, Ruth'd get 'er chance."

"Aye, but that's just it, yer not back ter yer old self, are yer? Yer 'ad one o' yer bad turns just nah."

"Stuff an' nonsense! Just gorra tickle in mi throat, that's all. I'm allus the same in this dry weather."

And worse in the wet weather, thought Nathan, but he kept his silence. He'd lost the fight before it had begun, and he knew it, not that anyone ever stood a chance when Lily had the bit between her teeth. He was wondering how to steer the conversation back to his other problem, but he needn't have bothered.

"So what's this step-up yer was talkin' abaht?"

"Oh yeah – that. General Overseer, but I 'aven't said I'll tek it, mind."

"Yer'll tek it or get mi big brush across yer ear!" quipped Lily with a teasing grin.

"Aye, well, mebbe that'd be berrer than General Overseer just at the moment."

She was puzzled, and abandoned the mock severity.

" 'ow come? Yer'll get more money, surely?"

"Oh aye, five bob a week more, but that's not the point."

"Well I don't know what other point there could be. 'ow many nights 'ave we laid awake wonderin' if we can really afford ter move ter the new 'ouse? 'ow many times 'ave you come 'ome at the end o' the week an' thanked the Good Lord that we'll 'ave food fer another week ter come? Dun't tell me that five bob a week's not the point, Nathan Slack, or I really will tan yer wi' mi brush!"

"I dun't need you ter tell me 'ow important five bob is, course I dun't," retorted Nathan sullenly, "an' I 'ain't forgot the new 'ouse. It's what I've got ter do forrit that bothers me."

"Everybody knows what an overseer does – even me," said Lily, tetchily, "an' it's 'igh time yer got yer just rewards fer all them years o' loyalty yer've given Robert Bradley. There's not a man in this yard would begrudge you a step-up, an' just like wi' Matthew an' Ruth, it's God's doin'. I can't understand what's got inter yer lately, Nathan. 'aven't yer got the stomach ter gerron in the world fer the benefit of yer family any more; is tharrit?"

"Don't be so damned stupid, woman!" He was close to exploding again, and as she stepped back a pace she feared for the first time in their relationship that he might be changing from the man she'd married to one who was just like the rest of them. There was an awkward silence, and Nathan looked down at his boots in shame.

"Yer see 'ow it's got me, lass? I'm sorry; I shouldn't be shoutin' at yer like that."

"No, yer shouldn't, but it's not like you, an' 'appen yer've got yer reasons. But there's still summat else botherin' yer, ain't there?"

"No. Well, yes . . . leastways . . ."

She reached out and took his hand. "What 'aven't yer told me?"

"Nowt. Not really, anyroad."

She clicked her tongue the way she always did when exasperated. "Then why 'aven't yer said yes, afore 'e gives the chance ter somebody else?"

Nathan's short laugh was a hollow one which contained no humour. " 'e'll not do that; there's no-one else 'e can trust."

"Wharrabaht Sam Pinkney? 'e's a God-fearin' man, and an 'ard worker, an' 'e's bin a journeyman longer than you. Yer'll need ter watch that yer don't get too prahd, Nathan. 'ow many times d'yer need ter be asked?"

"Yer dun't know what 'e's askin', that's just the point."

"Well, tell me then, instead o' carryin' on like a daft lad."

" 'e's wantin' me ter tell on the others, that's what!" If Nathan was expecting some outraged reaction, he was disappointed.

"An' why not? That's an overseer's job, ain't it?"

"Not just ter do wi' the work – ter do wi' the meetin's an' suchlike."

"But yer dun't go ter meetin's."

He sighed as patiently as he could. "O' course I dun't. But I gets to 'ear who does. There's lots o' things I could tell, things I 'ear bein' said. The men trust me as well, dun't yer see? 'ow could I respect miself if I started tellin' on them ter Bradley?"

"These things you 'ear, is it abaht the cause, an' all this wickedness?"

"Yer can call it wickedness if yer like, but ter me, it's mostly just 'onest men as can't tek any more worries. It's all right fer us, lass, it's allus bin all right fer us, ever since all this bother fust started. An' I'll not deny that the latest trouble – all the fightin' an' raidin' an' suchlike – is bein' stirred up bi men as I've no time fer. But a lot of 'em that's gerrin' caught up in it is decent men, an' some of 'em is men I've worked wi', an' still do. I'll not do the bosses' dirty work, not fer five shillin's a week, not even fer five sovereigns a week."

She shook her head disbelievingly. "Next Sunday, when we go ter chapel, yer'd best sit in another pew, Nathan Slack, 'cos you an' me's worshippin' a different God."

He was shocked. "What's God got ter do wi' owt?"

"Everythin'. You an' me's allus agreed, up ter nah, anyroad, that Robert Bradley's a fine example of a Christian employer. Now 'e needs the 'elp of other good Christian men, an' the one who's best placed to 'elp 'im – the one whose family 'e's 'elped ter raise up in the world – won't lift a finger in 'is hour o' need. Yer should be ashamed that 'e even needed ter offer yer five shillin's; or was yer waitin' fer thirty pieces o' silver?"

He sank down in his chair. "D'yer really think that abaht me?"

She had felt deep remorse as soon as the words had left her lips, and she reached down and ran her hand through his tousled hair. "No, love, no I dun't, an' I'm right sorry fer sayin' that. It's just that I feel so strong, deep dahn, like, that we should be 'elpin' Bradley all we can. 'e's done 'is best fer us, an' 'e's set a fine example ter the other bosses, an' I remember that 'enson feller sayin' in that square that the cause 'ad no quarrel wi' the decent bosses."

"Aye, an' if 'enson were still in control o' what's bin 'appenin', we'd not be 'avin' this conversation. Burre's not. Some feller called Ludd's tekken ovver, an' the likes o' Cadby an' Collishaw are right in wi' 'im. A fine cause they're likely ter be fightin' fer!"

"All the more reason why good Christian men should be standin'

agin 'em. Soldiers fer Christ are more use than them ruffians up at
the barracks. One of 'em pressed his unwanted attentions on young
Rosie Plummer, did yer know that?"

Nathan resisted the temptation to point out that whatever a
soldier might have pressed on Rosie Plummer was unlikely to have
been unwanted, and stuck to the main point. "Yer right abaht them
sojers. They're only mekkin' it worse, an' mekkin' fools o' themsens
at the same time. They ain't caught a single man yet, I 'ear."

"Like I said, Nathan, only the likes o' you can 'elp Bradley, an'
it's yer Christian duty ter try. Look what 'e's done fer Matthew, an'
nah Ruth. An' wharrabaht yer Christian duty to us? D'yer think I
want ter stay in this yard all mi life?"

He studied her face, then stood up and took her hands in his.
"You've changed yer tune all of a sudden. Are yer tellin' me yer willin'
ter go at long last?"

She shook her head despairingly. "It's a good job fer you that
I came along, Nathan Slack, 'cos what yer know abaht women yer
could gerron the tip of a darnin' needle. I've allus wanted ter gerraht
o' the yard; it's just that the woman o' the 'ouse 'as ter mek the best
o' what God gives 'er. God gev me you, an' where you go, I go. It'd
be so much nicer aht o' the yard, that's all."

Nathan held her to him, and gently kissed the top of her head.

"An' I reckon yer've made the best o' me that any woman coulda
made. I'm not up ter much on mi own, an' that's a fact."

"I dunno abaht that; yer up ter General Overseer, ain't yer?"

It was the knowing, triumphant smile of a seductive twenty-
year-old, and Nathan was helpless in its path. "All right, you win.
General Overseer it is."

His lips pressed once more into her whitening hair, but his
eyes gazed far away across the top of her head, into the gathering
storm clouds.

CHAPTER NINE

Turning the screw

"YOU MAY as well tell us without any more playing around, because me and my companion here, we know that you know. And what's more important, the authorities know that you know."

Clarrie Sharp sniffled more loudly into her cloth, pausing only from time to time to wring her hands on her apron. Ben Sharp stood behind the chair she was sitting on, while the two official-sounding strangers loomed in front of her, the taller man's head almost touching the cottage ceiling.

Conon and Baker had been well briefed for their trip to Arnold. On their first morning, after reporting for duty at the office of the Town Clerk, they'd been directed to the second-floor office of the Superintendent of the Watch, where they'd been given a full account of what had been learned from Ackroyd. The next morning at around eleven, the coachman had dropped them off in the village with directions to Thomas Bolton's premises; before they alighted, Baker had paid the coach fare and asked for a document of receipt, which Conon had cautiously pocketed before Baker could alter it in his favour.

Bolton had lost no time in offering them a warming glass of port wine, wishing them all the best for their enterprise, and directing them on to the Sharps' neat but modest cottage halfway down Church Lane. They had been there for over half an hour, declining repeated offers of tea and parsnip scones from Clarrie and ignoring the hostile stares of her husband Ben, as they tried every approach they knew to get the all-important information from her without giving away just how important it was.

"Like I said, there were that much noise goin' on that I couldn't rightly 'ear their voices."

"Mrs Sharp," Conon persisted with as much quiet menace as he thought appropriate in the circumstances, "that's not what you told some of your neighbours, in particular a Mr Simon Ackroyd."

"Simon's all right, but 'e's that full o' drink these days that yer can't really trust a thing 'e sez, 'onest."

It was Baker's turn to apply the pressure. "Look, missus, from what we've 'eard, this geezer Ackroyd were as sober as ninepence till them bullies turned the village over, so I reckon that you're tellin' us a little naughty there."

"My wife doesn't tell lies!" Ben Sharp protested.

"Pardon me, sir," responded Conon in the tone he had perfected over the years with junior officers for whom he had no respect, "but it's your wife we're talking to, not you. Unless, of course, you can tell us who this gentleman might be."

"Ben dun't know nothin', 'onest!" insisted Clarrie urgently. "I were free fer courtin' when I took up wi' Ben an' even if it were this feller yer reckon it were, well that were long afore I took ter courtin' Ben."

Conon sighed with irritation. "I don't know how long you intend to keep up this pretence, but I can tell you that we are authorised to hand over five gold sovereigns to anyone who can supply the name of anybody involved in the events of that night. And since we were reliably informed that you'd been telling everyone in the village that you'd actually been engaged to be married to one of them some years ago, we thought we'd begin with you. On the other hand, there are severe penalties for withholding such information."

Clarrie began sniffling again, and Ben came to her assistance.

"Look, like she said, it were noisy. The bastards was tryin' ter smash us door in, an' they was all shoutin' at once. It were in the middle o' the night an' all, so . . ."

"We've heard that excuse already!" thundered Conon, his face colouring with fury. Baker placed a warning hand on Conon's arm, and the latter reverted to the breathing exercises he'd been taught by the drill sergeant who'd encouraged him to box, and later trained him to control his murderous anger. Baker took up the conversation as Ben scuttled out through the front door.

"Look, maybe it was this geezer and maybe it wasn't. Just give us 'is name anyway and we'll be on our way rejoicin'. If you're right, you'll get your money, and if you're wrong, well the good gentleman can tell us that for 'imself, now can't 'e?"

Clarrie twisted miserably in her seat. "I can't tell yer, 'cos I'm not sure, an' I've 'eard wharrappens ter people when them sojers get 'old of 'em. Yer can both stay 'ere all day an' I'll still not give yer 'is name."

"I used to be a soldier," replied Conon coldly, "but at least I did my duty for King and Country. You, madam, are serving neither with your stubborn attitude, but this does not entitle you to insult the memory of those who died defending the likes of you. Good day to you!"

Conon turned smartly on his heel and all but marched out of the cottage, an action somewhat inhibited by the need to stoop under the lintel on his way out. Baker looked back apologetically at Clarrie. "Sorry, missus, but he can get a bit excited, like, when someone speaks ill of 'is fallen comrades. I'd better get after 'im, before 'e does sumfin' silly. Mornin' to ya."

He caught up with Conon a few yards down the lane, and the latter was about to fill the embarrassed silence with an apology when they heard a hiss from behind a tall yew hedge that bordered a narrow track running at an angle to the lane. They turned their heads simultaneously, and were surprised to see Ben Sharp beckoning them into his hiding place.

"In yer come, only I dun't want no-one seein' me talkin' ter yer; no offence, mind, but there's still a lot o' feelin' abaht wharrappened at Jack Westley's funeral. 'e were a local man, yer know."

Not having the faintest idea of what he was talking about, and having even less desire to find out, Conon maintained an impassive silence, and it was left to Baker to sense success in the offing.

"That's all right, me friend, we knows 'ow ya feel. Nasty business all round and no mistake, specially since your good lady seems to 'ave 'ad time for one of 'em in the past."

"Aye, well in the past," growled Ben, "but that didn't stop the bastard tryin' ter see 'er again when 'e came up 'ere on his bloody flour cart twice a week. I finally 'ad it aht wi' 'im, an' knocked the silly bogger inter the middle o' next week wi' a straight left 'ander. We never seen 'im no more, till that night when 'e come up 'ere wi' all them others."

Upon learning of the man's apparent prowess with his fists, Conon began to show signs of renewed interest in his story, but Baker sent him their well-rehearsed silent signal to leave matters to him, while as far as Ben knew, the friendly little man with the ginger hair was merely scratching his head.

"Sounds as if ya gave a good account of yourself," Baker commented. "No wonder 'e came back and tried to ruin ya. All the more reason for 'elpin' us put 'im in irons. You'd be doin' yourself a favour as well, like."

Ben's furtive eyes looked from one to the other of them, then back down the track he had come along. "Five sovereigns, yer said?"

"Ah, yes," coughed Baker cagily, "that was if your good lady give us the name. As it's you, then I'm afraid it's only three. All to do wiv 'quality of intelligence', as our boss in London calls it."

"All right," sighed Ben. "Times is tough enough at the moment, an' three sovs is three sovs. The bastard's name's Luke Johnson, an' 'e used ter work fer Baxter's Bakery in Barker Gate, in the tahn. I did 'ear as 'e'd gorranother livin' nah, but like as not they'll tell yer at Baxters where yer'll find 'im."

"Thank you, kind sir," chirped Baker as he counted out three sovereigns into Ben's hand. "It was a pleasure talkin' wiv you and your good lady."

Without another word, Ben pocketed the coins and scurried off back down the track. Baker grinned across at Conon, handed him one of the two remaining sovereigns and pocketed the other.

"For the next stage of this little job, we do it my way, agreed?"

Conon grinned back at him and nodded.

"You've got a damned impudence, is all I can say. You take over the cause, turn the men against any possible peaceful settlement, steal the name I came up with, and now you come to me for help when you've run out of ideas."

Henson had waited knowingly for this moment, but took no pleasure in it. Cadby, on the other hand, was pleased, and not a little relieved, that the wiser and more experienced man was still even speaking to him, because he needed his help, and badly.

The raids had recently intensified in number and ferocity, and even a substantial increase in the size of the local Watch, a rise in recruitment into the district militias and the dispatch of more royal troops – in the form of the returning Scots Greys, along with a contingent drawn from that most elite of guards regiments, the Blues – had failed to stem the flow of nightly outrages against frame owner and stocking knitter alike. Indeed, it seemed that the more troops the authorities committed to the suppression of the cause, the more arrogant and confident its supporters became.

A typical example had been a recent raid into villages south of the Trent, conducted by St. Mary's men with the assistance of local guides and sympathisers. Twenty frames had been smashed in Clifton, while on the same night a further fourteen had gone under the hammer in nearby Ruddington. Mounted messengers had been sent into the town by the terrified defenders, and within an hour or so the bridge crossing the Trent had been secured by a combination of hussars and local yeomanry, hoping to catch the raiders on their return. However, the lookouts, whom the raiders had learned to employ to good effect, had alerted their comrades to what lay in waiting for them, and they made short work of commandeering several boats moored under the river cliffs at Clifton, crossing the river by the swirling narrows on the river bend at Beeston, firing several pistols into the air in triumph, then dispersing into the western approaches to the town on the Trent's north bank.

Pistols had also featured in a raid closer to home, at Bensons of Carter Gate, in which eight frames were destroyed in as many minutes, but so silently that no sound of what was going on had been audible even in the street. The next night it had been the turn of Noble of Radford, whose premises were entered at six in the morning just as the lady of the house was preparing breakfast. She had been held at gunpoint and eventually pistol-whipped to suppress her screams, while the body of the invading force broke four frames in the upper room, using a sword in the process to cut all the threads already wound into one of them ahead of the day's intended work. On their return downstairs, they discovered that neighbours drawn by the screaming had attempted to fasten the main door from the outside. Undeterred, those inside had broken out by kicking in the door panels, raced into the street armed with pistols and, threatening death to anyone who attempted to follow them, had made good their escape before anyone in the Park Barracks had even been alerted.

The military were even more embarrassed by an incident the same week in Basford, when a Mr Barnes had made good use of his nephew being an officer in the town militia in order to secure the presence on his premises of two infantrymen armed with muskets, whose apparently simple task had been to guard access to his frames in the upper room. Unfortunately, their host had made them too comfortable, and lulled by the ale supplied to them, and by the warmth of the fire beside which they were now comfortably ensconced, they were too stupefied to react quickly enough when a group of seven raiders rushed them, seized their muskets, and smashed four frames in the upstairs room before cackling off victoriously with the muskets themselves and enough shot to fight a minor military engagement.

And on it went, with the authorities seemingly powerless to stop it. As the outrages became more brazen, so the responses seemed to be less. Following the loss of nine frames in the relatively distant northern village of Linby – north of Hucknall and almost within sight of the Newstead country seat of local peer Lord Byron – an alarmed frame owner from Kimberley, to the northwest, sought to bring his valuable wide frame into the relative safety of the town on a horse and cart which was attacked in broad daylight near Aspley by a large man wearing a goatskin over his face as a disguise, and wielding a large hammer with which the frame was rapidly demolished before its owner's eyes.

More ominously, in the town itself, a Mr Harvey of Highcross Street had been awakened at five in the morning by a man armed with a pistol, who had climbed a ladder and entered the upper chamber of the house via an open window. He in turn let in four companions who smashed five valuable warp-lace frames before they all escaped down the ladder. A local woman raised the hue and cry and was fired at with a pistol, which mercifully missed. But the most disturbing aspect of the entire episode had been the fact that none of the neighbours who ran out upon hearing the noise saw the need to apprehend the men descending the ladder, due to the presence at its foot of what appeared to be a detachment of armed troops. Only after they had all run off laughing had it become apparent that the 'sojers' had in fact been 'Ludd's men', disguised in stolen uniforms and carrying stolen muskets.

It was the very success of these, and similar, escapades, with no apparent resistance from the authorities and no sign of any response to their grievances, which had made the leaders nervous. While some, and perhaps the majority, were content to keep up the raiding which had become a nightly pleasure of sorts, and from which they were profiting handsomely in money, goods and opportunities for sexual and other assaults to gratify their violent appetites, there were others who could see that their activities were having no effect, and who feared that before long the cause might dribble to a halt because it was achieving nothing. If this happened, reasoned some of its ringleaders, the resulting slackening of tongues might result in their being identified. This supplied them, in turn, with a motive to keep up the momentum, preferably with some sort of truce or official pardon as part of the final agreement, before the men finally lost their taste for lawlessness. To achieve this, they needed to go back to the man who seemed to possess the necessary political ideas and connections.

"Yer right abaht one thing," asserted Cadby. "You started all this, an' the least yer can do is give us an 'and ter finish it."

Henson stared him out scornfully. "No doubt you're only concerned with saving your own neck, but a lot of innocent people have got mixed up with what you've been promoting, and if only for their sake, I'll tell you what I know. The authorities are not interested in meeting with me, or anyone associated with me, to discuss any sort of truce. In fact, as you probably know, Parliament recently brought in new laws against frame breaking."

"They already 'ad laws," Cadby objected. "What do they need new uns for?"

Henson glared back angrily. "What do you care about laws, Cadby? They only get in the way of how you choose to live your life." His expression softened as he turned to the others gathered in the room with them. "The rest of you might be interested to learn that what you've been doing almost every night for the past year could, until recently, have been punished by what they call 'transportation'. That's a trip to a prison farm in Australia. But now the government's replaced that with the death penalty. Carry on following this man here and you could finish up on the end of a rope!"

The silence was palpable, and it was Jack Cossall who broke it. "We can't go back nah, gallows or no gallows. We asked ter see you 'cos you know best 'ow ter mek the authorities listen."

Henson sighed. "And like I said, you've got a cheek, all of you. I told you a year back how best to do it, and you chose not to listen. The authorities won't give in to violence; they'll just throw more soldiers at the problem."

"Then we're fucked," responded Cossall.

"Not necessarily," said Henson. "The town aldermen aren't really the people who run this town, as I'm sure you've had occasion to learn over the years. There's a lot of political power in money and position, and the people in this town best supplied with that are the people you work for, or in some cases, used to work for."

"The bosses?" enquired Cadby scornfully. "Them's the bastards we're aimin' at!"

"Indeed," replied Henson patiently, "but so far your aim has been woefully misdirected. You've been taking it out on village middlemen, local frameworkers and small-time merchants. You've not yet really attacked the big names in the trade – they're the ones who run this town, in the sense that they control the mayor and aldermen. In fact, many of them are aldermen. Get to them, and you get to the authorities. Through them you get to London."

"We've already done Solley and Bradley," argued Cadby, "an' nowt's 'appened yet."

"That," suggested Henson acidly, "is because all you've done is throw bricks at their windows and damage the odd frame here and there. If you used your brains and your undoubted influence in St. Mary's more intelligently, you'd realise that you can affect them more if you remove their livelihood completely."

" 'ow do we do that – burn dahn their places?" asked Luke Johnson, for whom this had all become a little difficult to grasp after his second quart of ale.

"No," replied Henson more patiently. "You persuade their

workers to down tools."

There was a stony silence, eventually filled by Cadby. "A fat lot o' good that did John Blackner an' 'is friends. Is that the best yer can come up wi'?"

"I didn't think you'd agree with me," admitted Henson, "because you've no real appreciation of the commercial forces at work here. There were only four of them when John Blackner and his friends took that bold stance, and Rankin was able to carry on without them. If every framework knitter in the town did the same as they did, the employers wouldn't last a month before they went running to the authorities for some sort of settlement."

Cadby snorted. "They'd run a lot faster if we burned dahn their buildings."

It was Henson's turn to make a derisive noise, as he eased his haunches from the table he'd been seated on and reached for his travelling cape. "I'm wasting my time with you, Cadby. But the rest of you, ask yourselves this before you follow this fool to the gallows; if you burn down all the hosiery houses in the town, where will you all work when, and if, the employers come round to your point of view?"

The total silence which greeted his departure from the Half Moon may have afforded him satisfaction of a sort, but his face was troubled and he wished that at least one amongst them could sense the futility of the course that they were on – a course which might one day cost some of them their lives. He turned his face against the spring shower, then bowed his head as he strode down Carter Gate, trying to persuade himself that none of this had really been his fault.

Cadby was quick to reclaim the initiative as soon as the door to the back room had closed behind Henson. "Right, you all 'eard wharre said - we've gorrer 'it the big uns again."

"But like 'e also said," added Jack Cossall, "we've gorrer mek it count fer summat this time, an' stoppin' work's only gunner mek it worse. If we've got no money comin' in, the women's gunner turn agin us an' all, then what?"

" 'e's right," Cadby agreed quickly. "Let's mek a list nah, an' agree when it's gunner 'appen, an' what we're gunner do. Only there's somethin' yer've all gorrer know fust."

As they waited in silence, Cadby was gratified to note how much power he could still command. He made his words as dramatic as he could. "As you all know, I've got mi contacts all ovver the place, an' lately I've bin 'earin' as 'ow the bosses 'ave got themsens peaches in the workforces who's gerrin' money fer warnin' 'em afore owt 'appens. Solley's got one, I'm told, an' Cossons an' Mellors." He looked pointedly at Jack Cossall, then added, "An' Bradley, it seems."

Cossall stared back at him with a blank look. "So?"

"So just guess who Bradley's peach is? Nathan Bloody Slack, that's who. Yer'd best get that son of 'is aht o' yer platoon before yer try owt on Bradley's, else son'll go peachin' ter father, an' we'll all be fucked."

Cossall was shocked and hurt in equal measure. "The young un's got no time forris dad, 'e's told me that often enough. An' 'e's proved 'is loyalty ter the cause time an' time again, you know that, Stan."

"I know 'e's gorra big mouth at meetin's, but the way I 'ear things, 'e's done nowt as would risk 'is neck when it comes ter raids. When were the last time 'e came on a night trip, then?"

" 'e'd like ter, I know, but 'is dad won't lerrim aht that late."

There was a guffaw of derisive laughter around the room, and Cadby's was the loudest. "Jesus Bloody Christ, Jack, is yer platoon full o' pansies as need their parents' permission afore they come aht at night?"

"Course bloody not, it's just that, well, wi' Tommy yer gorrer go careful, like yer said, 'cos of 'is dad an' all . . ."

"Fust thing we do, then," interjected Cadby deviously, "is test 'ow good yer team is. We'll start wi' the biggest mealy-mouthed bastard o' the lot, Bradley 'imsen. All 'is frames in broad daylight, Nathan Slack or no fuckin' Nathan Slack. But afore yer can do that, we're gunner 'ave ter test the son – see which side 'e's on when the shit starts flyin'. But yer can leave that ter me, as usual."

Cossall looked apprehensive. "Steady on, Stan, there's nowt wrong wi' the lad – it's just 'is dad that's the worry, specially nah that 'e's Bradley's peach."

Cadby beamed back, delighted to be settling an old score. "You just worry abaht the son, Jack. Leave the old man ter me."

As the meeting broke up, one of those who had been in attendance weaved his way carefully along Fisher Gate. It was a muggy evening now that the showers had returned, and Luke Johnson wished he'd stuck to his one usual quart. As it was, he could still walk a straight line, but he'd be glad to reach his home in Pepper Alley, down Narrow Marsh, all the same. As he approached the Plumptre Hospital he became dimly aware of the argument going on as he drew close to a doorway on his left.

"Get off me, ya big ox! I've done me turn for the day, and there's no encores just for you. So get your sticky paws off me feathers and piss off!" The woman sounded more angry than frightened, but the little man who was obviously the source of her annoyance clearly didn't want to take no for an answer.

"Aw come on, Belle, just a few minutes. It was me what got ya the turn in the first place. Don't I always do the right fing by me best dancer?"

"Yeah, but don't ya always expect special favours in return? You're just an old goat, Isaac Blunt, and the answer's still no."

The man pulled the woman even further into the recessed doorway, and as she looked around in exasperation, she appeared to see the approaching local for the first time.

"Hey you – mister – ya couldn't 'elp a lady out in 'er hour of need, now could ya?"

"Oh fuck me," exclaimed the man in the doorway with her, adding, as he scuttled off down the street in a flurry of frock coat and top hat, "I'm not ready for the likes of 'im. I'll see ya back at the theatre tomorrow."

The woman laughed scornfully after him, then pulled her rescuer towards her by the front of his jacket. "Thank ya, kind sir; you've saved an innocent lady from a difficult fix. Only 'e's me theatrical booker, ya see, so I can't just call in the authorities every time 'e gets a bit frisky, now can I?"

"Theatre?"

The woman chuckled, throwing back her head and removing her bonnet so as to allow her long fair hair to cascade over the feathered collar of the velvet jacket.

"Sorry love, where's me manners? Belle Carson, actress, dancer and acrobat queen of the stage. You'll see me name on them posters outside the Royal next week. Just arrived in this lovely town of yours to be in that new production, and me lodgin's is down 'ere in Red Lion Square. That greasy goat ya just saw off, Isaac Blunt if you've 'eard of 'im, 'e manages all the big names in Lunnun. 'e was meant to walk me 'ome, seein' as 'ow we've 'eard that this place can get a bit lively of a night-time, but 'e's only after the one fing, if ya get me meanin'. 'e's not a nice genl'man like you."

" 'e's right abaht these streets, though. Yer shouldn't be walkin' dahn 'ere on yer own at this time o' night."

"That's what we 'eard from the theatre folk. Ya couldn't see your way to escorting a lady back to the safety of 'er lodgings yerself, could ya? Only, a strong young man like you on me arm'll see 'em all off, like ya did Blunt."

They were nearly at Red Lion Square and he had to go that way to reach Narrow Marsh, but uncertainty still showed in Luke's face. Belle moved closer towards him, and as she brushed her gloved hand lightly across the crotch of his trousers, he caught the whiff of an exotic perfume.

"I'd be ever so grateful, and when Belle's grateful to a genl'man, all sorts of nice fings can 'appen."

It was too good a chance to miss, and he relented. "All right, then, seein' as yer a bit on yer own aht 'ere."

She giggled girlishly and steered him by the arm into Red Lion Square, where a tall rooming house dominated one corner on the opposite side. They slipped into the side alley entrance, and with a light peck on his cheek she urged him through the ground floor door, down the inside passage and into a room on the right-hand side.

He barely had time to register that the door to the room appeared to have opened of its own accord, when he was seized by two burly arms covered by a frock coat and whirled round to face the centre of the shabby, unfurnished room, in which stood a mountain of a man with a scowling face and a large bald head, who stepped forward, grabbed him by the throat and lifted him clean off the floor with one hand.

"I presume I have the pleasure of choking the living daylights out of Luke Johnson, former flour cart driver and now enemy of law and order?"

Luke Johnson could hardly be expected to reply, struggling as he was for his next breath, and the tall man continued.

"Alfred Conon's my name, not that we'll be acquainted for long. The gentleman behind you is my associate Frederick Baker, and I see you've already met Miss Smollett, the third member of our expeditionary force into this shit-hole of a town. I'm perfectly happy to give up our names since we're here on official business, and you might not be alive for much longer, anyway."

A gurgling noise was all that could be heard from the man in his grip, whose face was beginning to turn blue.

"But where's my manners? You can't introduce yourself while I'm blocking your windpipe, can you? So relax for a moment; but only for a moment."

Conon removed the grip he had been maintaining with his right hand, and almost immediately delivered a driving left-handed blow under Johnson's ribcage which threatened to split it in two, and sent him sprawling to the floor, vomiting up much of the ale he had consumed earlier. Stepping carefully around the vomit, Conon loomed over him and aimed a kick at his left kneecap which wrung an agonised scream from Johnson.

"Now then," encouraged Baker from the rear corner of the room, carefully removing the frock coat and top hat which had to be returned to the Superintendent of the Watch the next morning, "a few easy answers to a few easy questions, and then me friend here'll be instructed to stop. On the other 'and . . ."

The carriage clattered and jolted up the rutted Turnpike road from Nuthall and on through Kimberley, the grimy town far behind them. Tangled hedgerows on either side reached out in search of the pale autumn sunlight. Above the dead husks of the wild brambles to the left, Nathan caught sight of a church tower, and he leaned forward to touch Matthew's arm, and pointed towards it with a look of enquiry.

Matthew cast it a casual glance. "St. Lawrence's in Heanor," he said. "You can see it better from the Ilkeston Road," before turning his body fully away from Nathan once more, and resuming his easy chatter with Lomas, Bradley's coachman, seated behind and slightly above him.

Lost for anything else to say, Nathan looked back down at the floor of the bucking carriage, then out towards Hucknall Woods away off to his right. He looked everywhere except at the other side of the carriage, where Ruth sat rigidly beside her older brother, sniffling without pause and trying not to disgrace herself by being sick all down the outside of the open carriage. Nathan tugged again at the new and unfamiliar collar which threatened to cut a slice out of his neck, and silently cursed the weakness which had led him thus far.

Lomas had arrived at nine that morning, and the whole yard had spilled out into Narrow Marsh to see the fine carriage which had arrived to take 'Little Lily' to her new life. Kitchen maid to Sir Francis and Lady Beardsall at Amberwood House, one of the finest modern mansions in the county. There had been many good wishes, and a little unwanted coarse advice, but all were sad to see her go.

All, apparently, except Lily herself, who had stoutly maintained her determination to the end, smothering Ruth's tears and pleas for a last-minute change of heart with a stern reminder that it was all God's doing, and that she would be showing her ingratitude to the Lord if she didn't take the wonderful opportunity He had given her. Lily couldn't go with them because of her poor health, and because of William. And because the minute the coach had pulled out of sight she had run back into the house and wept so hard that she eventually passed out on the floor, and it would not have been seemly to do so in public.

It was coming on for eleven when the upper storeys of the house became visible through the elm trees which lined the southern side of Amberwood Park. Matthew was in his element, and waved to a couple of gardeners who were mulching the rhododendrons to the left of the main drive. They waved back, and wished 'Young Master Matthew' a good day. Lomas shot a backward glance at the young man, remembered the yard from which the journey had started, and wondered what the world was coming to.

Once through the gap in the ornamental hedge which fronted the house itself, the carriage swung sharply to the left and onto the narrower driveway which led round to the rear of the house, well out of sight of the Georgian pillars of its imposing front entrance. It turned in the stable yard, and travelled back a few yards in the direction from which it had just arrived, before stopping alongside a heavy oak door in the side of the main building.

"Everybody down," commanded Mattthew as he leapt out and dashed towards the kitchen door without waiting for anyone else. He threw the door open and strode inside, from where Nathan could hear welcoming cries of recognition. Lomas held the horses by the bridle as Nathan helped Ruth down from the carriage, and lifted out the simple bag which contained her few possessions. It was as light as a feather, unlike Ruth, who had to be almost dragged from the carriage in the direction of the still-open kitchen door.

"Come on, lass," Nathan urged her, "yer know as well as I do that I can't tek yer back ter yer mam – she'd tan us both wi' 'er broom."

Ruth wanted to laugh, but instead the tears she'd held back for the entire two-hour journey finally broke free, and Nathan held her shaking shoulders tightly to his chest as he ran a comforting hand through her recently washed hair.

"Dun't, lass; yer'll 'ave me roarin' an' all."

"Dad!" she gasped between gulping sobs, "dun't leave me 'ere, I'm so frightened!"

"There's nowt ter be afraid of, 'onest; they're all good folks 'ere. A bit lah-di-dah mebbe, but good folks enough. It's a big chance fer yer."

"I dun't wanna big chance – I just wants ter go 'ome ter mam!" She choked and coughed between words, and her girlish face was already red and swollen.

"An' what's all this, then?"

Nathan looked over Ruth's head, and saw an enormous woman in the kitchen doorway, wearing a white smock the size of a ship's mainsail, and glaring at them. Ruth looked around in mortal terror at the huge apparition, and for a moment forgot to cry.

"That's berrer," added the woman, advancing from the doorway while wiping her hands on a cloth. "You must be Ruth."

"Indeed it is, ma'am," Nathan confirmed with an unaccustomed nicety of manners. "Ruth Slack. She's expected, I think."

"Aye, an' it's a good job she is, 'cos for all the manners that young scamp of a brother of 'ers's got, she might as well be the fishmonger's girl."

Nathan looked back down at Ruth, and gently pushed her away from his side. "Ruth," he prompted, "where's yer manners?"

Ruth turned round fully, looked furtively up at the formidable bulk, and executed an unsteady version of the curtsey she'd been practicing for days. The woman chortled, and every part of her wobbled in unison.

"Lord save us, lass, there's no need to curtsey ter me! I'm only the cook. Yer can call me Mrs Bennett, an' later on, mebbe, Polly. Yer'll be seeing a lot o' me, an' Lord 'elp yer if yer live up ter yer name!" Ruth looked bemused. "Slack, ain't it?"

Ruth still didn't comprehend, and Nathan had heard the joke too often to even pretend to laugh, so Mrs Bennett contented herself with handing Ruth a clean cloth which she took from the belt around her apron.

" 'ere, yer'd best wipe yer face afore Mrs Trentham sees it – the 'ousekeeper," she explained, with a knowing look at Nathan, who hadn't a clue what she was talking about. He put one arm around Ruth and led her to the kitchen door, through which they entered into a new world full of steam, bustle and unfamiliar hot smells.

Luncheon was about to be served upstairs, and much frantic energy was being expended on the task of ensuring that the expected high standard was maintained. Several girls, who appeared to be much older than Ruth, struggled with large pans and bubbling cauldrons, while Mrs Bennett reverted to berating and encouraging them in equal measure. Matthew reappeared from the stairwell that led up to the interior of the main house, accompanied by a gaunt, consumptive-looking individual in full formal dress and a wing collar. Matthew brought the man straight over to Ruth.

"Here she is. My only sister. She's a bit cheeky sometimes, but she's hard-working. Oh yes, and this is my father."

Nathan nodded in the direction of the newcomer, whose face twitched in the faint imitation of a smile he had long forgotten how to deliver.

"Hardiman. Butler to the Beardsall household."

Nathan nodded again, not sure how one addressed a butler, and it was Matthew who filled the uneasy silence.

"Now then, Ruth, come and meet Amy and Beth. They'll show you how to find your way around the servants' quarters, and Emily will show you how to behave in the kitchen when Mrs Bennett's not around, and . . ."

"Master Slack!" boomed Mrs Bennett, in a stern voice which was simultaneously neutralised by an almost motherly grin, "I'll thank yer ter let me instruct mi new staff in their duties. While I'm doing that, I'm sure you an' yer father would like a cup o' tea an' some pastry after yer journey."

And so it went on for almost another hour, the father trying to come to terms with the unfamiliar scenes around him, while the son took great delight in demonstrating how well accepted he had become in the big house. Amy and Beth took Ruth in hand, and when they brought her back from the servants' quarters complete with apron and cap, all three of them looked like tiny dolls in a dolls' house kitchen. Nathan's eyes filled with tears of love and pride, and Ruth smiled back sheepishly at him. For the time being at least, the excitement and novelty of it all had dried the tears.

Mercifully, she hardly noticed when it was time for Nathan and Matthew to leave her there, and Nathan's last sight of her through the kitchen door was an excited one-handed wave as the other hand cut out gingerbread men on one corner of the huge kitchen table. The Beardsalls would later enjoy afternoon tea in the library, probably unaware that they had another kitchen maid, one who already knew how to make gingerbread men.

The journey back took longer than the outward trip, partly because the horses had not been fully refreshed or changed, and partly because they had to call in at Babbington Mill for flour for the Bradley household, which Nathan helped them load onto the baggage rail under Lomas's feet, then off-load once the coach had come to a halt at the stables behind the house. During the return journey, Lomas had hardly spoken to father and son, both of whom seemed to have lost the power of conversation themselves.

Lomas had sniffed audibly when Matthew had leapt from the carriage at the Bradleys' front door, and knocked as if it were his own. When they had finished unloading the flour, Nathan thanked Lomas warmly for all he had done for them that day, and walked briskly out into High Pavement, then down Garner's Hill and into the gathering dusk of Narrow Marsh. He was alone as he passed under the archway into Tanners Yard, and was instantly glad that he was.

CHAPTER TEN

In the enemy camp

THE LETTERING was crude, and the words were misspelt, not that Nathan would have known. All he knew was that they were on his door, and they didn't look friendly. They had used some sort of red mud, and Nathan was just considering how best to get it off when the door itself opened, and Tommy strode out to meet him.

"Sorry, Dad – I were aht when they done it. Burrit's only Leen muck, an' it'll soon come off wi' a bit of a scrub."

"What's it say?"

Tommy looked uncomfortable as he read the words to himself. "Best yer dun't know, I reckon. But they're not best pleased abaht yer new job at Bradley's."

"Who's 'they'? An' what new job? I'm workin' mi frame, same as usual."

"That's not what I've 'eard, but nemmind, we'll soon get this shit off."

Nathan ignored him and instead gave voice to the nagging thought which had remained with him since he had first entered the yard. " 'as yer mam seen it?"

"No, she 'ad one of 'er funny turns after Ruth left, an' old Nancy gev 'er summat ter mek 'er sleep. I came 'ome only a while ago misen, an' Will Draycott told me as four men did it while I were aht. I were just gunner wash it off when I saw yer."

"Right, let's both do it, then p'rhaps she'll never find aht, unless someone in the yard tells 'er."

"I dun't think that'll 'appen, Dad. These days it's safer ter keep yer mouth shut rahnd 'ere. I got a lend o' Scuff's big pail, burre asked me specially not ter tell anyone who gev it me, in case they reckon 'e was 'elpin' a boss's man." His face instantly registered remorse for his blunt words, and he was about to offer some sort of apology when Nathan butted in.

"Boss's man or not, I can still look after mi own family, an' this lot's comin' off right nah."

Five pails of water and a lot of scrubbing later, all that remained was the faintest of mud smears which would soon dry into a fine but formless powdery stain. It would be enough to get Lily's tongue clicking in disapproval, but hopefully she would remain blissfully ignorant of its origins. They were just standing back to admire their efforts when Matthew entered the yard and looked at them quizzically.

"Why are you washing the door down? It's not Monday."

"Nemmind abaht that," Nathan replied sharply, "yer mam's tekken one of 'er bad turns, so yer'd best get inside an' see to 'er."

Matthew's face wrinkled in disapproval. "I hope I'm not going to have to replace Ruth, now that she's moved up in the world."

Nathan pushed the door open with his foot, and gestured for Matthew to go inside. "Yer might be 'ighly thought of in the kitchens o' the wealthy, but things 'aven't changed in Tanners Yard. When yer've seen ter yer mam, yer can find aht where William is an' see to 'is tea. Nah gerrin there, an' no backchat!"

Matthew mooched through the open door, and Nathan turned to thank Tommy for his help, but he was gone. He had used the brief diversion to slip under the archway and out of the yard, and a few minutes later he could be seen striding purposefully along Narrow Marsh, heading for the Half Moon. He was red in the face, whether from anger or exertion it was impossible to tell until he burst through the back door of the alehouse, elbowed his way through a group of men and grabbed Caleb Mason by the throat.

"Yer cowardly bastard! Yer wait till mi mam's all on 'er own, then yer treat us like enemies ter the cause! I'm gunner flog the rotten shit aht o' yer!"

Tommy was immediately grabbed by several men who pulled him back and pinned his arms to his side. As Mason massaged his bruised throat and tried to compose himself, one of his rescuers produced a sharp knife and held it up to Tommy's nose. Tommy in turn spat in the man's face, and things did not look good for his immediate wellbeing.

"Leave 'im be!" commanded a voice from the doorway, and as Tommy shook himself free of his captors, Stan Cadby appeared before him. "So yer got the message, then?"

"Some bloody message!" Tommy yelled back at him, his face still as red as his hair. "If yer wanted ter see me, yer coulda put the usual word aht. Mind yer, I guessed you was prob'ly be'ind it – nobody but you'd be daft enough ter send St. Mary's men on a job in Tanners Yard. Caleb got noticed."

"Who by?" asked Mason, forcefully.

"Fuck off! I'm not tellin' you, just so yer can paint some other poor bogger's door!" He glared back at Cadby. "An' as fer you, yer should be ashamed o' yersen, pickin' on one o' yer own. 'ave yer got nobody berrer to attack these days, or are yer just too soft in the 'ead wi' all that drink ter think o' summat different?"

"Yer needs ter watch what yer says, Tommy Slack," warned Cadby. "There's a few arahnd these parts as reckon yer goin' the same way as yer dad, specially since yer sister's gone inter service in that big 'ouse, an' yer brother's all set ter join the Bradley family bi all accounts."

"That's shit an' yer know it," Tommy snapped back. "It's just the way things've turned aht, that's all. Yer s'posed ter be goin' fer the bosses, not the poor sods that's got nowt."

"Aye," said Cadby, "but when we do, 'ow does we know we can count on the likes o' you ?"

"Gimme a try, that's all," suggested Tommy rather unconvincingly.

"Oh yeah?" was Cadby's reply. "An' wharrappens the fust time we send yer on a raid, an' you 'as ter ask yer dad's permission ter stay aht late?"

There was a ripple of laughter, and Tommy felt himself being tested. "I'm 'appy ter move aht o' there, so long as you mad boggers don't do owt else agin 'em. So then I won't need no-one's permission, norreven yourn!"

"So yer gunner join us full time?" Cadby queried.

"I allus meant to," Tommy insisted, "burra can do more if yer've got somewhere else I can stay, rather than bein' treated like a prisoner back there in the yard."

Cadby smiled encouragingly. "That's easy fixed. Jack's got room at 'is 'ouse since 'is eldest run off. So when d'yer wanner start?"

"Doin' what?" demanded Tommy.

Cadby smiled again, and signalled for everyone to gather closer round him as he spelt out his plan. "It's time ter do some real damage ter the big nobs in the middle o' tahn, an' I thought as 'ow we might start wi' Bradley's, seeing as 'ow young Tommy 'ere knows the place berrer than any of us. What d'yer reckon, Tommy, can yer still remember 'ow things is laid aht in there?"

"Course I bloody can," Tommy responded petulantly. "The frames is on the second floor be'ind them big winders, an' the stairs goes up the side from the bottom door dahn the alley. Yer'll need a lantern ter find yer way dahn the alley, mind."

"Only if we goes at night," observed Cadby as he turned a triumphant face around at the mesmerised assembly before adding, for special effect, "but this un's gunner be in the daytime."

There was a startled hiss of indrawn breath, and Tommy protested. "Yer bloody mad! There's six big blokes up in that frame room, plus a few more dahn on the packin' level. They're all St. Mary's men, like you lot, an' they'll know who we are – especially me, since mi own dad's one of 'em an' I used ter work there. I thought the idea was ter keep yersens secret!"

"I know yer think I'm mad, but I'm not seriously suggestin' that we bust in there while there's folks workin', yer daft prat. They 'as days off, dun't they?"

Tommy thought briefly before replying. "Only Sundays. Right enough, I dun't s'pose anyone in this room'll miss goin' ter church." There were several guffaws, and someone broke wind noisily.

"There's other days an' all, like 'olidays," added Cadby. "An' one o' your jobs is gunner be ter find aht when they're 'avin' one o' them."

" 'ow can I, if I'm not livin' at 'ome any more?"

"That's fer you ter find aht. There must be others yer know that's workin' fer Bradley, surely."

Tommy remained doubtful, but let the point pass. He was more concerned about being expected to lead the raiders into the building even though it was empty of workers, and what they would be expecting him to do once they got in there. He was glad that Cadby began to address the company again generally, and left him to his thoughts.

"It won't be soon, anyroad, folks. There's a lot o' plannin' ter do, an' we need ter work aht who's doin' what on the day. We'll need lookouts an' everything, as usual, but this time we won't 'ave the dark ter 'elp us, so we'll all be wearin' disguises. An' we'll be torchin' the buildin' when we've done wi' the frames. We'll need ter meet up wi' the Rookeries men afore long, an' watch 'ow they do Solley's, 'cos we'll be doin' Bradley's the same way. We've agreed that they get ter go fust."

There was a great deal of general discussion and a number of suggestions, all of which passed over Tommy's head as he began to contemplate what he had just got himself involved with. As the meeting slowly broke up, Tommy sidled back to Cadby's side and sought reassurance. "Nah that I've thrown mi 'and in wi' yer, will yer leave the Slacks alone?"

"All except you, yeah. But the threat's still there, mind, if yer play us false. Yer dad ain't ter know any different, neither, so dun't go tellin' 'im 'e's off the list."

"Aye, right. But 'ow come yer need me ter guide the men inter Bradley's? You know the place as well as I do."

"Used to, Tommy, used to. An' anyroad, what berrer way is there fer you ter prove that yer still wi' the cause, despite wharrit might look like to others? I'm doin' yer a favour lad, believe me."

Just then Jack Cossall took Tommy by the arm and led him out of the alehouse and round the corner to his new quarters in Wool Alley. Jack would have preferred his own son back with the family, but this young un seemed like he had the right spirit. He would have been disappointed to learn how low, in reality, Tommy's spirits had just sunk.

———— ·◇· ————

Nathan sighed with irritation and tried to ignore the puffy, haughty-faced young man who strutted up and down the frame room as if he owned it, which in time he no doubt would, perish the day. A less experienced stockinger than Nathan would have had enough to do keeping his mind, eyes and hands co-ordinated for the task of running out 'Lincoln knit' warp lace, but so skilled had Nathan become over the years that working the frame was now second nature, allowing his mind to run wherever it wished.

He had given up worrying where Tommy had got to for the past week or so, and had almost given up inventing various excuses to the increasingly befuddled Lily, who seemed to think that Tommy had gone to Eastwood with his sister, and in the end it was more merciful to let her take refuge in that belief. A well-meaning neighbour had reported seeing Tommy in an alehouse with Jack Cossall, but given that man's known friendship with Stan Cadby, it was not a line of enquiry that Nathan wished to pursue.

Certainly, if he came across whoever had enticed Tommy away, there would be blood spilt, and it added salt to the wound to see James Bradley so brazenly enjoying the fruits of his father's efforts without any obvious entitlement or noticeable talent. Even Tommy had known more about warp-frame knitting by the time he was six years old, and used to sit on the floor of the frame room and watch Nathan at work after bringing him the food which Lily had prepared at home. They had seemed like difficult times then, but if only he had been able to see into the future Nathan would have savoured them more gratefully. What was lost to time could never be reclaimed, it seemed.

"You'll have to go at a faster rate than this when we cut the hours back," James said, nonchanantly, without realising that his reedy voice could not be heard above the rhythmic clonking of the frames. Nathan could tell by his moving lips that James was trying to communicate with the entire frame room at once, and he allowed himself a silent smirk. He dropped his gaze when he saw James looking at him, but it was too late, and James walked over to his frame and stood in front of it.

"I say – Slack, isn't it? Could I have a word?"

"Pardon?" shouted Nathan, well aware of what James had said, but intent on teaching him a lesson in frame room communication. James cupped his hands to Nathan's ear, and as he bellowed out his next instruction Nathan caught the distinct odour of port wine.

"Could you stop your machine for a moment? I want to talk to you."

Nathan deliberately took his time over it, mumbling some nonsense to James about having to wait until he came to the end of a row, which the latter seemed to regard as a piece of technical intelligence specially intended for his enlightenment, when in fact it was a standard joke perpetrated on all fresh-faced apprentices. Nathan's neighbour, Sam Pinkney, saw Nathan closing down his frame, and some sixth sense urged him to do the same. It was suddenly much quieter, and James took full advantage.

"I was saying that you men will have to go a lot faster when the hours are cut back." Sam shot Nathan a warning look, but was wasting his time.

"An' 'ow much faster would that be, exactly?" enquired Nathan in an innocent tone which those who knew him had learned to be wary of.

"Oh I don't know – just faster, that's all."

"Well nah, there's the problem you see, young Mr Bradley, sir. These 'ere warp frames, they only goes at the one speed, an' that's the speed that the men working them decide on."

"So if the men work quicker, the machines will?"

"They're called warp frames, young Mr Bradley, sir. The only machines in 'ere are the poor sods who 'as ter mek the frames go full speed 'cos the likes o' you sez so."

"Nathan!" Sam warned him softly, but he knew from experience that there was no stopping the man once he had warmed up.

"I'm not sure I like your tone one little bit," James retorted, "but it's important that you let the men know that we're cutting back the hours from next week, and that we expect the same production, so they'll need to speed up. Have I made that clear?"

"Very clear, young Mr Bradley, sir, but why should I 'ave ter tell 'em?"

"Because you're the senior man around here, I'm told."

"That's as may be, young Mr Bradley sir, but you're the boss.

Or, more properly speakin' your father is. So perhaps you'd berrer tell 'em, then at least you'd be doin' somethin' useful while you're 'ere. Nah, if yer'll excuse me, I need ter increase mi production, it seems."

Sam couldn't quite suppress the spontaneous chortle, but he managed to convert it into a fake cough just as James whipped around to glare, first at him, then back at Nathan. Nathan's frame was back up to its normal working rhythm in no time, and his eyes were firmly glued to it by the time that James stormed out of the frame room and down the stairs towards his father's office.

"That weren't very clever," commented Sam unnecessarily above the combined din of both their frames.

"It were worth it, all the same," Nathan yelled back with a grin. "Nah let's wait an' see if the boss 'imself cares to explain what his little pipsqueak meant bi 'cuttin' back the hours'. He shoulda known berrer than ter send young pisspot."

Robert Bradley would have been less concerned about the nickname which his son had acquired on his very first morning in the business than the way in which his instructions had been blatantly challenged, particularly since James deliberately exaggerated the events which had just transpired when he burst into his father's office, red faced and very aggrieved, and demanded that Nathan be dismissed for insolence.

"Hold on there a minute, son," urged Robert. "Nathan Slack's worth 'is weight in salt, and I'm relyin' on 'im ter keep the others in order."

"Then God help you, is all I can say," exclaimed James as he reached for the port bottle without invitation. "If he's the one you've chosen to keep the others mindful of their positions, then it doesn't say a lot for the others. I won't tell you what he told me to do, but it was the same thing that Adam said to you that night you caught him in the parlour with the brandy."

Robert needed no reminder of that embarrassing confrontation, and he had hoped that James himself had forgotten it as rapidly as Adam himself seemed to have done once he had sobered up. James had obviously got well onto the wrong side of Nathan, and Robert knew he would clearly have to step in before things got worse.

"Did yer tell the men about the Saturday closure?"

"Didn't get a chance. I tried telling Slack himself to tell the men, and I got the reply I just mentioned."

Robert sighed. "I asked you to tell them yourself. Yer can't expect any respect from your workers if yer don't speak to them personally and get ter know them. Never mind, leave it with me. Perhaps yer'd better go down and check the production figures with Danby."

"Will the Slack boy be down there? I've had enough Slacks for one day, to be perfectly honest."

"No, 'e's back with the women in packin' and markin' up. And the sooner yer learn to treat him with respect, the faster the father'll come around ter you."

"I doubt it somehow, not after what he said to me," grumbled James as he loped out of his father's office, port glass still in hand.

Robert sat for a long moment, thinking it through. He was not particularly surprised that James had proved unpopular with the workers, given the arrogance and air of superiority which he displayed even at home. What was of concern to Robert was the fact that Nathan Slack – one of the few men employed on the premises whom he thought he could rely on to support the Bradley family business, particularly since his daughter and younger son had been so well treated by the Bradleys – had evidently seen fit to side with the other workers.

It never occurred to him to doubt that Nathan had said what James had accused him of saying, and he needed to talk to Nathan, not only about that, but about some important changes which had to take place without delay. But how could he re-enforce his authority on a workforce which must be on the point of open rebellion, if someone so normally polite and deferential as Nathan could feel emboldened enough to say something as disgusting as that to his future employer?

Nathan, for his part, had no idea of what he had been falsely accused by James of having said, but was still disappointed that Mr Bradley had opted not to announce the forthcoming changes in working hours to the men the way he always used to do – in person. And since James had failed dismally in what should have been a simple task, Nathan was fairly certain that Robert would seek to cover the blunder by requiring Nathan to be the bearer of bad tidings.

It was hardly the most auspicious of backgrounds for a meeting which was to have such serious consequences, and Robert feared the worst when he saw the mutinous look still lingering on Nathan's face when he was ushered into his office by an overly-nervous Danby some thirty minutes after the confrontation in the frame room. Because he felt challenged, Robert was uncharacteristically brittle in his opening remark.

"I'm cuttin' out Saturday work as of now."

"Aye, so yer boy said," growled Nathan. "Leastways, I think that were what 'e were tryin' ter say."

Robert's face darkened further. "As General Overseer, I expect you ter show the lad a bit o' respect, Nathan. After all, 'e's goin' ter take over from me one day."

"Aye, an' 'opefully bi the time 'e does, 'e'll 'ave learned that respect is summat you earn, like you 'ave. It can't be bought, an' it can't be forced on folk."

"Neither, apparently, can good manners," retorted Robert, who immediately wished that he hadn't, but felt obliged to continue what he'd started. "Your Matthew is a credit to any family, but that lout of a brother of 'is clearly didn't acquire any manners."

The mention of Tommy made Nathan even more guarded and eager to terminate the interview. "Let's not talk abaht families, 'cos I'm not exactly in the mood fer showin' mi gratitude right nah. Just tell me what ter tell the men, an' let's 'ave done wi' it."

"Very well," replied Robert coldly. "There'll be no openin' next Saturday, or any other Saturday in the near future. But if the men can keep the production at present levels they'll get paid the same rates, so they'll not lose out."

"Owt else?" queried Nathan in the most insulting and confrontational tone of voice Robert had ever heard him use. Robert could feel his temper rising, and wanted this over with before his anger and feeling of betrayal spilt out and made things even worse.

"Yes. Once word gets out that the place is empty on Saturdays, we'll become an even bigger target fer the mob. Sundays are fine, because I've fixed up fer some o' the Watch ter look in from time to time, but on Saturdays they're kept too busy in the Market Place, so yer'll have ter show yer face once or twice. Make it different times every Saturday, and that should fool 'em."

Nathan rose from his seat, and for the first time in their long relationship Robert did not feel the urge to invite him to stay. Their eyes met in sad recognition of what was happening, before Robert broke the silence. "Right, yer can go."

Nathan successfully suppressed the urge to touch his forelock in sarcasm.

The back door was old and dry as parchment, yielding to the first axe. Within seconds it was hanging in shards, as eager men collided with each other in the narrow entrance hall before racing up the staircase to the upper floors. They were well drilled and even better rehearsed, and each played his part to perfection. Neighbours who had heard the noise, but nervously chose to remain behind barricaded doors of their own, first became aware of the sweet smell, and then the crackling spit of burning wood. They heard the pistol shots which had come to signify the end of a raid, and the more curious of them peered cautiously out around their doors to see the factory well alight on three different levels. This much was clear even though it was only two o'clock on a weekday afternoon. Mercifully, none of the workforce had been there when it happened.

The first to arrive were the Watch, who set about passing pails of water in a human chain up the staircase, pressing spectators and passers-by into service. Then came the militia, who kept the curious away from the burning building and cleared a space for the cavalry to gallop in, a full twenty minutes after the event. Eventually the flames were extinguished, but it would be weeks before Solley and Sons would be back in production.

In the Exchange Hall, two days later, an irate George Coldham was berating the two men who had been escorted to his office by two officers of the Watch like condemned prisoners being led onto a convict hulk. The taller of the two looked sullen and resentful, but the shorter, red-haired one was trying to make light of it.

"Like I said, Your Worship, we've got a definite line on one of the clowns what's be'ind all this, and we'll 'ave 'im in irons in no time."

"All I know," boomed back the far from convinced Town Clerk, "is that while you two have been living at considerable public expense in some of the best accommodation in this town, a very good friend of mine – and a very good friend of our immediate past mayor – all but lost his entire livelihood in a fire caused by the very people that you are supposed to be tracking down."

"Not exactly the case, sir, with the greatest of respect," corrected the taller of the two, without apparently moving either his mouth or any other part of his head. "These cowards hunt in different packs, it seems, and the fire in Fletcher Gate was the work of a different pack from the one we've locked onto."

"But they must all co-ordinate their efforts, surely?"

"That, again with respect, sir, suggests a level of organisation which we have yet to detect," continued the tall man, his bald head glistening with sweat from the exertion of selling his explanation of recent events and controlling his temper. "The men we're onto may well drink with those who carried out the attack on Solleys, but they weren't directly engaged in it."

"So what do you suggest I tell the mayor, who has summoned

me to his chambers this very afternoon, for a report on what we're doing to prevent these outrages?"

"That's easy," chipped in Baker, who was anxious not to forfeit any of the credit. "Tell the good mayor that we've got the breeches off one of the key men in the local outfit, and we can put a finger up 'is nasty whenever we choose."

It was difficult to tell which of his audience looked the more appalled by the imagery, but it was Conon who did his best to retrieve the situation. "What my colleague means is that we have secured the co-operation of a leading hand in the St. Mary's raiding party, and he is now, happily, more afraid of us than he is of his companions in crime."

"But if you have the man in the town gaol, how come I wasn't informed earlier?"

"He's not in the gaol yet, sir, because we need him to identify the others. Right now he's at home, and fearful of setting foot outside his own door without seeing us standing there, so he may as well be in gaol. But we didn't want to alert the enemy to the fact that we're on to them, if you follow my reasoning, so we left him as free as a chained hawk, so to speak, ready to do what we tell him, when we tell him."

"How did you discover where he lives?" enquired the Town Clerk.

"Pathetically easy," sneered Conon with a cold, cruel set to his mouth, that made even Coldham shiver with apprehension. "Once we'd given him his first lesson in loyalty, he was unwise enough to direct us to his dwelling so that we could assist him home. It will, by now, have penetrated his cretinous brain that we can come back for him whenever we wish, and if he seeks to escape, well . . . shall we just say that he has a wife and two daughters?"

"So what do I tell the mayor?"

"Tell him that the leaders of the St. Mary's raiding party will be in irons within a matter of days."

"I will, and with the greatest of pleasure. The Capital Bill was passed just in time, it seems; perhaps we shall see a hanging or two out of this miserable business even yet. But mind, gentlemen, you have until Thursday coming to live up to your promises, or Mr Ryder shall hear of it."

He was gone in a swish of coat-tails, leaving the taller man to smack his ginger-haired companion across the side of the head.

"You and your bloody mouth will get us hung one of these fine days."

"But not before some of our little chickens," came the perky reply.

CHAPTER ELEVEN

Two star-crossed lovers

"MR PAUL SOLLEY," announced Adam in his best drawing room manner.

Robert Bradley rose from his chair to meet him, and, taking him gently by the elbow as if he were an elderly invalid, steered him towards the place of honour at the tea table, where Solley paused to bow formally to Catherine, then walked around it to shake hands with James, before taking the proffered seat across the table from all three of them. Lucy was attending one of her Sunday School meetings, and the conversation had not been deemed suitable for Rebecca, who was taking tea alone in her room.

"Paul," said Robert in a condoling tone normally reserved for funerals, "we're so glad yer could join us, and the Good Lord alone knows that yer'll be relieved ter be surrounded by your dearest friends at a time like this. I can't begin ter comprehend what a shock it must have been ter you and Margaret, comin' home ter find all that."

"I'll not deny that it was a shock," agreed Solley, "although word had reached us in Loughborough, so it wasn't as if we weren't prepared for what we saw. But even so, Margaret had to take to her bed for two days – she sends her most sincere apologies by the way, but she's still not up to facing company."

"Quite understandable," Catherine reassured him. "Please let her know that I'd be happy to call on her once she's fully recovered, and in the meantime, if there's anything . . ."

"That's very thoughtful of you," said Solley, almost by way of interruption, "and her physician did recommend some sort of diversion. I'm only too glad we moved house when we did, so that we don't have to stare at it, day in and day out."

"I went down there the day before yer got back," Robert told him, "along with other members of the Association, ter see if there was anything we could do, and James tells me that we can lend yer some standard knit fer any incomplete orders yer may still have on yer books, but even so, if there's anything . . ."

Solley grimaced ruefully. "You're very kind, as always, Robert, but as you can well imagine it's going to take an age before we can get back to the way we were. The frame room's almost gone completely, along with the frames themselves of course, and most of the stock's perished from the water that the Watch threw in. I'm not blaming them, of course; without the Watch we'd have nothing left."

"I can loan yer a few warp frames," offered Robert as he listened with deepening sadness to the full account of his friend's reversal of fortune, "and ter tell yer the truth, if the stories I've been 'earin' are reliable, my frames might be safer in your building, anyway."

Solley looked across at Robert with raised eyebrows as he paused in the act of reaching for the china cup. "You reckon you're next?"

"So I've 'eard. Not from the man who's paid ter tell me, mind you. Someone else, who got it from a reliable source in the Town Clerk's office. Seems as if all the leading master hosiers are on the list – you were just the first."

Solley shook his head sadly. "It's a bad business all ways round. My overseer, Pollard, was away visiting his sick mother in Mansfield when they hit us, although everyone to do with the place knew that it was closed for a few days while we were in Loughborough. Ordinarily he'd have arranged to keep watch on the building, and my first thought, naturally, was that he had made up the story of his mother just so he wouldn't be there when it happened. How much can you trust your man?"

" 'e's the best I've got," Robert replied, to an answering snort from James which came close to spraying buttered muffin across the tea table. "James isn't so sure," Bradley explained, "but I've got no reason ter doubt that Slack's heart is in the right place if it comes ter the push. The problem I 'ave is that my man doesn't ever seem to 'ear anything. Or if he does, 'e's not tellin' me."

Solley leaned across the table closer to Robert in a conspiratorial gesture, adding, "There's something else you should know," while flicking his eyes towards the young girl in the white apron who stood silently by the serving board. Robert was not slow on the uptake.

"That'll be all fer the time being, thank you Sarah. We'll ring if we need anything else."

The girl curtseyed in the customary manner of domestic servants everywhere, and slipped silently from the room. Robert looked expectantly across at Solley, who cleared his throat in some embarrassment.

"The fact is, Robert – and mind, I've no way of proving this – but the fact is that there was only one person apart from me who knew that Pollard was not going to be making his rounds of the building on the day it was raided. That was a girl called Kate, who we took in some months ago when we found her begging in the alleyway at the side of the factory; we gave her a position in the scullery, where according to our cook she's been progressing very well. But when we got back from

Loughborough, not only was half the business gone, but so was she."

Robert was concerned, but puzzled. "But 'ow did a scullery maid get ter know what arrangements you'd made ter guard yer business premises?"

"That's just it. Ordinarily of course she wouldn't, but it just so happened that Pollard got the news about his mother late one evening, after we'd closed, and thought it best to come straight to the house to ask if it would be possible for him to set off for Mansfield that very night, and take off the two days he would need to get there and back. He came to the back door, where the scullery is, of course, and according to my man Henshaw, when he went to bring Pollard into the sitting room to see me, he and Kate were deep in conversation about his sick mother. Henshaw only realised that it might be connected to what happened when Kate disappeared the same day that we were attacked, then he told me."

Catherine had been following the conversation with interest, and saw her opportunity. "You must feel very bad, having shown such Christian charity to the girl, only for her to repay you in that wicked and ungrateful way. As you pointed out a moment ago, had it not been for the Watch, you could have been completely ruined."

"Like I said," Solley responded, "I have no way of proving that my suspicions are true, but if they are, then of course you're right. I'm only telling you and Robert all this because I know that Robert's allowed Miss Lucy to bring a boy from Narrow Marsh into your house, and I don't want you good people to suffer the same fate."

"It's worse than that," complained James as he clattered his cup down noisily on his saucer, causing his mother to wince with embarrassment, "the same boy's been allowed into the paperwork side of the business, where he can find out what's happening. And what's more," he added triumphantly, "that same boy's father is the General Overseer that my father's relying on to keep the men under control. All it needs is for the father to take a day off, and the boy will be free to tell half the town about it, if he wants to."

Solley looked alarmed. "Robert, is this true?"

Robert looked uncomfortable, and Catherine drove the poison further in.

"Absolutely, and it would seem from what James has been observing since he joined the business that both father and son are beginning to display considerable disloyalty since they were shown such generosity by Robert. Admit it, Robert, they're beginning to behave as if they have no duty of gratitude towards any of us."

Robert squirmed uneasily in his seat. "The father maybe," he conceded, "although James can be the most exasperatin' person to deal with. No, James, don't put on that sulky look, it's true, as you and I have had occasion to discuss. But as fer the boy . . ."

"Oh really, Robert!" Catherine protested. "You know as well as I do that the boy behaves as if he's part of the family. Young Rebecca's manners have quite degenerated since she's been associating with him, and his presence in this house has gone far beyond the decent bounds of Lucy teaching him basic reading and writing. We're creating a rod for our own backs, if you ask me."

Solley was embarrassed at having caused this tense exchange between husband and wife but he could not take back what he had said, and instead could only emphasise the point more strongly.

"Robert," he interposed, "you won't have forgotten that at that meeting of the Association, not only did we pledge to appoint our best men to defend our interests, we also decided to root out those who might be a threat within our organisations. That must obviously include family situations as well, and surely you don't want to have to think twice before you say anything in your own drawing room?"

"Well reminded, Paul," Catherine encouraged him. "I, for one, feel very uncomfortable when that Slack boy's around our house. It's as if he's here to find out all he can about us, then pass it on to his horrid friends in that dreadful yard."

"There you are, Robert," confirmed Solley, "even your wife feels that you're taking a risk harbouring this young man within your walls. No-one will deny that you demonstrate the finest principles of Christian charity, but there are limits, particularly these days, when everyone has to clearly show which side of this terrible affair they want to be on. If your business were to go up in flames next week, could you ever be certain that it wasn't your misplaced trust that caused it?"

In the ensuing silence, all eyes were on Robert, whose own eyes in turn were downcast at the half-eaten muffin which lay on his plate as he struggled with conflicting emotions. Finally he looked up, not at Catherine but at Solley.

"Very well, Paul. The boy has ter be told that he's gone too far, at least in the estimation of some people." This time he allowed his gaze to drift sideways in order to encompass the wife and son seated to his left. "But the father 'as ter be given the chance ter prove that I didn't misjudge 'im, and ter be perfectly 'onest I wouldn't feel safe replacing 'im with anyone else at this time. So let's leave it at that, and talk about something a bit more cheerful, shall we?"

Some thirty minutes later their guest had taken his leave, James had set off to join his friends at the theatre, and Catherine had swept gleefully into the drawing room, where she penned a hasty letter to her sister, warning her to be careful of what was said in front of 'the Slack girl'.

Robert remained seated at the table, brooding over the decision he had been forced into making, and picking absent-mindedly at more leftover food than was good for him. Eventually, he rang for Adam, and gave him a brief instruction which he hoped he would never regret.

"Adam, when Miss Lucy returns home, please be so good as to send both her and Miss Rebecca in here to see me."

———————————

It was a small meeting at the Half Moon, but this was all that was required and there was a need for urgency. Cadby counted them in mentally - Geordie Packer, Jack Cossall, Jim Collishaw, Tom Darby, Caleb Mason, Stephen Perry, Arthur Peters, Jacob Rawlings and Tommy Slack. He was surprised to see Luke Johnson limping in as well, since he'd been missing for some time. He got straight down to business, before they could get noisy.

"Right, sorry ter call yer in at such short notice, but we've bin told ter do us bit on Sat'day comin'." There was a surprised gasp and he continued. "All right, I know it's a bit sudden like, but we've bin told ter strike again afore the memory of Solley's is lost, and . . ."

"Told by who?" demanded Cossall.

"Never you mind," retorted Cadby. "You still wi' us, or what?" Jack fell silent, as Cadby resumed. "We all know where, an' nah yer all know when. All we've got left to agree is – 'ow."

"We still talkin' abaht daytime?" enquired Collishaw.

"O' course we are; broad bloody daylight, while folks is safely dahn at the market. Only one man left in the place an' we all know who tharris," said Cadby, with a stern stare across at Tommy, who simply shrugged.

" 'ow do we know the lad won't tell 'is dad?" asked Mason.

Tommy flushed with anger, and hit back. " 'cos 'the lad', as you call 'im, ain't no lad any more. Just don't kill 'im, that's all I'm askin' yer."

"That's not 'ow we does things, as yer well know," replied Cadby quickly. "An' anyroad, 'e'll be given a chance ter clear off an' say nowt. We know where the Slacks live, an' Nathan Slack's no fool when it comes ter 'is family's wellbeing."

Tommy fought down the fear and anger in order to clarify something. "Am I expected ter go in wi' yer? I can't promise mi dad'll keep quiet just 'cos 'e sees me there an' all. An' 'ow do we know 'e won't 'ave me tekken up bi the Watch?"

Cadby smiled with satisfaction. "Why d'yer think we've gone ter so much trouble ter keep yer hidden dahn in Wool Alley? Bi all accounts, yer dad's already bin tryin' ter find yer, burre's got nowhere. Anyroad, once we're in, show 'em the way up ter the frame room an' show me where Danby's room is these days, then your job's done an' yer can go."

"So who's goin' in?" queried Collishaw.

Cadby puffed out his chest in self-congratulation as he revealed his plan. "Tommy does the door, Luke an' me'll see ter the lower floors, an' the rest on yer do the frame room. In an' aht in ten minutes, then leg it."

"An' Nathan Slack?" enquired Cossall nervously.

Cadby glared across at Tommy. "If 'e can be persuaded ter stand back, then leave 'im be, but dun't lerrim aht o' the place in case 'e calls the Watch. If 'e won't stand back, then 'e'll 'ave ter be 'eld dahn or summat."

Tommy's stomach lurched as he contemplated what the 'summat' might involve, and it occurred to him that there might be another way, although he wasn't about to explain it to Cadby, who was clearly anxious to call the meeting to a close.

"Right then, that's it, apart from the exact time. Ten o'clock bi St. Mary's chimes an' the side door goes in. Bi then most folks'll be at the market, but black-up or wear summat ovver yer 'eads, just in case there's any still left in the street. See yer all in the side alley, an' good luck. General Ludd's abaht ter strike another blow fer the cause."

It was not a happy company which left the Half Moon in twos and threes and it wasn't just Tommy who was doubtful about the likely success of the plan. The Rookeries men who'd raided Solley's had enjoyed the advantages of surprise and the absence of the overseer, but this time the authorities would be more prepared, and although Saturday was market day, this generally meant more people out and about to witness what was happening. The Watch would be alerted almost from the start and behind them would be the soldiers, keen to erase the humiliation of past months. There were several who thought that Cadby had become too ambitious, or was being controlled by those who were more interested in shocking the town than they were about the safety of the men whose actions they were commanding. Finally, there was the fact that frame smashing had become a hanging matter.

There were even some who were unhappy about the prospect of hurting Nathan Slack; those who knew him were well aware of his bluff but generous nature, and that he was a family man who meant no-one any harm. Now that the cause was reaching out to harm such men, it was time to reconsider whether or not some values had become twisted – after all, wasn't he one of the very people that the cause was supposed to be helping?

No such thoughts troubled Cadby, who was more focused on getting away from the meeting and reporting back his success. In order to do that, he would be required to shake off Luke Johnson, who seemed intent on recounting yet again why he had been missing for the past two weeks on account of the knee he had injured when he slipped in the road while wending his inebriated way home from the last meeting he had attended. They were still walking along Carter Gate, Johnson hobbling to keep up with Cadby, who was weighing up in his mind the best way to shake him off, when two oddly matched men stepped out of a doorway ahead of them.

"Just stay right where you are," commanded the taller of them, "and you might want to take a look behind you."

Cadby did as suggested, and less than twenty yards behind them were three heavily armed officers of the Watch, two of whom rapidly approached and grabbed Cadby by both shoulders. One of them spoke. "Stanley James Cadby, I'm taking you into custody on suspicion of sedition."

Cadby may not have been familiar with the precise legal definition of what he was being arrested for, but there was no mistaking their intent. It did not even occur to him to ask what Luke Johnson was being arrested for, as he was led, protesting and pleading in equal measure, up Hollow Stone towards the town gaol. The two men who had originally intercepted them followed a few yards behind, and as they passed the third officer of the Watch, with his hand loosely holding the shoulder of the stationary and terrified-looking Johnson, the shorter of the two spoke.

"It's all right, officer, ya can let 'im go. As for you, Mr Johnson, you've kept your part of the bargain, and ya won't be seein' us again, unless, of course, ya decide to blab, and then you'll be seein' us all too soon. Now sod off and keep your mouth shut, if ya knows what's good for ya."

He knew well enough. For Luke Johnson, the nightmare was over – for Stan Cadby it was just beginning.

Matthew was a mass of churning emotion as he stood in Halifax Lane, across the road from Sion Chapel, which he'd left a few minutes earlier. The Bible Reading class had passed off normally enough and as usual he had been the star pupil, weaving his way expertly and confidently through the Epistle of St. Paul to the Corinthians, boring and apparently meaningless though it might be. When Lucy had asked him to stay back after the rest had left, he had imagined that it was in order that he could be praised once again for the example which he was setting to the others, or that there might be news of another family trip somewhere. The reality had hit him like a blow to the stomach.

It had fallen to Lucy to explain to Matthew that her father had decided that in view of the 'difficulties' which the town was currently experiencing, it would be best if Matthew discontinued attending for his lessons at the Bradley house, and that, for the time being, Rebecca would be receiving religious instruction at home. Lucy didn't even begin to explain how Matthew's attendance at the Bradley house might in some way be connected with the rising violence in the streets, but for Matthew her message conveyed only one meaning – he was not to see Rebecca any more, even at Sunday School.

Matthew had enough about him these days to take the news with apparent good grace, and Lucy would later recount to her father, with a profound sense of relief, that it was all over and how 'refined and mature' he had been in accepting the new arrangement. But once he had left the chapel, and watched from the darkness of a bootmaker's doorway as Lucy made her way back down the lane towards Pilcher Gate in the company of Adam and two off-duty Watch officers hired by Robert to ensure her safety wherever she went on foot, Matthew had let the tears flow, and allowed his anger to vent itself on the doorpost of the dilapidated shop.

He had still been idly kicking at the badly dented wood when he heard someone call his name. He looked out into the lane, and it was Billy Howell, the same Billy Howell who, his tortured memory reminded him, had been a silent witness to his flogging by Tommy on that magic day almost two years before when he had first entered the Bradley household, and had first met Rebecca, whom he was no longer to be allowed to see.

"What do you want?" he asked in a gruff tone which he hoped would mask the emotion in his voice; for the same reason he kept his tear-stained face well back in the gloom of the doorway.

"I've gorra message for yer."

"Yes? What?"

"Nine o'clock where yer grandad's buried."

"What? What sort of stupid message is that?"

"It's wharra was told ter tell yer. Nine o'clock where yer grandad's buried."

"And who gave you the message?"

"Can't tell yer that, else I can't keep mi penny."

"All right, keep your penny, and thanks for the message."

Billy skipped off into the darkness, no doubt in search of a sweet vendor whose desperation for business drove him to remain open until late in the evening, in the hope that a young boy might have a penny to spend on barley sugar. Matthew, meanwhile, turned the possibilities over in his head.

Rebecca knew well enough where his grandfather was buried, since they had often walked past the burial ground in Barker Gate on their chaperoned promenades after Sunday School. There was no headstone, but more than once he had pointed out the raised mound near the back, between the permanent stone memorial to a former employee of the Town Corporation and the alabaster tomb of a departed cheese maker. She must have chosen this way of meeting him, despite her father's ruling, and under the cover of darkness they could renew their vows of undying love and perhaps exchange clandestine kisses. He knew that it was well after eight, and that he should lose no time in proving his love and devotion in return.

He was standing before old Joe's grave, silently praying for some of the old man's courage in the face of adversity, when he heard the bell tower clock of St. Mary's ring out the chimes, and as he counted the last of the nine in his head he heard a footfall behind him. He turned eagerly, ready to embrace the angel to whom he had given his heart gladly and freely, but the silhouette which stood before him was taller and more angular. As it stepped forward into the half-light of the unclouded new moon, it also had that unmistakable mop of unruly hair, although it was much thinner than when he had last seen it.

"Tommy?"

The two brothers embraced awkwardly, and Tommy stepped back to get a better look at his younger brother. He was clearly fighting back emotion as he choked out a greeting. "Yer'll do. Glad ter see that mam's still feedin' yer."

"Actually, dad does most of that, now that Ruth's gone. Why don't you come home, Tommy? We all miss you, and Dad's been looking for you all over the place."

"So I 'eard, but there's no time fer that. I'm gunner 'ave ter rely on yer ter do summat that's real important. Can I trust yer?"

Sadness at the realisation that the message had come from Tommy and not Rebecca was deadened somewhat by curiosity, as Matthew hastened to reassure him. "I'm your brother, Tommy. You can trust me with anything, you know that."

"I'm not so sure yer'll think that when you 'ear wharrit is, but I'm left wi' no choice."

"What is it, Tommy? Are you in some sort of trouble?"

"No, not yet, anyroad. It's dad that could be, unless yer does wharra tells yer."

"What's dad done?"

"Nowt, except be stupid enough ter fight Bradley's battles forrim. An' by the way, nowt I'm abaht ter tell yer must get back ter the Bradleys, understood?"

"Of course," Matthew agreed, unwilling to explain that it would not now be possible, anyway.

"Well, it's like this," continued Tommy. "Next Sat'day – Sat'day comin', mind – yer've got ter stop dad goin' up ter Bradley's."

"Why?"

"Nemmind why; just do it, right! I can't tell yer, 'onest I can't, but if yer love Dad, yer'll keep 'im away."

This was the second piece of bad news Matthew had received that evening, and he hoped it was to be the last. "It's Bradley's turn, isn't it? First Solley's, now Bradley's. Tommy, why did you ever get yourself involved in all this?"

"It dun't marrer. What marrers is that dad dun't do summat stupid, like tryin' ter stop it. An' if 'e is there when it starts, well I dun't care if he is ar dad, I'll say it anyroad, 'e's daft enough ter try."

Matthew nodded sadly in agreement. He also knew their father well enough to realise that if his loyalty were to be tested, Nathan would give his life if necessary. And Nathan had never left anyone in any doubt where his loyalty lay. "But how do I stop him? You know what he's like."

"I dun't rightly know; you're the clever clogs in the family. All I can tell yer is that it's gunner 'appen at ten o'clock on the nose. If yer can keep 'im aht till after then, that should do it, I reckon."

Matthew began thinking deeply, and as he did so Tommy's shadowy form merged into the night, and his boots could be heard retreating back towards Wool Alley and his new lodgings. Matthew called after him once, then thought better of it. It had been quite a night, he reflected, as he, too, walked back out into Barker Gate and headed home in the opposite direction.

After two days in the solitary, filthy cell on the lowest level of the town gaol, Stan Cadby was ready to sell his mother for something decent to eat, or at least some fresh water. The pallet of straw on which he was expected to sleep had already been verminous when he had been forcibly thrown into the room by two turnkeys in moth-eaten gaol uniforms, who clearly had a vocation for cruelty and were thoroughly dedicated to their work, whilst the bucket, into which he was expected to void his bladder and bowels, itself reeked of fear and desperation.

He had not seen a living soul in all that time, apart from the scrofulous underling who twice a day placed a bowl of gruel and a lump of stale bread in the hatchway cut into the solid oak door which was his barrier to the outside world. It was bitterly cold down there, and he had no way of knowing whether it was day or night. Even when the hatch was opened, the corridor outside was so far beneath ground level that even the bringer of food needed a lamp to guide his way. The pail of water had not been changed since he had been thrown in there, and rats appeared to have been nesting in the metal cup from which he was apparently expected to drink.

He was curled up in the corner, trying to calculate in his mind how long it had been since the last food delivery, when he heard a faint noise outside, which proved to be the turning of the key in the lock. His hopes raised, he was about get to his feet when the door opened, and as his eyes adjusted to the glow from a hand-held torch he could just make out the bizarrely mismatched figures of his original captors.

The taller man held the torch up high, as the little one with the face like a pumpkin grinned down at him triumphantly. "Mr Cadby, nice to renew the acquaintance, if only for a little while. Sedition is a short but messy end, they tell me. But to judge by the smell in 'ere, you've already got one of them."

The taller man clucked in disapproval, and took over the conversation. "You'll have to excuse my associate here, but he recognised the smell because he comes from a long line of shithouse rats himself. Me, I have a little more breeding, after several years under His Majesty's banner, and it's on His Majesty's authority that I am here to speak with you this morning. The little matter of your co-operation in restoring tranquility and order to this town. The opposite of sedition, if you prefer."

It was doubtful if Cadby had understood half the words being addressed to him, but he was crafty enough to sense a line to freedom if he played the game correctly. For the moment, it was, he decided, best to say nothing. The tall man continued, and there was a smile in his voice, if not on his face. "We appreciate that you have been, to a very great degree, the victim of circumstance, and that only the humbling experience of being without work led to you being the trusting dupe of others. On that basis, and for those reasons, we are prepared to allow you the privilege of advising us of the current whereabouts of Mr Ned Ludd."

Cadby's hopes sank before his eyes, and he struggled to think of something equally valuable which he could offer instead. His silence was misinterpreted by the pumpkin-faced one. "Let's not piss each other about," he urged Cadby. "We know that you work for 'im, and ya must 'ave met 'im more than once, so why not be kind to yourself? Me and my friend 'ere, we've not only got the keys to this 'ere shithole, but we can walk right out of 'ere wiv ya, release ya into the street, and not a word more said on the subject. On the uvver 'and, wivholding information vital to the authorities could be taken as a sign that you're still one of 'is followers, and that's what they call sedition. That's a polite word for treason, and the last time I saw anybody topped for that, 'is wife were given the remains in four roughly equal bits."

Cadby finally found his tongue, but missed the exchange of triumphant looks between the two men as he began to tell them what they had come to hear. "I can't give yer Ned Ludd, 'onest I can't, 'cos the truth is 'e dun't exist. That's why nobody's ever bin able ter tek 'im, 'cos 'e's not a real person. Them what calls the shots in this business just let 'is name get used, 'cos it keeps the attention from them."

It was the turn of the taller man to move the conversation on. " 'Calling the shots' is a military term. Are you telling us that these raids have been conducted along military lines?"

"Dun't know abaht that," confessed Cadby. "I were never in the army misen, although mi dad were, so mi mam reckoned, anyroad. Wharra can tell yer is that each part o' the tahn 'as it's own gang what does the business when it's told to. Me, I've just bin in the St. Mary's mob."

"Don't be so modest, Mr Cadby," said Baker. "Accordin' to our sources, you're the big chief around the St. Mary's company – Captain Cadby to General Ludd, so to speak."

"I told yer, 'e dun't exist," persisted Cadby, who somehow felt that he should be offering something more promising if he was to regain his freedom. His opinion was obviously shared by his two interrogators, who turned back towards the cell door at the same time, as if by telepathy but in fact as the result of a concealed hand signal from Baker.

" 'ere, dun't go. I might 'ave summat ter tell yer!"

The two men turned back, and the taller one handed the torch to his pumpkin companion before squatting down on his haunches to stare into Cadby's face with what was far from being a friendly expression. "Please don't disappoint us this time, Mr Cadby, because if you do, two things will happen. The first is that my companion here will roast your nuts with that torch, and the second is that we will not waste our time returning to this verminous hole, even if you could deliver Napolean on a silver platter. Now, have I made that clear?"

Cadby nodded, his vocal chords frozen in terror. But when he was finally able to speak again, the words came out in a torrent. "Like I said, there's no Ned Ludd, but yer right, I do 'appen ter command a few men in St. Mary's who does wharra tell 'em. I can't tell yer where I gets mi instructions from, 'cos it's a different feller every time, burrit's allus the same place, an' that's the Newton's 'ead, in Glasshouse Street, every Monday at noon. I can tek yer there next Monday, if yer likes, burra can do berrer than that. Yer see, this Sat'day comin', there's gunner be a big do at Bradley's Hosiery in Stoney Street. It's all set ter go off at ten in the mornin', an' if you good gentlemen would care ter call in the sojers just as it goes off, I reckon 'is Majesty would be most impressed wi' yer efforts. Your reward would be my reward, so ter speak, if yer could see yer way clear ter gerrin' me aht of 'ere."

Baker was all smiles until Conon wiped them off with a warning look. Without changing his expression he drew himself up to his full height and glared down at Cadby. "One thing I learned in the service of His Majesty is that broken men will say anything to save their own skins. I don't necessarily believe that we can trust you, and just in case I'm correct in this view, you'll be coming with us on Saturday morning. If what you're telling us turns out to be correct, we'll review your legal status. If not, you'll have me to deal with. And just so that we understand each other, I've seen worthier causes than you hanged for cowardice. Good morning, Mr Cadby."

As the two men left, taking the torch with them, a turnkey appeared from the corridor to relock the cell. Conon issued brief instructions to him. "The same regime as before, but change the shit bucket. And don't take anything in there that he can harm himself with, or I'll have your guts."

Cadby lay down on the cold earth floor and wept, mainly for himself.

CHAPTER TWELVE

Let slip the dogs of war

SATURDAY MORNING was overcast and blustery, but Matthew was up and about even before Nathan came down the narrow staircase, carrying William in the bedding shawl which Lily had taken such pride in knitting out of some wool she had been given by the chapel. Matthew had lit the fire as usual, and was already heating the water for the morning tea as Nathan began to mix William's breakfast feed of flaked wheat and fruit, plus whatever else might be available. He tutted as he opened the stone storage jar and looked inside it. "There's no cheese left; yer mam must 'ave forgot again."

Matthew looked across at him hopefully. "We could go down to the market and get some more."

"Later, mebbe," was Nathan's only reply.

Matthew tried again. "It's fresher first thing. Why don't we go now?"

Nathan looked sideways at him, one eyebrow raised. " 'cos I've gorrer go ter Bradley's fust, that's why. It might be Sat'day, but I 'as ter go twice every Sat'day; yer should know that bi nah. An' anyroad, 'ow come you're so keen ter go ter the market? Yer normally wouldn't be seen dead in the place. Are yer finally learnin' what life's all abaht, nah that yer not gerrin' all them fancy ideas from the Bradleys?"

Matthew let the matter rest, stung by Nathan's seeming lack of concern for his heartbreak over being excluded from the Bradley household. And here was his father, about to put his life in certain danger by arriving at Bradley's factory just as Ned Ludd and his followers were planning to attack it. And the way Matthew felt about Robert Bradley just at the moment, they could burn all his frames with Bradley himself at the top of the pile, but he couldn't let his dad just walk into the middle of it without making some effort to stop him. He couldn't warn him, either, because Nathan would almost certainly alert the Watch and they would call in the soldiers, and Tommy would probably be in the raiding party.

At least that explained why there had been no more writing on their door, Matthew reasoned. Nathan didn't know that Matthew had been told all about that by one of the neighbours, and Nathan also didn't know that Tommy had thrown his hand in with those who had been responsible, in order to prevent any further trouble for the Slacks.

Yes, there was a lot that Nathan didn't know – including what was planned for that morning – and yet his stupid pride kept him loyal to what he believed to be right, even though both his sons had suffered as a result. Matthew asked himself again why he was wasting his time, when he heard Lily coughing and calling out for Nathan, who immediately poured a small portion of the herbs that old Nancy had left for them into a mug of hot water and hurried upstairs with it, and Matthew needed no further reminder of what mattered in life, and what didn't. But keeping Nathan away from the factory was going to be even more difficult than he had first imagined.

Matthew's brain was working feverishly as Nathan clumped back down the stairs with a gloomy, "Yer mam's cough's bad again."

"Maybe you should stay home and look after her." Matthew realised the futility of that suggestion as soon as he had made it, and was onto his next thought while Nathan was still giving him the answer he deserved.

"That's your job, or are yer above all that nah?"

"Course not, it's just that she's always happier when you're around, and when she's happy she doesn't cough so much."

"Tripe. She coughs 'cos o' the weather, and in case yer've not noticed yet, it's blowin' a gale aht there. The sooner I get the fust check ovver the berrer, then I can get back an' 'elp you wi' yer mam. Meantime, dun't let 'er dahn 'ere till that fire's roarin' proper. All right?"

"I thought I might come with you."

Nathan stared hard at him over the top of his tea. "That'd be the fust time. What's the marrer, dun't yer even want the job o' lookin' after yer sick mam? An' wharrabaht William? Somebody's gorrer see ter 'im while I does mi job. I'm sorry if this little place ain't what yer used to, but it's all yer got left nah that yer fancy friends 'as dropped yer."

Matthew wanted to scream out in sheer frustration, "you stupid, stupid bogger, you're going to get yourself killed just because you're too stubborn and set in your ways to listen to what I'm trying to tell you!" But just as he bit his lip to stop the words coming out, he heard St. Mary's chime eight o'clock, and he had another idea. The raid wasn't due to start until ten o'clock, and Nathan was usually back from his Saturday inspection duties within an hour. If he left now he could be back before it even started. Matthew tried another tack.

"Sorry Dad, you're right of course. You set off now and I'll look after things here. I'll see to William and I'll wash the pots and make sure that the fire's properly banked up for mam; you just get off straight away."

Nathan shook his head, wondering what went on inside the heads of boys of Matthew's age. "I'll go when I'm good an' ready. I've 'ad nowt ter eat yet, so pass me that bread, an' see ter the fire. Then yer can tek yer mam a cup o' tea."

Each minute seemed like an hour as Matthew watched his father cut the bread and spread it with some lard, then swirl his tea meditatively around his mouth as if rinsing his teeth in it. More than once he was tempted to urge Nathan to hurry up, but realised that it would have no effect other than to make his father even more suspicious than he already seemed. At last Nathan stood up and reached for his coat, as Matthew made a show of clearing up the dishes from the table and taking them to the pail in which they could be rinsed in hot water. Conscious of his son's eager eye on him, Nathan couldn't resist a parting shot.

"I 'ope yer'll be as keen ter see me come 'ome. Mind yer mam's tea."

Matthew heard the church clock chime nine at the same time that Nathan's boots rang out in the tunnel exit from the yard, and he prayed that the inspection wouldn't take as long as usual and that somehow his father would be out of there by ten. He would have endured further mental agony had he been able to watch the tragic scene unfolding, with Nathan standing at the top of Garner's Hill, chatting casually to several acquaintances about the windy weather which seemed to have swept in from nowhere, and would require the lighting of home fires for several more days at least. Pleased to have secured the promise of a share of some copse wood recently cut near Sneinton to make way for some new houses, Nathan finally opened up the side door to the factory a few minutes before ten.

All seemed to be in order as he made his way up to the frame room and looked out through the high windows down into the street below. Stoney Street, a main thoroughfare from St. Mary's into the town centre, appeared normal for a Saturday morning, with small groups of local residents wending their way past the junctions with Barker Gate, Wool Pack Lane and Goose Gate as they headed towards the market with their baskets and, in some cases, their small handcarts.

There was a group of men in the alleyway across the road from the Free Grammar School. Nathan might have paid them no attention had they not been in the process of painting their faces a dark colour with something they were sharing in a pot held by one of them, whom he recognised as Jim Collishaw. Jim and his wife should by rights have been in the Market Place, where they earned a few coins on Saturdays cleaning the shoes of the wealthier patrons who were obliged to step through the same orange mud as everyone else.

Several of the men in the group were looking around as if waiting for someone to join them, and as one of them turned to look down the alleyway back into the street, Nathan made out the gaunt features of Jack Cossall. Nathan was weighing up in his mind whether or not to go down and ask if the rumours were true, and that Tommy was staying with Jack these days, when his brain registered that each of the men appeared to be carrying a weapon of some sort. Suddenly, he snapped out of his reverie and ran for the staircase.

As he raced down them two at a time, his mind set on alerting the Watch who could always be found lounging around the old graveyard, he was aware of a cold draught of air coming up from the side door. He had just passed the door to Bradley's office on the first floor, and was trying to remember if he had left the side door off the latch, when the office door opened behind him and he was felled on the spot by a savage blow to the back of the head from a young red-haired man wielding a cudgel.

"Sorry Dad," muttered Tommy, "burrit were the only way. P'rahps Matthew forgot ter tell yer, or yer didn't listen, as usual." He grunted and heaved Nathan's inert form through the door into Bradley's office, leaving him behind the large mahogany desk which took up most of the room, before hurrying back down to the side door. A group of men was running along the alley towards him, and he searched their faces anxiously.

"Where's Cadby?" asked Tommy.

"Fuck 'im," replied Jim Collishaw, already out of breath, "it's just chimed ten an' we're goin' in, like we planned." The others had already started up the staircase, and Jim was now the last man in, as Tommy ran back up the stairs behind him. Instead of going up to the frame room, where he could already hear the smashing of wood and the gleeful cackles of his companions, he went back into the office where he had left Nathan unconscious.

There was no sign of any movement from him, and Tommy felt panic rising in his throat as he looked around in desperation for some water to throw over his father's face. His eyes lit upon a half-empty bottle of brandy on the desk, and he was just in the process of balancing Nathan's head onto his knee in order to pour some of it down his throat when the door flew wide open to reveal a terrified and breathless Matthew, who had run all the way after hearing the ten o'clock chimes.

"Yer were s'posed ter stop 'im comin' in 'ere terday," said

Tommy frantically. "I 'ad ter drop 'im an' 'ide 'im afore the others fahnd 'im. If they see you, yer'll be 'orse meat an' all. Rub this on yer face, an' quick abaht it!"

He handed Matthew a jar containing pungent black grease which Matthew recognised from the frame room, and he rubbed it into his open pores without a second thought. Upstairs all was chaos, as the men ran from room to room pulling out anything which might burn quickly and fiercely. Then from outside came the sound of musket shot and the shouting of orders, and they both heard Geordie Packer hollering down the stairs in panic.

"Sojers! I can see 'em from the winder, an' they're comin' forrus!"

Outside, in Stoney Street, a curious crowd of market goers had stepped aside to allow the contingent of militia to march down the middle of the street with bayonets drawn. They had stayed put to watch the excitement as the line of redcoats wheeled on command and formed three ranks in front of the Bradley factory. On a further barked command from an officer mounted on a large grey horse at their head and slightly off to their right, the front column fired a volley of musket shot into the air, then dropped to their knees to reload, as they had rehearsed time and again in the Castle grounds.

From out of Barker Gate, six officers of the Watch ran into Stoney Street and headed up towards the redcoats. One of them ran to the officer on the horse and saluted. "Leading Watchman Bonthorn, Town Watch. At your command, sir."

The officer declined to look down as he acknowledged the arrival of the locals. "Colonel Whitbread, Notts. and Derby. My men have just put up a warning volley, so we can expect the rats to leave the sinking ship at any moment. I suggest that you position yourselves at the doorway down that side alleyway. I'll send my right column as backup. Arrest anyone who comes out of there."

"Sir," was the clipped response as the senior officer of the Watch ran back to his men to pass on the instruction. As he did so, thirty mounted hussars clattered in from the town end of the street, having very recently scattered several hundred terrified citizens around the Market Place as they galloped through from the Derby Road. The horses wheeled and whinnied as their riders pulled harshly on their bridles to bring them to a halt, then allowed them to sidle in behind the rear row of infantry. Their captain rode across towards the colonel of militia and saluted.

"Pultney, Queen's Bays, sir."

The colonel looked disparagingly at his rank flashes. "You took your time, Captain. I'm claiming rank here; put your men on both flanks of mine and use your horses to block any resistance from that lot behind us."

"Quarter, sir?"

"None whatsoever, Captain. These men are enemies of the State and they've made a mockery of law and order in this town for quite long enough. We need a few examples set. Any resistance and you have my authority to kill, as do my own men."

"Sir!" grinned back the hussar, as he wheeled his horse back to his own cavalry with the good news.

The first of the raiders spilled out from the doorway halfway down the left-hand side of the alleyway, to be met by three officers of the Watch, two of whom wrestled him to the ground while the third knocked him senseless with his staff. Geordie Packer had both knees shattered by a blow aimed at them by a fourth Watchman as he tried to slip past, and as Jim Collishaw tripped over his writhing form, he was bayoneted in the side by an over-eager militiaman. The last of the raiders stopped in their tracks as they tumbled out through the side door and viewed the carnage, and for an uneasy few seconds they and the remaining infantrymen from the front rank of the militia eyed each other warily.

From the back of his horse, and the safety of the open street, Colonel Whitbread commanded the raiders to remain where they were in the name of King George, and one by one they were placed between two soldiers, each with a drawn bayonet, and marched out into the street where a restless crowd had begun to voice their disapproval. Captain Pultney instructed his hussars to sidestep their mounts in front of the crowd, as both a physical barricade and an implied warning. For this reason, he was late in spotting Tommy make his bid for freedom.

Tommy had remained in Bradley's office with Matthew and the still-unconscious Nathan until he had heard the last of them run down the stairs. Wishing Matthew good luck with Nathan, and apologising one final time to his inert father, Tommy peered surreptitiously out through the window overlooking Stoney Street and saw Jim Collishaw and Geordie Packer being carried off bodily, screaming in pain, by soldiers in red coats. There were soldiers on horseback too, and Tommy calculated that he might just be able to rush out into the street and down into Barker Gate, where he could hide among the familiar gravestones in the burial ground.

He crept down the staircase to the side door, and taking the deepest breath of his life, skidded into the alleyway and raced full pelt for the street. There was a militiaman to his left, busy cleaning the blade of his bayonet, and a Watch officer to his right who had his back to him. Ducking between them, and elbowing the Watch officer in the small of his back, Tommy made it out into Stoney Street and began running for the junction with Barker Gate. A roar of approval from the crowd alerted the hussar captain, who spurred his horse down the narrow, uneven thoroughfare, overtook Tommy in a matter of yards, and leaning out from his horse administered a slashing right-hand blow from his sabre which all but severed Tommy's head from his shoulders. There were screams from the crowd, a small girl fainted and at least one onlooker began to vomit into the gutter.

Pultney clattered to a halt, turned his mount round and walked it back to where Tommy's corpse lay at a grotesque angle. He yelled back towards two of his men who were cantering towards him. "Throw this into the infantry's baggage wagon before the crows get it, or the mob keep it as a souvenir."

If the mob had been in the mood for souvenirs, these would more than likely have come from the ranks of the military, who now had their work cut out keeping the crowd from open warfare with them. The remaining hussars were using their horses as crowd restraints, and trying to avoid being pulled from their saddles, while the militiamen were being ordered back into line to face the crowd, with their backs to Bradley's factory. Ominously, they were also told to prepare to volley into the crowd on command.

In the midst of all this, it occurred to several of the Watch that there might still be raiders left in the building, which they entered cautiously with their staffs held high in the air. They split up on the first landing, and as one of them kicked open the door to Bradley's office he found Matthew, his face painted as black as the others, crouched over his father, with a blood-smeared cudgel a few feet away on the floor. The officer shouted out a warning, and a colleague came back down the stairs and surveyed the scene with him. Not realising why, Matthew obeyed the instruction to get to his feet and allowed the officer to lead him down the stairs and into the alleyway, where he was handed over to several red-coated soldiers and marched down Stoney Street towards High Pavement and the gaol.

Robert Bradley failed to recognise Matthew's blackened face as he passed by on the far side of the street in the company of more Watch officers, who had been sent to his house in order that he might confirm the extent of the damage. The militia colonel dismounted and saluted as Bradley approached, and not wishing to be outdone the captain of the Queen's Bays cantered over, saluted the colonel and reported.

"One dead, nine prisoners, sir. I'll have my men remain in case of any further trouble from these civilians."

"Very well, Captain. Thank you for your assistance, and I'll see to it that your men's actions today are mentioned in my report."

"Thank you, sir," replied the captain, as he wheeled his horse after a polite nod to Robert Bradley, who was trying to clear his thoughts above the clamour of the baying crowd and the noise of horses. Suddenly he remembered something important, and turned to the Watch officer on his right.

"Are you in charge of things inside the building?"

"Not specially, no sir. Benny Bonthorn, Leading Watchman. Some of mi men was in there earlier, but the sojers done most o' the dirty work, I 'ave ter admit."

"Only there might have been one o' mi workers in there, mi General Overseer in fact. Name o' Slack."

"There was a party lyin' in one o' the rooms, so I'm told. Nasty blow ter the 'ead, apparently, but 'e'll be all right, so they say, an' 'e'll be aht in a minute. Funny abaht that name, though, 'cos we arrested a young lad bi the same name what were in there wi' 'im, an' 'e's bin tekken ter the gaol."

"A tall youth with red 'air?"

"No sir, that sounds more like the one what gorrimsen killed dahn the road there. No sir, this one were on the short side, wi' dark 'air."

"That can't be right," mused Bradley aloud. "That sounds like the younger son, and 'e wouldn't get 'imself involved in anything like this." But then Solley's warning came back to him, and he added, under his breath, "But who can be sure, these days?"

Safely out of sight, in the shadows of a nearby alleyway, three men had watched the whole gruesome episode unfold. Satisfied that the morning's operation had been successfully concluded, Baker and Conon quietly quit the scene by way of the back alleys, leaving a tormented and terrified Stan Cadby to find his own miserable way home.

There was to be one more death that night. It was well into the afternoon before the crowd was finally persuaded to disperse by a magistrate reading the Riot Act, and a reserve platoon of militia called up from the Park Barracks to fill the street with military uniforms and stern reminders of who had the upper hand in the matter of weaponry. But the last of the crowd to leave were far from happy, and there was much disquiet and the occasional angry shout, as they abandoned all thought of the market and headed instead for the alehouses.

In the taproom of the Golden Fleece, two of them could be heard bitterly bemoaning the fate of the recent martyr to the cause.

"It's allus the same," protested Amos Bullock. "They leaves the common folk ter starve ter death, an' the minute somebody tries ter do summat abaht it, aht comes the sojers. There were no need ter kill 'im, fer Christ's sake!"

"Just bloody target practice afore they goes ter France," commented Will Draycott on his left, who was determined to keep quiet about his role in previous raids, and the fact that had it not been for his recurrent back complaint, he might have been on this one. "That lad what got cut dahn bi the sojer on the 'oss, 'e used ter be one o' mi neighbours. Tanners Yard, 'e lived."

"Bad bloody business all rahnd," Bullock continued, unabated and unimpressed. "It's the fust time anyone's bin caught, mind yer. It were like they was waitin' forrem."

"They was," came a voice to their left. Will turned his head in startled surprise to look down at the little man seated near to them, and Bullock leaned across to make sure that he had not been hearing things.

"Beg pardon?" asked Will.

"They were waiting for 'em. I was there in the gaol when it all got planned."

They both stared hard into the watery eyes, and took in the unruly ginger hair sticking out from under his hat. Will was suspicious.

"An' 'ow come you was in the gaol, then?"

"Little misunderstandin' about some jools I was sellin' in the market two Sat'days ago. The beak give me seven days, and I 'eard it all on me fourth day in there. I was in a stinkin' 'ole next to this bloke who was singin' like a canary to two geezers from Lunnun, just like meself. That's what made me listen in, ya see; I'm not normally one for listenin' in."

Will snorted with laughter, exhaling a mouthful of Bodleys Best in the process. "Yer was bloody well listenin' in to us, yer nosey shit! Anyroad, what was it you 'eard?"

"Well," continued the ginger-haired stranger, unabashed, "seems like this geezer in the next 'ole to mine was tellin' these fellers all about this business ya was just talkin' about – when and where, and all that. Only this was two days before it 'appened! They 'ad the door open, like, and the food flap'd been left undone in my door, so I copped the lot good and sweet. The geezer was doin' a trade for 'is freedom, far as I could 'ear."

"Dun't s'pose yer gorris name?" asked Will, hopefully.

"Well now," came the reply, "I could probably remember better if I wasn't so thirsty." The cheeky, enquiring, look seemed perfectly at home on the face, and in next to no time there was a fresh quart pot in front of it. The man leaned in closer.

"I made a point of askin' as I were leavin', since ya never know when that sort of information might buy ya a drink. 'is name were Cradley, or sumfin' very close to that."

"Not Cadby?" queried Will with a murderous look on his face.

"Aye, that were it right enough. Cadby. I saw 'im once as they were puttin' me in the 'ole next to 'im. Little fat geezer wiv very little 'air on the top."

" 'scuse me!" cried Will, as he pushed his way roughly past his informant and interrupted a conversation between three other men on the far side of the room. There was a shout of rage and disbelief, and all four men ran out into the street, spitting blood and yelling oaths into the still, night air.

Just under an hour later, the tall, bald-headed man guarding three travelling bags outside the Exchange Hall ceased his anxious pacing up and down, and half ran over to the shorter man who had just emerged from the end of Smithy Row, while his female companion uttered obscene words of relief from behind the bags.

"Where did you get to?" demanded Conon. "We thought you were going to miss the coach."

"What, me miss the chance to get back to good old Lunnun, and leave Miss Smollett 'ere wiv you as a travellin' companion? I couldn't do that, now could I?"

"Fred Baker," the woman complained in a strident tone, "you'll make an old woman outa me yet, ya great poltroon! Where the 'ell 'ave ya been?"

"Me?" grinned Fred. "Just tyin' up a few loose ends."

The loose ends were finally tied up several hours later, so far as the authorities could deduce. Certainly they were well tied up before two constables of the Watch, bringing in a protesting burglar, found the sack lying on the top step of the town gaol entrance. The contents had once been Cadby, although certain essential parts of him were never found. If God had extended a mercy Cadby didn't deserve, they would have been cut off after he died.

CHAPTER THIRTEEN

Taking instructions

A GREAT DEAL happened during the ensuing weeks, although most of the main players only saw some of the unfolding events, and even then partly through a fog of shock and disbelief. Nathan was carried down from Bradley's office still barely conscious, and when told of what had happened he seemed to have formed the idea that Matthew had been the one who had hit him on the head. Bradley had seen Nathan being carried out by two Watch officers and had insisted that he be taken to the General Hospital in The Park, where he remained for less than twenty-four hours and was treated for a superficial head wound, before leaving and making his way back to Tanners Yard, against all medical advice.

They had delayed telling him about Tommy's death in the belief that it would hinder his recovery, but once he learned the truth it proved to be the final incentive for him to rise groggily from his bed in the Poor Ward, thank the treating surgeon for his kind attentions, and stride somewhat unsteadily through the town streets back to Lily and, as he expected, Matthew, to whom he believed he owed his life, after learning how he had been kept hidden from the raiding party.

Lily had been informed of Tommy's death within a few hours of the raid by a well-meaning neighbour, who also informed her that Nathan had been taken to the hospital. She was still comatose when Nathan walked under the tunnel archway and into the yard and was intercepted by a devastated-looking Aggie Draycott. Aggie explained, between tears and unnecessary apologies, that William had been in her care since the previous afternoon, ever since Lily's wailing and screaming had brought the neighbours running to her door, to find her on her knees in front of the fireplace, pleading with God to give her back her eldest son. They had carried her to bed upstairs, where she had remained ever since, occasionally waking for long enough to resume her wailing, until eventually old Nancy persuaded her to take a cup of hot tea laced with something she would not identify to those who asked, and which she kept hidden in her apron on her way in and out of the house.

Nathan rushed into the house and climbed the stairs in trepidation, wondering why Matthew was nowhere to be seen, and peeped in over the threshold at the sleeping bundle wrapped in every warm blanket and coat that Nancy had been able to find. Even so,

Lily was shivering and coughing in her sleep, and an occasional burst of unintelligible words would tumble from her tortured dreams onto the old prayer cushion covered with muslin cloth that passed for a pillow, which Lily had proudly made for Tommy's birth, and which had in turn served each of their children.

He was about to go back down and build up the fire for when Lily came downstairs again, when a creaking floorboard betrayed his presence, and she stirred.

"Tommy?"

"Nay, lass. It's only me, Nathan."

"I know mi own 'usband, yer daft donkey," came the words from somewhere deep down in the pillow, and Nathan felt the tears rising in his eyes and throat. He crouched awkwardly by her side and took one of her hands in his.

"I'd still love yer even if yer didn't. Nah get back ter sleep; yer need yer strength."

"Is it true abaht ar Tommy? Is 'e really dead?"

"Aye, lass, 'fraid so. But dun't tek on, 'e'll be wi' God nah."

"Is it right 'e were killed by a sojer?"

"Aye, but it were a mistake, so they say," Nathan lied.

"An' 'ow come yer finished up in that there 'ospital? Did they get you an' all?"

"Nay, lass, I just banged mi 'ead, that were all. Nah get back ter sleep."

"Can yer send Ruth up when she's finished wi' William?"

Nathan faltered, horrified and saddened by the extent to which she had lost her grip on reality, but he was saved by a hammering on the outside door.

"There's somebody at the door. I'll just see to 'em, an' come back wi' some tea."

"If it's ar Tommy, tell 'im ter tek 'is boots off. 'e's allus comin' 'ome mucky."

Nathan swallowed down more tears, and flung open the door to reveal Sam Pinkney, a picture of embarrassment and discomfort.

"Ey up there, Nathan. Good ter see yer back 'ome. I've just bin ovver ter the 'ospital but they said yer'd already left. Any chance of a jar 'o tea? I'm right parched after that walk."

Nathan realised at once that this was not purely a social call. In the twelve or so years that they had been workmates in the frame room their families had never socialised, and neither man had ever visited the home of the other, except once when Nathan had been entrusted to deliver Sam's wages at the end of a week in which he had gone down with the flu. But that was years ago, and Nathan could not imagine that Sam had come to see him unless he had something important to say. Nathan closed the door behind him and the two men stood in the yard in the midday sun, Sam with a dejected look on his face.

"Nowt personal, Sam," Nathan reassured him, "it's just that Lily's a bit poorly at the minute, an' I dun't want 'er 'earin' things she shouldn't. We can 'ave that jar o' tea in a shake, but what yer got ter tell me fust?"

"Bloody 'ell, Nathan," exclaimed Sam, "there's nowt gets past you, an' that's a fact. 'ow d'yer guess?"

"The look on yer face were enough, but apart from that, yer've not come all this way wi'aht Bradley sent yer. I'm not blamin' yer, mind – 'appen yer the new General Overseer nah that I'm aht."

"Who sez yer aht? An' anyroad, after wharrappened ter you, 'e could promise me owt, an' yer'd not see me tekkin' on that job. No, mi friend, yer see, I bumped inter Mr Bradley at the 'ospital – 'e were there ter see you an' all – an' 'e 'ad a message fer yer. Said ter tell yer that Matthew's bein' looked after, an' yer job's waitin' fer yer whenever yer up to it again. There's three frames left, an' one of 'em's yourn. Burrit's number four, since your frame were the fust ter get smashed. But they left yer tools alone, so that's summat."

Nathan formed a quick mental picture of the warp frame on the other side of Sam's, but closer to the wall and away from the natural light, and he caught himself wondering what it was going to be like working with less light, before he checked himself with a slight feeling of guilt. "What's that abaht Matthew? What d'yer mean, 'e's bein' looked after?"

Sam looked even more uncomfortable as he spelt it out for Nathan. "Truth is, Nathan, 'e were tekken up bi the Watch. There's nine of 'em altogether, although they reckon Jim's in a bad way. Anyroad, they're up fer a special court or summat, but Bradley sez ter tell yer that 'e's gerrin' a lawyer bloke ter look after Matthew, an' not ter worry 'cos . . ."

"Yer bloody kiddin'!" thundered Nathan, relieved at his foresight in keeping their conversation out of the house. "I've already lost one son in all this shit, an' Matthew were the one who saved me; they can't charge 'im wi' owt!"

"That's not 'ow they see it, Nathan. 'e were fahnd in there like the rest of 'em, an' – Jesus Christ, I 'ate ter 'ave ter be the one ter tell yer – but they reckon that they're gunner do 'im for the raid along wi' the rest of 'em."

"A load o' fuckin' shit!" bellowed Nathan at the top of his voice, to Sam's astonishment. He had never heard Nathan use language that strong in all the time they had worked together, and he was concerned at the level of anguish that must have provoked it. His measured response was as mild and conciliatory as he could make it.

"Aye well, like I said, Bradley's mekkin' sure that 'e gets a lawyer fer if 'e 'as ter go ter court an' everythin'. 'e also said ter tell yer that yer wages is safe fer as long as yer need ter get well again. Wharre didn't tell me ter tell yer is that yer gunner be missed arahnd the place, but yer can tek that from me."

"Aye, thanks Sam," said Nathan absently, still trying to get his thoughts up-to-date with this latest information. "Nah, just tell me where they've got Matthew, an' then we'll 'ave that jar o' tea. But dun't say owt ter Lily when we goes inside. I'll tell 'er when she's feelin' a bit stronger, like."

If Nathan was confused by the turn of events, Matthew was even more bewildered. He had left Bradley's factory in the company of two militiamen under the impression that they were escorting him home for his own safety, and the truth had only begun to dawn on him when they had almost reached the junction of Stoney Street with High Pavement and he had seen Robert Bradley on the other side of the street, and had stepped out of line intent on speaking with him. One of the soldiers had grabbed his arm, stuck his bayonet under his nose and warned him not to step out of line again or he would reap the consequences. When he had asked where they were going he was brusquely told to shut his mouth before it got slit open permanently.

Inside the town gaol he was led into a large room in which there were some half a dozen men who glared at him resentfully as he was thrust down on one of the bench seats by a uniformed turnkey, and told to stay where he was until they were ready for him. He assumed from the whispered conversations and blackened faces around him that his companions were some of the raiding party, and he heard the name Slack mentioned at one point, as curious eyes looked surreptitiously at his own still-blackened countenance. He recognised one of the men by sight – having seen him once in Tommy's company – and realised that they must know who he was. He was also wondering whether or not Tommy had managed to get clean away when he heard his own name being mentioned again, but this time more loudly, by the turnkey who had put him in the room and was now calling him out of it again.

After being ordered rudely to wash his face in a pail outside the door, he was taken roughly by the arm into a larger room and up to a high desk, behind which sat another uniformed gaol officer who asked for his name and address, fiddled with some papers, announced 'C 12' to the man who still had Matthew firmly by the arm then went back to poking his ear with the end of his quill pen. What followed was a confusing journey through locked doors, down dank and gloomy passages and around endless corners, before Matthew was told to halt and remain still in front of a heavy wooden door which his escort opened with a large key from a monstrous bundle of them hanging from his uniform belt. The door was pulled open and Matthew was pushed inside; by the time his eyes had grown accustomed to the dim light from the oil lamp high on the wall, the door had been slammed shut and relocked from the outside, and Matthew began two weeks of isolation.

He was able to follow the course of the days from the routine lighting and extinguishing of the lamp by a little old man dressed in some sort of cast-off tunic and smelling of fish oil and onions, who made it very clear to Matthew on the first evening of their acquaintance that there was no conversation allowed. Sometime, roughly in between each of these two visits, another man, equally poorly dressed but slightly less odorous, would bring in the bare essentials for Matthew's existence – bread, water, sometimes a sort of gruel and very, very occasionally something that resembled one of his mother's pot stews, but with hardly any meat and no vegetable that Matthew could identify.

The nights were, in a sense, no different from the days, in that Matthew was not allowed anything to read, and when he asked the lamplighter, the latter expressed surprise that Matthew could read, before reminding him that "The rules sez I can't talk ter yer." But when the lamp had been extinguished for the day (if indeed it had been the day, because no natural daylight penetrated his cell), Matthew was left alone with his thoughts, which at first centred upon Rebecca, his parents and Tommy, but over time lost some of their clarity and finally merged into a resigned expectation that 'this was it' and that, whatever he had done, he must have deserved it.

Then came a day when the cell door was opened at an unusual time, and Matthew was ordered out into the corridor. His first thought was whether or not, by being absent, he would miss the meagre rations which were routinely delivered in the middle of the day, which by Matthew's rough estimation could not be far off. Then his mind was distracted by being told that "Yer attorney's 'ere, an' wants ter see yer," and as he allowed himself to be led back down the maze of corridors and through the confusing series of doors, he tried to recall where he had heard the word 'attorney' before. He was sure it was during some conversation at the Bradley house, but he could no longer remember what else they had been talking about at the time.

He was finally led into a brightly lit room with a high ceiling, two chairs and a table, at which was seated a young thin-faced pale-looking man who reminded Matthew of an alabaster figure he had seen on a tomb in St. Mary's Church, but clothed entirely in black and wearing an equally black hat which seemed incongruously tall on his tiny head. The man didn't get up to greet him, but simply motioned him into the chair opposite and continued reading through some papers which were spread out before him, as the gaoler closed the door behind him and noisily locked it from the outside. The man looked searchingly into Matthew's face for at least a minute before he spoke.

"Matthew Slack? I'm Timothy Shand, Barrister-at-Law, and I'm here at Mr Bradley's request to defend you."

"Defend me from what?" asked Matthew, surprised at how husky his voice sounded after so long without using it.

"This criminal charge, of course. Haven't you been informed of what's being alleged against you?"

"Nobody's said anything to me except 'shut up', 'stand up, 'sit down' and 'here's your food, shithead' for what I think has been twelve days, although I'm not sure."

"I see," Shand replied, somewhat surprised at the lad's ability to express himself, and wondering whether or not it might somehow come in useful at trial. "Well in that case, I have to advise you that you are charged with one count of frame breaking in company, and that a special preliminary hearing has been set down for a date next month in the Guildhall. Mr Bradley has retained my services as your attorney, which means that I will be doing my best to persuade any subsequent jury that you have been falsely accused."

For all his recently acquired learning, Matthew had found this last communication a little perplexing and unfamiliar, and it showed in his face. Luckily for him, Timothy Shand had thus far spent most of his post-Oxford and Middle Temple legal career representing the criminal classes, the more innocent and less experienced of whom found the criminal justice process a confusing challenge, so he began again.

"They say that you were one of those who broke into Bradley's

Hosiery and destroyed some of the fittings and fixtures in there."

"That's not right!" protested Matthew fiercely. "I only went in there to warn dad – sorry, my father – that Bradley's was going to get done that morning, and then, when . . .' "

Shand raised a hand in the air to stop the flow of information, and looked down quickly at his papers. He also picked up a pen, dipped it deep into an inkwell set into the table, shook the excess off the end of the quill and began writing on the top sheet of a pile of parchment in front of him.

"Sorry Matthew," he explained, "we have to take this step by step, so that I can write it all down. Your father – that's Nathan Slack, correct?"

"Yes," Matthew confirmed. He waited tensely until Shand had finished writing and looked up at him again before asking, somewhat tentatively, "Is my father all right?"

"He's recovering from a nasty blow to the head, if that's what you're asking me," said the attorney. "But the allegation is that you were the one who knocked him senseless."

"No, that was Tommy," insisted Matthew, adding almost as an afterthought, "he's my brother, and he was one of the lot that did Bradley's. But he knocked dad to the floor and hid him from the others. He can tell you all about it; he's the one who can tell the truth about what happened, but then . . . look, I'm not going to get Tommy into trouble, am I? I'd rather stay here forever than do that."

It was fortuitous that Shand had not yet received his copy of the entire Crown Brief of Evidence in the matter of Rex versus Collishaw and Others, nor had he spoken to anyone else about the case in the few days after being advised by his clerk that he had new instructions to defend one of those 'from that do in Stoney Street', about which he had not bothered to consult any newspaper beforehand. Had he done so, he might have learned of Tommy's death, and his face might have given things away. As it was, his lawyer's instinct told him that a line of defence might suddenly be opening up before him.

"Let me see if I've got this right so far, Matthew. Your father was the General Overseer at the Bradley premises, and he was making a routine inspection that Saturday morning when a group of Ludd's men broke in, intent on breaking frames and so on. What you're now telling me is that you were there yourself, but that the person who knocked your father to the floor in Mr Bradley's office was your brother Tommy?"

Matthew hesitated before replying in the affirmative, and his hesitation was not missed by Shand, who checked his papers before continuing. "But if it helps – and bear in mind that at the end of the day you may have to tell the truth about your brother if it means saving your own life – I can tell you that Tommy is not on the list of those who are charged along with you."

Matthew looked both relieved and mystified at the same time. "That's the best news I've had since they brought me in here. He must have got away after all. But what did you mean about my life?"

Shand had been required to do it before, but it was never easy. "I'm sorry, Matthew, but evidently no-one's told you. The charge you're facing is what they call a 'capital' charge. That means, I'm afraid, a possible death sentence if you're found guilty, but no doubt the judge in your case could be persuaded against it, given your age – sixteen, isn't it? Please, Matthew, listen to me and try not to get upset; it's important that we talk some more."

Matthew had begun to cry like the boy that, in truth, he still was, and Shand reminded himself again of the savagery of a law which took no account of the frailty of those in reduced situations, with no life experience and no role models with moral fortitude and conviction which they could pass on to them. He pulled a large handkerchief from the top pocket of his frock coat and handed it to Matthew, whose composure was restored when he remembered the last time that someone had handed him a handkerchief, which he still kept with him all the time, and he reminded himself that the person who had done that would expect more courage from him at this time. After all, he was innocent, and he had nothing to fear in the sight of God.

"Sorry," he mumbled. "I don't normally do that, and I won't do it again; promise."

"Think nothing of it," Shand breezed, happy to have his client back in a state in which he could give instructions. "There's still one thing you have to tell me, though."

"What's that?" enquired Matthew.

"How did you know that Bradley's was to be raided that morning?"

"Tommy told me," Matthew replied. "He wanted me to keep dad away from the place that morning, and I tried, but dad insisted on going anyway and when I heard the church strike ten I knew that it would all be happening and dad would be in the middle of it, so I ran to Bradley's and there was dad on the floor of Mr Bradley's office, and Tommy told me he'd done it, and . . ."

"Whoa, whoa!" cried Shand, almost laughingly. "I've got to write all this down, remember? Now, give me a minute or so, and I'll get all that down, then read it back to you and you can make sure that

I've got it right."

When he had done so, there was still one more matter to be clarified."Is it true that your face was painted black, like all the rest of them?"

"Yes it was," said Matthew without realising the significance of this evidence against him. "Tommy told me to do that so that the rest of the gang wouldn't realise that I wasn't one of them."

"And unfortunately," mused Shand, who was beginning to gain confidence in the task ahead of him, "neither did the Watch, who took you for one of the raiders. It's possible that if we can get all these facts into evidence, the jury can be persuaded to acquit you."

"But won't that mean Tommy getting into trouble? I don't want that!"

Shand was touched by the boy's misguided loyalty to his brother, all the more so because his experience of criminal defence work thus far had been just the opposite, with co-accused almost tripping over themselves in their enthusiasm to run 'cut-throat' defences blaming everything on each other. But the boy had to be made to face reality.

"Look, Matthew," he explained, "it seems to me that the entire case against you will collapse if Tommy can be persuaded to tell the court what really happened, and how you were not directly involved in any of it. You may be able to afford to feel the way you do, but in your best interests I have to think differently. Right now, my main concern is how to persuade Tommy to come forward and tell the truth. Where can I find him?"

"Dunno," was Matthew's quiet and reflective reply. "He left home weeks ago and we don't know where he went. But the others might know. Who are they?"

Shand consulted the papers in front of him and found his copy of the charge sheet which would, following a Grand Jury hearing which he was now thinking of defending, be converted in due course into a capital indictment. He began reading from the list.

"James Collishaw, John Cossall, Ralph Darby, Caleb Mason, George Packer, Stephen Perry, Arthur Peters and Jacob Rawlings. Do you know any of them?"

"Don't think so. I might know them by sight, but I don't know their names."

"Very well, Matthew, you just leave things with me for the time being. I'll be back to see you again in a few days but what you've told me already's been a great help. Try to keep your spirits up, and if you can think of anything else that might help, just remember it until we meet again – all right?"

Matthew nodded, and the lawyer gathered up his papers before hammering loudly on the inside of the door. The turnkey unlocked the door and Shand slipped down the corridor, leaving Matthew reflecting with mixed feelings on the conversation which had just taken place.

As the turnkey made his way back down the labyrinth to return Matthew to his cell, Timothy Shand heard the big front doors slammed shut behind him by unseen hands. He stood on the steps looking down at Weekday Cross, and felt confident enough to take his first deep breath for two hours.

———————

The three men stared pessimistically down at the table between them, as each contemplated the enormity of what lay ahead. Any comfort which Robert Bradley might have derived from being seated in his own office had dissipated rapidly with the news which the lawyer had brought him, and, difficult though it might be in the current circumstances, he could not avoid sending a messenger down into Tanners Yard to summon Nathan to join them. After all, it was his son's life they were dealing with.

It was fortunate that Robert had the presence of mind to impress upon the man he had sent – who had known Nathan Slack for as long as anyone in Bradley's employment – that Nathan had to be told that the meeting was solely to do with Matthew's forthcoming trial, and nothing else. Robert knew enough about Nathan's stubborn pride to realise that he would not attend in respect of any other agenda, and after Nathan had appeared awkwardly in the doorway, and been introduced to Timothy Shand before being invited to take the remaining chair, Robert let the latter do the talking.

"The fact is, Mr Slack," Shand admitted, "that we have encountered a problem in the preparation of your son's defence. I had been led to believe that your other son, Tommy, could be the means of securing Matthew's acquittal if only he could be persuaded to testify. Matthew tells me that it was Tommy who knocked you out and hid you from the rest of the raiding party, and that he – Matthew that is – only came in afterwards. Obviously, if Tommy could tell the court that, then Matthew would have to be acquitted. But now Mr Bradley here tells me that . . . that Tommy's . . ."

"Aye, 'e's bloody dead, right enough," responded Nathan in a voice gruff with suppressed grief. "So yer can forget that."

"Nathan," interjected Robert gently, "someone's got ter tell Matthew."

" 'e's gorrenough ter worry abaht, wi'aht addin' that ter the list."

"What Mr Bradley means," continued Shand in his best negotiating manner, "is that without Tommy, we have to think of some other way of getting out in evidence what really happened that morning."

"Well, I dun't bloody know, do I?" retorted Nathan, irritated by the calm way in which the lawyer could talk about one of his sons being dead and the other facing the gallows. "A fat bloody lot o' use I was, as it turned aht, an' nah I can't tell yer wharrappened 'cos I were aht fer the count – 'ere in this very room, as it 'appens."

"Surely, Matthew can explain it all ter the court?" suggested Robert. "After all, 'e's a very well-spoken young man fer one of 'is class. Oh, shit, sorry Nathan."

"Aye, yer right – fer one of 'is class. Yer oldest daughter took care o' that. But 'ow's 'e gunner do in front of all them lawyers an' such?"

Sensing the mounting tension between the two very different men, Shand sought to defuse it. "Mr Bradley's idea is a very logical and sensible one. But unfortunately, the law won't allow it."

"What?" exclaimed Nathan. "Yer mean that a man can be on trial fer 'is life, an' 'e can't even speak up forrissen?"

"Not in the normal sense, no," the lawyer replied. "Every witness normally has to give their evidence on oath – that is, after swearing on the Bible – but the law has never allowed the accused himself to do that. Many lawyers like myself believe that to be wrong, and many of us are arguing for reform, but that won't happen in time to help Matthew. He can give what is called an 'unsworn' statement from the dock, but juries never afford them the same importance, and it's usually a mistake to even attempt it, even if your client is as articulate as Matthew."

"So what d'yer suggest yer can do?" demanded Nathan, who was clearly still in a state of high irritation, and was wondering how on earth he could explain all this to Lily.

"All I can do," said Shand, "is build the best case I can for Matthew with what little bits of information I'm given. Even then, there's no guarantee that I'll be allowed to ask questions of the witnesses they call against Matthew. But leaving that aside for the moment, and beginning with you, Mr Slack, please tell me everything you can still remember about that morning. Even if it doesn't seem important to you, it might be important for Matthew."

Nathan stared despondently across the table at the far wall. "Like I said, I dun't remember 'owt after I got 'it on the 'ead."

"Did you by any chance see who hit you?"

"No. Fer a while there I thought it were Matthew 'cos 'e'd bin actin' a bit funny all that mornin', in a manner o' speakin'. But if Matthew reckons it were Tommy, then it musta bin."

"What do you mean by Matthew acting strangely that morning?" queried Shand.

"Well, it were like 'e were tryin' ter stop me from goin' ter Bradley's as normal fer a Sat'day. 'e knew that mi duties involved checkin' aht the place, an' it were as if 'e were tryin' ter find excuses why I shouldn't go."

"Was he behaving as if he knew what was going to happen?"

Nathan thought for a few seconds before replying. "Aye, yer right; that's exactly 'ow 'e was. But 'ow could 'e 'ave known?"

"According to what Matthew told me, Tommy had warned him that there was a raid planned for here that morning, but he didn't want to tell you outright in case you called in the Watch and Tommy got arrested. All along it seems that Matthew's first thoughts have been for you and his brother."

"Aye, that's Matthew at 'is best," agreed Nathan, wiping his face with the sleeve of his coat, and shaking his head when Robert made an inviting gesture towards the bottle of brandy which was sitting between them on the office desk.

After pouring himself one, and offering a glass to Shand, who politely declined, Robert observed, ruefully, "I still say it's a shame and a sin that Matthew 'imself can't speak out with the truth. It's not as if 'e can do 'is brother any harm now. Sorry, Nathan, but that's the truth of it. The fact is that Matthew would give a very good account of 'imself if 'e was allowed to."

Shand's face lightened for a moment. "Perhaps you could speak for him, Mr Bradley?" he suggested. Both Robert and Nathan looked at him in surprise, as he continued. "Somehow we have to show the jury that Matthew is in a different category from the rest of the men who are charged along with him. We can hardly expect any of them to admit that they were in the raiding party, and that Matthew wasn't, because they're obviously going to have to try to argue that it's all a matter of mistaken identity or something. How they conduct their defence is their concern, but if a fine upstanding member of the community like yourself could tell the jury what Matthew is really like as a person, and how his loyalties are more likely to have been with you than with the raiders, that might make all the difference.

After all, you were the victim here; what I mean is, you were the target of their activities."

He had added this correction as soon as it had occurred to him that the true victims of what had happened were probably Nathan's two sons, and he didn't want to antagonise Nathan any further because he might have to call him as a witness.

Robert appeared to experience some awkwardness with the proposal which had just been put to him, and he looked apprehensively across at Nathan. "I'd be more than 'appy ter do anything I can fer such a fine young man," Robert confirmed without taking his eyes off Nathan, "but 'e's your son, and I don't want ter be seen to meddle in matters which aren't mine."

"Very kind o' yer," acknowledged Nathan gruffly. "Yer may as well, since there's nowt 'is own father can do forrim."

Sensing that he had probably achieved all he could for one morning, Shand took his leave after arranging a further meeting for the same time the following week, which would apparently be only a matter of days before the presentation of the 'true bill' application. As he left, Nathan also stood up to go, and Robert felt obliged to say something supportive, while at the same time feeling almost completely useless.

"I wish I could say something that would make things better, Nathan."

"So do I," agreed Nathan as he walked towards the open door. Then he stopped and turned to look back at Robert. "An' I wish yer could tell me 'ow to explain ter Matthew that after all 'e tried ter do, 'is brother's still dead."

The next two weeks passed slowly and miserably for Matthew, who remained locked alone with his own thoughts for day after day, with only one more visit from Timothy Shand to break the monotony. In some ways Matthew wished that this second meeting had never occurred, because his lawyer seemed even less sure of how matters were to proceed and was evasive whenever Matthew tried to bring Tommy into the conversation.

Matthew assumed that either they had been unable to find Tommy (who, if he had any sense, was probably deep in hiding anyway), or that they had found him and he wanted nothing to do with telling the truth. Either way, things did not look promising, and as Matthew was taken from his cell and transferred into a large room under the courthouse, and ordered to remain silent, he comforted himself with the thought that at least something was now happening and he was out of that lonely cell.

There was a brief whispered conversation between the other prisoners before a trapdoor in the ceiling was unlocked noisily from the other side, and Matthew finally realised why there had appeared to be a flight of stairs in the middle of the room, apparently giving access only to the upper floorboards. One by one they shuffled up the stairs and into the centre of one of the largest rooms Matthew had ever seen. There were muted cheers from a crowd sitting in a row of what looked like church pews in an upper gallery running all round the room, which were silenced immediately by the stern old man seated in a high-backed chair with gilded sculptures on its top, who slammed down some sort of hammer onto the bench in front of him and warned those seated there that any more noise would result in the entire public gallery being emptied for the day.

Each of the prisoners was in ankle shackles which had allowed just enough freedom for each of them to mount the stairs, and once they had been told to sit down in the long box which contained them, a chain was passed between each of their sets of shackles and attached to bolts at either end of the box. Matthew was seated at the very end of the line on the right-hand side, and as he gazed up at the mass of people looking down at him from the gallery, he caught sight of his father's anxious face, which broke into the ghost of a smile of recognition as their eyes met.

Matthew switched his attention to the old woman who was being held upright by his father, and with a pang of horror and guilt he recognised his mother beneath the green bonnet which she always wore for Sunday best, mouthing words silently to herself as she gazed into the distance, her cheeks hollowed by suffering and her eyes robbed of all expression. She seemed in even poorer health than when he had last seen her, but of course, he was unaware of Tommy's death and the pain and anguish his mother had endured when she stood by his graveside a few days after the military had handed over his body for burial, then had come back apologetically an hour later with the head.

She was sitting between Nathan and Aggie Draycott, and Matthew tried to catch her eye without success; then he tried to raise his hand to wave, but the manacles which also constrained his wrists would not allow any upward movement unless the man sitting to his left allowed it. Matthew looked sideways at Jacob Rawlings' grim expression, and decided against even asking.

All the while, Matthew had been vaguely aware of people talking to the old man with the hammer. A large man in a uniform of the Watch had just sat down, and Matthew got a rear view of Timothy Shand as he rose to address the Bench.

"I seek leave to appear for the prisoner Slack, and I am instructed to offer no evidence at this time."

The old man frowned. "Your name?"

"Timothy Shand, attorney-at-law. I appear on private instructions which I claim privilege against disclosing, and since this is a capital matter . . ."

"Yes, yes!" interrupted the old man testily, "but as we are both well aware, if I grant leave to appear now, it will carry over into the trial, where one of His Majesty's judges may well have occasion to criticise my decision. This is most inconvenient."

There was a polite cough from the Clerk to the Justices sitting below him, who craned his neck backwards and upwards from his bench as the elderly magistrate leaned forward for a whispered conversation with him. The magistrate sat back up straight and addressed Shand.

"Very well. I am advised that since the authorities wish there to be no suggestion of unfairness or irregularity in this matter, it is a suitable one for the grant of attorney audience. But what about the others?"

"I understand," continued Shand, "that they are not represented this morning, and indeed have received no legal assistance thus far. Perhaps, if Your Worship is subsequently obliged to commit this matter to the Special Assize, suitable arrangements might be made for the others under the Poor Prisoners' Act?"

Matthew was just asking himself why he didn't come within the definition of a 'poor prisoner' and wondering exactly how Mr Bradley had come to be paying for Mr Shand to speak for him, when the magistrate gave all the remaining men in the dock a bitter glare and asked, "Do any of you wish to say anything at this time?"

One by one they lumbered to their feet and answered 'No', the last of them before Matthew's turn came – Jacob Rawlings – half dragging Matthew to his feet in the process. He had just succeeded in sitting back down when the magistrate looked down and across to his right at a group of men sitting in a separate area fenced off with polished wooden railings, and enquired, "Do you need to withdraw?"

One of the men stood proudly to attention, touched his forelock, and replied, "No, Your Worship. We find a true bill."

"Very well," responded the old man, who then commanded the

prisoners to stand, before pronouncing, "Committed to stand trial for the capital offence of frame breaking, contrary to section two of the statute of our sovereign majesty King George enacted as chapter fourteen of the fifty-third year of his reign. You will be held in close custody until your trial, which by order of the Lord Chancellor will commence at Special Assize in the Shire Hall on the second day of August next coming. Take the prisoners below."

Back down the stairs, Matthew was relieved to learn that they were to be transferred by wagon to new cells under the Shire Hall, to await their trial. He was less happy when advised that they would not be occupying a cell each, but were required to double or triple up for their new accommodation. They were offered no choice, but were manacled back together in smaller groups as their names were called, and they were led off in twos and threes. In Matthew's case it was a duo, and he shuffled alongside Jack Cossall, to whom he was attached by ankle chains, and from whom he would learn a great deal in the weeks to come.

CHAPTER FOURTEEN

Trial and tribulation

"ALL THOSE having business before My Lord the King's Justice, of oyer, terminer and gaol delivery, let them now draw near and they shall be heard. God save the King."

The door behind and to the right of the highly polished Bench opened to reveal a liveried flunkey bearing a mace, behind whom walked the High Sheriff of the County of Nottinghamshire, the Vicar of St. Mary's in whose parish the court was located, and whose presence was required at the hearing of all capital charges, and finally His Lordship Mr Justice Buller, of the King's Bench of the High Court. They each reached their seat behind the Bench, turned inwards to face the courtroom, bowed solemnly and took their seats. The potential jurors fidgeted nervously, and even those in the packed public galleries were reduced to silence by the contrived majesty of the occasion.

The Special Assize had been convened as soon as word had reached London of the first arrests under the new law, regardless of what might be the outcome of the Grand Jury deliberations. Hastily arranged late night consultations within the corridors of power had resulted in the appointment of Sir Montgomery Buller KC as the Assize judge, partly on the basis of his judicial seniority, and partly due to his proven preference for the Crown case in any criminal trial. The Crown case itself would be led by Jeremy Manning KC, Senior Treasury Counsel and Member of Parliament for a safe Tory seat in Sussex, which boasted that no two of its dwellings were less than one hundred yards apart, and who was widely tipped as the next Solicitor General. His junior in the matter – and the member of the team with the firmest grip on the facts contained within the Prosecution brief – was Mr Hugh Burnett, a London barrister with a largely Equity practice in the Chancery Division of the High Court, selected by his 'leader' because he owed him a considerable amount of money following a card game at their London club.

The two Crown Counsel sat at the right-hand end of the bar table, as viewed from behind by the eight men in the dock. They were one less in number than those originally arrested, since Jim Collishaw had died from complications arising from his injuries a week after he had been thrown into a cell like Matthew's, but without any medical assistance. At the other end of the bar table sat Timothy

Shand, who announced his appearance for Matthew after the same had been done for the other prisoners by the counsel sitting to his right, Charles Daubney, who had accepted the 'Paupers' Brief' on behalf of all the others in the hope that a tentative foray into matters criminal might breathe some life into his otherwise moribund, and thus far largely commercial, practice.

Even the venue had been carefully selected. The offences themselves had occurred well inside the town boundaries, and ought therefore to have been heard in the Guildhall, attached to the town gaol and the normal palace of justice for crimes committed within the town. However, the Shire Hall had been chosen because of its greater dock capacity, the availability of the larger holding cells beneath the courtroom itself, and the greater ease with which it could be defended from the mob, should the need arise. There were also the added – but unspoken – reasons that the space in front of its massive outer doors already contained a convenient set of holding brackets for the gallows, and that a County hearing required a County jury, which could be drawn from a population less likely to be sympathetic to those town men who had regularly and brutally raided the outlying villages during the preceding eighteen months or so. All it had then required was a commission for a Special County Assize, and a 'forum of convenience' application, in respect of both of which the Lord Chief Justice had been only too willing to oblige.

Nor had they spared any expense in the matter of security. Mindful of previous performances by the Nottingham mob when displeased with the dispensation of justice, the front row of what would otherwise have been the minor lawyers' benches, located behind those of counsel, with only a narrow walkway in between, was occupied by ten specially selected infantrymen from the Royal Berkshire Regiment, their red coats set off with the gold and white of their plumage and dress coat appendages. Each man sat bolt upright, seemingly oblivious to the proceedings, but each holding a musket, complete with fixed bayonet, between his knees, the stock firmly planted on the floor ahead of him. Thirty more sat in readiness in a specially created space behind the courtroom, which had once been a court record store, but which now boasted direct access to a spot immediately behind the judge's seat on the Bench via a recently created doorway which was hidden behind a wall hanging depicting The Martyrdom of St. Anthony.

To Matthew, it all seemed as if it was happening to someone else and he couldn't focus his mind on the fact that this was it, the end of all the effort which had been made on his behalf, all the hopes which people had held for his future and, in a slightly unreal sense, possibly the end of his life. He was worried what that might do to his mother, who, as before, was seated in the gallery between Nathan and a neighbour, a different one this time whom Matthew thought might be old Nancy, but he wasn't sure, since it seemed so long ago that he had last seen her.

Nathan had been allowed to visit him earlier that day along with Mr Shand, and when Matthew had asked for his mother, Nathan had explained that only one of them had been allowed into the special room set aside for the meeting, and that "Yer mam's still a bit poorly, like . . ." She certainly looked it, huddled up to Nathan with the neighbour holding her steady from behind, and Matthew was alarmed to see Lily stare directly at him without any sign of recognition. Still, it must be unbearable for her, losing one son and now watching another one, as likely as not heading the same way.

Nathan hadn't had to tell Matthew what had happened to Tommy, because Jack Cossall had told him the minute they had been left together in their cell. Matthew had broken down, and Jack had cradled him in his arms like the son he had never shown any affection for until it had been too late, and Jack had also confirmed what Matthew had suspected all along, that Tommy had only played Cadby's games in order to protect the rest of the family. And now here was he – Matthew – facing trial for also trying to protect their father. If only they could all have been allowed to live their lives like normal folk, without any of this shit about 'the cause', Matthew reflected grimly, they could have been the happiest family in the yard, perhaps even in Nottingham.

He began to allow his thoughts to drift towards Rebecca, who, he felt sure, would be ashamed. Not ashamed of him being accused of attacking her father's business – he liked to think that she knew him better than that – but ashamed and embarrassed that he'd been so stupid as to get involved and then get caught the way he had, and he wondered whether she had been the one who had persuaded Bradley to find a lawyer to defend him. His daydreaming abruptly came to an end as he was jerked to his feet by the rest of those attached to his wrist manacles suddenly standing up at a command from a man in the well of the court wearing the same sort of silly grey wig as the judge, but without the red robes.

The jury had been sworn in and the indictment was being read to each of the prisoners in turn, beginning with Jack Cossall. They all said what Matthew had been told by Mr Shand to say, and when it came to his turn he took a deep breath and prepared to sound as manly and convincing as possible.

"How say you, Matthew Joseph Slack, do you plead Guilty or Not Guilty?"

"Not Guilty."

"Very well, the prisoners may now resume their seats," intoned His Lordship in the voice which normally left the accused quaking in the dock, but this time seemed to have had no effect, to judge by the sullen looks on the faces of the eight prisoners who had just been arraigned. Hopefully they would show the same lack of emotion when he finally got to cover his wig with the black cloth sitting conspicuously on the Bench, in order to pronounce sentence of death on each of them in turn, in accordance with his instructions.

Justice Buller looked, thought Matthew, like one of the spaniel dogs he had played with at Eastwood, with heavy jowls that wobbled every time the grey earpieces on his full-bottomed wig flapped around as he moved his head. If this was the majesty of the law, it was lost on Matthew, who reminded himself to pay attention to what was going on in case he missed something important.

There was an ill-tempered exchange between the two defence counsel and the judge, as each of them insisted on maintaining their right to appear for their clients, the judge for his part questioning the sanity and good judgment of the magistrate who had granted them this right in the lower court. Matthew caught some reference by the judge to matters being 'slowed down to walking pace', and a look of relief on Timothy Shand's face as he turned briefly at the end of it all to smile encouragingly back at him. At least Matthew still seemed to have a lawyer to speak for him, not that he could imagine what could be said on his behalf.

The first witness called by Manning, for the Crown, was Nathan. Matthew had seen him being beckoned out of the public gallery by a uniformed court officer, and had been wondering what was going on until he saw his father climb into the narrow witness box, raise his right hand and repeat the words of the Oath administered to him by another bewigged flunkey who to Matthew resembled one of those performing monkeys he had once seen at the Goose Fair.

The first few questions put to Nathan were straightforward enough, dealing with his profession, his years of employment at Bradley's Hosiery and his current status as General Overseer. He was then taken through the events of that morning, question by carefully worded question, and he recounted how he had been on his way back down the stairs past Bradley's office when he had been hit on the head from behind. His next recollection had been of coming to in Bradley's office with a concerned-looking Matthew bending over him, just before two officers of the Watch had helped him to his feet, and then removed Matthew before coming back for him.

"Let me see if I have this right, Mr Slack," repeated Crown Counsel. "There's no doubt in your mind that when you came round, it was your son Matthew who was in the room with you. We'll hear that his face was blackened at that time, so how did you know it was him?"

"By 'is voice; it's softer an' berrer spoken than Tommy's is . . . er, used ter be."

"But you still insist that Matthew wasn't there to begin with, as far as you can recall?"

"No, burre musta followed me there."

"But how can you be sure of that, Mr Slack?"

"Well, 'e were at 'ome when I left ter go ter Bradley's, an' I didn't see 'im go past me on the way there."

"But the fact remains, Mr Slack, that you didn't actually see the person who hit you, did you?"

"No, but . . ."

"And," cut in Manning before Nathan could fully answer his question, "you were hit from behind, were you not, so you couldn't possibly have seen who your assailant was, could you?"

"No, but . . ."

"Thank you, Mr Slack. No further questions, My Lord."

Charles Daubney had only one question for Nathan in cross-examination, but it was one which he no doubt subsequently regretted having asked.

"Mr Slack, I represent all the accused persons in this case other than your son Matthew. As I understand it, you never got to see any of the persons who raided Bradley's Hosiery that morning, did you?"

"Not once they came in, no."

Looking slightly bemused, Daubney sat down, and glanced apprehensively across at Junior Counsel for the Crown, Hugh Burnett, who was furiously scribbling something on a piece of paper which he handed across to his leader. Looking sympathetically back at his fellow defence counsel, Timothy Shand rose to his feet for the second time that morning, and cleared his throat before addressing Nathan.

"Mr Slack, as you know I am representing your son Matthew in these proceedings. In answer to one of my learned friend's questions earlier, you told the court that the last time you saw Matthew on the morning of the raid was back at your house, and that he was still there when you left."

"Aye."

"Could you please describe to the court your son's demeanour that morning, before you left?"

"Eh?"

"Sorry, let me put it another way. What sort of mood was Matthew in before you left the house?"

"Kinda funny. It were like 'e were tryin' ter stop me from goin' up there."

"As if he was trying to protect you, you mean?"

"Aye, that's right."

"Thank you, Mr Slack."

Shand turned briefly to smile at Matthew, then sat down. Jeremy Manning rose to his feet to re-examine Nathan, armed with a far less pleasant smile.

"Mr Slack, you told my learned friend Mr Daubney that you didn't recognise any of the raiders 'once they came in', as you put it. Did you see them at any time that morning?"

"Yeah, when they was across the road from Bradley's. They was in an alley across the road in Stoney Street, an' they all 'ad weapons o' some sort."

"And were their faces blackened at that time?"

"No. They began doin' that while I were watchin' 'em from the frame room winder o' Bradley's."

"So you saw them all before they effected their disguises?"

"Aye," said Nathan, a little uncertain of what 'effected' meant.

"And did you know any of these men by sight?"

"Two of 'em, yeah."

"And who were they?"

"One of 'em were Jim Collishaw, but 'e's dead now, so they tell me."

"And the other?"

Nathan squirmed uncomfortably as he looked down at the courtoom floor, just beyond the witness box in which he was standing.

"Mr Slack?" insisted Manning.

Nathan coughed feebly, before replying, in a low voice. "It were Jack Cossall."

"Jack Cossall?" repeated Manning in a loud clear voice, for the benefit of the jury. "And do you see him in court today?"

Nathan raised his head to look across towards his left at the eight men in the dock, his face a picture of misery. With what passed for a smile of abject apology, he replied. "Aye – 'e's the one on the far end – the fust un."

"This one here?" enquired Manning, moving triumphantly to the side of the dock, and waving a bony finger at Jack Cossall.

"Aye," confirmed Nathan miserably. "Sorry Jack, burrit's the truth, an' I'm sworn ter tell the truth."

"Yes, thank you Mr Slack, and no doubt we can rely on you to tell the truth in regard to another matter. You said that your son Matthew was behaving in a 'funny' way, as you put it, before you left the house that morning. Assuming, by that, that you didn't mean that he was behaving in an amusing way, you meant that he was behaving oddly; is that correct?"

Timothy Shand shot to his feet immediately. "I object to that question, My Lord. He's clearly leading the witness."

Justice Buller fixed him with one of his legendary glares of irritation. "No he's not, Mr Shand. He's merely seeking clarification of a matter which you deliberately left in an uncertain state. Proceed, Mr Manning."

"Thank you, My Lord," replied Manning with one of the unctuous, ingratiating smiles for which he was equally famous, before he turned back to address Nathan once more.

"Was your son Matthew behaving oddly that morning, Mr Slack?"

"Aye, 'e were," said Nathan.

"He didn't want you to go to Bradley's that morning, did he?"

"No, 'e didn't," confirmed Nathan happily, not realising that a trapdoor was about to open beneath his feet.

"And one reason for that might be that he knew what was planned for that morning, might it not?"

"Aye, but . . ." Nathan began hesitantly, before running out of words.

"But what, Mr Slack?"

"Nowt," Nathan conceded, in a defeated tone.

"And as you told the court a few moments ago, there was a brief period during which you were looking into Stoney Street from the frame room window of the Bradley premises, correct?"

"Aye," agreed Nathan, who this time could see what was coming.

"And during that time, Matthew could have crept into the premises, entered Mr Bradley's office, and been waiting to hit you on the head when you came back down."

"Matthew wouldn't do that!" Nathan protested.

"Really?" responded Manning gleefully. "Is it not the case that when you were first found by the Watch, lying on the floor in that office, you conjectured that Matthew might have been the one who had hit you on the head?"

"My Lord, I must protest!" yelled Shand, rising to his feet instinctively, regardless of the likely consequences. "He's cross-examining his own witness!"

"And very effectively too," commented the judge with a sadistic smile. "Sit down, Mr Shand."

"Thank you, My Lord," beamed Manning, already half-seated. "I have no further questions of this witness."

Matthew was still trying to decide what it all meant and why his father looked so defeated as he left the witness box, when the judge announced the luncheon adjournment and the court began to empty. The prisoners were led in shackled convoy back down the stairs and fed a thin gruel in the room below. Matthew tried to avoid looking at Jack Cossall, who for his part didn't seem to want to look at anyone anyway, and after what seemed like hours they were all led back up through the trapdoor and into the dock while the courtroom filled up around them. Timothy Shand walked up to speak to him as the shackle bolts were being reconnected to the sides of the dock.

"Chin up, Matthew. They've still not eliminated the possibility that all you were doing was trying to protect your father, and we've still got Mr Bradley's evidence to come."

"Thanks anyway," said Matthew in a resigned tone, "but that judge doesn't seem to like you very much."

"Leave me to worry about him," Shand replied, then turned round as a knocking on the door behind the Bench indicated that His Lordship had finished his lunch. "I've got to get back to the bar table. I'll talk to you later."

The first afternoon was taken up with evidence from various Crown witnesses who had been present during the aftermath of the raid, who one by one recounted how the raiders had run from the building straight into their waiting arms and had then been taken away. Jeremy Manning, for the Crown, seemed to dwell particularly on the fact that all the men concerned had their faces blackened, and had only been identifiable later, after they had been compulsorily scrubbed inside the gaol, after which they had given their names and addresses. He dwelt gloatingly on the evidence-in-chief of Roland Kettley, one of the two officers who had found Matthew inside Bradley's office with Nathan, and who happily confirmed that Matthew had his face blackened like all the others and seemed no different from them in appearance.

Timothy Shand did his feeble best against a credible witness who could not really advance Matthew's case anyway.

"Am I correct in suggesting that my client – young Mr Slack, on the end of the line there – offered no resistance when you asked him to accompany you from the building?"

"Aye, that's right."

"If I were to suggest to you that he had no idea why you were removing him and that he didn't realise that he was being arrested as a frame breaker, would you agree with that suggestion?"

"I dunno, do I? It were 'is business what were goin' on in 'is 'ead. But yer right that 'e didn't give us no trouble."

In re-examination, Manning experienced little difficulty in re-establishing his advantage. "Matthew Slack was the last to be removed from the building, was he not?"

"As far as I know, yes."

"And by then, those who had resisted had been dealt with, how shall we put it – 'forcibly' – by the military?"

"There were one dead in the street, and another one bleedin' 'is guts inter the alleyway, if that's what yer mean."

A low rumble of disapproval began to spread through the public gallery, silenced instantly by the fall of the judge's gavel and a demand for 'Quiet!' Manning passed hastily to his final point.

"In all the time that you were with Matthew Slack in that room, did he once express any concern for the condition of his father?"

"No, sir."

"And did he at any time try to explain that he had not been a member of the raiding party?"

"No sir, not once."

"Thank you, Officer Kettley. No further questions, My Lord."

In what was all-too obviously a prearranged submission, Manning rose to his feet and addressed the judge.

"My Lord, the Crown clearly cannot complete its case this afternoon. We have a further group of witnesses who can attest to the identities of those apprehended at the end of the raid which has led to the bringing of these charges, and it might be in the best interests of justice that they all be heard during the same session. In view of the time, Your Lordship might think it best if we . . ."

"Yes, you may well be right," agreed His Lordship, on cue. Turning to the jury, he added, "I am adjourning these proceedings until ten o'clock tomorrow morning. You are free to go back to your homes for this evening, but you must return here then. I must also, as a matter of law, charge you not to discuss the evidence you have heard today, either with each other or with anyone else, in the meantime. Thank you, Mr Bailiff."

The same liveried officer who had borne the mace ahead of

the opening procession stood up and called out, "Court adjourned until tomorrow at ten o'clock in the forenoon. God Save the King," before leading the Bench party out through the door into the judges' corridor, securely separated from the public section of the building. The turnkeys began to disconnect the shackles in the dock, and the first day was all over.

That night, they were lodged once again in the cells below the courthouse, and Matthew sat awkwardly on the floor on the far side of the cell from where Jack Cossall sat on the sole bench seat which the sparse accommodation possessed. After what seemed like hours of silence, he grinned at Matthew. "Cat got yer tongue, son?"

"No, it's just . . . well, I mean . . ."

"Yer dad 'ad no choice, boy. They'd 'ave put 'im in 'ere wi' us if 'e 'adn't told the truth. Can't blame a man fer tellin' the truth afore God."

Matthew looked across at him with an enquiring look. "I had no idea that . . . that . . ."

"That I were a God-fearin' man, yer mean?" Cossall's face took on a reflective look as he called up old memories from years now long past. "Aye, I were – once. Then came the drink; yer dun't drink, do yer, boy?"

"Not really," confided Matthew.

"Aye, well, you mek sure yer never start. It were the ruination o' me, an' that's the real truth on it. All the rotten shit yer've no doubt 'eard about me – floggin' the missus an' beatin' the boy 'alf stupid – it's all true. Mi life's fucked, an' I deserve what's goin' ter 'appen, so dun't you go worryin' that yer dad told the truth when 'e got the chance. Yer should be prahd of 'avin' a dad like that. Tommy were, I could tell, fer all that 'e didn't agree wi' the way yer dad sided wi' Bradley an' all that 'e stood fer. If yer learn owt from all this, son, mek sure that yer tek after yer dad an' follow 'is example."

"I may not live to do that," Matthew countered sadly.

"Aye, yer will, if there's any justice left in this world. In the same way that God's waitin' fer me wi' a big length o' wood, 'e'll mek sure that you gerraht o' this mess, unless yer've done summat I dun't know abaht, tharris."

An hour later each of them had fallen asleep, exhausted by the day's ordeal. They awoke the next morning to the cell door being thrown open by two turnkeys carrying water, cloths and pumice blocks. They also had two bundles of prison clothes.

"Right, 'ere yer go," said one of them. "Get yersens washed an' changed. There's bin complaints from the courtroom that yer all stinkin' the place aht. Can't 'ave that nah, can we?"

It was the first water Matthew had seen for weeks that had not been for drinking, and although embarrassed by the reason for its appearance he nevertheless made sure that he put it to good use, in case his mother was allowed in to see him that day.

In fact, there was no-one to see him that morning before they all began the now familiar shuffle up through the ceiling. Matthew looked anxiously through the faces in the galleries which ran around three sides, and finally, directly behind and above him, caught sight of Nathan and old Nancy with a wizened stick of a human being propped up between them, staring into the middle distance and mouthing silent prayers to no-one in particular. He was wondering who was looking after William when the customary knock was heard on the outside of the door leading onto the Bench. Day two of Rex versus Cossall and Others had begun.

For the entire morning the evidence was boringly repetitive, if essential to the Crown's case. One by one, those who had been responsible for the apprehension of the prisoners told how they had handed them over to officers of the militia, and then those officers took it in turns to relate how they had delivered them to the town gaol and had remained until each of them had given a name and address. By this painstaking process it was established that those now in the dock, including Matthew, were the self-same individuals who had been removed from Bradley's, and the Crown had deftly got around the potential difficulty arising from the fact that each of the raiders had his face blackened when first apprehended.

During the luncheon adjournment that day, the two defence counsel were deep in conversation with Jeremy Manning.

"Are you calling Robert Bradley?" enquired Shand.

"And why should I?" demanded a complacent Manning in his usual arrogant tone.

"Because if you don't," Shand reminded him, "you have no evidence that any damage was done inside the building, only that the accused were where they shouldn't have been."

Manning gazed inquisitively into Shand's face. "You obviously want to cross-examine him, but I can't for the life of me understand what about. Why don't you call him yourself?"

"Because then, as you well know, I can't cross-examine him. But apart from that, why should I do your job for you? Without

Bradley, your case falls apart."

"I've a couple of unremarkable witnesses left to go, then I'll consider my position. But I still don't see what you're up to."

"Call Bradley, and you'll see," Shand chirped back, before adding, "don't call him, and we'll both be submitting that you've no case, won't we, Charles?"

"Er . . . yes, that's so," replied Daubney without conviction, as both men left the robing room in search of a late luncheon.

It was mid-afternoon before Manning opted to take the bait, announcing that the final witness for the Crown would be Robert Bradley. Bradley climbed into the somewhat rickety witness box and took the Oath, looking a little surprised when the questions began to come, not from Timothy Shand, but from a counsel he had not seen before, and who had not taken the trouble to visit him as he sat for two days in a witness room, waiting on the off-chance that he might be required.

Bradley's evidence-in-chief was confined to a largely formal confirmation of the fact that when the business had closed for the week on the Friday evening prior to the raid, everything had been in order, and he had been the proud owner of twelve warp frames. By the time that he was allowed back into the premises the following day, this had become four warp frames and a great deal of matchwood. He also described the damage and destruction to his stock-in-trade committed by raiders in search of things to burn, which action they had fortunately not been able to complete before the authorities had moved in. Finally, and for the record, he stated that the only person with authority to enter the building that day had been his General Overseer, Nathan Slack.

"Thank you, Mr Bradley," concluded Manning, but then added, with a sideways glance at the two defence counsel, "please remain where you are in the witness box."

After Charles Daubney had confirmed that he had no questions to ask of this witness, Shand rose slowly to his feet and adjusted his wig slightly as he looked down at his papers.

"Mr Bradley, I believe you know the young man on the far left-hand end of the line of prisoners there in the dock, my client Matthew Slack?"

"Yes, I do."

"In fact, he was one of your employees, was he not, apprenticed to his father, the Mr Nathan Slack who gave evidence at the start of this case?"

"Yes."

"And in fact, he became a little more than an employee, as time went on, was that not the case?"

Shand became aware of the trial judge raising his head from his notes, to stare intently at Bradley, obviously curious to hear his answer.

"Yes, in a sort of a way. 'e showed great promise as a clerk, after my daughter took 'im on as a pupil, and . . ."

"A pupil?" echoed His Lordship. "Is your daughter a teacher?"

Bradley went on to recount how Lucy had discovered Matthew's latent talent in her Sunday School class, how she had brought him home with her one Sunday, and how he had slowly become a friend of the family and a regular companion to his younger daughter Rebecca. His Lordship's derisive snort conveyed his overall opinion of this arrangement.

"And no doubt, Mr Bradley," His Lordship suggested, "you have now come to regret such charitable generosity?"

"I'm not sure what you mean," Bradley persevered. " 'e never showed any sign of disrespect when 'e was in my company, and I can't believe that 'e could have got 'imself mixed up with the lot that attacked my business premises."

"But you wouldn't be the first person in your position to clasp a viper to your bosom, would you?" was the response from the judge. "And in these dark and dangerous days of Jacobins and revolutions, one could be forgiven for being too trusting, holding out the hand of Christian charity, only to have it bitten off by those with darker purposes to serve."

Shand sat down slowly and sadly, having decided not to give the judge yet more opportunity to engage in his legendary amusement of baiting defence witnesses. The judge looked down at him disapprovingly.

"Mr Shand, I take it from the fact that you have resumed your seat that you have no further questions of this witness. Mr Manning, do you wish to re-examine?"

Manning rose to his feet with another unctuous smirk. "No thank you, My Lord. Your Lordship has, if I may respectfully say so, done that for me more than adequately."

Shand was still quietly fuming at the judge's lawful, but unnecessary, interference as he followed Charles Daubney in confirming that no witnesses would be called for the defence. Due to the lateness of the hour, His Lordship, with the consent of all counsel in the case, adjourned the trial to its third day to allow ample time for closing addresses, the charge to the jury, and their deliberations, hopefully without the need to accommodate them overnight at public expense. The prisoners were then allowed to trundle back downstairs for another night under the Shire Hall.

At least Matthew was allowed visitors on that final morning, although his mother was not among them. Explaining that she was 'still proper poorly', Nathan gave what little comfort he could in the circumstances, while Shand confined himself to apologising to Matthew for the entire criminal justice system which had brought him there, and seemed reluctant to hand him back. Shand sought to justify not having asked all the questions of Bradley he had been planning to, explaining that judges had what the law called an 'ex proprio' right to ask any question of a witness which they felt was necessary in the interests of clarifying an issue for the jury, and that some judges, like Buller, could not entirely excise from their systems, when they rose to the Bench, the gladiatorial instincts which they had displayed while at the bar table in their younger days. Most of which was lost on Matthew as he prepared to join the morning procession of the hopeless up through the ceiling.

Since none of the prisoners had led any evidence in their own defence, it fell to Jeremy Manning to close the case for the Crown, leaving the two defence counsel with the last word before the jury retired to consider its verdict. Manning rose slowly and solemnly to his full six feet two inches in height, melodramatically threw his papers down on the bar table in front of him, and, without thereafter referring to a single note, pierced the jury with the clearest slate-grey eyes at the English Bar.

"Good gentlemen of the jury," he boomed, "there never was, in my submission to you, a clearer case of guilt of a heinous crime than that against each of the prisoners who are ranged before you in the dock of this court. You have heard each of them in turn identified by lawfully appointed, honourable and God-fearing officers of the State as persons who were seen running for freedom from the premises of Bradley's Hosiery on the Saturday morning specified in the indictment. Inside those premises, later that day, the owner of those premises – whose evidence you also heard given in a straightforward honest way before God – found the wrecked remains of what had once been his livelihood, the shattered remnants of his years of commendable industry, which in turn provided the means of sustenance to honest, ordinary folk like yourselves; men like the good Nathan Slack, whose evidence you also heard and who almost gave his life in defence of his employer's hard-earned interests.

"Would that this country had more men like Nathan Slack, men prepared to be counted, and prepared to stand firm against the slow and insidious growth of sedition and revolution which now threaten the very existence of all those among us who ask nothing more than the right to work hard for our families, fear God and respect the laws of this land. The dark forces you have heard so much about in the past few days would, had they not been brought to account by those brave men, some of whom are even now defending our realm against the French, have continued with their evil schemes and ambitions in the very alleyways, courtyards and byways of this town, as well as the helpless and vulnerable villages from which many of you have come in order to see justice done, villages which have already witnessed the evil which such wicked conspiracies can bring down upon innocent communities.

"Today, you have the opportunity to show your support for, and admiration of, those who strive tirelessly to preserve our nation from the perfidy of foreign revolution. You may today show Nathan Slack that, though he may have been deserted even by his own sons when he stood for what was right, yet the hearts and minds of true God-fearing people everywhere will always uphold the honest cause which he symbolises, and will always reach out a comforting and supportive hand in the fight for justice and freedom in which he has gladly joined on your behalf.

"Gentlemen, I ask you to find each of the prisoners guilty as charged."

The atmosphere in the courtroom remained almost mesmeric as Manning sat down with a flourish of his robes, but slowly returned to normal as Charles Daubney rose to close the case for the other accused. In doing so, he made much of the fact that the case against all the prisoners – Matthew included – was almost entirely circumstantial, consisting as it did of the fact that each of them was seen leaving Bradley's at a time shortly before the damage was discovered.

"Not a single witness was able to say that he saw any of the accused raise so much as a fist in anger," Daubney argued loudly, in a voice that still seemed weak by comparison with Manning's stentorian tones, "and not a single person was able to swear on oath to having seen any of these men break a single frame. The damage which was described could have been inflicted at any time the previous night, and not even the General Overseer, Mr Nathan Slack, deponed to having seen or heard any riotous activity before he was struck down by a person who has never been identified.

"It is on the basis of these flimsy facts that my learned friend for the Prosecution asks you now to condemn eight of your fellow citizens to a brutal death. As His Lordship will shortly advise you, you may only find these men guilty if you are satisfied of their guilt beyond reasonable doubt. I say to you that it is impossible for you to do so solely on the basis of the evidence which has been given before you. Thank you."

It was finally Timothy Shand's turn, and he smiled weakly back at Matthew as he rose to his feet and continued the attack on the Crown case.

"First of all, gentlemen of the jury," he began confidently, "let me adopt and commend the submissions to you by my learned friend Mr Daubney. This is indeed a tissue of innuendo woven by the Prosecution around a few bare threads of circumstantial fact which, even taken together, go nowhere near proving that these men were responsible for the crimes of which they now stand accused. There is not a single piece of evidence in this case pointing directly to the guilt of any of these men, and of none of them is this more true than my client Matthew Slack.

"The only evidence against him is that he was found in the same room as his injured father, the witness Nathan Slack. I draw your particular attention to the fact that he had made no attempt to leave the building, a fact of which my learned friend for the Prosecution made much when seeking to emphasise the guilt of the remaining prisoners. If attempting to leave the building that morning is to be taken as a sign of guilt, then not even that may be urged upon you in respect of my client. On the contrary, the fact that he did not must surely count in his favour. We do not even know why he was in the building at that time, or what circumstances led him to be there. Even his own father had believed him to be back at home as he entered the building, and he only became aware of Matthew's presence in that room after he had been unconscious for an unknown length of time.

"You may ask yourselves why Matthew Slack has not entered the witness box himself and told you on oath why he was there. This is because the law will not allow him to do so, and so we may only speculate as to the reason for his presence at the scene. Even his own father, in his evidence, hinted at the possibility that the boy may have entered the building to assist him, or to save him; certainly, he was not able to testify that Matthew had been among those whom he had seen gathering outside the building before he was struck from behind. He was not even able to testify that it was Matthew who had struck him.

"And so, gentlemen of the jury, the case against Matthew Slack consists of nothing more than the fact that when officers of the Watch entered the building that morning, they found him beside his father, in circumstances which were equally consistent with the suggestion that he was there to render succour and aid to him, as would any decent boy for his father. Is this the evidence upon which he should be condemned to hang? Thank you, gentlemen."

A brief outburst of applause drifted down from somewhere in the public gallery, to be instantly silenced by the fall of the judge's gavel. After glaring individually into every face in the courtroom, resting noticeably longer on the tense faces of the men in the jury box, His Lordship began his closing charge to the jury.

After first explaining that theirs, and theirs alone, was the task of finding guilt or innocence in the case of each of the prisoners, he advised the jury that the only duties allocated to the trial judge following the closing addresses of counsel were those of summarising the law, and directing them on the evidence. The law he summarised in little more than one sentence, advising the jury that this was the first time under English law that the recently enacted capital crime of frame breaking had come before a jury, and that to them fell the honour of ensuring that it was employed in the manner which Parliament had intended. Having clarified what 'beyond reasonable doubt' meant, he then turned to the evidence which had been heard.

"This, gentlemen, was in short compass, and it was substantially to the effect that shortly after the authorities received intelligence that an outbreak of frame breaking was in progress at the premises of Bradley's Hosiery, officers of the Watch, supported by contingents of both infantry and cavalry from the local barracks, apprehended each of the prisoners in turn either in, or endeavouring to escape from, those premises, and that further inspection of the premises revealed that a considerable number of what I noted were called 'warp frames' had been destroyed, and that a sizeable quantity of the stock-in-trade of the business had been disarranged.

"Mr Daubney, on behalf of all of the prisoners except the one named Slack, urged upon you the fact that this evidence was what we lawyers call 'circumstantial', by which is meant that it merely pointed to the guilt of the prisoners, and did not prove it directly. Be that as it may, gentlemen, I must advise you as a matter of law that circumstantial evidence is perfectly capable, in and of itself, of proving the guilt of a prisoner. I myself presided in a case at the recent Gloucester Assizes in which a wretched woman was accused of killing her husband by administering arsenical poison in his food. There was no 'direct' evidence in that case, either, in the sense that any one person could be brought to testify that they had seen her administer the poison. But the Court heard from other witnesses of the woman's previous threats to 'do away' with her victim after he began consorting with a female neighbour, of her having clandestinely obtained a quantity of arsenic from the tannery in which she was casually employed, and of a certain financial benefit which she enjoyed from the unfortunate man's death, and these factors, taken together, were sufficient to secure a finding of guilt against her.

"Likewise in this case, you must not be dissuaded from your duty by counsel's description of the evidence as circumstantial. All cases in law are made out by circumstances, and it is the solemn duty of every jury to assess those circumstances in accordance with the gravity which they deserve. You have been summoned to serve on this jury because you have been judged to be men of intelligence and experience. Use that intelligence and experience in this case, and ask yourselves whether or not the evidence you have heard can admit of more than one conclusion.

"Mr Shand, for the prisoner Slack, sought to raise issues of particularity, over and above the case against the prisoners generally, and it is in the interests of justice that I deal with them before you withdraw and consider your verdict. It was suggested by him that the presence of Matthew Slack in the building at the time of its entry by the authorities might be explained away on the basis that Matthew Slack was there to assist his father Nathan Slack, and, by extension, was therefore in the process of defending the interests of Mr Bradley against the depredations of the remaining prisoners. It is important that you approach this suggestion with caution, if justice is to triumph in this case.

"First of all – and I am sure that it was merely a lapse of attention on the part of that learned and experienced counsel – Mr Shand suggested to you that the witness Nathan Slack had not testified to the effect that it was his son Matthew who struck him from behind. In fact, according to my notes, Mr Slack was asked, in re-examination, if he had told one of the officers of the Watch that he did believe it had been Matthew. This point may be of considerable importance when you come to assess Matthew Slack's motivations for being in the premises in the first place.

"Which leads me to another point on which, with considerable regret, I am obliged to correct something said to you by Mr Shand.

While he is correct in stating that the law of this land does not permit a prisoner to testify on oath in his own defence, it does not prevent him from entering the witness box and giving his account of events. If he does so, of course, he is liable to be cross-examined by opposing counsel, and having seen Mr Manning's admirable powers of advocacy, and the tenacity with which he can ferret out a lie, you may legitimately ask yourselves why Matthew Slack chose not to take that risk.

"The precise reason why Matthew Slack was in that room that morning seems, therefore, destined to remain a mystery and you must not speculate on that reason. Instead, you must confine yourselves to the evidence you have heard. What you did hear was the evidence of Mr Robert Bradley, who recalled how a member of his family, as it were, took Matthew Slack in off the street and provided him with a free education. You also heard how the same Matthew Slack almost became accepted as one of the family. For this reason, Mr Bradley found it difficult to believe that Matthew Slack could have been involved in the attack on his business.

"But did that same closeness within the family bosom motivate Matthew Slack to reward the kindness and Christian charity of the Bradleys when they were under threat from the mob? If, as has been suggested, Matthew Slack's purpose in being inside the Bradley premises was to protect his father, then you must ask yourselves two questions. The first is – how did he come to know that his father might be in danger? And one possible reason for that, as you heard suggested by Mr Manning, was that he knew that the raid was planned for that day. Whether or not you conclude that the reason why he knew that fact was that he was associated in some way with those who were planning that raid, you may legitimately ask yourselves the second question – why did he not immediately run, with all his strength, directly to his benefactor, Mr Bradley himself, and warn him of the impending threat to his business interests? You heard from Mr Bradley that he learned of the attack from the authorities only after it was all but over. He did not hear it from the ingrate who had been so generously lifted from the gutter by the God-inspired charity of the man whose warp frames were being smashed to matchwood even as Matthew Slack was skulking in the office with his face blackened. But, as I have already indicated to you, these are all matters of speculation, and you must be guided by the evidence.

"Shortly, the Bailiff will escort you to a room in which you will find all you need in the way of comfort while you consider your verdicts in this case. Feel free to take as long as you wish, but once you have begun your deliberations you will not be free to disperse from this building as individuals until those deliberations are completed. Should you not have reached your verdict before nightfall, arrangements will be made for your accommodation at public expense. You must also be 'unanimous' – by which I mean that you must all be in agreement – before you may find each of the prisoners guilty. Yours is a solemn and thankless duty, but as I have already indicated, the evidence in this case is both short in length and clear in its implications. Gentlemen, please retire to consider your verdicts in this matter."

Popular criminal practice folklore asserted that it was never a good sign for an accused person if the jury came back with a verdict after only a short time, and this ominous indicator of how things had gone in the jury room was supported by another of these beliefs, which was to the effect that a jury which had decided to convict could never look a condemned prisoner in the eye.

The twelve good men and true made their way slowly back into the jury box after only thirty minutes, their eyes firmly cast down at the floor. Their elected foreman tugged nervously at the cloth tied around his neck as the Clerk of the Court asked for their verdicts in respect of each of the prisoners in turn. Beginning with Jack Cossall, each of them was pronounced guilty, and Matthew received the same verdict with a numb sense of inevitability.

To save time, the Clerk administered the allocotus to all of them as a group, asking if any of them knew any reason why sentence should not be passed upon them, and, if so, to speak out. It was now the turn of the prisoners to stare down at the floor as they sadly shook their heads, and only Matthew stared straight ahead of him, remembering that Timothy Shand had one more task to perform for him – to save him from the gallows and to argue instead for transportation to the colonies, wherever they might be.

"My Lord," Shand began, "I rise in mitigation of sentence of my client Matthew Slack. He is not yet seventeen years of age, and since the jury has, by its verdict, indicated that it believes him to have been guilty, then in my respectful submission it was the intemperance of youth, and nothing more, which led him to become associated with those who stand next to him in the dock. If I might anticipate – with considerable regret – the course which Your Lordship is about to take in respect of the remaining prisoners, might I also urge upon Your Lordship the same Christian charity of which Your Lordship spoke so eloquently earlier today? There are those who regard the maximum sentence prescribed for this offence to be brutal enough in the case of an adult, but to apply it to a young man with all his life before him – a life, which we have heard, is the more hopeful because of the advantages which he has received – would, in my respectful submission, be beyond brutality. I respectfully urge Your Lordship to temper the hand of justice with the spirit of mercy. We have great need of young men such as him – young men with spirit and promise – in our recently founded colonies, where he may prove himself a valuable member of society in a land in which starvation and hopelessness does not drive good people to commit bad deeds. Thank you, My Lord."

His Lordship obviously required little time to formulate precisely what he was about to say, and the confidence with which he said it suggested that it was both long practiced and recently rehearsed.

"Prisoners at the Bar, you have all been found guilty by a jury of your peers – quite rightly, in my opinion – of the crime of frame breaking by day, an offence in respect of which, in its infinite wisdom, Parliament recently prescribed the sentence of death. It is only in respect of one of your number, the prisoner Slack, that I have received a most earnest submission that I should not impose that ultimate sentence. It is urged upon me that you, Slack, are a young man, and that your crime was the result of youthful intemperance. However, it may also be said, as your own counsel conceded, that you had more advantages than most people of your age and class, largely as the result of the benevolence of the very person you then took it upon yourself to attempt to ruin.

"We hear much in London of the hardships claimed by the artisans and labourers of this town, and their related assertions of justification for the wanton and wicked acts which they have recently inflicted on this once peaceful community. You above all, Matthew Slack, had the opportunity to rise above all this, and be the person which others thought you capable of being. You threw those opportunities back in the face of your benefactors, and I see no reason for believing that your rebellious spirit would be of any assistance to those in our distant colonies, most of whom have succeeded without your advantages. I see no reason to treat you differently from the rest. The prisoners will now stand."

They struggled to their feet in the same manacled line that they had occupied throughout the trial and faced the front with as much courage, and, in some cases, mute defiance, as they could muster, as the judge at long last finished the business he had been sent north to conduct. He reached out his hand for the black cloth which had sat before him on the Bench for the entire trial. For a brief moment the courtroom was presented with a view of the black cloth in midair, before His Lordship draped it solemnly across his grey wig, and repeated words with which he was all too familiar.

"John Cossall, Ralph James Darby, Caleb George Mason, George Henry Packer, Stephen Perry, Arthur John Peters, Jacob Esau Rawlings and Matthew Joseph Slack, you have each been found guilty by a jury of your peers of the capital crime of frame breaking by day. It is the judgment of this court that you be taken from here to a place of detention until such time as suitable arrangements can be made, and then taken from thence to a place of execution and there hanged by the neck until dead. And may the Lord have mercy on your souls. Amen."

The 'Amen' – which was echoed by the vicar as his sole contribution to the proceedings – was drowned in a communal howl of rage and protestation. To a man, the contingent from the Royal Berkshire Regiment rose on a command from their sergeant and presented bayonets in anticipation of a riot. Above all the confusion could be heard a piercing and heart-rending scream which Matthew thought he knew; he looked up at the public gallery and saw his father and old Nancy attempting to revive an inert bundle on the floor in front of them.

CHAPTER FIFTEEN

Open wide the stable door

ROGER COURTNEY sighed with irritation as he hovered at the entrance to the Members' Lounge in case the two senior gentlemen required any further port or brandy, although the Good Lord knew they had consumed enough already. He noted that they had barely started on their last round, and resigned himself to the fact that he would be there for at least another hour, by the time that he had tidied up and locked down the shutters which gave access to a privileged view of St. James's Street and the Mall which lay beyond it, running down to The Queen's House.

However, being Assistant Secretary of the most exclusive gentlemen's club in London had its privileges, and he was normally addressed by his first name by both of the patrons who seemed reluctant to call it a night. The Lord Chief Justice had been a member since his early days at the Bar, and it was hard to imagine the club without the current Secretary for the Home Department on its membership list as well. And there was always the third-floor apartment which went with the post, where Miles would be waiting as usual when Roger had completed his duties for the day. Roger had been selected primarily for his discretion, mainly because he had a certain matter of his own over which to remain discreet.

The more portly of the two members sensed that he might be running out of time, and there was one more matter yet to resolve.

"Mr Secretary," he continued, in the same judicial tone of voice which normally won all arguments on whatever matter he chose to dispute, "there is finally the matter of the Nottingham Luddites."

"Yes," responded his companion in a reflective tone, "damned fine result that. Please congratulate your man for me. Buller, wasn't it?"

"Yes, Home Secretary, but they've appealed."

"Beg pardon?"

"They've appealed. Against both conviction and the death penalty which followed. The matter's before me next Wednesday."

"Damned impudence!" For once the professional politician looked out of his depth. "No real prospects of success, I take it?"

"No, not from what I can see of the written pleadings. And I can soon put a stop to any attempts to improve on them during oral submissions."

"Well then, why bring the matter to me?"

"Because one of them is still only sixteen and there's talk of his seeking the King's Pardon in exchange for transportation."

"Out of the question, assuming that I'm consulted. His Majesty can be relied upon to do the right thing, of course, but that son of his can get some strange ideas into his head sometimes. The sooner the current Regency's over the better."

"How is His Majesty?" enquired the Lord Chief Justice.

"As mad as ever, they say. Began drilling the ducks on Hyde Park lake last week, they tell me, just as if they were infantry, by all accounts. Fortunately the Horse Guards were on escort duty so we got him home without further incident. But it doesn't make it any easier to run the country at a time like this. These Luddite fellows – you going to hang them publicly?"

"Not up to me, ultimately. A matter for the Lord Lieutenant, but he normally toes the line when word comes direct from Westminster. Actually, we've already been in communication on the self-same matter. Apparently there was something of a disturbance after the sentences were handed down, and the Duke has requested permission to hang them in the private yard inside the gaol where they're being held at the moment. There's a lime pit goes with the yard, I understand, so we can dispose of them quickly before they become holy relics or something."

The older man thought deeply as he took another swig at his brandy and water. "You still got any gibbets up there?"

The Lord Chief Justice's eyes widened in surprise. "I've no idea – but gibbeting was only meant for traitors."

"And how would you describe these scum? If I recall correctly, it was one of your predecessors in title who extended the practice to highwaymen, so why not to Luddites?"

It was the lawyer's time to reflect. "I'll have to look the point up, but I have a mind that it has to be specially ordered on sentence."

"Or on appeal?"

"Point taken. But what about public disturbances? As I've already mentioned, the Lord Lieutenant is worried about the mob's reaction even if we just hang them publicly. If we hang them in gibbets afterwards that's bound to provoke a riot, and we'll get lower types seeking bits of the bodies to put on display."

"They couldn't be more on display than in a gibbet, could they? What's the current maximum sentence for interfering with a corpse?"

"Seven years' transportation, from memory."

"Good. I'll write to the Town Clerk and make sure that the

Town Crier earns his stipend for once. And for those who can read, we'll put warning notices on the gibbets."

"So the sentences are to stand?"

"I think I've made myself abundantly clear on that point, Sir Edward. Now, if I can just attract Roger's attention, I'll have my carriage brought round. Can I offer you the services of my coachman to Chelsea? It's on my way home."

There had indeed been disturbances in the town following the handing down of the sentences, but this time they had been confined to the town itself and the authorities had been well prepared. Those leaving the Shire Hall screaming their anger and grief into the wind had found the streets lined with redcoats, and the squares filled with mounted hussars on restless horses. Even the alehouses seemed to have acquired officers of the Watch as door staff, and apart from a few taproom brawls brought on by excessive ale consumption, the Establishment survived the immediate aftermath of the trial.

It was as if the life had gone out of the cause well ahead of the barbaric ritual which would claim the eight who had been convicted. Although there was much muttering on street corners, and in the courts and alleyways from which the raiders had been drawn, the authorities, had they but known it, had bullied the stuffing out of the people's resolve to improve their circumstances. Faced with an organised and brutal regime orchestrated from London, and one which furthermore had the lawful capacity to hang their opponents by the neck in public, few could be found with enough moral courage, or physical stamina, to keep the fight going. Apart from the odd sporadic incident which owed more to the settlement of private scores than anything which represented continuing organised activity on the part of General Ludd and his army, there were no more frames broken in the weeks which immediately followed the trial.

But this did not mean that nothing was happening. With the spirit of generosity which seems to be granted only to the truly destitute, the people rallied round their fallen heroes and their families, collecting food, money and clothing which was delivered anonymously where it was most needed. Some even found its way through the corruption of the gaol system into the stomachs, and onto the lice-tormented bodies, of the condemned men themselves, now separated from each other into individual cells stripped of all items which might enable them to deny the hangman his fee. Three of those sentenced to hang had young families whose daily intake of food, the likes of which some of them had never tasted before, relieved the widows-to-be of some of their most immediate anxieties. But for everyone, the days were passing in a dull monotony of anticipation as the date fixed for the appeal drew closer, and the days which they had been counting down became hours.

Ahead of their journey to London, Timothy Shand and Charles Daubney became local legends, whose names would never be forgotten among the uncomprehending but fearful townsfolk whose last hopes they carried in the blue barristers' travelling bags which contained their wigs and court gowns, crisply starched jabots and freshly cleaned bar jackets.

They had asked for no fees in return for conducting the appeal on behalf of the convicted men, but as they scurried through the gathering drizzle from the Exchange Hall up to High Street and into the courtyard of the Blackamoor's Head to join the London Mail coach, a small bag of gold sovereigns was hurriedly handed to each of them by two highly embarrassed delegates of the anonymous but compassionate local tradespeople who depended for their livelihood on the likes of those who were in peril of being despatched on the end of a rope. Timothy Shand was too overcome to admit that he had already been paid more than adequately for his services by Robert Bradley, and as the coach lurched and clattered along Bridlesmith Gate on its way south to the river bridge, he handed his bag of coins to Charles Daubney with the laconic observation that, "I'm only for one of them, and I've an easier case to argue."

As the town waited anxiously for news, Nathan turned his immediate attention to Lily and William. Now over three years old and more than capable of feeding himself, William presented a whole new chapter of challenges as he experimented with his newly discovered mobility, specialising in walking into sharp wooden furniture edges and wobbling dangerously near the open fireplace. Lily was altogether a different concern.

In addition to the recurrent chest complaint which had plagued her since William's birth, and the increasing bouts of confusion and memory loss which had developed since it, the mental strain of losing one son to a sabre blow and facing the loss of another in the ignomy of what, rumour had it, was to be a very public hanging, had added occasional blackouts to her growing list of ailments. They normally left no residual symptoms, although after her collapse in the courtroom she seemed to have less control over her right arm, which trembled slightly whenever it was extended, and occasionally even when it wasn't.

But Nathan's concern was the same for her as it was for William, that she would harm herself when and if she fell. At the same time he risked a severe tongue-lashing if Lily ever noticed him "followin' me abaht like a love-sick puppy", whatever one of those might behave like. This combination of responsibilities was, however, sufficient to justify, in Nathan's own mind his continual absence from Bradley's where, if the truth be told, he was reluctant to return anyway, given the phantoms which now stalked the building waiting for him.

He had been obliged to return several weeks before, when summoned by Bradley's messenger to attend a meeting with Timothy Shand to discuss how Matthew's appeal was to be organised. The legal arguments went straight over the top of Nathan's head, as usual, but he had not missed several pointed remarks by Bradley regarding his ongoing concern for the safety of his business in the absence of a General Overseer, and the loss of business revenue from the spare warp frame. Nathan knew that he would have to make a final decision on a day not too far distant, and that day nearly came in the middle of September, when word reached him that his presence was required at the office of the Housing Development Family Trust in Pelham Street. Leaving his two charges in the capable hands of his neighbour Aggie Draycott, he was gone for over two hours, and returned clutching a handful of papers and wearing a hesitant look of triumph.

"Lily, look 'ere, lass, the new 'ouse is finally ready forrus."

"What new 'ouse?"

"Yer know, the one ovver at Radford. Dun't yer remember goin' up there wi'. . . wi' me an' Ruth?"

"That's summat else, Nathan. That young Ruth's gerrin' a bit unreliable lately. I sent 'er aht fer bread this mornin', an' she's still aht in the street somewhere."

Nathan was used to fending off confusion like this, and was determined to get through to her.

"Nemmind 'er fer the minute. The 'ouse in Radford – we can go in there any time after November. We just 'as ter tell the Trust when we wanner start livin' there."

"An' why would we want ter leave 'ere? Imagine if the boys came back an' fahnd they'd no 'ome ter come back to. I could never forgive misen."

Nathan was close to screaming in frustration as he felt his brief elation ground down by Lily's confused state of mind, to which her instinctive stubbornness refused to take second place. He took several deep breaths, but even so he was perhaps blunter than he would have wished.

"Lily, they're not comin' back, leastways not Tommy anyroad. Tommy's gone ter join 'is grandad in 'eaven, so 'e'll not be comin' back 'ere. Ruth'll be back afore dinner time, an' as fer Matthew – well, we 'as ter pray 'ard, that's what."

He watched apprehensively as Lily creased her forehead in her efforts to absorb it all, then finally smiled, and asked in her best coy, girlish voice, "Does that mean we can go ter chapel this Sunday?"

The request took him completely unawares. Due to Lily's uncertain health, they had not attended the Halifax Lane Chapel for quite a few weeks and it was one of several unattended matters which had been nagging at Nathan's conscience whenever he had time free from his other responsibilities, which had not occurred very often recently. During that time, Lily had not referred once to church matters, although much of her conversation of late had been of "God's infinite mercy", "God's good grace", and all the other benefits which the Good Lord seemed, to Nathan, to bestow on all those except his most loyal followers. Perhaps a return to chapel might ease her mental torment, and help her see more clearly that there were things happening in which Nathan needed her usual advice and blunt wisdom, things which he could not face alone.

"All right lass, if yer want. It'll p'rhaps do yer good. But we need ter talk abaht the new 'ouse an' all."

"I'm not goin' – I told yer," seemed to be her last word on the subject for the time being.

Sunday evening duly arrived, and with William safely installed with the Draycotts, Nathan took Lily's arm a little more firmly than he used to do as they walked out of the yard, up Garner's Hill and along Market Street to Halifax Lane and the chapel. Lily seemed physically bolstered by the service, and she was almost back to her old self as she sang along with the familiar hymns in her usual voice, almost childlike and slightly lacking in volume. There seemed to be no sign of confusion or memory loss as she repeated the Lord's Prayer, and there was even some colour back in her cheeks by the end of the service as they made their way out of their pew towards the front door of the chapel, where the Reverend Hepworth was waiting for them with his characteristic beam.

"Nathan, so good to see you and Lily back amongst us after all your troubles. It's so easy for a man to lose his faith in our Heavenly Father after events such as these, and I've been praying for you both daily."

"Aye, well yer might spare a few o' them prayers fer Matthew while yer at it, Reverend. That appeal business is on next week in London, an' 'e's gunner need all the 'elp 'e can get from you, an' God, an' everyone."

"Of course, Nathan. I'll be conducting the Hour of Prayer meeting in person this coming week, and I'll make sure that we include Matthew at the very heart of our devotions."

"Very kind o' yer, I'm sure."

"That's what God requires of all his workers, of course, so it's a very small effort for someone in my position. But make sure you thank Him too, in your prayers."

"Aye, right. Thanks."

"And of course we'll be praying for Lily as well. How's she bearing up at this difficult time?"

Nathan followed Hepworth's distant gaze back over his left shoulder, and suddenly realised that Lily was not standing next to him, as he had assumed. Instead, she was deep in conversation with a young girl who looked familiar, and it was clear that the girl was very upset by something.

" 'scuse me, Reverend," Nathan mumbled, as he worked his way back into the body of the chapel through the outgoing tide of the congregation. He reached Lily and the girl just as the latter ran off towards the vestry, clutching a handkerchief to her face.

"What's up?" Nathan enquired as he watched the disappearing figure. Lily was smiling for the first time he could recall in months, as she replied.

"That were young Rebecca; you remember, Matthew's friend. Lucy's young sister."

Nathan did not need to be reminded of who Rebecca was.

"So? Why were she cryin'?"

"Just tears o' joy, that's all. Matthew's gunner be comin' 'ome soon."

Nathan was mortified by the thought that Lily had been rambling away to Rebecca in her confused state of mind, bringing her false hope, and it brought it home to him more strongly than ever how many other people were going to miss Matthew if the worst came to the worst.

The worst came to the worst on Friday of the following week, as the overnight mail coach from London rattled into town shortly before noon, bringing a letter for Robert Bradley, and despatches from court correspondents which would find their way into the late afternoon broadsheets. Soon, the whole town knew that the appeals had been dismissed by the Lord Chief Justice, and that the executions had been set for two weeks' time, and would be followed by public gibbeting. This particularly sadistic practice was now located so far back in public memory that those seeking literary immortality in the more salacious publications made a considerable effort to explain to their readers precisely how, once the bodies of the condemned had been cut down, they would be placed in metal frames and hung up to rot in full view of passers-by, as a warning against future wrongdoing. None of which did anything to ease the grief of the families concerned, or dampen the ire of the mob. The Shire Hall lost several more windows before it then acquired a round-the-clock frieze of redcoats.

Nathan heard the news being called out from a distance by the broadsheet hawkers, and for the first time in his life he raced up to Weekday Cross, handed over a penny ha'penny, received a paper in return and hurried down to the chapel, where a tearful and horrified Reverend Hepworth confirmed the worst as he left off briefly from supervising arrangements for the next day's christening. A shattered Nathan directed his feet automatically back towards the yard, thinking hard about how to keep the news from Lily.

On the way, he had to wage the biggest war he had ever conducted with his own conscience. His heart told him that she was Matthew's mother – the one who had brought him into the world – and that she, above all others, had the right to know. But his head also reminded him that she could not survive another shock like this one, and that she had two other children who still needed her, even though one of them was still in Eastwood, "gerrin' on in life" as Lily would put it. It said much for Nathan that not once did it occur to him to reflect on how much he needed Lily, particularly now. He lifted the latch and re-entered the house still deep in thought.

"What's up wi' you?" Blunt as ever, Lily was on good form as she stirred the pot hanging over the fire, while keeping a wary eye on William, who was pulling himself up and down from a seated position with the aid of a table leg.

"Eh?"

"Yer look as if yer've lost a sovereign an' fahnd a shillin'. Cheer up, we're 'avin' neck o' lamb stew fer dinner. Aggie 'ad some spare neck an' she were worried it'd go off."

Nathan appreciated only too deeply the sacrifice which Aggie Draycott had made in handing over even such a cheap cut of meat, and he told himself that Lily had earned the whole family this sudden flood of kindness in their darkest hour. In better days, for them, it had been Lily who had kept others alive, and now they were returning the favour. Not that Nathan felt hungry, but it would help to build up Lily's strength, and William seemed capable of eating everything that came within arms-length these days, even if it wasn't meant for eating.

As usual, Lily placed six dishes on the bare table, and as usual Nathan tactfully removed three of them while she wasn't looking. As she came back to the table with the stew pot and ladle she looked momentarily puzzled, then began to serve the meal as if they were accustomed to eating alone. Given the thoughts spinning around in his head, Nathan could only toy with the stew with the assistance of a piece of bread and a knife, and Lily was offended.

"What's wrong wi' mi cookin'? Yer've 'ardly eaten a bite, an' lamb's one o' yer favourites."

"Aye, it were once, but just lately, wi' things the way they are . . ."

"There yer go again, allus lookin' on the black side. There's folks a lot worse off than us, yer know – yer should give thanks ter God for the fine children 'e's given us, an' the steady work. Nah what's up wi' yer?"

A tortured glaze of horror and incomprehension on his face, Nathan rammed the paring knife into the surface of the rough-hewn table, and ran from the yard screaming oaths and obscenities which could be heard halfway down Narrow Marsh.

He was to learn afterwards that he had wandered all that night and into the following day, when he had finally been found just in time in the East Croft. His recollections of the night were somewhat hazy, but he had a very clear memory of an incident just before he had been found, which he put down to a dream he must have had; either that or he was going as daft as Lily.

He had found himself in the meadows leading down to the river, and his mind had begun to drift back to happier days, when the whole family had attended the Sunday School Union celebrations that Lily had been so proud to be a part of. As he walked on through the marsh grass he was reminded of what had happened, bit by bit, to his own family, and he cursed himself for having been persuaded to rise above his natural station into a venture which had robbed him of his two sons, and his life's companion of her senses.

Without realising, he had reached the section of the river by the remains of the overhanging willow tree, where Matthew had pulled Howard Bradley from an almost certain death by drowning. Most of the remains of the tree had now fallen into the fast-flowing and powerful river, and Nathan swallowed the bitterness in his throat as he recalled that it was now Matthew's life which was to be taken, and he asked himself how Lily could be stupid enough to believe that "God provides everythin' in due season", as she was so fond of saying. Life was just a fucking fix, that was all, and if you were at the bottom of the heap, those above you would just step on you to get higher.

He found himself looking across the broad expanse of water at a woman on the far bank who appeared to be kneeling in prayer, her hands clasped together and her face raised towards the sun. Although the river was some sixty yards wide at that point, there was something very familiar about her face, which seemed to become larger and clearer as Nathan stared at it more intently.

The recognition hit him like a blow in the chest, and momentarily he stopped breathing. It had been many years, but he could still remember the grey-green eyes and the small mole above the upper lip on the left-hand side. She might have been dead these past thirty odd years, but hardly a day of that time had passed without Nathan recalling that kindly and reassuring smile, always there when he fell and hurt himself, or when he came off second best in a fight. She had always been there when he really needed her, and here she was, back from the dead to offer him the comfort that only a mother could.

As he smiled across the river at her, she smiled back. Then he heard his name being called and he saw her mouth opening in a loving welcome as she stretched out her arms for him to come to her. Without a second thought he waded in, boots and all, and was at waist height before he realised that the voices he could hear calling his name were those of his neighbours Will Draycott and Scuff Needham. He turned back towards the sound, and saw them waving furiously from the riverside. He looked away from them and pointed across the river, meaning to proclaim the miracle of his mother's return, but saw only a tinker woman washing clothes, who to judge by the expression on her face was wondering what on earth was transpiring on the town side of the river.

Feeling more than a little stupid, he waded back to the riverbank, where both his neighbours seemed to be mightily excited about something. He began to explain that he had just needed to get out of the house, and had started to ask after Lily when Will Draycott interrupted him.

"Fer God's sake shurrup, an' listen, Nathan. It's Matthew – 'e's escaped!"

At first Nathan didn't grasp what he had been told, but the men seemed so delighted with their news that he reasoned that it had to be good. Then suddenly the penny dropped.

" 'e's bloody what?"

"Escaped, that's bloody what! Dun't ask me 'ow, but 'e's gone like a rat from a shit'ouse. Gorraht during the night, they reckon; didn't even know that 'is case'd bin turned dahn in London. Lily knows, but Aggie reckons that she's not tekken it in proper yet. It were Lily as told us that yer'd not bin 'ome last night, an' then we 'eard that yer'd bin seen dahn 'ere, so we came lookin' just in case, like . . ." His voice tailed off in his indecision.

"Aye, thanks Will. It musta looked as if I were gunner do misen in just nah, an' one day I'll tell yer all abaht it, but right nah I've gorrer get 'ome an' see ter Lily an' the boy."

"William's wi' Aggie, an' the last we saw o' Lily she were in bed, singin' hymns an' stuff, so mebbe she did understand after all."

"Aye, it's 'ard ter tell wi' Lily at the moment, I know. Look, thanks fer everythin', Will; yer've bin more than a friend ter the 'ole family, leastways, what's left on it."

"Shurrup, yer daft prat," said Will gruffly. "If it 'addnt've bin fer the Slacks, we'd all 'ave died them past two winters back, so it's nice ter be able ter repay yer when it's you that's needin' us. That's what friends is for, ain't it?"

"Aye, p'rhaps yer right," agreed Nathan, as he grasped Will by the shoulder and allowed the two men to escort him back across the meadows, a warm noonday sun raising the steam on his breeches as he made his way home with new hope in his heart.

"Where the 'ell 'ave you bin?" Lily demanded from the upstairs room, as he peeled off his still-damp clothes in front of the fire.

" 'ow d'yer know it's me?" Nathan answered back playfully.

" 'cos no-one but you'd be fool enough ter come 'ome to a daft old nag like me," she replied, as she came slowly and carefully down the stairs in her nightclothes and folded herself into Nathan's arms and began to sob.

"Careful, lass. I got a bit wet, like; fell in the river."

"If yer think that's a good enough excuse fer me ter let go o' yer, then yer wrong," Lily whispered tearfully, as she held him even tighter and closer.

"Aye, but . . ."

"Aye but nowt, Nathan Slack. I'll let yer go when yer promise ter eat that leftover stew. It'll not tek a second ter warm up in the pot."

Nathan suddenly realised that he was hungry again, and needed no further persuasion to sit in front of the fire with the bowl on his knees, while his clothes slowly dried. During the necessary silence he was wondering how much he could tell Lily of the latest news, but she saved him the trouble.

"Did yer 'ear abaht ar Matthew? 'e's bin released by God, just like I asked 'im. God provides everythin' in due season – it just teks time, that's all."

"Aye," said Nathan, wondering how much had sunk in about Tommy, and whether she remembered that Ruth was now in service. As if she'd read his thoughts, she continued.

"An' I know that I sometimes forget abaht Ruth, but yer'll 'ave ter be patient wi' me, not that I'm sayin' that yer not, but, well, sometimes I can get a bit muddled, like . . ." Her words tailed off into silence, and as Nathan mopped up the last of the stew with the remaining hunk of bread she moved close to where he was sitting, her chest heaving uneasily.

"Nathan, d'yer still love me?"

He didn't know whether to laugh or cry. Instead he got up, folded her into his arms and fought back the tears as he replied. "More than the day we walked dahn the aisle. More than that fust day when yer came inter the yard. More than the day Tommy . . ."

He stopped abruptly and braced himself for what might follow. The silence was, however, brief.

" 'ave I got that bad that yer think yer can't even mention Tommy? I've accepted that 'e's wi' God, Nathan. Nowt'll bring 'im back, I know that, but 'e's only dead as long as we never speak abaht 'im, so promise me we will."

With a sigh of relief and thanksgiving, Nathan pressed her even closer to him and kissed the top of her head, now a mass of white hair with an occasional stubborn brown streak hanging on to remind him of her younger days. As he held her to him, he was conscious of how frail her body had become, and he promised himself that he would take over the cooking – everyone always put on weight when he was in charge of meals.

The afternoon turned into evening, as they sat quietly holding hands by the fire. Lily seemed disposed to dwell on the happier days of their life together, and Nathan comforted himself with the thought that it would probably help to keep her mind on an even keel, and that happy memories would be good for her. There was still the question of the new house to be broached again, but that could wait. However, as the evening wore on, Nathan became aware that Lily's conversation was becoming more vague and hesitant, and eventually he found the courage to ask.

"You feelin' all right, love? Only yer seem ter be gettin' a bit tired, like. D'yer want ter go back ter bed?"

"Ter tell yer the truth," she admitted, "I'm gerrin' a bit light-headed or summat. I've bin gerrin' like that these past few weeks, ever since I took them funny turns when I fainted. I'll be all right, but yer right – I think I'll go back ter mi bed."

Nathan let go of her hand and stood up. "Yer not goin' up them stairs on yer own. Just gimme a minute ter go aht ter the privy, an' I'll go up wi' yer. Ter tell the truth, I'm proper boggered misen."

"Nathan Slack," she grinned back at him, "yer may be gerrin' older, but yer language ain't improvin' one little bit! That's one thing abaht yer that Lily Parker never did get ter change."

"Aye, well," Nathan muttered as he opened the outside door and walked across the yard towards the privy. As he was walking back, he heard a crash from inside the house, and, fearing the worst, raced back inside to find Lily lying in a crumpled heap at the foot of the stairs, the top of her nightclothes stained red with blood. He knelt beside her and prayed to God that she was still breathing. Thanking God that she was, he lifted her over his shoulder and carried her up the stairs, laying her gently down on the bed.

It took him less than no time to run next door to the Draycotts and tell them what had happened. Satisfied that William would be taken care of, he ran down a little further and hammered on old Nancy's door. She was also dressed for bed, but threw an old cloak over her nightclothes when Nathan blurted out his news, and they hurried back to number seven and up the stairs.

"She's 'ad another of 'er faintin' fits," Nancy confirmed. "Did she tell yer abaht 'em?"

"Aye, but this is the fust she's 'ad fer weeks. What's that blood doin' comin' aht of 'er ear?"

"Busted head, likely. Nowt we can do abaht that 'cept keep watch on 'er, an' keep 'er strength up. Not that she's gorra lot o' that these days, all things considered. But I've got two women in the yard what's due any time, so you're gunner 'ave ter do most o' this yersen."

"Aye, all right. Owt else yer can suggest?"

Nancy looked at him almost in pity. "I know yer've 'ad ter do a lot o' this lately, burrit never does any 'arm. Pray, Nathan. Pray."

CHAPTER SIXTEEN

Balancing the ledger

THE DAY dawned dull and windy. Just before first light, a silent but sullen group assembled at the foot of the Shire Hall steps, as far as they were allowed to go by the hand-picked detachment of redcoats who barred the front entrance, parting only once in order to allow the official party to pin the judicial execution notice on the board. Not many could read, but none of them needed to, because a nervous Town Crier read from his copy. The first spattering of rain hit the tower of the parish church across the road as some yelled their protest, while some of the women cried for those who had paid the ultimate price in the execution yard shortly before dawn.

The heavy showers which followed served only to dampen further the spirits of those who had supported them to the end, as they trudged back to their homes through patchy bursts of warm autumn sunshine which raised steam from the ground and mocked their grief with the added discomfort of humidity.

As usual, the sunlight was late in gracing Tanners Yard, where Nathan remained resolutely indoors, dully performing the domestic chores which somehow seemed so meaningless now that Lily was not in a position to direct them. She lay motionless among the bedding in the upstairs room, an occasional tremor on her lips reassuring everyone that she was still alive. Around mid-morning a solitary tear rolled down her cheek, just before Aggie Draycott came in and coaxed Nathan into taking some tea and bread. He did so out of politeness, but he had no appetite for it.

It was the day that Matthew should have swung along with the rest of them, and Nathan wondered for the fiftieth time where he might be now. Hopefully he'd made his way to one of the seaports which his grandfather had often talked about, from where he could work his passage on a coaster to another part of the country, or a cargo jammer to foreign climes – at all events, to some place where his name would not be known. Whatever his fate, it was doubtful whether Tanners Yard would ever see his once cheery face again.

It was early afternoon before Nathan persuaded himself that today was the day when it had to be done. There was no fitter way of honouring the memory of those who had died in the cause than for a man to make the best of what God had given him, and support his family as best he could. For Nathan, that meant working a stocking frame, and although he knew deep down within himself that he could never comfortably resume what he had been doing before – at least, not where he had been doing it – he couldn't expect Robert Bradley to keep sending him money for no good reason, and he had to be honest with him regarding his intentions. Whether or not he could secure employment with another merchant hosier remained to be seen, but at the very least he would need the tools of his trade, which hopefully were still there for him to reclaim.

But to walk to Bradley's meant that he had to pass the Shire Hall, which stood across the road from St. Mary's Church, a few yards ahead of where High Pavement met Stoney Street. By now, there would be seven corpses hanging in gibbets on either side of the entrance steps – eight, had the law taken its destined course – and Nathan asked himself once again whether Matthew was really the lucky one, living the rest of his life under the threat of the discovery of his true identity. He pulled on his jacket and took William round yet again to Aggie Draycott's and asked her to keep an eye on Lily from time to time. Aggie took no persuading; Lily had always been generous towards the Draycotts, particularly during their hardest times, and William was no trouble for a woman who'd had nine children of her own.

He scuttled past the Bradley house on the other side of the road from the Shire Hall, his eyes fixed firmly on the road below his feet. But his ears couldn't block out the noisy creaking of seven old and rusty gibbets straining in the gusty wind, and just before he came to St. Mary's Churchyard he couldn't resist raising his eyes to the grisly scene across the road.

He stood for a moment, stunned by the full horror of the obscenity, and appalled by the official brutality which had ordered it. There was a small crowd of onlookers with nothing better to do, but most of those who were obliged to pass this spot did so with their eyes meekly averted. Soon they would no doubt need to cover their noses as well, and Nathan said a silent prayer that the authorities would put a merciful end to the whole hideous display of judicial barbarity before the autumn sun and the hungry pigeons wreaked their final blasphemy.

"Penny for the Guy, mester?"

Nathan looked down, white with anger, and saw a boy of about nine, urchin-faced and innocent in his total ignorance of what was going on. Nathan was reminded of Matthew at about that age, face aglow on his birthday with the new knife that his grandfather had made for him. Strangely, he couldn't remember Tommy at that age, but in remembering Matthew his anger had quickly dissolved. He nodded across the road.

"D'yer know what tharris, lad?"

"Course I do – it were some fellers what was wicked, so they 'ung 'em."

"Why were they wicked?"

"Dunno, but mi mam sez they was. Mam sez they'll 'ang me if I'm wicked like they was."

"Well, you just remember that, an' do what yer mam tells yer. 'ere's a penny, but only if yer go right away from 'ere, 'cos it's not a nice place fer a lad like you ter be."

"Ta, mester!" enthused the young boy, as he grabbed the coin and ran off in search of bullseyes, the sickening scene already forgotten.

Nathan finally turned into Stoney Street, as if in a dream. Although the road ahead of him was so familiar from the almost countless number of times that he had walked halfway down its length on his daily journey to work, it was if he were seeing it for the first time. The same buildings were in the same places, along with the ruts in the road which he knew by heart, but somehow it had all changed.

There was an occasional soldier in uniform to be seen among the people passing lawfully about their business; the soldiers, on the whole, looked slovenly and arrogant while the ordinary townsfolk seemed subdued and timid. Nathan passed several people he knew and made a great effort to acknowledge their presence, but the only replies he received seemed reluctant and embarrassed. Either they didn't want to be seen associating with the family of a condemned criminal, or they didn't trust themselves to say the right thing to a man who had lost two sons. Whatever the reason, they didn't know quite what to say, and Nathan consoled himself with the fact that neither would he in these circumstances.

He reached Bradley's almost without realising, and had to backtrack a few yards in order to enter the side alleyway. Ahead of him stood that fateful side door. He hadn't thought much about it the last time he was here – to talk to Timothy Shand about Matthew's appeal – but now the memories of that ill-fated Saturday morning came flooding back. He should never have ignored what Matthew had clearly been trying to tell him, and he should never have let Tommy enjoy so much freedom in his last few months. Perhaps he wasn't fit to have had sons. Perhaps he shouldn't have selfishly thought only of his own happiness by marrying Lily and then subjecting her to the tragic life for which he, and he alone, had been responsible. Once, they'd been too happy, too comfortable, but he'd been a blind, stupid, stubborn fool. Dear God, what were they to do now?

Punishing himself by taking the side stairs two at a time, and in the hope of getting it over with as quickly as possible, he was up in the frame room in no time. The frames were clonking away as usual, all except one which he realised was meant for him, but which he would never work again. He stood looking at it, repeating in his mind the intricate series of movements which it demanded of its operator. He had acquired a lifetime's skill – some never did master it – and yet he was not sure in his own mind if he could ever bring himself to work one again. He needed to forget, and the main consequence of mastering the frame was that the physical actions became automatic, leaving the mind of the frameworker free to wander wherever it wished.

He sighed and reached down for the bag of tools, neatly wrapped in cloth. Someone had written his name on it with marking chalk and he smiled with satisfaction to think that the bag had lain untouched all this time. At least he had some friends left in this world, and he was just wondering which of them could make the best use of his tools when a familiar voice cut into his thoughts, straining as usual to be heard above the noise.

"There's nowt gone – they'd've 'ad ter get past me fust."

"Thanks, Sam. Ter tell yer the truth I'm not sure if I want 'em after all, so I reckon you should 'ave 'em. You were allus a good friend ter me, an' your Walter'll be comin' inter the trade soon; mebbe 'e could mek good use of 'em. I were gunner gi' 'em ter Tommy anyroad."

His voice choked slightly on this last sentence, and Sam couldn't help but put a comforting arm around his shoulders.

"I'll not 'ave 'em, Nathan, nor will ar Wally. We'll not be party ter yer leavin' this place. An' there's not a man 'ere would take 'em off yer, neither. An' right in front of yer's yer frame, when yer finally come ter yer senses. We'll not be lettin' anyone else tek it, yer can be sure o' that."

Nathan wanted to break down and cry on Sam's shoulder, but instead he forced a smile. "Thanks, Sam, but mi mind's made up. Memories, yer see. I can't stand bein' 'ere even nah, an' it'd half kill me ter come an' work 'ere every day."

"That'll pass, yer'll see, an' then yer'll be needin' a job. Even if yer dun't come back 'ere, at least keep yer tools. If I mind right, they was yer dad's anyroad, an' 'e'd've given yer a right smack in the 'ead if yer'd given away 'is tools that easy."

In all the recent trouble, Nathan had almost forgotten that the long tradition which had required that he pass on his tools to Tommy, had been the means by which they had been passed on from old Joe to him, and this further memory of better times was almost too much for him to bear. Not trusting himself to say another word to Sam, he simply gripped his arm in a silent farewell, kept a firm hold on the tools with his other hand, and stumbled back down the stairs, made blurry by the tears which were stinging his eyes.

He passed Bradley's office in a daze, forgetting that the main reason for his visit was to see Robert, and he'd just made it out through the downstairs door into the alleyway when a commanding and all-too familiar voice called him back, and he suddenly remembered why he was there. His undying sense of duty made him stop and turn round to face what was coming. "May as well get this ovver with," he told himself, "an' that way I never 'as ter come back 'ere, fer owt."

The silence was painful for both men, and as usual it was Bradley who was obliged to speak first, as he cleared the last of the stairs and came fully out into the alleyway to stand a few feet away, facing Nathan.

"You and me's got some talkin' ter do, Nathan."

Nathan summoned all the strength he had left in order to keep his voice calm and level, and betray none of the emotion which was churning inside him.

"I dun't see as 'ow it'd do any good, beggin' yer pardon Mr Bradley. I'll allus be grateful fer what you an' yer family 'ave done for me an' mine ovver the years, an' specially these past weeks, burra can't change what's in mi 'eart an' in mi 'ead. I can't come back 'ere, an' that's all there is to it."

"I'm goin' ter be blunt with you, Nathan Slack, because I reckon it's time that somebody was. You're bein' a fool ter yerself and a fool ter yer family. You're a good skilled frameworker with a secure future 'ere, in one o' the most prosperous hosiery 'ouses yer'll find in this town. There's not many that can say that around these parts, and you're about ter chuck it all away. And fer what? What's 'appened is a tragedy, we all acknowledge that, and you've all been constantly in our prayers. But you're not goin' ter change a blessed thing, or bring anybody back, bi throwing yer livelihood down the privy."

"An' I'll be blunt wi' you an' all, if yer'll pardon the liberty. But since yer've spoken ter me, man ter man, yer must let me do the same. The truth is that I never want ter see this place ever again as long as I live. It's not you, an' it's not the work. It's the memories, yer see. Everythin' I'd bin workin' for fer the past twenty years was tekken from me that Sat'day mornin' in 'ere, an' I couldn't bear ter come back 'ere every day fer the rest of mi life. I dun't expect yer ter understand, 'cos it's not you it's 'appened to. It's all right fer you."

"No, it's not all right for me!" Robert retorted. "Quite apart from owt else, I'm losin' mi best worker fer no good reason I can see."

Nathan was close to breaking down completely, and losing the stern composure he had always prided himself on maintaining in his employer's presence, and he made one last desperate attempt to save face by channelling his grief into what he hoped sounded convincingly like anger. He threw his head back proudly and yelled back down the alleyway, trying his best to choose words which Tommy would have approved of. "Well, it's a good enough reason fer me! But then, we think different, we basic classes. We never could find enough gratitude ter thank the likes o' you fer goin' inter business an' mekkin' a fat livin' off ar backs!"

Robert was deeply shocked and hurt, and his face clearly showed it. "You think I''ve done all that I've done just fer mi own ends?"

"An' why not? Yer'd not be the fust, nor the last I reckon. It teks five years ter train up a good framework knitter, an' yer could allus rely on me fer an 'onest day's work. I even agreed ter peach on the rest of 'em for yer, though God alone knows 'ow much I 'ated it, an' 'ow scared I was. I thought I'd 'ave ter pay dearly forrit one day, burrif I'd known just 'ow dearly, I'd've told yer where ter shove the job, free education or no free education. No, I reckon it's yer conscience that's troublin' yer – assumin' yer've got one. Or is it yer fallin' profits?"

" 'ave yer quite finished?"

"Oh, I could stand 'ere an' go on all day, burra reckon I've said more than's good fer me already."

Robert, unlike Nathan, was now genuinely angry, and still very hurt. As he became more emotional his Nottingham accent became even more pronounced, and any semblance of upper class pretension was driven out of his voice by the strain of the occasion.

"Right then, it's my turn ter say summat I might regret later, but I'm gunner say it anyroad. There's bin a closeness between ar two families in recent months, an' speakin' fer my family it was – an' still is – genuine enough. Young Matthew were almost one of us, an' we feel the loss almost as much as you, especially Rebecca. I dun't s'pose yer know she locked 'erself in 'er room fer two days after Matthew were sentenced? No, yer didn't, 'cos it never occurred ter yer that we might be grievin' an' all. Just dun't bloody stand there, full o' yer own self-pity, an' tell me that we dun't care wharrappens ter you an' yours, 'cos yer dun't know the 'alf on it. I'll tell yer this much – Matthew wouldn't be alive today if we didn't care!" He could have bitten his tongue out the minute he'd said it, and he quickly cleared his throat to move on to another topic. But Nathan had heard, even if he didn't understand.

"An' what exactly is that s'posed ter mean?"

"Nowt."

"Yer never say owt fer nowt. So what were yer gerrin' at?"

"Nowt, really. Just a manner o' speakin'."

"I may be poor, burram not daft. Yer meant summat all right, an' I reckon yer owe it ter me ter tell me what yer on abaht."

Robert chewed his lip and looked shamefaced.

"Well, the truth is – an' this is strictly between me an' thee, right? – well, I did summat I rightly should be ashamed of, 'cept I'm not. I did it 'cos I believed it were right, an' I still do. It saved Matthew's life, anyroad."

There was a heavy silence, and exasperated by the continuing uncomprehending look on Nathan's face, Robert spat it out.

"Well, yer dun't imagine 'e just walked aht o' there, do yer?"

Nathan's mouth slowly opened.

"Well, do yer?"

Nathan's mouth closed again.

"Look, if yer must know, one o' the gaolers were bribed. By me; or at least wi' my money. It's not 'ard, yer know – at least, not in there it ain't. I dare say that come the Great Day o' Judgment I'll 'ave some explainin' ter do, but there it is. Call me dishonest an' interferin' if yer like, but fer pity's sake say summat, instead o' just standin' there!"

"All right, then – why?"

"Why? Why the 'ell d'yer think? We were all fond o' the lad, that's why, an' we knew as well as you did that 'e were innocent. We weren't gunner stand by an' watch 'im 'ung!"

There was another lengthy silence while Nathan took it all in, then his eyes narrowed.

"If yer expectin' mi thanks, I'll not disappoint yer. On be'alf o' what's left of mi family, I thank yer. It were a brave thing yer did, an' yer likely ran a serious risk in doin' it. We'll allus be grateful, o' course, but let's not pretend yer did it just fer Matthew."

Robert's face darkened. "I beg yer pardon?"

"Yer know wharram gerrin' at well enough. Yer did it fer Rebecca, who were daft enough ter get all sweet on a young lad below 'er station in life. She'll soon get ovver it, I dare say."

"By God, Nathan Slack, there are times I could strangle yer wi' mi own bare 'ands, yer that pig-'eaded! I can see nah where that eldest lad o' yourn gorris ideas from. Yer so wrapped up in yer own class thinkin' that yer can't accept any good in anyone from my side o' the street. Yer just can't accept that anyone in my position would want ter 'elp the likes o' you, can yer? Dedicated to a cause, the whole bloody lot on yer! That's 'ow all this started, let me remind yer, an' I dare say it's not ovver yet, not bi a long chalk. All right, let's leave it like this – you saved my son's life, an' nah I've balanced the ledger. If I thought like you, I'd say that yer only fished Howard aht o' the Trent ter get well in wi' me. Only I know you berrer than that. I know, fer a start, that yer can't swim any more than Matthew could . . . can. No, yer did it 'cos deep dahn somewhere inside yer there's a good Christian man, when 'e's not wallowin' in his own self-pity. Yer acted wi'aht any thought fer yersen, but apparently I'm not ter be credited wi' the same qualities. Fair enough. Good day, Nathan."

He turned to walk back into the building, but stopped and whipped around again when Nathan called after him. "Look, I didn't mean ter . . ."

"Didn't mean what? Ter mek me lose mi temper? Bothers yer, does it, seein' good old Robert Bradley losin' 'is rag? Well dun't worry, I've said mi piece, apart from one thing. Yer still think I did all this just fer Rebecca, dun't yer? Well, as a matter o' fact she knows nowt abaht the part I played in the business, an' I'll thank yer not ter tell 'er. An' ter tell yer the absolute truth, I didn't exactly do it just fer Matthew, neither. I did it fer one o' the most genuine Christian women I've ever met, an' one o' the most loyal. God alone knows how she ever came ter be married ter you!"

He turned angrily on his heels, and was almost through the door before Nathan shouted back. "I dun't s'pose she'll ever thank yer forrit, the way it's worked aht!"

Robert stopped dead, one foot on the first step. He turned it over in his mind briefly, then decided that this time, Nathan deserved all he got. He walked right back up to Nathan, looked him squarely in the eye, and delivered the coup de grâce.

"She oughta thank me – it were 'er idea!"

Nathan turned pale, and as his knees began to buckle, Robert grabbed him and gently lowered him to the ground. At that moment his senior bag-hosier, Josh Akers, appeared in the alleyway entrance from Stoney Street and between them they carried Nathan up the single flight of stairs to Bradley's office, where they eased him into the visitor's chair. Robert produced a bottle of brandy and two glasses, and the colour began to return to Nathan's cheeks as he coughed at the unaccustomed liquor.

"Tek yer time, Nathan; yer've had a nasty shock. I'm sorry."

"Yer'd best tell me owt else I dun't know."

"There's nowt else, 'onest – apart from the details."

"Well, yer'd berrer let me 'ave 'em, then."

Robert looked embarrassed as he cleared his throat.

"Well, it were when we got back from chapel a couple o' Sundays ago, an' Rebecca 'ad this 'ere bit o' paper that your Lily 'ad written me a note on. She musta bin a bit wanderin' in 'er mind, if yer'll forgive me sayin' so, 'cos she seemed ter think that I could go marchin' up ter the gaol an' demand Matthew's release in God's name. I lay awake 'alf the night feelin' useless an' guilty, 'cos your Lily were obviously relyin' on me; then this idea came ter me. I tried ter purrit away, 'onest I did, burrit kept comin' back ter me, after I began rememberin' stories I'd 'eard abaht prisoners bein' allowed to escape if the money were right. The next day I started mekkin' a few discreet enquiries, an' yer know the rest. He were aht o' there in no time."

Nathan twisted the glass in his hands, his eyes rooted to the floor. "Look, I'm not very good at sayin' thank you, any more than I'm any good at sayin' sorry, but . . ."

"Think no more abaht it, Nathan. Yer shouldn't be thankin' me, anyroad – it's Lily yer owe the thanks to. It were the thought of 'er lyin' there wi' all 'er trust in me that finally made me do it. God alone must know 'ow strong 'er faith is, an' 'ow much it must all 'ave tekken aht of 'er. But there's summat else, which I nearly forgot. I'd've told yer later, I promise."

"What's that?"

"A letter from Matthew. Rebecca gorrit yesterday – 'e wrote ter say that 'e's safe an' well up north an' hopin' ter make it ter Hull or somewhere bi the end o' the week. 'e sends 'is love ter you all, an' sez not ter worry."

" 'ow can we be sure it's from 'im?"

"Well, fer a start, both Lucy an' Rebecca would know 'is writin' a mile off, an' 'e sent back a handkerchief which ar Lucy gev 'im years ago. Must've kept it all this time. 'e also said ter tell you an' Lily that 'it were God's doing' – says yer'd know what 'e was meanin'.' "

Tears welled in Nathan's eyes as he was reminded of one of Lily's favourite phrases. He rubbed his sleeve across his face before replying in a choking voice. "Aye, that's Matthew right enough."

"I'm afraid I insisted that Rebecca burn the note, in the circumstances – I 'ope yer understand. But no doubt there'll be more, an' we'll pass 'em straight onto yer when they come. We should've done that this time, I know, but we just didn't think."

"That's all right. It's me that should be apologisin' ter you, all things considered."

"Well, let's just say that we're equal nah, shall we?"

Nathan looked up, sadness tingeing his still-moist eyes.

"We can never be that, can we? Never equal, you an' me. I dun't care what the church sez, an' I dun't care 'ow close ar families might 'ave got fer a while there. Tommy were right, yer see, even if 'is methods were wrong. There's a gap between the likes o' me an' you that'll never be crossed in ar lifetimes, an' we both suffered fer thinkin' we could cross it. Even if folks'd let us, we still dun't even think the same way. If we did, mebbe I'd still 'ave two sons ter go 'ome to, instead of a wife who's 'alf daft, an' a baby boy wi' a dirty family name ter live dahn as 'e grows up. All the likes of you an' me can do is show each other decent respect, but from different sides o' the street. My sort dun't mean you an' your sort any 'arm, when it comes dahn to it. So dun't be scared on us – just respect us an' leave us be. Anyroad, I'd best be gerrin' back ter Lily."

Robert gazed at Nathan in open-mouthed astonishment. It was certainly the longest speech he'd ever heard from him, and perhaps the longest he'd ever made. Robert also had a strong suspicion that Nathan was right, but it wouldn't change his attitude to his workforce one little bit. And, he reminded himself, there was need for men like Nathan in that workforce if the gap was ever to be closed.

"Nathan, when yer've 'ad time ter think things ovver a bit more, there's still a job fer yer ter do 'ere."

Nathan smiled back sadly as he rose to leave.

"Thanks, Mr Bradley, an' I really do appreciate all yer've done forrus these past few years, burra dun't think I'll be back. No, stay there – I know the way aht."

He plodded slowly back up Stoney Street, and turned automatically right into High Pavement, his feet knowing the way home as well as he did. He was still trying to absorb it all as he walked. Lily, of all people! She must have forgotten that God sees to everything in due season, and that it was a sin to try to deflect his will. But then, she hadn't been quite right in the head, and perhaps never would be again. His depression intensified with every step, and he looked up again at the stiffening corpses in the sideshow, creaking and groaning in the early sunset. "Lucky bastards," he mumbled to himself, "some of us 'as ter carry on."

The moment he emerged into the yard from under the archway,

he knew that there was more to come. There was a deathly silence; no children playing their usual shrill games across the muddy courtyard and no neighbours conversing in doorways. Aggie Draycott was standing in the doorway of number seven, twitching wretchedly at her apron, her white face red at the eyes and nose. He looked beyond her and through the open door, where he could see old Nancy unfolding their best sheets.

He walked steadily up to Aggie, who dropped her gaze down to the greasy ground and sniffled. He placed a reassuring hand on her shoulder.

"Yer needn't fidget fer the words, lass; I can guess. She's gone, 'asn't she?"

"Aye. Not long after yer left. Just a gret big sigh an' nowt more – that were it. There was nowt ter be done, an' no pain as I could mek aht. Our Mary's lookin' after William."

"Aye, she's a good un, your Mary."

He stepped in quietly and Nancy looked up from what she was doing, an unaccustomed tear rolling down her cheek. Lily was laid out on the floor by the fire, wrapped in the best bedding Nancy could find in the house, and with a promise that she would return after nightfall she respectfully withdrew, leaving Nathan alone with his grief.

The lines had gone from Lily's face, along with the little bit of colour she'd had left. Nathan hadn't really noticed how the grey of her hair had turned to white during the past few weeks, but there were still those few stubborn brown streaks to remind him of her former colouring. Above all, she looked peaceful, as much like a young girl as the first day he'd met her. All those years of work, all the childbearing, all the worry, all the caring for others; all snuffed out like a candle. Gone to the Heaven she'd never seen, but always believed in. He hoped she was right, and he allowed himself a grim chuckle as he imagined her inspecting the place for dust before she agreed to go in and sit down.

He glanced up, and it was getting dark outside. He closed the door then went back and knelt beside her, both knees on the floor. He took one marble hand in his and began to tell her how much he loved her, as the emotions he had been holding back all day finally broke free, and he slumped forward onto Lily's icy shoulder and let the racking sobs burst through him, wave after wave.

It had turned fully dark when, suddenly, he felt a soft hand on his shoulder. Startled, he turned round. There was a shadow there, something quite small and the smell of camphor and soap. It rustled slightly as it stepped backwards.

"Can I light the lamp, Dad?"

He peered into the gloom, disbelievingly.

"Ruth?"

"Who else were you expectin'? I've come 'ome, Dad."

" 'ow did yer find aht so fast?"

"Abaht mam? I didn't know owt abaht 'er till I got inter the yard, an' Aggie dashed aht an' told me. She gev me a mug o' tea, an' I 'ad a bit of a teary, an' then she told me I'd find you wi' mam in 'ere."

Nathan opened his mouth to say something comforting, but she cut him off.

"An' yer needn't tell me abaht Tommy an' Matthew, 'cos I already know, includin' that Matthew gorraway. That's why I'm back 'ere, really. Got mi marchin' orders from the 'ousekeeper, didn't I?"

"Yer mean they chucked you aht just because o' Tommy an' Matthew?"

"No skin off my nose; they was rotten pigs, anyroad. The master an' missus was all right, an' Polly the cook, but that Mrs Trentham were a right old cow. They reckon 'er 'usband drank 'imself ter death just ter gerraway from 'er. Anyroad, she 'ad it in fer me right from the start, an' was allus findin' excuses ter criticise mi work. When the news came abaht mi brothers, that were it. A week's notice, then aht on mi arse."

" 'ow did yer get back 'ere?"

Ruth smiled knowingly, and Nathan felt his blood run cold.

"The baker's boy were comin' inter tahn this mornin' fer flour. 'e were only s'posed ter go as far as Basford Mill, but the silly bogger told Polly 'e were sweet on me, so I gorrim ter drop me off at the Cross, norrat the yard – didn't want folks thinkin' I were a trollop or summat. Nah, can I light that lamp, or what?"

Without waiting for a reply, she went through the motions which were second nature to her, and which she had clearly not forgotten during her time with the Beardsalls. Realising that Nathan was still on his knees, she looked down at him sternly.

"That floor's damp."

Nathan gazed up at her forlornly in the meagre light from the lamp. There was no obvious physical change, apart from a slight loss of weight and a definite gain in height, but she was far from being the tearful child he had all but abandoned at the kitchen door in Eastwood. Her eldest brother had been killed, her second brother was on the run from the gallows, her mother lay dead in the same room, and she hadn't even asked about William. There she stood, only fourteen, and already as hard as the mending-room sluts he used to come across at Bradley's. What in God's name had they done to her up there?

It took them a few days to get to know each other again, and even then it was not until after the diversion of the funeral that they had the chance to plan for the new house and the future which hopefully lay beyond that. As for the funeral itself, if Nathan had entertained any doubts about the high regard in which Lily had been held in every community she had touched, these were fully dispelled when the chapel donated a coffin, the ladies of the chapel decorated it with flowers, Robert Bradley sent a coach (but not his own), and every man and woman, and even most of the children, from Tanners Yard, walked behind it in a laying to rest that outshone even the one bestowed on old Joe some four years previously. However she may have been received on the other side, Lily Slack née Parker definitely left this side wreathed in glory, and surrounded by love.

"I'm just the same as I've allus bin, Dad," Ruth insisted as she poured Nathan another mug of tea one evening a couple of days after the funeral. "Mebbe yer seein' me different, after all yer've bin through. Well, yer've got me ter look after you an' William nah, so there'll be no more talk o' me goin' back inter service, I 'ope."

"No, that were yer mam. But she meant well."

Ruth took the news of the move to the new house with gleeful anticipation, as he knew she would. It was almost like having Lily back at full strength, particularly when Ruth began to tell him how best to organise his life. But there was something else there, a hardness which Lily had never possessed, and it came out most noticeably whenever money was being discussed.

Ruth had tutted most derisively when Nathan had explained to her that he couldn't go back to Bradley's, but she eventually accepted that it would be a long daily walk to and from the new house, particularly in the winter months. She also passed some remark about Bradley 'doing his bit', and he chose not to ask what she meant, nor why she was missing from the house several times during those few weeks.

On those days in which the late autumn sunlight found its way into the yard, Nathan could be seen sitting on the doorstep of number seven, taking in the warmth, while indoors could be heard the bustle and clatter that those with recent memories associated with Lily in her prime. If Ruth was now increasingly known as 'Little Lily', it was also not unusual to hear Nathan described as 'Old Nathan', and indeed he was looking much older than his years, and it was generally doubted – by those who discussed it – that he would make the old bones that his father had.

Three weeks after the funeral he was summoned to attend Ashley's Lace Manufactury on Derby Road, almost within sight of the recently completed house in Radford which had their names on the tenancy papers, with three names tactfully removed from the final draft. He was most surprised to learn that Ashley's needed an experienced 'leading hand' warp framework knitter, and that he had been highly recommended. Twelve shillings a week guaranteed, take it or leave it. He took it, wondering, but not quite wondering, how this had all come about. The glint of satisfaction in Ruth's eye said everything, and the fact that Patrick Ashley was a distant cousin of Letitia Beardsall and Catherine Bradley said the rest. While waiting to start in his new position, he sat out in the yard, thinking of the future and deeply proud of his young daughter.

Then one morning, they were gone. A horse and cart had been all they needed, and it had appeared without asking at the Narrow Marsh exit from the yard, just as Ruth had predicted. The driver would only say that 'a certain party dahn Stoney Street' had ordered and paid for it two days in advance, and the satisfied smile on Ruth's face gave Nathan all the other information he needed.

He sat on the left-hand side of the cart, watching their earthly possessions wobbling and shifting as the driver did his best to navigate the rutted roads through the town, and as they finally breasted the top of the Derby Turnpike, and turned into the road to Ilkeston, he looked past the driver and down the hill. Below them, and slightly to the right, lay twenty-three Coldham Street, and a new life. Lily would have been so excited, and so proud. And yet, he reflected, perhaps she was here after all, in the example she had set. He looked across at Ruth, her eyes shining with all the eagerness of youth which the world had not yet quenched. She returned his look, and smiled.

"Mam woulda loved this."

"Aye, lass, she would. But nah it's your turn."

CANARY CHILD
by David Field and Alan Dance

A supernatural mystery drama – at times tragic yet immensely humorous.

In 1968, in a small Nottinghamshire country churchyard, an embittered divorcée has a strange encounter with the apparition of a girl who claims to have died in an explosion at a nearby First World War shell-filling factory fifty years before. Unable to dismiss from her mind the girl's desperate plea for help, Dorothy Younger begins her search for further details surrounding the events leading to the girl's death, in the hope of finding the child left orphaned by the blast.

Enlisting the help of veteran army officer Tim Mildmay, together they learn of one of the greatest wartime civilian tragedies, which claimed the lives of almost 140 workers. Dorothy and Tim grapple with the mystery of a young woman who apparently died in the explosion, but who was never officially there, and the survival of another who should have been blown to pieces but was later discovered safely at home.

Of those who died in the tragedy, there were no doubt many tales which could have been told of their lives and the events which led to their last, fatal, few moments on earth. Perhaps this is one of them.

Praise for *Canary Child*

"This absorbing tale, based on a tragic explosion in Nottinghamshire during the Great War, had me rushing to Attenborough churchyard to pay my respects at the gravesides."

John Holmes, BBC Nottingham

"An unravelling mystery mixed with an incredible real war story and some cracking Nottingham dialect. And, always a good thing, a bit of love. It's a powerful mix."

William Ivory, screen writer

Canary Child is published by Arundel Books
ISBN 978-0-9558133-6-8
Available to order from all good book shops, price £6.99
or **post-free** direct from the publisher.
Also available as a Kindle eBook.

NARROW MARSH

A R DANCE

An exciting historical saga set in Nottingham in the early years of the 19th century

Nottingham, 1811 - a time of fear and hardship for the town's framework knitters. With low wages and long working hours, desperate men turn to direct action. And when a man is killed, someone has to pay the ultimate price. Young William Daniels witnesses the public execution, and from that day onwards he develops a burning desire for justice and freedom. But his chance encounter with the headstrong daughter of a wealthy factory owner sets in motion a tumultuous chain of events that will change his life forever. Set in early 19th century Nottingham, in an era of bitter social unrest, Narrow Marsh is a dramatic story of life, love and hope.

Praise for *Narrow Marsh*

"One of the best novels I have read. The story just flew through my fingers and I couldn't turn the pages fast enough."

East Midlands Arts

"A highly evocative story of early 19th century high and low life. At its heart, one of England's most notorious slums. Unputdownable."

John Brunton, journalist and author

"The sense of overriding hope against unrest and misfortune will stay with you long after you finish this rewarding novel."

Nottinghamshire Today

Narrow Marsh is published by Arundel Books
ISBN 978-0-9558133-0-6
Available to order from all good book shops, price £7.99
or **post-free** direct from the publisher.
Also available as a Kindle eBook.

LEEN TIMES
A R DANCE

The dramatic sequel to Narrow Marsh

Having returned to Nottingham from exile in France, William Daniels has now settled in his home town and is developing a successful business as a canal carrier. But ever resourceful, and always looking to the future, he also becomes involved in plans to bring the railway to Nottingham. Meanwhile, on the other side of the world, one man has not forgotten the past. Residing at His Majesty's pleasure in a penal colony in Van Diemen's Land, an old adversary of William waits patiently for the day when he will become a free man again. And as he waits, he carefully plans his revenge against the one whom he regards as responsible for his downfall.

Nottingham in the 1820s and 1830s, an era of brutal and uncompromising change and of fierce political upheaval, is the setting for the dramatic sequel to Narrow Marsh. A fast-moving story of retribution, radical politics and criminal conspiracies.

Praise for *Leen Times*

"Excellent story-telling. A fascinating marriage of fact and fiction."

Andy Smart, Nottingham Post

"A thrilling sequel to Narrow Marsh, with as many twists and turns as the courts and alleys of 19th century Nottingham. I never knew my ancestors' town had experienced so much turmoil, political chicanery and mob violence."

Jean Boht, actress

Leen Times is published by Arundel Books
ISBN 978-0-9558133-1-3
Available to order from all good book shops, price £7.99
or **post-free** direct from the publisher.
Also available as a Kindle eBook.

THE WESTBROOK AFFAIR
A R DANCE

Young Joseph Lambert has enjoyed all the childhood privileges befitting the son of a wealthy Yorkshire squire. But when his widowed father is mysteriously killed in a riding accident, his comfortable world is suddenly torn apart. Joseph's elder brother, the dissolute and self-indulgent Miles, inherits the estate and promptly abandons his young brother, leaving him to fend for himself.

Determined to seek his fortune, the thirteen-year-old orphan makes his way to Sheffield where he secures an apprenticeship in a cutlery factory. Seven years later, now an accomplished and skilled craftsman, he marries Hannah and soon a daughter, Eliza, is born.

But barely is Eliza old enough to know her father, when tragedy strikes. Hannah is struggling to support herself and her daughter, when one day an old lady arrives with an astonishing tale to tell.

And slowly, a forgotten family secret begins to unfold.

Set in Yorkshire and Nottinghamshire in the mid-nineteenth century, The Westbrook Affair is a gripping story of poverty and wealth, betrayal and greed, and ultimately the search for justice and the truth.

The *Westbrook Affair* is published by Arundel Books
ISBN 978-0-9558133-5-1
Available to order from all good book shops, price £7.99
or **post-free** direct from the publisher.
Also available as a Kindle eBook.

The Right Fist of God – Bendigo

by Alan Dance and David Field

A rip-roaring romp through Georgian and Victorian England. There's never a dull moment as William Thompson – better known as Bendigo – fights his way from the poverty of a Nottingham slum, via the workhouse and street brawls, to fame and fortune as champion bare-fist boxer of all England. With twenty prize fights to his name, and many more barrels of ale under his belt, Bendigo became the most famous son of Nottingham since Robin Hood first ventured from the leafy glades of Sherwood Forest to taunt the Sheriff.

Later, sinking into a wretched haze of drunkenness, with numerous spells in the House of Correction, Bendigo was finally saved from an ignominious end when a chance encounter with an evangelical preacher turned his life around. Abandoning the evils of strong drink he took to preaching the word of God, once again fighting the good fight, but this time from the pulpit rather than in the ring. A legend was born, and when he eventually departed this life at the age of nearly seventy, thousands followed his coffin the five miles to the burial ground.

This book is a novel based around the true story of one of England's greatest sporting heroes.

The Right Fist of God — Bendigo

by Alan Lance and David Hall